Praise for *THE BODY OF DAVID HAYES*

"*The Body of David Hayes* is gripping and engaging. Pearson has constructed yet another taut and intense thriller."
—*Chicago Tribune*

"This is another of Ridley's spellbinders."
—Paul B. Kincade, Detective,
Washoe County Sheriff's Office

"Pearson shows his usual mastery of the intricacies of structure and the subtleties of suspenseful pacing."
—*BookPage*

"The latest Ridley Pearson book about Detective Lou Boldt is a fast-paced and exciting tale. Pearson has obviously done thorough and meticulous research into crime scenes and forensic science, creating a story any professional in the field would enjoy."
—Donna J. Meade, Forensic Scientist II,
Idaho State Police Forensic Services

"Pearson cares deeply for these characters."
—*Entertainment Weekly*

"Intriguing, exciting, and highly recommended."
—*Library Journal*

Praise for *THE ART OF DECEPTION*

"Beautifully orchestrated."
—*The New York Times Book Review*

"Better than a guilty pleasure."
—*Entertainment Weekly*

"A one-sitting read that shows why Ridley Pearson is the grandmaster of the police procedural."

—*The Midwest Book Review*

"A dramatic finale . . . this series remains one of the genre's greatest pleasures."   —*Booklist* (starred review)

"No one blends crime fiction and realism like Ridley Pearson. In *The Art of Deception*, he transports readers into uncharted realms—the eerie, subterranean ghost town that is Seattle's 'Underground'—and the groundbreaking relationship between John LaMoia and Daphne Matthews. A 150-proof thriller!"

—Greg Iles, author of *Dead Sleep*

"Realistic police work, real people, real suspense. Ridley Pearson always delivers."   —Tami Hoag

"Ridley Pearson has been called 'the best thriller writer alive,' and . . . there's no disagreement here."   —*New York Post*

"Pearson tells an irresistible tale."

—*The Los Angeles Times Book Review*

"Pearson excels at writing novels that grip the imagination."

—*People*

Praise for *PARALLEL LIES*

"Pearson has written another terrific thriller."

—*Library Journal*

"Pearson remains near the top of the genre."   —*Booklist*

"Pearson handles the complex plot with grace and speed, packing a potent blend of action and procedural information into his work. A must-read for thriller fans." *—Chicago Tribune*

"The gadget man is back with a bag of new toys. You don't have to be a techno-nerd to get wired on this scary stuff."
—The New York Times Book Review

"Pearson weaves psychology and suspense into this tale of high-tech clues and complex motives." *—Playboy*

"Ridley Pearson is an unequivocal success. I'm hooked again."
—Entertainment Weekly

Praise for *NO WITNESSES*

"Tough and intelligent." *—Fort Worth Star Telegram*

"Up-to-the-nanosecond techno-thriller." *—New York Times*

"Infused with astonishingly effective overtones." *—Boston Globe*

"Good old-fashioned storytelling." *—Washington Post Book World*

"A serious, well-researched, complex thriller."
—Los Angeles Times

Praise for *THE ANGEL MAKER*

"Exceptionally gripping and full of amazing forensic lore: a top-flight offering from an author who has clearly found his groove."
—Kirkus Reviews

"A chilling thriller."   —Dell Publishing

Praise for *HARD FALL*

"Pearson excels at novels that grip the imagination. *Hard Fall* is an adventure with all engines churning."   —*People*

"Mesmerizing urgency."   —*Los Angeles Times Book Review*

"Nifty cat-and-mouse caper. Crisply written tale."

—*Chicago Tribune*

Praise for *UNDERCURRENTS*

"Neatly constructed plot. Hair-raising denouement. Remarkable insight and understanding of the motivations of the criminal mind."   —*Publishers Weekly*

"*Undercurrents* is a roller-coaster ride in the dark."

—*Book-of-the-Month Club*

CUT AND RUN

RIDLEY PEARSON

HYPERION NEW YORK

Mass market ISBN: 0-7868-9002-9

Hyperion books are available for special promotions and premiums. For details contact Michael Rentas, Assistant Director, Inventory Operations, Hyperion, 77 West 66th Street, 11th floor, New York, New York 10023, or call 212-456-0133.

FIRST MASS MARKET EDITION

10 9 8 7 6 5 4 3 2 1

For Marcelle

ACKNOWLEDGMENTS

Special Thanks to Laurel Shaper Walters and David Walters and Marcelle for the multiple reads of the manuscript; to Paul Kenny, for a place to hang my hat and pen; to Ed Stackler, for his patience in editing many revisions; Leslie Wells, my editor at Hyperion; Al Zuckerman, friend, editor, agent; Amy Berkower, Writers House; Matthew Snyder, CAA; Susan Steiger, attorney; at Hyperion: Karin Maake, Bob Miller, Ellen Archer, Jane Comins, Katie Wainwright. Thanks also to Nancy Litzinger and Louise Marsh for their day-to-day office support.

For helping me with the details: Andy Hamilton, Assistant United States Attorney (retired); Eric Robertson, U.S. Marshal for the Western District of Washington State; and to many who choose to remain anonymous.

ACKNOWLEDGMENTS

P R O L O G U E

SIX YEARS EARLIER

The forty-first day was their last together.

Roland Larson was holed up in a truck stop's pay phone, half-mad from guarding her round-the-clock while denied any privacy with her whatsoever. He resorted to calling her on the phone. He'd slipped her his cell phone, and now dialed his own number to find her breathless as she whispered from her hardened bedroom, the aft cabin of the bus, not thirty yards away.

"I can't stand this," she said.

He found himself aroused by the hoarse, coarse sound of her. Forty-one days, under every conceivable pressure, and this the first complaint he'd heard from her.

"Us, or the situation?" he asked.

Hope Stevens had been moved on three separate occasions: first, to a wilderness cabin in Michigan's Upper Peninsula, the kind of place Larson could see himself retiring to someday, a lethargic life so different from the one he lived; then she'd been moved to a nearly abandoned Air Force base in Montana, the desolation reminding him of a penitentiary, a place he knew well; and finally, into a private coach, a customized diesel bus that Treasury had confiscated from a forgotten rock band, its interior complete with neon-trim lighting and mirrored tables. Painted on three sides as a purple and black sunrise, the coach comfortably slept six and converted to club seating by day. Three deputies, including Larson, two drivers, and the witness traveled together—one of only a handful of times in the U.S. Marshals Service's long history of witness protection that a "moving target" policy had been adopted. The last had been aboard a sleeper train in the mid-'70s.

Ironically, the more attempts made upon her life, the more importance and significance Hope Stevens gained in the eyes of her government. It wasn't for her keen understanding of computers that they guarded her, nor for her fine looks or sharp tongue (when she did bother to speak); it was instead for a few cells and chemicals inside her skull and the memory trapped there, living now like a dog under the front porch, cowering with a bone of truth in its jaws.

The problem for Roland Larson was that the longer he guarded her, the more he cared for her—cared intensely—a situation unforgivable and intolerable in the eyes of his superiors and one that, if discovered, could have him transferred to some far outpost of government service, like North Dakota or Buffalo. But the few private moments shared with her overwhelmed any sensibility in Larson.

After just seventeen days of protection, the Michigan cabin had gone up in flames—arson; in the resulting firefight, a shadowy ballet in the flashes of orange light from the mighty blaze, two deputy marshals had been injured.

When, at the Montana Air Force base, mention of "persons unknown" had been intercepted by some geek in an NSA cubicle, the marshals had been instructed to move Hope yet again. Larson wasn't much for running away from a faceless enemy, but he knew well enough to follow orders and so he did.

As a former technical consultant to an industry probe of fraudulent insurance practices, Hope had connected a string of assisted-care facilities to millions of dollars in wrongful charges. The names she'd eventually given Justice—Donny and Pop Romero and, by inference, the young scion of the crime family, Ricardo Romero—were well known to federal law enforcement's Organized Crime Unit. The Romeros, notorious for inventive white collar crime on an enormous scale, also played rough and dirty when required, the arson and the shoot-out at the lake a case in point. Hope's value to Justice was not only her initial discovery of insurance fraud—a scheme involving billing Medicare long after the patient was dead—but, more important, her interception of a series of e-mails sent to and from the Romeros that proved to be murder-for-hire contracts. Five executives of the same health care consortium that had called for the probe, all referred to in the correspondence as whistle-blowers whose actions threatened the Romeros, had later been found brutally murdered, the victims of so-called Serbian Spas—laundry bleach enemas that burned the victim from the inside out over a period of several hours, their families tied up and forced to watch their prolonged deaths.

Intended perhaps to implicate the Russian mob, these horrific tactics did nothing of the sort. The FBI had immediately placed the Romeros onto their Most Wanted list and their two remaining witnesses, Hope Stevens and an unnamed accountant, had been placed in protective custody.

The e-mails had been electronically destroyed; they existed now only in Hope's memory. Government prosecutors believed a jury would convict based primarily on her testimony. And so they sequestered her on the garish bus, never allowing her off, never risking her being seen in public, and never stopping the bus for more than fuel or supplies. The strategy had kept her alive for the past ten days and left everyone on board with a bad case of cabin fever. Discussions had begun to once again relocate her, this time to a "static," or fixed, location, probably a federal facility, quite possibly a short stint inside an unused wing at a federal penitentiary, or in an ICU at a city hospital. They had myriad tricks up their sleeves if left to their own devices. They seldom were.

"Isn't there something you can do?" Hope asked. "Order us to stop at a motel, and arrange for you to guard my room? There has to be something."

"I'm only guessing here," Larson answered, "but I think a few of the guys might see through that tactic." He caught his reflection in the polished metal surrounding the pay phone's keypad. No one was going to call him pretty, although they had as a child. He'd grown into something too big for pretty, too hard for handsome, like a puppy growing into its feet. Pedigree be damned.

She sputtered on the other end, not quite her trademark laugh but a valiant effort.

He said, "You could make like a heart attack, and I could give you mouth-to-mouth."

A little more authentic this time.

At the cabin, and then again at the Air Force base, they'd managed to find moments together, though not the moment both of them longed for, one he repeatedly daydreamed about. But once onto the bus, they'd barely shared a glance. A phone call was as much as they were going to get.

"It's probably better this way," she said. "Right?"

"No. It's decidedly worse."

"As soon as I testify . . . as soon as that's over with . . . they'll put me into the program and that will be that. Right? We should have never started this, Lars."

Her testimony against Donny Romero—the fraud case—would

come first. The capital murder charges were likely still a long way from prosecution—a year or two—but he knew better than to mention it. One didn't talk about the future with a protected witness, the reality far harsher, the adjustment far more difficult than they understood. In practice, breaking off all contact with one's former life proved traumatic, invariably more difficult than the witness imagined.

"Seriously?" he asked. "Because I don't see it that way at all. I wouldn't trade one minute with you for something else."

"You're hopeless."

"I'm hope*ful*," he said, an intentional play on her name that he immediately congratulated himself for, though no doubt one she'd heard before.

His feeling for her had come on like a force of nature, as unavoidable and inexplicable. Together, they communicated well; she accepted teasing in the face of all the madness; they fit. And when you found that, you held on to it.

Nearly ten minutes had passed since he'd left the bus. Members of his small squad would be wondering why the delay. Ostensibly, he'd left the bus to settle the bill—with cash, *always cash*—but ten minutes was pushing it.

"My gut tells me we'll work this out somehow," he lied. He couldn't see them ending this now—not before they tested the boundaries. He'd attended the seminars on avoiding emotional attachment with the witness. Brother bonding with the male witnesses was as dangerous as what he and Hope had stumbled into. It screwed up everything, risked everything, and he well knew it. It could not possibly have a happy ending. Still, he encouraged her to stay with him while he looked for some way around it all, a way that he suspected wasn't there. At this moment, after what they'd been through together, letting her go was not an option.

"Lars," she spoke, yet again in a hushed whisper, the crisp sibilance rolling off the *s* and causing a ripple of gooseflesh down his left side. It snaked into his groin and lodged there. But rerouted by a synapse, it suddenly sparked across a gate in his brain that translated it differently, albeit a beat too late: This was nothing short of the sound of panic.

"Hope?"

"Oh, my God."

The line went dead.

The bus.

Larson dropped the receiver and ran, losing his balance as he took a corner too quickly on wet tile, ignoring the yellow sandwich board written in Spanish and English with an icon of a pail and mop and a splash of water. He went down hard. He scrambled to his feet, knocked over a corn chip display, and hurried out the truck stop's main door, the cashier's cry of complaint consumed by the high-pitched whine of highway traffic.

"Rolo?" This came from Trill Hampton, a member of his squad, a fellow deputy marshal. Approaching footfalls of shoes slapping blacktop came on fast. Larson's running had sent a signal. Hampton was in full stride, already reaching for his piece.

Larson's arrival into sunlight temporarily blinded him. They'd stopped at far too many truck stops over the past ten days for him to immediately recall the layout of this one. They'd parked out here somewhere. A spike of fear insinuated itself as he considered the possibility that the entire bus had been hijacked, for he didn't see it anywhere.

But then, as Hampton caught up to him and edged left, and the two of them moved around the building, Larson spotted the rows of diesel pumps and the bus where they'd parked it, wedged amid a long line of eighteen-wheel tractor-trailers.

Hampton walked gracefully, even at double time.

Leading at a slight jog, Larson assessed the bus from a distance, seeing no indication of trouble and wondering if he'd misinterpreted Hope's distress.

"What's up?" Hampton asked, not a sheen of sweat on his black skin.

He wasn't about to confess to phoning the witness from the truck stop. "A bad feeling is all."

"A bad *feeling*?" Hampton questioned. "Since when?" He had a flat, wide nose, too big for his face, and a square, cleft chin that reminded Larson of a black Kirk Douglas.

Larson wasn't exactly the touchy-feely type; Hampton saw through that.

Larson sought some plausible explanation for Hope hanging up on him. He seized upon the first thing he saw. "Why isn't Benny stretching his legs?" The older of their two drivers had been complaining to anyone who would listen about a bad case of hemorrhoids. Larson saw Benny through the windshield, sitting behind the wheel.

"Yeah, so?"

They drew closer. Benny not only still occupied his driver's seat, but his head was angled and tilted somewhat awkwardly toward his shoulder, as if dozing. This, too, seemed incongruous, as Benny rarely slept, much less napped.

"Rolo?" Hampton said cautiously. Now he, too, had sensed a problem with Benny. Hampton and Larson went back several years. Hampton had come out of one of New Haven's worst neighborhoods, had won an academic scholarship to a blue blazer prep school, and had gone on to graduate from Howard University. He'd wanted to be a professional sports agent, but had become a U.S. marshal as an interim job, at the urging of an uncle. He'd never left the service.

"Radio Stubby," Larson instructed.

Hampton attempted to raise Stubblefield, the third marshal, who remained inside the bus, but won only silence.

"Shit!" Hampton said, increasing his stride. The man could cover ground when he wanted to.

The two were twenty feet away from the bus now, Larson adjusting his approach in order to come from more of an angle to avoid being seen, his handgun, a Glock, carefully screened.

He instructed Hampton: "Hang back. Take cover. Lethal force if required."

"Got it." Hampton broke away from Larson, hurrying toward the adjacent tractor-trailer and taking a position that allowed him to use it as cover.

Larson found the bus door closed—standard procedure. Benny would typically open it for him as he approached, but that didn't happen, sounding a secondary alarm in Larson's head. He slipped his hand into the front pocket of his jeans, searching amid a wad of cash receipts for the cool, metallic feel of keys—the duplicate set to the bus that, as supervising deputy, Larson kept on his person.

Benny remained motionless, not responding; Stubby not answering a radio call. But who could storm a bus through its only door—a *locked* door, at that—and overcome two drivers and a deputy marshal?

Larson heard thumping from inside. Banging. Just as he turned the key, out of the corner of his eye he caught sight of a state police car parked beyond the diesel pumps and he thought: *Benny would open the door for a uniform.*

As Larson opened the door and entered, the banging stopped abruptly. Larson both tasted and smelled the bitter air and knew its source from experience: a stun grenade—an explosive device that uses air pressure to blow out eardrums and sinuses and render the suspects temporarily deaf and semiconscious.

The narrow stairs that ascended to the driver prevented him from seeing into the main body of the bus. He saw only Benny, whose shirt held a red waterfall of spilled blood down the front. Larson's first assessment was that the man's nose was bleeding—typical with stun grenades. But then he saw a precise line below his jaw, like a surgical incision. His open eyes and frozen stare cinched it: Benny was dead.

Weapon still in hand, Larson kept low and climbed the bus stairs, ready for contact. The banging he'd heard had been someone attempting to breach the hardened door to Hope's cabin. He saw Stubby, unconscious or dead, on the left side, behind a collapsible table. Clancy, the other driver, sat upright in a padded captain's chair opposite Stubby, his head tilted back. A game of gin rummy between them had ended abruptly. No blood or ligature marks on Clancy.

No sign of a state trooper either, the aisle empty, a sleeping cabin on either side.

One of Stubby's golf clubs lay broken in front of the rear cabin's door, which appeared intact and suggested Hope remained safe, a source of great relief. The intruder had been trying to use a club to pry the door open.

There was only one key to that door, hidden in a Hide A Key in the rear engine bay. Larson edged forward.

He went down hard as a strong hand gripped his ankle and pulled from behind. The gun hit the carpet and bounced loose. The wind knocked out of him, Larson reeled.

The intruder was a stringy guy with frog-tongue reactions. He seized Larson's hair from behind and pulled. But Larson rolled left and the razor blade, intended for his throat, missed and caught the front of his right shoulder instead. Larson broke loose, dived forward, and grabbed for the gun. He spun and squeezed off three rounds. Two went into the mirrored ceiling, raining down cubes of tempered glass, and blinding him in a silver snow.

A crushing force caught Larson in the jaw, snapping his head back. He inadvertently let go of the gun for a second time. The intruder had fallen onto him, and Larson realized he'd hit him with one of the three shots. Larson grabbed for the man and felt fabric rip.

A uniform. Larson fought back, the wounded man keeping him from the gun. Larson bucked him off, but his cut shoulder caused his arm to flap around uselessly, refusing all of Larson's instructions. Tangled up with the man, Larson drove his left elbow back and felt the crunch of soft bone and tissue, like an eggshell breaking.

He then heard a series of quick footfalls and looked in time to see the intruder hurry off the bus.

Landing out on the parking lot's pavement, the uniformed man's voice shouted, "Someone call for help!"

Larson came to his knees. His head swooned. He looked around for his gun through blurry eyes.

Hampton saw the slender state trooper throw his hands in the air as he called for help. He was bleeding. The man sank to his knees in front of the door to the bus.

Hampton held his weapon extended and stepped out from behind the tractor-trailer. "Hands behind your head," he called out, not feeling great holding a gun on a man in uniform.

As the trooper sat up, Hampton saw a yellow-white muzzle flash. He took the first round in the thigh, driven back by the impact and losing his balance. He sprawled back onto the hot blacktop, rocking his head to the right and watching the suspect run off. He fired two rounds from his side.

———

As Larson dragged himself toward the front of the bus, he tried to lock down anything he remembered about the intruder: thin and wiry; strong; the uniform; a scar. He focused on the scar. The lines of pink, beaded skin crossed, forming a stylized infinity sign on the inside of his forearm. Larson's vision filled with a purple fringe, the dark, throbbing color coming at him from all sides. His shoulder was cut badly. Sticky down to his waist. He felt faint. Sounds echoed. Again he smelled the tangy air, laced with black powder and sulfur. Bitter with blood. His stomach retched. He felt as if he were being pushed and held underwater—dark water—by a strong, determined hand. He resisted, but felt himself going. Deeper.

His last conscious thought was more of a vision: not an infinity sign at all, but two triangles facing inward, touching, point-to-point.

Like a bow tie.

CHAPTER ONE

THE PRESENT

Of all things, Larson thought he recognized her laugh. Here, where he least expected it. It carried like a shot, well past his ears and spilling down into the audience where it ran into a waterfall of others—though none exactly like it—and broke to pieces before the footlights and spots that made the dust in the air look like snow. It might as well have lodged in his chest, the way it stole his breath.

He'd started the day perfectly, the way he wished he could start every day, busting his body into a sweat while pulling on twin sticks of composite carbon painted on the scoop in a diagonal of rich burgundy and black, the owner's college colors no doubt, driving the borrowed scull through swirls of no-see-ums and gnats so thick he clenched his teeth to filter them out, the occasional dragonfly darting swiftly alongside as if challenging him to a race. He'd been up before the birds, and would be done—put away and showered, Creve Coeur Lake behind him—before the rush-hour traffic made the city's famous arch stand still.

He'd taken in the play on a whim, calling the box office to see if there were any singles available, a guilty pleasure he wouldn't have told anyone about if he hadn't engaged the receptionist, Lo-kisha, in a discussion of Shakespeare on the way out the door.

The fact was that in over five years of secretly searching for Hope at Shakespeare festivals and performances—in places as far away as Ashland, Oregon, and Cedar City, Utah—he'd become passionate about the Bard himself: the violence, the romance, the lies and deceptions, the cunning, the manipulation, the *symmetry* of the plays. It had never occurred to him that he might find her here in his own backyard. The belief in coincidence had been trained out of Larson in the way a dog could be made to lie by the dinner table and not look up to beg.

He'd felt his BlackBerry purr silently at his side several times over the past ten minutes, but it was after hours and it did that for any incoming e-mail, spam or legitimate, and he wasn't about to bother the people sitting next to him by lighting up a pale blue electronic screen in his lap while they tried to remain firmly in the sixteenth century. The intermission was fast approaching. He'd check e-mail and messages then.

This city was the last place—the absolute last place—he might have expected to hear her laugh: a combination of wild monkey and a Slinky going down a set of stairs. Even almost six years later he would have known her musical cackle anywhere. But St. Louis, in the Fox Theatre? Not on your life. Not on hers, either.

But it was Shakespeare, which he knew to be in her blood. If he were to find her, it would be at a performance like this—and so a part of him was tempted, even convinced, that he'd finally found her.

The balcony. He imagined her selecting a seat that offered the strategic advantage of elevation, because that was just the kind of thing he'd taught her.

Onstage, Benedick, having dived into a horse trough, addressed the audience, his black leather riding pants and billowing shirt-sleeves leaking water. Another volley of laughter rippled through the crowd, and there it was again. Larson felt like a birder identifying a particular species solely by its song.

He was no longer laughing along with the others. Instead, driven by curiosity, he was turned and straining to look up into the balcony.

Being too large for the closely crowded seats, his temperature spiked and his skin prickled. Or was that the possibility running through him? He represented Hope's past, her former self. Would she want that as badly as he did? Had she somehow found out about his transfer? Through all his training, coincidence nipped at his heels. Baffled, unsure what to do, he stayed in his seat.

The Fox Theatre, a renovated throwback to a bygone era, dwarfed its audience. Its combination of art deco, gilded Asian, quasi-Egyptian splendor, with anachronistic icons, like a twenty-foot-tall cross-legged Buddha, lit in a garish purple light, looked intentionally overwhelming. Despite the vastness of the hall, Larson felt impossible to miss. At well over six feet, and with shoulders that impeded both the theater-goers on either side of him, he would stick out if he stood. It seemed doubtful she might spot him, might recognize him from the back at such a distance, but he hoped she would. He glanced around once more, amused and concerned, intrigued and feeling foolish, his muscles tense. His shoulder ached, as it had ached for the past six years every time a storm drew near. He'd carried the same badge all these years, though now his credentials wallet showed a different title, Larson having been reassigned, along with Hampton and Stubblefield, to the Marshals Service's elite Fugitive Apprehension Task Force. Part bounty hunter, part bloodhound, part con man and actor, FATF marshals pursued escaped convicts and wanted felons in an effort to return them to their predetermined incarceration.

If she spotted him before he spotted her, what would come of it? Larson wondered. Would she fight through the crowd to be in his arms? Would she run? Again he put his own training onto her, deciding for her that she'd selected an aisle seat near an exit. She'd probably make for that exit rather than risk running into him.

He'd lost all track of the play. The audience erupted in laughter, and he'd missed the joke. He continued to imagine various ways this could possibly be her, but none made sense. Not here. Not St. Louis. Not unless she, too, were looking for him.

Six years. It seemed alternately to him like both a matter of days and a lifetime. What would he say to her? Her to him? Would she even care?

Larson wiped his damp palms on the thighs of his khakis. Again, a wave of laughter washed over the crowd. But this time, something different: her distinctive laugh was no longer a part of it. Larson turned again in his seat, scanning various exits. No sign of Hope, but slightly behind him, a pair of men in dark suits stood with an usher, both dutifully scanning the crowd.

In an audience of twenty-five hundred, there were plenty of men wearing suits—but none quite like these two. Conservative haircuts, thick builds. The big guy looked all too familiar. Federal agents, like himself. Though not like him at all. FBI maybe, or ATF, or even Missouri boys, working for the governor. A WITSEC deputy? The federal witness security and protection service was now a separate entity, but had recently been part of the Marshals Service.

Larson knew many of those guys, but not all. These two, WITSEC? He doubted it.

He might have thought they were looking for Hope, but the big one looked right at him and locked on. This man somehow knew the row, the seat—he knew where to find Larson. Cocking his head, the agent directed Larson to meet up with them. Larson held off acknowledging while he thought long and hard about how to play this, the earlier buzzing of his BlackBerry now more persistent in his memory.

As with Hope's laugh, two deputy marshals, or agents, materializing at the Fox was anything but coincidence.

He felt tempted to check the BlackBerry but didn't want to leave his head down that long. The big guy's posture and the way he bit his lower lip revealed a gnawing anxiety, a nagging unrest. This wasn't a social call.

A nearby woman wore too much perfume. He'd been struggling with it through the performance, driven to distraction. Only now did he find it nauseating.

The audience laughed uproariously.

Larson chanced a last strained look toward the balcony, then gave it up.

Hope didn't miss anything. Whether she'd seen Larson or not, she'd likely have spotted the suits by now, and therefore was already well on her way to gone.

Intermission arrived with a wave of crushing applause. The stage fell dark. By the time the houselights came up, Larson had already slipped past four sets of knees, avoided a handbag, and laid his big hand on a stranger's shoulder.

Hope would now head in the opposite direction from the two agents; she would quickly put as much distance between herself and the theater as possible. Seek cover. Avoid public space. She would never look back and would not hurry, no matter how desperate she believed her situation. Her walk would be controlled, yet deceptively swift, her demeanor casual though determined. She would never return to the theater again, no matter what the show. If he were to catch her, he would have to run; and if he ran, the two bloodhounds were sure to follow; and if they followed, and if he led them to her, then he'd prove himself a traitor to her.

Stuck. Larson tested the agents' purpose by mixing himself

into the throng and making for the opposite exit. But his head traveled a full head above most, like a parade float.

As expected, the two immediately followed, rudely pushing open a route to attempt to intersect Larson's path. Larson got caught in a snag of people as a wheelchair blocked the aisle. He cut through a now-empty row, working away from the men. Copies of *Playbill* littered the floor. He joined the right flank and pressed on toward an interior lobby, where people mingled looking lost.

Out of habit, he tested his skills, scanning the crowd for any woman wearing a headscarf or a hat, any woman making quickly for the main lobby and the doors beyond. He didn't spot her, and all the better. He had no desire to get her tangled up with these two.

Someone shouted and he knew it was for him. Adrenaline pricked his nerves. His stomach turned with the mixture of human sweat, cologne, and perfume. He pushed on to his left, his swollen bladder taking him down a long, wide set of elegant stairs as he joined a phalanx of men eager for urinals. He heard his name called out and cringed. It reminded him, not favorably, of being singled out by a coach, or the school principal.

He hazarded a look: The big one with the leather face and edgy disposition was following him, the younger one immediately on his heels.

He stopped on the stairs, and the current of impatient men streamed around him. He addressed his two pursuers as they drew closer, the face of the more senior of them revealing his surprise that Larson would allow himself to be caught.

"Gimme a minute of privacy," Larson said as he continued down, determined to appear unruffled.

Reaching the basement level, he entered a cavernous anteroom that held only a mirror, a small wooden table, and twin tapestry chairs that looked to be from a museum. Beyond this anteroom was the actual bathroom, about the size of a soccer field. Sinks straight ahead. To his left, a room of stalls; to his right a roomful of old porcelain urinals—there must have been thirty or forty of them. Built into the wall and floor, and so obviously antiques, the urinals looked surprisingly beautiful to him.

Larson took his place in line and emptied his bladder. One of the great pleasures in life.

"We need to talk." The same low voice, now directly behind him. The big one had followed him down. Junior Mint was no doubt standing sentry at the top of the stairs, ensuring that Larson didn't slip out.

"And I need to pee," Larson said, not looking back, but the magic of the moment spoiled.

A hand fell firmly onto his shoulder.

"Fuck off!" Larson shrugged and wrenched himself forward, dislodging the grip. Thankfully the man stepped back and let him finish. As he washed his hands he saw two images of the big pain in the ass in the cracked mirror.

"That was unnecessary," Larson cautioned. He wanted to establish some rules.

The agent said, "We were told you could be slippery. To respect that in you. That's why the hardball."

The guy at the next sink over stopped washing and eavesdropped on them.

"You trying to butter me up?" Larson asked. "You've got a funny way of doing that."

"I'm trying to get a message to you."

Larson had to stare down the man at the adjacent sink to get him to leave.

"So, deliver it."

"Here?"

Larson turned and faced the man, Larson taller by several inches. "Here."

Seen close up, this other guy's face carried an unintentional intensity—something, somewhere, was very, very wrong.

The man cupped his hand and leaned in toward Larson, who did nothing to block him, as his own hands were now engaged with a paper towel. The guy's breath felt warm against Larson's neck, causing a shiver as he said, "I was told to tell you that we've lost Uncle Leo."

Larson dumped the towel into the bin and heard himself mumble, "Oh, shit."

CHAPTER TWO

Larson had picked up people from private jets before: a supervisor; some WITSEC brass; a witness or two came to mind. But he'd never flown in a private jet himself, so although the cause was a man's disappearance, and the resulting tension inside the aircraft nearly palpable, he got a kick out of it nonetheless. Leather seats the size of first class held his large frame comfortably. Wood trim, polished like the dash of a Jaguar, surrounded a wall-mounted flat-panel TV that currently displayed their flight route over ground but probably could have handled a video, had either of the agents been interested in some entertainment. There was even an air phone that none of them had permission to use. Heady stuff, despite the lack of any offer of food or drink, beyond bottled water, and the general mood of its inhabitants, both of whom bordered on morose.

Larson wished his parents had been alive to hear about this, but he'd lost them both to twentieth-century plagues: his father to smoking, his mother to drink. He'd had a sister once, but she'd gotten lost in her high school years and had run away, never to be heard from again. He'd never used his tracking skills to hunt her down, and he wondered if someday he might.

The explanation for him taking this flight had been cryptic at best—Uncle Leo had gone missing. The wherefore and how had yet to reach him. But the promise of a nearly instant return flight once there, also on the private jet, had convinced him not to challenge this assignment. Few people could summon a government jet at a moment's notice; fewer still to transport his rank of deputy marshal. He was considered little more than a glorified bounty hunter, so why the special treatment? He'd decided to ride this one out, despite his tendency to question orders and cause headaches for his superiors, because he suspected that Scott Rotem, his immediate superior and boss, was behind the order. Neither of his companions would confirm this.

He thought once more of the woman's laugh in the Fox, and the state of panic in him that it had caused. He laughed out loud at his flight of fancy, then covered his mouth with his hand and tried to wipe the grin off his face: Of all the unhealthy indulgences. Why her? Why now?

The agents looked at him like he was supposed to share the joke. Both of his keepers carried Justice Department credentials. The older one with the pained eyes answered to one of those names that rang familiar to Larson: Wilcox. Larson knew a couple different guys named Wilcox, one a running coach at a private college, the other a former FATF deputy said to be one of the most reliable and most entertaining stakeout partners out there. This guy was neither of them and, whereas Larson felt a little tired, Wilcox saw eleven o'clock pass still rigidly upright and wide awake in his padded seat, like he had a broomstick up his ass. He typed aggressively, as if the laptop had pissed him off in some way, or else the report he was generating was his last will and testament.

"What about Hampton and Stubblefield?" Larson asked suddenly. Hampton and Stubblefield had survived their wounds. The two had transferred with him and were members of his FATF squad. Larson depended upon them. "Have they been called?"

Wilcox pursed his lips and returned to his typing. "You find out when we get there."

Larson stared out the window, the night's black canvas mixing with his own reflection of deep set green eyes, lips set in a constant smirk, and skin that needed a shave. Below, city lights shimmered, small and clustered. The world looked so simple from above.

Hope's offer, six years earlier, had been straightforward enough itself. The bus incident, the failed attempt on her life, had forced the Marshals Service to request her immediate placement into WITSEC, an unusual but not unheard-of pretrial tactic.

There had been nothing romantic or sentimental in Hope's proposal perhaps because, like him, she feared they were being watched. There was never time for just the two of them. While Larson appeared at briefings covering the bus incident, Hope had been placed into a safe house—the Orchard House, an old farmhouse out of town—and guarded by Larson's team, limiting Larson's contact with her. The days ticked down toward a full "identity" wash, after which Hope Stevens would cease to exist, even for Larson.

"Come with me," she'd said in a businesslike tone.

They were standing in the safe house's backyard. A winter wind blew through his clothes; this was how he explained to himself the full-length shiver that swept through him at that moment.

His fantasy and the culmination of his fears. "What?"

"Request a new identity and come with me. We'll start over together."

She knew—they both knew—that this was nothing short of a proposal of marriage. Where she was going, it was permanent. Once into WITSEC, there was no going back, no reconnection to one's past. It was a case of self-invoked amnesia. Suddenly it seemed to Larson that on so many levels they barely knew each other. Could he make this decision without thinking it through, without a chance to say some important good-byes?

Adding to the difficulty was his insider's knowledge of how difficult—*impossible*—WITSEC could be on the protected witness. Even the most hardened criminal cracked when shut off from all contact with family members. Many ended up attending baptisms, weddings, or funerals, exposing themselves, breaking the anonymity of their protection, risking their lives for a few minutes of the familiar.

How long would Hope hold up? What if he gave up the years of his training and employment only to have the relationship self-destruct six months into the struggle to remake themselves? How well would *he* hold up?

He didn't speak any of this, didn't voice his concerns, but he clearly wore them on his face, for she grew pale, turning away from the wind and him along with it.

"Oh," she said.

"It's not that . . . It is just so out of the blue is all . . ."

"Is it?"

"Me joining the program? WITSEC? Yeah, it is. It's like a doctor becoming a patient. The warden becoming a prisoner. It's just something you don't ever see happening to you, when you're on this side of protection."

"Well, I'm asking you to see it."

"Will they even let me? I doubt it." He had no idea how such a request would be treated. Fraternization was discouraged, sometimes punished. All deputies were instructed to avoid what most protected witnesses wanted most: safety in the form of friendship with the marshals. "It's complicated."

"No, not really," she said. "It's about as simple as it gets, Lars. You either see us together or you don't."

He coughed out a nervous laugh, and this hurt her. He wished he could take it back.

"There's a lot to get done," he said.

Her face brightened. He knew it was the right decision.

She came into his arms eagerly but tentatively, like a child asking a parent for forgiveness. "I'm not asking you to suffer with me, I'm asking you to live with me."

"Don't worry, you'll suffer plenty with me in your life," he teased, returning the hug.

"Penance I'll gladly endure."

"I have to make some calls, say some good-byes. Clear this through channels." The list grew longer in his head.

"What if they refuse you?"

Only then did he fully understand the extent of her proposal, and he had to wonder if this was her original intention all along. "I can't do that, Hope."

"Can't or won't?"

"Sneak you out of here somehow? Run away with you without the . . . the firewall . . . of WITSEC to protect us? I'm one person. It doesn't work like that."

He realized immediately she underestimated WITSEC's importance to her—to their—survival. This, in turn, caused him to reassess his own willingness to destroy Roland Larson in the coming twenty-four-to-forty-eight-hour period, all in the name of love. A love less than three months old. A love fashioned under the threat of death and in the heat of battle.

"Rotem will try to talk me out of it. At the very least they'll make me meet with a psychologist or psychiatrist. There will be papers to sign, releasing them of responsibility. It's not a matter of breaking out the champagne and waiting to be relocated."

"Second thoughts?"

"It's too soon to have second thoughts. These are original thoughts," he said. "I just need a little time to think it through and put it together."

"There isn't any time, is there? Do you think they're going to warn you before they take me off? Do you think they're going to warn me? No way." She was right. It would be done in the dead of night, like a criminal act. Two or three vans all leaving at the same moment, all heading different directions. She'd be inside one of them, gone for good. She'd already been placed on the fast track. Her new identity would arrive any moment.

He explained his situation again, detailing his need for a day or two at least. "I *do* love you. But I owe some explanations. I won't leave my friends in false grief. I've seen enough of that."

They kissed, though for the first time without passion, and that kiss would haunt him as he told Rotem of his plan to join her, and later considered her offer through the night, phone off the hook, his bed not slept in.

In the morning, his mind made up, he returned to the farmhouse.

He found it empty and deserted. Even the tire tracks had been swept out of the dirt, as if no one had been there in years.

He blamed Rotem, though never to his face. He blamed her for waiting so long to ask. He blamed himself forever for wavering, for leaving her side, even for a moment, that day.

Touchdown returned him to the present and delivered the requisite black Navigator to the jet's stairs. This kind of service made Larson feel both important and uncomfortable, neither of which pleased him. The three federal employees were whisked off by a driver, who also carried Justice Department creds. Larson was once again reminded of how serious this must be.

Uncle Leo. It was little more than a name to Larson, but it carried weight, of legendary import in the realm of WITSEC. Uncle

Leo had had something to do with the witness protection program's modernization which had begun in the mid-1990s. Leo's name spoke as much of secrecy as anything else, as did so much of the WITSEC program's overhaul. It was the equivalent of the program's very integrity, its security, and the security of its protected witnesses. Uncle Leo's predicament had rallied the big hitters. It might be nothing more than an unscheduled vacation, or a trip to a hospital, but Uncle Leo had disappeared and Rotem had obviously been ordered to move heaven and earth, along with a sizable private jet, to find the man. It was as if WITSEC and FATF, separate entities, with one rarely having anything to do with the other, would be working together. The presence of these Justice agents spoke volumes. This was the varsity squad; if Larson was being called off the bench, as it appeared he was, then people wanted Uncle Leo found. The desk jockeys were ready to sit back and watch people like Larson work.

This particular October night in Princeton, New Jersey, left Larson wishing he'd brought a sweater, rather than the black jeans and black blazer he'd been wearing at the play. The smell was of car engines and tire rubber as he climbed out of the Navigator, stepping onto a blacktop driveway alongside a modest, unremarkable home in what was probably called a "nice neighborhood," a place where kids could ride bikes and skateboards at any hour but the current hour of four A.M.

Larson, for no reason other than his own experience, had been expecting a crime scene—local cops, a crime scene unit, maybe an effort to hold back the press. Instead it was the Navigator, a Town Car, and one other Navigator, also black. The house was dark, and it took him a minute to realize someone had taped black Visquine or garbage bags over the interior windows. He followed his two escorts inside.

He was struck both by the hideous color of the living room's yellow carpet and the abundance of printed matter—books, magazines, and more magazines. The owner was a reader. The place was a litter basket. The furniture wanted to be contemporary but stopped at modern and so looked like the before-shot of a custom-renovation ad. A '50s ranch for a scientist who belonged in *Back to the Future*, judging by the few shots of Uncle Leo and various dignitaries and politicians that hung on the wall amid copies of Warhol lithographs and some fairly decent black-and-white portrait photography that included John F. Kennedy and Ronald Reagan.

"He knew everybody, once upon a time." Scott Rotem, forty-one or -two going on fifty-five. He sported bulging eyes a comedian would kill for if they'd been capable of carrying any expression at all. A patch of missing hair cried out for Rogaine. Rotem was all right if you liked your bureaucrats with zero sense of humor, a mean streak burnished into a crease between the eyes, and the vague aura of foot odor following one about. The man not only woke on the wrong side of the bed, he also willingly entered it from that side, too. Not simply a stick-in-the-mud, but a phone pole, pile-driven at that. Larson liked him, though it confounded him exactly why this was. It might have been the beauty and polish of Rotem's stubborn persona, that never-give-an-inch, bastard-at-a-glance attitude that made him both an asshole and yet someone Larson could rightfully respect. Rotem was consistent, if in a vaguely pernicious way, and that struck Larson as a noble attribute in this day and age.

"You owe me half a performance of *Much Ado about Nothing*. Your guys pulled me at intermission."

"Come in here."

Larson followed. Whenever possible he took the high ground against Rotem, took it early and fought to hold it, because the man had a way of getting under his skin, getting him to do things, to take assignments he didn't want. Larson would say yes before he meant it, even if the one time in his life he should have, he hadn't.

The moment he entered the side hall, now passing framed snapshots of what had to be family, he smelled the blood. Once you've been around it a few times, your nose can pick it up at a distance, and Larson had been around it more than a few times, so the memories attached to that odor like ticks. Each step down the hall was a step down memory lane, only the snapshots on the walls of his recollection were all of victims.

He found the silence of the house disturbing. He wished Rotem would say something. He caught himself humming and wishing he could carry a tune better than he could.

The smell grew riper now. All of a sudden, it reeked like someone had opened a long-ignored trash can. It hit Larson like twisting the cap off a bottle of ammonia. Hit him in the eyes and deep up into his sinuses where he knew it would lodge and remain for hours to come. Days perhaps. It came from a Macy's parade balloon, facedown in a vanity bathroom, fallen to the linoleum floor, the body so swollen and distorted that the wrists puffed out above the shirt cuffs, straining the buttons. Two to three weeks. Decomposition so advanced that the skin on the back of the neck had split as it swelled, leaving a set of narrow trenches running from the shirt collar up under the hair.

"It's not Leopold Markowitz," Rotem informed him.

"Not Uncle Leo?" Larson asked. "Then this was . . . ?"

"One Emerson Brighton Doyle. Name's not important. A graduate student. Markowitz's personal assistant. Against the university's bylaws—unpaid personal assistants—but fairly common practice, especially for the emeritus types like Markowitz. He did consulting for Princeton, Markowitz did. Consulted all over the place. We're collecting that information now."

"Did or does?" Larson sought to clarify the tense.

"You catch on quickly."

"You wanted me to see Emerson Brighton Doyle in person. I don't get that."

"A picture wouldn't have done it," Rotem said.

"Aromatherapy?"

"Come around this side."

As Larson stepped across the pale log of a khaki-clad leg, Rotem continued. "The moment they move him, disturb him, some or all of this will be ruined. He's going to come apart like an over-cooked brisket. You're right about me wanting you to see this. But it's not as if I'd wish this upon anybody," he said, displaying what was for him a rare moment of humanism.

"Then why?" Larson asked, as it turned out, a little prematurely. For by then Rotem had pointed toward the head, which looked more like a horrific beach ball. Larson backed off a step, his back now pressed against the coolness of the wall between the corner sink and toilet, his left arm on the roll of toilet paper like an armrest. That chill found its way through the blazer and shirt and into his skin and bored down into him like a dentist's drill. Rotem was right, moving the body would have likely destroyed it. At first blush, it looked like nothing more than another of the series of chins—Larson counted nine or ten of the folds despite the heavy bloating. But the pink one just below the man's right earlobe was more than a tear or a split. It was too precise, the slight smile of a curve that started at the ear. Too intentional.

"Benny the bus driver," Larson finally said. "Christ almighty. The Romeros?" Hope rose in his thoughts again. Hope and her long history with the Romeros.

"We can't be sure," Rotem said, but his heart obviously wasn't in it.

The medical examiner had written up Benny's sliced throat as a precision cut intended to sever the trachea while simultaneously laying open the carotid arteries. An extremely efficient cut for someone wishing to both silence and kill a man. Benny had bled out while drowning in his own blood, his larynx cut and inoperable. Larson hadn't seen anything like it in the past six years.

"Can't call it a signature cut," Rotem continued.

"Can't we?"

"But I wanted you to see it."

"Scott, maybe I'm punchy because it's four-thirty in the morning, or maybe it's from all the chitchat with the two wonderful conversationalists you sent to abduct me, but I'm squatting by this pile of stink looking at what it is you brought me here to look at, and I'm telling you it is a signature cut, which must be exactly what you want to hear, or why would you bring me? So if you know something else, would you just fucking say it?"

Larson wanted out of there. He wanted to find Hope—tell her the Romeros were on the move again. *On the move? They had Leo Markowitz! Good God.*

"Leopold Markowitz wrote the code for *Laena*."

Larson had assumed as much. *Laena* was the name given to WITSEC's master witness protection list, the most carefully guarded database in the Justice Department. Larson's insides did another little roll. Anything and everything to do with the identity and location of Hope Stevens was contained in *Laena*.

"*Laena* became inoperable yesterday afternoon at around four, eastern. They can't open it; they can't access it."

"So they've got the list," Larson said.

"The list, but maybe not the names *on* the list." Seven to eight thousand people, including dependents—women, children, spouses and relatives. "The encryption's a significant obstacle."

"Not for Markowitz, though," said Larson. "Right?"

"Even for Markowitz, decrypting *Laena* will take time."

"We've been tapped to find him."

"You have. By me. Yes."

Larson held his breath, disentangled himself from the toilet paper roll, and leaned forward to study the cut more closely. There was too much rot and decomposition for him to determine if a razor blade had been responsible, though he knew this would ultimately be the judgment of the coroner or medical examiner. It all proved a little overwhelming. He stood, hurried out of the bathroom, down the hall, and outside where he gasped for clean air, or what passed for it in New Jersey.

Rotem was right there behind him, more agile and quick than Larson might have given him credit for.

The treetops fluttered and stirred in a breeze, swaying back and forth like a gospel choir.

Larson coughed up a clam and spit it into a nearby shrub and heard it glob down from twig to leaf and finally trickle into the sodden mulch. The taste lingered at the back of his throat, hanging barely above his retching point. "Fuck," he muttered.

"Judging by this, he has a two-week head start on us," Rotem said. "Three at most."

"So does he have the names or not?"

"I'm told by WITSEC that it's possible but doubtful. Not yet, but any day now. Not only is the master list encrypted, but each individual record within it as well. Think of it as a safe-deposit box inside a bank. Markowitz not only has to break into the bank, but then open each and every safe-deposit box in order to win a protected witness's identity. Three weeks to a month, and only then with the fastest computers out there—the Crays and Silicon Graphics. Gives us a week to ten days more to find him."

"Which means finding the Romeros. I thought they up and vanished after Donny checked into our federal facility."

"We know better than most, Larson," Rotem said, "that no one ever fully disappears." He paused. "Excepting maybe Hoffa."

With Donny's initial conviction on fraud charges, Pop, Ricardo, and others had gone to ground. If the government knew where to find them, it was news to Larson. The remaining Romeros had never been prosecuted, leaving Larson wondering why. Hope's testimony would be enough to convict; she remained a living threat to the family.

Rotem added, "Any one of the big families would kill to have that list. Pay millions. Why not the Romeros? If Markowitz gives them Laena—every assumed identity of every protected witness in the WITSEC program . . ." He let it hang there. Then he said, "That's a lot of motivation."

"But the point of making the list digital was to make it bulletproof," Larson said.

"Right. And the *Titanic*'s unsinkable. Listen, WITSEC is reassembling the list through paperwork, but it's a hell of a lot of paperwork."

"There's got to be some kind of backup, right?"

"I suppose they might get it back online. What do I know? We're supposed to find Markowitz. Period."

"We do this in secret?"

"You do everything in secret," Rotem said.

"Yeah, but something this big . . . It's gonna be a task-force effort, right? FiBIes, us, ATF . . . who else?"

"Us."

"I said us."

"Us," Rotem repeated, the light from his butane lighter now

catching his oversized eyes and throwing two noses onto his face as he lit a cigarette. Larson didn't know this about the man—that he smoked—and he found it disconcerting to have served five years on the Fugitive Apprehension Task Force and only now learn this.

His head was spinning. He still couldn't get that taste out of his mouth. Then, as Rotem coughed, Larson understood the cigarette. It was Rotem's way—as a nonsmoker—to purge the lingering taste from his own throat.

"Does that really work?"

"Yeah," Rotem answered.

"You mind?"

Rotem passed Larson the burning cigarette. Larson took it between his thick fingers, looked down at his own hand, and then passed it back. He tried a stick of gum instead, and for a minute it worked, but when he swallowed he thought he might upchuck.

The panic hit him again, ran right through him like venom. Hope—first in line for execution by the Romeros.

"Donny Romero," Larson said.

"Is coming up for parole. Yes."

Larson had heard only rumors. "How does he pull off a parole hearing if he's still a suspect in capital murder investigations?"

Rotem sized him up, sucked on the cigarette. "Government lost its star witness. No witness, no prosecution. The other Romeros are in the wind."

Larson cringed. "Lost the witness . . . to spoilage?" The service's euphemism for killed witnesses.

"AWOL."

"This is Hope Stevens we're talking about?" So she never had testified—the rumors were true.

The look that came back from Rotem was paralyzing. Rotem knew the connection. He nodded.

Is that why he picked me for the job? Larson wondered. Rotem wanted as much added motivation in his men as he could find.

Some kind of critter scampered through the undergrowth. A rat, Larson thought, though he didn't get a look at the thing.

"Markowitz could be bent," Larson said. "This could be some kind of ruse."

"One hell of a ruse. My gut says Romeros. Yours?"

Larson's silence signaled his assent.

"We'll bring in forensics," Rotem said. "But I guarantee you that cut'll end up matching Benny's."

Larson wondered, with the master list gone, with Hope AWOL from WITSEC, how he would find her before the Romeros did. No matter what Rotem assigned him, *that* was the task at hand. With Donny's parole on the line, the Romeros wouldn't want a witness as potentially damaging as Hope changing her mind and stepping forward. In fact it didn't seem out of the question that they'd gone after the list specifically to find Hope and prevent her from testifying.

Larson spat again, trying to rid himself of that horrid aftertaste. The rat or squirrel—whatever the fuck it was—rattled the underbrush as it ran off into the night.

CHAPTER THREE

Rotem flew him back commercial. Larson should have seen that coming. The rush had been getting him there, not flying him home. Coach, of course, so he ate his knees and felt his lower back for the entire flight.

A layover in Chicago, of course, because TWA had sold to American and thus the demise of nonstops to St. Louis. Progress.

Weather delay, of course, because this was Chicago's O'Hare. Larson wasn't sure he'd ever had a perfect connection here.

Tired, of course, because he'd been up all night. He'd managed to doze for an hour or so on the plane; it held off the headache but did nothing for the gloom, the underwater-like efforts of movement, and the persistent buzz of panic in his gut.

He couldn't get past Hope being a likely target. The Romeros wouldn't know that she'd fled WITSEC—but unless she'd done everything perfectly, that would only make her easier to find.

By the time the second delay in boarding for the homeward leg was announced, Larson had already spoken twice with Rotem and finally connected with Trill Hampton. He needed to lead Hampton down the garden path in order to disguise his own intentions to locate Hope Stevens and somehow get her to safety. And, he needed to do so without violating the secrecy Rotem required of him.

"The trail's ice-cold," he told his next in command. He'd caught him up on Markowitz's disappearance and the murder of the man's assistant, but not the professor's role in the creation of *Laena*. Rotem had been adamant about the need for secrecy. The future of WITSEC itself depended on their team's ability to contain *Laena*, *and* the news of its compromise. And yet Larson felt his guys worked better when they understood the stakes. It took a special mindset to work fugitive apprehension. Your guys deserved to know what to expect on the other side of the door. And Larson felt like giving them the benefit of the doubt. But to keep his word with Rotem, he'd have to lead Hampton into discovering Markowitz's role for himself. Hampton and Stubblefield didn't have the rank within the service to have heard of Uncle Leo.

Larson said, "I'm told a couple of our guys canvassed Markowitz's associates this morning. They were pretty tight-lipped. Claimed he traveled so much he was hard to keep track of, and that no one knew he'd gone missing."

"A guy his age, traveling a lot?" Hampton, who was not yet forty, related everything to age. Larson had long since decided it was some kind of phobia with Hampton. He was terrified of growing old and saw anyone over fifty as long gone. He'd focused so much on age that he'd missed the hint Larson had dropped.

Larson again. "Markowitz was, or is—we don't know yet which—doing a lot of consulting work as well as speaking engagements. Must have been raking it in."

"And no one knew his schedule?"

Larson sank the hook. "*Our guys* didn't get anything out of the canvass." His point here was that FATF, not the FBI, had done the canvassing. That should have sounded alarms for Hampton.

"His last known?" Hampton had missed again.

"A little slippery. His assistant might have helped there. We're left to fill in the gaps, and his most recent schedule is among them. We've confirmed Palo Alto, Raleigh-Durham, and our own Wash U. Airline records show he'd been commuting between these three and back to Princeton regularly for the past couple months. That's where you and Stubby will start. Phone-canvassing the three universities. Face-to-face follow-ups, if needed."

"This guy qualifies as a fugitive? From what, an old folks' home?"

Closer, Larson thought.

"We're gonna need his full financials, his medical records, and a psychiatric." Hampton's voice bordered on complaint. "Does a guy that old have a love life?"

Larson carefully considered what he said next. He wanted Hampton making the connection that no other law enforcement was involved, that Leopold Markowitz had put the witness protection list at risk. He owed his guys that much. He looked for another way around it.

Okay. "The assistant's wound was nearly identical to Benny's."

The pause on the other end of the call said enough. "Did you say our guys did the canvassing?" *Bingo*. "Why are *we* investigating this, anyway?" Hampton asked. "Where the hell's the Bureau in this?"

Larson nodded on his end of the call. "They're *not* in this, which should tell you a lot. That, and the fact that it may be the Romeros behind the disappearance, right at a time Donny's coming up for parole review."

"Why the fuck would the Romeros care about some old computer geek?" Hampton asked. "What is it you're *not* telling me, Rolo?"

"Now you're getting the idea."

"They've got you gagged on this."

Relief swept through him. He thought this was probably how "people close to the investigation" leaked things to the media. You didn't have to say things to say things. You could let them speak for themselves. He was somewhat new to this.

"Who else did this geezer consult for besides these three universities? Do I smell federal government?"

"Hell of a nose you've got, Hamp."

"Romeros," Hampton said. "Organized Crime Unit?"

"Colder. Think Benny."

"Justice?"

"Scalding hot."

"WITSEC." The inflection was gone. Hampton had made it a statement. "Wait! Was he involved with the reorg of the master list?"

Pure poetry. Larson knew Hampton would see the full scope of it now. They were not pursuing some old man who was missing his college lectures but—if Hampton was able to take it one step further—the man behind the *Laena* list, the lives of more than two thousand protected witnesses and their five thousand dependents. What came with that was a level of personal risk unlike anything associated with their typical day job: chasing down escaped convicts and wanted felons.

"Our primary is Markowitz. He's believed to need access to a supercomputer for whatever reasons. They want us interviewing the people running the computers at these places in hopes of intercepting him."

"Supercomputers? You go for that?" Hampton asked.

"It has merit."

"Money, women, and work," Hampton said. "That's how you find a guy."

"No argument there."

"Why's he need the computer?"

"That's off-limits for discussion, as is most of this."

"The Romeros?"

"You're warm." Hampton would put it together. It just might take a day or two.

"Scrotum's taking his orders from WITSEC? What's with that? Since when?"

"If this plane ever takes off, I should be landing before noon." But another idea had surfaced. He would not be on the next plane out.

"You want me to pick you up?"

"That would be good. My car's downtown. But I'll call you when I leave. Meanwhile, you and Stubby get cooking. Rotem's got the contacts for you."

"Riddle me this, Rolo," Hampton said, still working out the information he'd been supplied. "Are you in Chicago on a layover or because the regional WITSEC office is up there? How involved are they? They wouldn't be *missing* something, would they? Something our very own Ben Franklin created for them about five years back?"

Larson wanted to congratulate the man, but he said only, "I'll call you."

His return to St. Louis was going to have to wait a few hours.

First things first.

CHAPTER FOUR

Chicago's North Shore, a string of bedroom communities developed a century before, retained some of its former heritage. Classic architecture lined the streets of the quaint villages. These townships had, for the most part, been spared the tract housing that swept across the American Midwest during the suburban sprawl of the postwar 1950s.

But to Larson it all began to look the same—Winnetka, Glencoe—hard to tell one from the other, the difference being the occasional golf course with a brick clubhouse.

On a Saturday afternoon the die-hard homeowners were out raking leaves. They wore creased khakis, leather deck shoes, and Izod shirts. The women had been released to jog, Rollerblade, and walk the dog, while their adolescent kids skateboarded or rode bicycles in packs.

The cars he followed, Lexus, Mercedes, Volvos, and Cadillac Escalades, carried golden retrievers or Labradors in the back, with soccer camp and hockey stickers on the rear window and foolish bumper stickers announcing their kids were honor students.

Larson's small house in St. Louis—one of those '50s ranches—would have fit into the garage of most of these palaces, though that space was probably reserved for the au pair or the Morgan or XKE. He double-checked the address and pulled over.

Traveling through suburbia, the reminders of family and what his life might have been had he accepted Hope's invitation without second thought, forced him to call Linda, the only person in whom he'd confided this past.

Linda had been his one and only relationship in the past six years. A recently widowed wife of a dear friend of Larson's, the two had shared a brief, but emotionally charged affair nearly three years earlier. Neither had entered the bed with any expectation beyond comfort and understanding, but both came away with a confidante for life. Linda often looked after Larson's dog, Tanner, when he was away for work. He'd left her a message from New Jersey, and decided to follow up.

She screened her calls, so he had to wait for her to call him back. She never asked him where he was or what he was doing.

"Tanner's fine," she began the call.

He thanked her for taking care of the dog on such short notice and she replied that it was no problem. She lived in a huge house with a giant backyard, a holdover from the marriage she would eventually have to part with. But not yet. They both knew she wasn't ready.

He said, "You remember that guy who I knew would know my friend's new persona?" No names. Nothing definite.

"Yeah?" She sounded worried. He'd expressed many times how pursuing this information might cost him his job.

"I'm parked around the corner from his house."

"Well, that's news."

"Am I crazy?"

"Of course you are. Crazy in love, right?"

"She's in danger."

"I'm sorry."

"I don't know if I'm just using this as an excuse or not, but here I am and I'm going through with it."

"Unfinished business."

"Exactly."

"If I could have had even five minutes with Jack . . . Well, you've heard this enough times."

Larson's friend had died while lecturing at a small New England college. Not for the fee, but because they'd asked. Forty-three years old. Way too early.

"I'm going to get my five minutes," he said, although it rang of hollow confidence. His odds of tracking Hope down were limited by a very tall wall erected to prevent such contact.

"Remember, you're the one pursuing her. You've had time to process the reunion and what it means. She won't have. Don't judge her by her first reaction. Give her time to sort it out. It won't be easy on her."

"It won't be easy on either of us."

"I'm happy for you."

He felt like an asshole, bringing Linda into this, rubbing her nose in his opportunity while she would have no such chance to reconnect.

He said, "If and when I find her, it may be me making the proposal this time . . ."

"I'll give Tanner a good home" was all she said.

He heard her voice tighten, could picture her at the kitchen table. He knew her patterns. He loved her as one of the good ones. They would miss each other.

"We'll see," he said.

She told him to take care of himself, that she loved him, and as they hung up he realized how very close they'd become, how much he would miss her.

Pulling back onto the road, the trees alive with color, Larson considered the career risk he took by coming here to the man's private home. He wasn't supposed to know the identity of any of the WITSEC regional directors, much less visit one unannounced. He had no idea what repercussions he might face.

He pulled to a stop in front of an impressive, three-story Tudor. Either Sunderland or his wife came from a wealthy family, or she had a hell of a good job, because there was no way a person on Sunderland's salary could afford this place. It sported four brick chimneys, leaded glass windows, and a fully landscaped yard—more like a park—including a slate walkway that led up to an arched-top wooden door that hosted a massive wrought-iron knocker in the shape of an ivy wreath. A pair of impressive oaks shaded the front yard, their leaves rattling at Larson's feet. Intimidated by the surroundings, he rehearsed not only what to say, but how to say it.

The door opened to a young teenage girl, self-conscious and wearing braces she tried to hide by covering her mouth as she spoke. She wore hip-hugger blue jeans, and a Gap T-shirt that showed her navel. Larson wondered what it was like being her parent.

"Marley? Your dad home?" He took a risk by using her name, but thought the familiarity might soften her.

She cocked her head. Curious. "May I tell him who's asking?"

The right words. The right schools. She didn't invite him inside. She blocked the door with her foot. The right training.

"Deputy Marshal Roland Larson," he told her, handing her his business card. "Tell him I'm with," he spelled it, "F-A-T-F."

"Sure. Wait here, please."

She closed the door. For the hell of it, Larson tried the handle and found it locked. Sunderland's kids had grown up to learn the complexities of living in the same house as a regional WITSEC director. Or maybe it was just suburbia. There were only four other regional directors who knew the program as intimately as Sunderland, but it had been Sunderland who had relocated Hope from the Orchard House.

Sunderland's face and his wrinkled clothes left the impression he hadn't slept recently. A pair of smudged reading glasses hung from his neck by a thin black cord. He smelled of popcorn—or maybe that was the house itself. He had ice blue eyes that projected contempt, a Roman nose, the silver hairs of which needed trimming, a cleft chin, and awkward ears. He wore his graying hair cut like that of his fellow suburban businessmen, well in disguise. His right hand remained behind and screened by the massive door, possibly concealing a weapon.

Larson caught a reflection in the narrow side window alongside the door. Two big guys, well dressed, completely out of place on a Saturday, stood back on the sidewalk between him and his car. Deputy marshals, no doubt assigned to protect the guy who protected so many. The loss of *Laena* had shaken WITSEC to its core.

"Creds," Sunderland ordered, fingering the business card.

Larson turned over his ID wallet, his moves slow and controlled for the sake of the two behind him. "We met once, six years ago."

"Did we?" he asked, still studying Larson's credentials through the half reading glasses on the bridge of his nose.

"A woman witness," Larson said, using this to jog Sunderland's memory because women were such a minority among protected witnesses. "It was a farmhouse, outside of St. Louis. You came down there to debrief her."

Sunderland glanced over the top of his glasses. "You do look vaguely familiar."

"Scott Rotem was in the field then. This is back before our protection squad was transferred to F-A-T-F."

"That's a nice promotion." He still couldn't place Larson. "Let me ask you this: my home? Are you out of your mind?" Sunderland's phone number went unpublished and was not listed anywhere in any government publication, nor on any Internet site, standard security for a WITSEC regional. The five regionals ultimately relocated all the witnesses in the program or oversaw their relocated identities. As such, the regionals were carefully protected.

"I traced you through Marley and Conner. You, or your wife, bought them each a cell phone about a year and a half ago. Marley's phone had the home address listed. It took me about thirty minutes to get it."

Sunderland grimaced and then waved off the two guards. As he closed the door behind Larson he asked incredulously, "You found me through my kids' cell phones?"

"It's what I do for a living."

The living room was Chippendale, handwoven area rugs, and floral arrangements that matched. Larson drank in the sweet smell of furniture polish, and the tang of ripe cheese. He heard a television running.

Sunderland led him past the kitchen, down a hallway lined with summer vacations, the television first growing louder then fading.

"Scott knows about this visit?"

"Not exactly," Larson answered honestly.

"Fugitive Apprehension has the utmost respect of those of us in the Service, Larson, and we're all aware it's you running field operations. Rotem can be a real prick. We all know that, too. But he gets the job done. So do you, I'm told, or I wouldn't have let you past the front door." In fact, he'd recognized Larson's name if not his face.

"How well do you know Markowitz?" Larson asked, once the study door was closed. Lived-in and somewhat disorganized, it appeared to be a maid's room he'd converted, for it was a door or two past the laundry room. It smelled of oil paint and whiskey. A partially completed, somewhat tacky landscape sat on a paint-stained wooden easel in the near corner, a canvas drop cloth beneath it.

"Calms the nerves," Sunderland explained, catching Larson staring.

Not when you look at it, Larson thought.

"Leo Markowitz is a brilliant designer and technician. I know him only professionally, of course, but I'm not sure there's much to Leo besides the professional. He took an unruly system for cataloging and . . . and tracking thousands of protected witnesses and . . . and created out of it not just a database, but an *encrypted database.* We paid a dozen convicted hackers to try to break *Laena,* and . . . and not one of them made it past first base. The man's a genius."

"How many within WITSEC knew what he was doing . . . knew it was him doing it?"

"Listen, if you're going where I think you're going, we're way ahead of you. We're on it. So's Rotem. If there's a mole— WITSEC, FATF, Justice—we'll ferret him out."

"I'm sure you will, but we're coming at this from an entirely different direction than you. You're trying to find a mole and turn him. We're trying to find Markowitz. And that means radiating out from anyone who knew his role in this and looking at their recent activities, calls, e-mails, contacts, finances. Some of the same stuff you're looking at."

"So, I'll get you the names. We'll e-mail them to you. There are about eight people total we're looking at."

"That'll help. Thanks."

"Which woman?" Sunderland asked. "The farmhouse," he reminded. "What was her primary?"

"Stevens. Hope Stevens."

Sunderland nodded. No one forgot Hope. But as it turned out Sunderland remembered her for other reasons than Larson might have thought. "She opted out, you know?"

"I heard." Larson took a deep breath. "I need to know what's in her WITSEC record. What someone might see if they went looking. I need to find her."

That half-cocked, tilted head of curiosity was something his daughter had learned from him. "Have you been assigned to do so?"

Delicate territory. Larson hesitated.

"Because, I don't know if you know this or not, but Justice would do backflips to find her right now. There's a case pending. She could be . . . influential."

"Donny Romero."

"You're beginning to impress me, Larson."

"Or am I pissing you off?" Larson could see it in the man's face.

Sunderland nodded behind an ironic smile. "Okay. That, too."

"You're not going to read this in any report, but Markowitz's assistant, the one we found dead in the downstairs bathroom, was killed by the same person that attacked Hope Stevens on that bus six years ago. You remember that incident?"

"Go on."

"I need to find her, because they'll come looking. Markowitz's assistant was either done by the same person, or a different one trained by whoever trained him, because it's a signature kill. We're never going to prove it was the Romeros, but that's not my job. And we're never going to prove this either, but Hope Stevens is at the top of the list of people they want dead. She reads about Donny's parole review and maybe she has a change of heart and comes out of the bushes. Are they going to risk that? And we have two choices: let them get her, let her be killed; or find her, lay a trap, and either arrest the killer on the way in and try to debrief him, or—and this is more to my liking—scare the shit out of him, drive him off, and hope the termite returns to the nest." He'd surprised Sunderland with all of this. In truth, he didn't care nearly as much about tracking the killer, but he knew Sunderland would want a bigger prize than protecting an AWOL witness. "The same nest that's containing Markowitz and *Laena*, I'm guessing."

"I told you: She opted out."

"You placed her into the program."

"I did. It's true."

"You created a new life for her, a life she may still be following, using, even if under an assumed name."

"I've put dozens—hundreds—into the program. What makes you think I'd remember this one?"

Larson had his own answer for that. He said, "When she opted out, was there any discussion, or did she just blow you off?"

Sunderland pursed his lips, studied Larson thoughtfully, and shook his head slightly. "I don't do this," he said. "I don't know what your agenda is, Deputy Marshal, but I don't discuss protected witnesses."

"The active list is missing. No one is protected. But what about the inactive list—those who've opted out of the program? Why do I think that those witnesses would have a list of their own?"

"Everything that's contained in *Laena*, or nearly everything, has a paper counterpart. We also have physical backups of *Laena*. All of that is being onlined as we speak. By Monday we'll be most of the way back." His tone indicated otherwise, but Larson didn't challenge any of that. The computer backups had probably been installed by Markowitz, and if so, they might not be so easily accessed. WITSEC most certainly had paper records, but how current were they, and how easily found and organized? He thought it was probably in more of a shambles than Sunderland was letting on. A couple years into depending on computers and paperwork seemed to calcify.

"I need anything you've got on her," Larson said.

He felt Sunderland resist.

"Why do you suppose there hasn't been a bloodbath?" Larson asked.

"I beg your pardon?"

"If Markowitz has cracked *Laena* and decrypted each of the protected identities, if the Romeros have all those names and locations, then why hasn't there been a bloodbath?" With Sunderland behind the desk, Larson stepped forward and took a seat in a comfortable red leather chair facing him. "They could sell the names off that list. No shortage of buyers. Every crime family in the country has someone on that list they'd like to see dead—most have hit lists they're just itching to get to. So why no bloodshed?"

"I'm sure Scott told you about the encryption. One identity at a time. That's a lot of work. Takes a lot of time."

"Why else?"

"They want to cherry-pick the list, I suppose. We're way ahead of you on this, Larson. Believe me, we have crews out there right now recalling dozens of witnesses."

"But not the ones who have opted out," Larson said.

"Actually, we're posting a prearranged general warning for *all* witnesses. It's a red flag meant to send them and their dependents to ground. They'll stay there until they get the all clear."

"And Hope will obey that?"

"If she's smart she will."

"If she's not smart," Larson said, "we miss a golden opportunity to catch a killer and find Marko."

"Are you always this confident?"

"Fugitive apprehension isn't like anything else. You have to learn to see around corners. That's all I'm trying to do here."

Sunderland stood and moved to his study door, trying to draw Larson out of his chair. "Come on," he said.

Larson didn't budge. "You've got to help me."

"Not here," Sunderland said. "Not in my home. I'm not discussing a protected witness—even one that opted out—in my home. We have a room downtown. It's clean. Both of us will have to be swept as well. I'm not doing this without taking that precaution."

Larson practically sprang out of his chair. Sunderland had agreed to give him Hope Stevens.

Larson was made to empty his pockets—billfold, credentials, loose change, handkerchief, pen—and to leave his BlackBerry and his belt, anything metal, with the deputy in charge. Sunderland did the same, but was carrying a lot less. Wands were waved over every limb and up and down their torsos, like an airport security check, before either man was cleared. They entered a plain-looking conference room.

Housed in the center of the offices, this room was without windows or decoration, and only the one door, a thick door that locked with a significant *click*. The pale green walls looked different to Larson, perhaps a special metallic paint had been used, or even a composite material that reflected radio waves. He'd heard of such rooms, but had never been in one. No phone, no computer. No electrical wall outlets. The recessed lights in the ceiling shone through some kind of thick glass or similar material, and Larson thought this material was probably also designed to ground out any random radio waves.

It had been a thirty-minute drive downtown, Larson in the rental following Sunderland's Buick. All this effort, he thought, an exercise in secrecy for a woman no longer in the program. He would never fully understand the government of which he was a part.

At his request, Larson was provided a simple wood pencil and a blank piece of paper.

"Hope Stevens was relocated under the protected name Alice Frizen," Sunderland began without ceremony. A man in a hurry. "Bakersfield, California. We set her up, as I recall, with employment in health care. Information technology skills, wasn't it?"

"Computers, yes."

"Yes. I.T. at a hospital, I'm pretty sure it was. No matter, because just short of a year after assuming her new identity, right at the time she was applying for a dependent, there was another of our witnesses, a man known to Hope Stevens, who was murdered while in a parking lot outside a Wal-Mart in Des Moines. His picture—it was a gruesome kill—went national before we could stop it. The Stevens woman went off our radar, just as the AUSA was putting a second case, the murder-for-hire case, together against Donny Romero and the others. Needless to say, those conspiracy and attempted murder charges were never brought."

Larson sat there, as if slapped across the face. Hope's application for a dependent's paperwork suggested the existence of a husband or a child or both. A new life, indeed.

"A dependent, singular or plural? Anything more on that?"

"There might be in her record. You're right about her information being filed separately. We *do* pull it once they opt out. But it's kept in *Laena* as well, because seventy-some percent of those who opt out eventually rejoin the program. By Monday I'll be in a better position to clarify this sort of request."

"And that's all? Alice Frizen voluntarily left the program." Larson scratched out notes for himself.

"Forfeiting a sizable stipend and medical insurance coverage, I might add."

"That's a lot to give up."

"It is indeed."

"No explanation of this dependent? Child? Lover? Relative?"

"None that I'm aware of."

"And that's that?" Larson had spent a career reading the faces of notorious liars, and he put Sunderland up there with the best of them—but a liar just the same. It wasn't all, and Larson knew it.

"The possibility of Mr. Romero's parole lit a fire under the U.S. Attorney's office. With it came a renewed interest in locating Ms. Stevens, a.k.a. Ms. Frizen."

"And?"

"And I don't report rumor or innuendo."

Larson studied the man carefully, awaiting another lie.

"It's one of those things you hear, is all," Sunderland said.

"Would you make the call for me?"

"On a Saturday?"

Larson answered, "You want to wait until Monday? I was told that if Markowitz doesn't have the entire list decrypted by now, he will *any day*. I doubt either of us has slept much in the last thirty hours, and I can tell you I for one won't be doing my best work by the time Monday rolls around."

"You'll have to wait here."

"I'm good at waiting," Larson answered, containing his excitement. "Government work, you know?"

Sunderland didn't appreciate the sarcasm. He left the room, Larson catching a glimpse of the deputy marshal standing guard by the door. After a minute Larson put his head down onto his arms and rested on the table. He sat bolt upright upon Sunderland's return.

Sunderland sat down beneath a great emotional weight, reminding Larson of some judges as they returned to the bench following jury deliberations.

Sunderland said, "An Alice Dunbar appears on a three-year-old health insurance group coverage for St. Luke's Hospital, Minneapolis. The social she provided is the same one we gave her for Frizen. She probably had no choice. It makes sense: Post 9/11, it's this side of impossible to get a counterfeit social. The name change to Dunbar was legit—done legally in California. There's also a social assigned by Treasury to one Penelope Dunbar, born in California, currently a five-year-old Caucasian female. The kid's social was mailed to a box number in Minneapolis. The investigator's report lists some calls made to the hospital there before passing this up the command. His report suggests the lead was promising at that time."

"And?" Sunderland now seemed to be dragging this out for dramatic effect and the change bothered Larson.

"No follow-up." Sunderland's face reflected Larson's exasperation. "You're the one who brought up government work: It looks as though he sent it over to us, to Justice, but not directed to the U.S. Attorney's office—and this is a little over three months ago. Apparently it never found its way to the U.S. Attorney's office. This deputy had not only the post office box number where the social had been sent, but a residential address he thought was good. It was very good work this guy did. There's been a lot of turnover at Justice since Ridge and Homeland Security—I probably don't have to tell *you* that. But as far as I can tell—and it's the same for the guy I talked to—it looks as if it died there."

"Right," Larson said, then, under his breath, "Or else she did."

CHAPTER FIVE

Minneapolis, Minnesota, streamed past outside the bus window as the passenger took a final opportunity to commit the face of his next victim to memory. He had to allow for added age, a change in hair color or style, weight loss or gain, so he focused on the green eyes, the soft curve of her chin and the placement of her ears, finding a tiny, hooked scar in the hairs of the eyebrow above her left eye. He put no currency in the name—Alice Frizen, Alice Dunbar—he thought instead of carving lines into her, shallow at first, deeper when necessary, the beauty of the rich, sanguine red against pale skin.

A hole in the knee of his worn blue jeans revealed the dark skin of his Latin heritage. His knee bounced with the vibrations of the city bus. The fabric moved, including the forest green sweatshirt he wore, but not the body within—every muscle flexed and taut, a cat ready to pounce. With the hood of the sweatshirt pulled up, the man's face remained like a monk's, in dark shadow, so that the curious little girl who studied him so intently from the row in front of him could make out no distinguishing features. Just two eyes peer-

ing out, impossibly dark brown to the point of appearing black at
the center. Those eyes looked down and returned to the crossword
puzzle in his lap.

3 across:
A knot, not to be undone.

The five-year-old girl smiled at him and waved with the tips of
her fingers so her mother wouldn't see. She clearly hoped for a
smile, but she got nothing out of him.

Paolo ignored the girl, his attention on the puzzle and occasion-
ally out the bus window, on the street numbers above or alongside
the door of a passing building. He awaited a particular address. For
all the rigidity of his muscles, he felt an internal calm. He followed
instruction; he did as he was told. He felt eternally grateful for the
opportunity he'd been given: a sense of family, a sense of *belonging*. Nothing, no one, would come close to stopping him.

Paolo had Philippe to thank for his training; he served him as a
lieutenant serves his captain. It had crossed his mind more than
once that his orders should have come directly from Ricardo,
Philippe's half brother, who now ran the Romero compound in his
father's "retirement." Philippe did not sit on the council as Ricardo
did, and was unlikely to have the authority to order this woman's
execution, but this was the woman responsible for putting Donny
away, and so Paolo followed the orders. Philippe was tangled up in
a family dispute, a power struggle to keep the family business in
health care and insurance, while his worthless half brother was
more of a street thug who favored cutting in on the Native American casinos and gaming. Paolo would follow Philippe to the grave,
if asked. Ricardo was an arrogant, spoiled snot. If the bastard son,
Philippe, was making a move for control of the Romero family, as
it appeared, then Paolo would gladly assist the transition. Philippe

carried a hard-on for his half brother's wife, an extremely fine-looking Italian woman named Katrina. Paolo grew heady with the thought of his own increased importance following the success of this job.

He felt the twinges of an erection and knew he must be close.

He looked up and caught a street number off a delicatessen's window. Yes. Nearly there.

GORDIAN

. . . he wrote into the small boxes.

He reached for the button to signal the driver: *next stop.*

Paolo scouted the back of the apartment building intent on finding an alternate point of entry. The crossword puzzle was now folded and tucked into a back pocket. He pulled down the sweatshirt's hood, aware that he exposed his face by doing so, but wanting his ears in open air, his hearing in top form. He pursed his lips and inhaled through his nose, collecting the various odors of the back alley—*cats, stale beer, human urine, decomposing trash, motor oil*—wiggled the fingers of both hands like a butterfly drying its wings, and briefly closed his eyes, containing himself in darkness before opening them again and seeing everything around him as new.

He saw it. The adjacent office building held a fire escape on the alley side that led to the building's roof. This office building physically connected to the apartment building, which had a similar fire escape, but one that used a weighted drop mechanism and was therefore impossible for Paolo to reach. It was an indirect route, but one that would serve his purpose.

Broad daylight, he thought. *Who expects to die in the morning?*

Hollywood had conditioned the public into believing murder only happened at night. He had them to thank for the ease with which he could surprise his victims.

He climbed strongly, his light frame moved effortlessly by a taut, lean musculature. He made no hurry of it, counting again on the public's conditioning. He climbed with confidence, a maintenance man perhaps, or a roofer making an inspection.

He crossed to the four-story apartment building, descended an exterior steel ladder, and worked his way down one level to the catwalk that fronted a string of eight large windows. Studying the top floor as he climbed down, he made it out to be two apartments, four windows each: kitchen, living room, and probably a pair of bedrooms.

From a distance no one would see the Tru-Feel surgical gloves. With his back turned to the alley it would be difficult, if not impossible, to make out the reflective sunglasses he now donned. They served the same purpose as the black box strung across eyes in photographs, effecting anonymity.

He had "Alice's" face committed to memory. Her body as well—what the photo showed of it. He made a point of slipping past the windows swiftly—a blur, a shadow.

He had the recent heat wave to thank for four of the six windows being either ajar or fully open. Two contained fans that spun noisily, helping to conceal his actions.

Apartment 3D would occupy the three right-hand windows. The first of these was open four inches and looked in on an empty galley kitchen. Paolo heard a woman's voice as well as synthesized New Age background music. *Not a human voice*, he discerned. *Electronic. A CD or television.* He hesitated just long enough to hear the instructions and realize it was yoga. "Tighten your abdomen, firm up the buttocks, and rock like a rocking horse . . ."

The next window was shut. Without exposing himself, he studied it from the side more closely: *locked*. But the third window—the bedroom—was also open.

He peered around the window frame, just far enough to see her. Facing away from him, and toward a television where an instructor went through the motions, "Alice" wore a black swimsuit or leotard that fit her lean frame tightly and was currently wedged up her buttocks and crotch as she rocked per instruction. She was damp with perspiration and some pubic hair escaped the edges. Paolo again felt the twinges of arousal.

He slipped the razor out from behind his belt buckle and sliced the nylon screen on the kitchen window.

A calculated risk. Nothing came without a price. If his diversion failed, things could get messy. Noisy. He might be forced to work incredibly fast. Nothing new in this world. The most promising situations often turned bad.

He reached through the slice in the screen and pushed a warm coffee mug off the counter. To his delight, it crashed to the tile floor.

His eye was to the second window by the time she came out of her pose, pulled her feet in front of her, and stood.

"Hello?" she called out.

She marched into the kitchen, pulling down on the backside of the leotard, her buttocks flexing nicely.

Paolo slipped past this window, cut the screen to the bedroom, and was fully inside within a matter of seconds. His heart beat wildly in his chest.

She was neat and tidy. *And dead before she knows it*, he thought.

He heard her picking up the pieces of the cup and dumping them into the trash. She ran water, probably for a sponge. She wouldn't see the cut in the screen, for his technique was to work the very edge, by the frame. With it tucked back into place as he'd left it, she'd have to push against the screen to reveal the damage. The cup falling would remain a curiosity. She'd blame it on wind, despite the weight of the cup and the air being still. She'd blame it on vibration from the dishwasher, though it was not running. People wanted to believe the easy explanations. If she had any fear, it was just now warming her. He hoped it might be pulsing strongly by the time he confronted her—he could work a person's fear like a potter with wet clay.

He hurried into the living room and drew the gauzy drapes shut, glad that on the television the forty-something, flat-chested instructor continued her smooth-voiced program. On the screen, the woman currently held both legs apart suggestively. Paolo was at the height of excitement, like an athlete before the starting gun.

He moved fluidly across the room, placing his back against the wall that joined the kitchen, awaiting her coming through the doorway. He was hungry now. He felt electricity sparking in the air. *I can smell her*, he realized.

Almost time.

It always ended too quickly. He hoped this time to drag it out as long as possible. It wasn't every day he did a woman, much less one as young and pretty as this one. One had to count one's blessings.

The woman stepped back into the small living space, prepared to reengage in her yoga, when Paolo collared her around the neck with a choke hold. The elbow and forearm grip cut off both her wind and the blood to her head. He lifted her off her feet as she kicked and struggled, putting up with her flailing elbows. He drove a knee into her back and, maintaining the choke hold, slammed her down onto her tailbone. He managed to secure her left arm and, releasing the choke hold, handcuffed both hands behind her back. He set the choke hold again to prevent a scream and dragged her into the center of the room, turning up the volume on the TV with his free hand.

Her nipples spiked under the leotard and he responded with an urge to have her. He grew excited by her frantic breathing, her heaving chest, and her legs slapping together. He decided to enjoy her before he killed her, or at least before she fully expired.

She shook her head side to side, eyes wide as saucers.

He abandoned the choke hold to cup her mouth and muffle the upcoming scream. At the same instant he used the razor to sever the leotard's shoulder straps, cutting into her skin as well. The pain from a cut of a sharp razor takes several long seconds to register.

A moment later, the trickles of blood began. He made no effort to expose her chest. Black and gray straps sagged down but the tight leotard held to her. He felt her shudder, the waves of fear quaking through her, and it pleased him. Saliva ran down the hand that covered her mouth.

"Say good-bye, Alice."

"I'm not Alice," the woman moaned. "I have money . . . a car . . . anything you want . . ."

A flash of heat filled his face. He would expect her to claim she wasn't Hope Stevens, but Alice? Could he possibly have the wrong woman? He spun her around to face him, and she must have known by the fact he didn't hide himself from her, what he ultimately had in mind. He struck her below the V of her rib cage and threw her back and onto the floor. "You say one word . . ." He hoisted the pink-edged razor to indicate his intention. He withdrew the photo and did a quick comparison. He looked for scars from implants or plastic surgery; he compared only the relationship of the eyes to the ears, not the look of them.

The eye color was wrong. Way off. He scrambled forward, pinning her beneath him as she writhed to be free. He liked the feeling of her warmth beneath him. Of her bucking to be free. The leotard slipped lower on her chest, a breast revealed. He grew hard as he steadied her. Then he reached toward her face, held her head in a tight grasp, and carefully spread open her left eye with his fingers, searching for a pigmented contact lens.

No lens . . . Not possible.

He felt tormented by the possibility he'd screwed this up.

"I'm not Alice . . . I'm not Alice," she repeated, in shock now, barely conscious. This was how he liked them. But the situation was not good. He tried to maintain his focus.

Her face was blotchy, snot all over her chin, tears oiling her cheeks. He used his bare hand to clean her up.

"Steady now," he cautioned. "You wouldn't want me to slip."

Again he produced the razor. As he lowered it toward her, she froze, obeying him. He cut into the fabric at her cleavage, and the stretch fabric came open like he'd lowered a zipper. This revealed a gray sports bra that he quickly cut and peeled back, exposing both breasts now. Her chest glowed an angry red.

"Much better," he said, knowing the power he gained by working against embarrassment and shame. Her nipples and areolas were dark brown going on black, puckered, and nut hard. He felt some drool on his own chin; he was salivating.

She raked her head side to side, her eyes locked onto the bloodied tip of the razor he held in his right hand. By now her shoulder cuts would be stinging. By now she understood what he intended.

"Tell me about Alice. This is her apartment." He knew enough to discern the spark of recognition. "Talk to me." He lowered the razor again, pulling on the cut stretch fabric to continue the line he'd started. That line led down. He exposed her navel, a ridge of carefully trimmed pubic hair. The less of the leotard, the more of his arousal. He wasn't sure how long he could contain himself.

"Mrs. Blanchard!" the woman coughed up. "Neighbor . . . Mrs. Blanchard. Mentioned, Alice . . . Alice . . . Alice and her daughter. 'Two peas in a pod,' she said. I . . . am . . . *not* . . . Alice. Please, God! Don't do this."

Paolo had a thing about God's name being invoked during his work. It seemed everyone summoned up the courage to get religion when a razor flashed before their eyes. Paolo had a grim relationship with God that few would understand, but one that caused him deep resentment when his victims begged for saving.

He cut through the rest of the leotard, careful not to nick her. He didn't want her all bloody and dirty there. The leotard now stretched in a long *V* from armpits to the dark tangle of brown hair. Her scent enveloped him, and he briefly swooned, like a patron in a pastry shop. This was fear. Pure fear. Heady. Heavenly.

The woman said, "I'm subletting. Alice . . . This Alice . . . IT'S NOT ME! I'm not her."

"Shut up!" He backhanded her, meaning it more for himself. He contemplated the ramifications of his mistake. He loathed the idea of disappointing Philippe. He would not call to inform him of bad news. And what of this child? What *child*? *What daughter?* He'd been told nothing of this, knew nothing of this. He drew a line at doing anything bad to children. He'd been one himself.

"Mrs. Blanchard . . ." the woman beneath repeated. "Talk to her. She knew Alice." The welt rose on her right cheek where he'd struck her. The dull look in her eye told him that she understood this was quickly coming to an end.

The television instructor was talking about "deep stretches," and he had a little deep stretch of his own to give her.

His mind made up, he cut off a piece of the leotard, balled it in his fist, and crammed it into her open mouth as she summoned a protest. She tried to bite him, but to no use. Her eyes wild, they opened to where he could see the crown of the eyeball itself. Again he noted no contact lens, nothing to explain the wrong color. He felt dizzy, both from excitement and confusion.

He slipped the razor away, unfastened his belt and let his pants down. Let her see what he'd done to himself. If he had seen fear in her face before, now he saw terror.

She humped her way backward, thrusting her bottom off the floor, trying to distance herself, but the humping motion of her hips only served to stimulate him all the more.

"That's it," he said. "Just like that. Don't run from me . . ."

Then he crawled forward and went to work.

Paolo rubbed a few small drops of blood deeper into the green fabric of his sweatshirt before knocking. An older woman he took to be Mrs. Blanchard opened the door. It had to be her: gray blue hair, cloudy ice blue eyes that sparkled with a hunger for companionship, even the companionship of a stranger knocking on her door.

"I think you may have known Alice . . . my dear, dear, friend," Paolo said by way of introduction, speaking as politely and calmly as possible.

Mrs. Blanchard took note of his color; he'd seen that look a thousand times before. "Yes?" A fragile voice. He was reminded of little glass horses on windowsills.

"I wonder if you might be able to help me find her? I have no other address for her than this."

"What dear girls, those two," the old woman said.

"Do you know where I might find them?"

"No . . . no, I don't. Just up and left one day. Not even a good-bye."

That fits.

Paolo cocked his head slightly, inviting himself in. "Would you mind? I'd love to hear anything you can tell me about them."

"I'm sorry," she said as sweetly as possible. "But I don't admit strangers."

"But with both of us their friends?"

She seemed to consider this. Then reconsidered. "I'm sorry. I'd be happy to meet you at Pete's—the diner next door. Say, twenty minutes?"

Her head tilted in curiosity as she heard the snap of latex on his left wrist, and she looked down. He calmly slipped his right hand into the second glove.

"What on earth?" She made a play to shut the door.

Paolo's shoe blocked it.

She looked up, her mouth gaping like a fledgling, too terrified to cry out.

"We just need to have a little talk." He seized hold of her, the loose skin of her throat rolling over the latex, lifted her off her feet by her neck, and stepped inside, nudging the door gently shut behind him.

"Nice place you have here," he said.

When it was all over, out of habit, Paolo chased down a vanilla milkshake and drank it slowly so that it wouldn't give him a headache. His temptation was to use the cell phone to call Philippe, but he could put that off a while. A second, much stranger compulsion overcame him: a desire to call *Mother* in Italy—a woman he hadn't seen in fifteen years. But the time zones were all wrong, and perhaps she wasn't even alive, though if she was he knew she'd be pleased to hear from him, just as she'd be pleased to hear from any of the dozens of boys she raised along with him.

Instead, following the milkshake, he gave in and placed the call he was required to make. The line rang three times and went silent. He typed in the code, *9645, waited for two beeps, and pushed 1.

"Go ahead," said the male voice on the other end of the call. Philippe.

"It got wet. It'll make the news and bring the dogs."

"Go on."

"She's not here. Moved on. There's a daughter named Penny." He knew this information would stun Philippe, so he gave that a moment to sink in.

"Do we know where she is? Where they are?"

"She worked at St. Luke's Hospital here. Maybe still does. I'm heading over there now."

"The girl . . . the daughter. We just doubled our odds of finding them," Philippe said.

"Yes," Paolo agreed, still not liking the development.

"When you get to the hospital, focus on the child. She's unlikely to change her daughter's name. Not her first name. Kids don't go for that. And that helps us—you. Use it. People love kids. Love to talk about them."

"True enough." Paolo liked kids himself.

"We'll see if there's anything we can get you from this end. Report back after the hospital."

Despite Philippe's businesslike tone, Paolo hung up feeling he'd let him down. For the past several years, Paolo had been top dog at the compound, Philippe's right hand. He had no intention of giving up that position.

If there were information to be gleaned from the hospital, he'd find it. If Alice still worked there, he'd find her and kill her. Reminded of his attack on the bus all those years before, he had no intention of repeating that failure. He was older now, more seasoned and experienced. He made it a point never to repeat a mistake.

CHAPTER SIX

FOUR MONTHS EARLIER—
Minneapolis, Minnesota

Burn victims were the worst, like fish skin left too long on the barbecue. The patient arrived sedated, rushed from the ambulance to the ER. Alice Dunbar watched the blur of blue scrubs pass as the ER nurses took possession and the paramedics surrendered control. A male nurse broke off the cavalcade to handle the paperwork; three others, all women, stayed with the patient, running the gurney toward the elevators in order to expedite delivery to the burn ward.

As the emergency room administrator, Alice could observe all this with a certain degree of detachment. She kept the health care machine working: admittance, insurance, scheduling, on-call assignments, and she attended administration meetings to convey the inherent problems, the personality conflicts, the budget overruns— all part of her daily life. The job had nothing to do with her technical expertise, but that had been the case for most of the past six years. As a former systems analyst and fraud investigator for Jamerson Ltd., a British-owned insurance underwriter, her computer skills had once proved incredibly valuable. Now those talents went unrecognized and uncompensated for, until a colleague had a problem with a PC. Alice was the unpaid computer geek of the emergency room administrative offices.

She'd chosen Minneapolis nearly at random, but in part because Garrison Keillor's show had let her imagine that good, simple lives were lived here. A wholesome place to bring up her daughter. And also because it had a robust theater community—including Shakespeare in the Park. Of course, if WITSEC ever came looking for her, Roland Larson would concentrate on cities offering Shakespeare first. He knew this about her. He knew too much about her.

Alice had been a redhead for the past six months—a fairly convincing color given that it was out of a box. Beneath the red was natural blond. She'd tried to gain weight, but to no use—her metabolism, her nerves, burned it off as fast as she could eat. The result was a slightly gaunt look, sunken eyes, pronounced cheekbones. *Unflattering*, she thought. She looked a little sallow, unable to spend the time she wanted outdoors, simply because she felt safer while inside. *They* were out there somewhere. She never forgot about *them*—not for a second. Not in the shower, not on her way to sleep, not now as she worked in St. Luke's. *Anybody, anytime*. This mantra had been drummed into her during WITSEC orientation. She could make friends, but she could not trust them. She could tell no one. She lived like the bubble boys on the sixth floor of this same hospital, insulated, isolated, and completely alone. *Except for Penny*.

"The new website is pretty cool, don't you think?"

That was Tina, sweet Tina, who worked as her administrative assistant. Tina, whose job it was to dig them out from under the pile of paperwork, but who toiled at it like a dog digging in sand. Perfect Tina, with her perfect body, her perfect kids, and her perfect husband. There were times Alice ached to trade lives with her.

"What website?"

"The daycare," Tina answered. "It went up over the weekend. Such cute shots! You should see you and Penny in the music circle. The two of you are adorable. And I'll tell you something, I like that they only use first names. You know? A little extra measure of safety."

Alice's ears whined, like standing too close to a jet airplane. She remembered the music circle, vaguely.

"Do you read any of the e-mail they send us?" Tina worked the keyboard of her computer, opening the website. "The coolest part of it is this . . ." She spun the monitor so that Alice could see.

On the screen, in a small box, Alice saw the jerky motion of kids playing, and she understood immediately that she was watching a *live* webcam.

"Are they *insane*?" Alice said, far too loudly for the small office. She dropped the pile of papers she'd been holding.

She broke into a full run as she reached the same corridor through which the burn patient had just been admitted. She felt burned as well.

Tina watched through the office's interior window. She called out, her voice silenced by the thick glass.

Tina inadvertently left the webcam up on her computer. Five minutes later, in that same jerky, almost inhuman motion, Alice entered into frame, snatched Penny into her arms, and looked once directly at the camera, with a face so full of fear that Tina flinched and backed from the screen.

CHAPTER SEVEN

THE PRESENT

Paolo entered the modern brick edifice of Minneapolis's St. Luke's Hospital with the small brown shoulder bag he'd borrowed from Mrs. Blanchard, the woman who'd told him about St. Luke's in the first place. He worked his way down the sterile corridors until reaching the administration receptionist, a Hispanic woman in her mid-twenties with long, acrylic fingernails.

He held up the bag, putting it on display, then slid his photograph of Hope Stevens across the counter, and through the open window. "I found this purse out in the parking lot. It says inside there is a reward if found. This picture was inside. Does this woman work here?" He let the woman take a look, and he took a chance. "The name on the ID is Alice . . . Alice Dunbar. There is a photo of a pretty little girl, too."

The woman answered him after a moment. "Alice? *This?* I'd barely recognize her." She looked up at Paolo. "You only found this just now?"

"Just now."

"Hmmm. She hasn't worked here in a long time." She eyed him curiously. "*Where* did you say you found this?"

"Have you got a forwarding address for me? I wouldn't mind that reward." He felt his pulse quickening. Legwork and patience paid off. It had been drummed into him by Philippe. The thrills—like those at the apartment—were short-lived, but well worth the wait.

The receptionist worked the keyboard with those long nails. "No, nothing," she finally said. "You might try Tina, down in ER admin. She and Alice were close."

"Tina."

The woman pointed to the left down the hall. "Follow signs to the ER."

"*Gracias.*"

"Good luck with the reward. And if you hear from her, tell her we could use a postcard."

The ER's waiting room teemed with noise and confusion, giving Paolo a moment to study the back of the brown-haired woman in the glass box of an office, a woman he took to be "Tina Humboldt, Executive Assistant," as advertised by the black placard by the sliding window.

Another woman, prim and proper, came and went from the same office. She carried an aluminum clipboard and hurried stiffly down the long corridor, her clothes neatly pressed.

Twice, a male housecleaner in green scrubs opened and entered a glorified closet that Paolo saw stacked with linens, cleansers, and supplies. This, he thought, would make a suitable interrogation room. He would need Ms. Tight Ass to be off on one of her excursions, and the busy waiting room to remain so. The more he worked it out in his head, the longer he waited, the better he liked it.

The officious one with the pointy tits and stiff walk came and went one more time. A sick Mexican laborer coughed up blood that threw his family into a frenzy. Paolo moved toward the office door and knocked loudly enough to be heard over the cacophony behind him.

"Hello?"

Tina glanced up at him, delivered a press-on smile, and pointed to the waiting room. "We're handling everyone as quickly as possible."

She'd probably mistaken him for a Mexican, and this pissed him off. A Brazilian, orphaned and raised briefly in Italy before being trained in Washington State, Paolo didn't care for the ethnic association. "It's about Alice," he said. "Alice Dunbar."

Tina spun on her office chair. She had a pleasant but not exceptional face. "You know Alice?" Her face brightened.

Paolo measured his chances of getting her out of the office and toward the closet. "I've heard from her . . ." he said. "She asked me to pass a message along to you, but it's . . . private . . . confidential, you understand." He looked behind him at all the noise and confusion.

"Please come in," she said, standing to reach for the door.

The phone rang, saving him. He gave it a distasteful look, its interruption unacceptable, and he said, "Maybe just over there . . ." cocking his head, "away from all this . . . stuff."

She nodded. "I get so used to it. I don't even hear it."

He stepped away, hoping she would follow, and she did, drawn by her curiosity. He felt a rush of satisfaction. When he found the right play—as he had just now—he could use the victim's own desires and needs.

He stopped just in front of the closet door marked PRIVATE, turned and faced her. "My name's Raoul," he said. "I helped to relocate Alice and Penny."

Tina's brow furrowed with concern. He knew that word would win her interest.

"Relocate?" she asked.

"Did she never tell you about *him*? The father? And what he'd done to her?"

Tina shook her head. He could see her thinking: *So that was it.*

The trick was to buy enough time to wait for the exact moment. He needed them to be invisible. He used a convex hallway mirror mounted overhead to keep an eye on the corridor behind him, another eye on the distraught Mexicans, while watching the small glassed-in office as well, in case the other woman returned. A doctor appeared in the waiting room and the Mexicans clustered around him.

Now!

Paolo reached out toward Tina with open hands, as if to console her. As she responded, her hands coming up reluctantly, Paolo grabbed her wrist, opened the closet door and spun her inside in one fluid motion. In a precise ballet of movement, he flicked on the light, caught her up in a choke hold, and eased the door shut behind him. The door wasn't made to lock, so he dragged her off her feet and away from the door.

He reversed her, his hand on her throat now, and pinned her up against the shelves, nearly lifting her again.

Tina proved herself a wily one. Maybe she'd taken a self-defense class, or seen the move in a film, but she reached back onto the shelf as he pushed her against it, and one-handed a steel brush at Paolo's face.

He saw it coming, deflected the effort, and knocked the brush from her hand. He was angry now.

She drove a knee for his crotch, but he blocked it, taking it on his thigh.

He delivered a fist to her solar plexus, and watched her pale, felt her sag. His rule, his automatic response to those who fought back, was severe punishment. He drew his razor from its hiding place behind his belt buckle.

"Listen to me, now," he told the whites of her eyes. "You know what happens to little girls who lie? They get religion."

He cut straight down through her blouse, neck to navel. He made it a shallow cut—a bleeder that wasn't close to life-threatening. Maybe because she worked in ER she'd know that about the cut. Maybe not. But either way he won her full attention. The second cut, made equally fast, ran breast to breast, completing the sign of the cross that seeped out into her clothes.

"I'll leave you to bleed out if you don't answer me. Do you understand?"

She nodded, terrified. He loved that look of panic in their eyes—that moment when they realized they'd lost all control.

Choking her as he was, he watched her grow slightly blue, and felt her begin to tremble from shock. "Hold it together. I'm going to let you go."

She nodded again, though her eyes rolled slightly back into her head, and he feared she might faint.

He loosened his grip and whispered, "Where did Alice go?"

She coughed. Tears streamed from her eyes. She whipped her head side to side, indicating "no." Perhaps in his outrage he'd pushed her too far. Perhaps she was a lost cause. If so, he knew the thing to do was to quickly finish her and get the hell out of here. He tried one more time.

"Where?"

"She didn't say . . ." Tina gasped. She was feeling the sting of the cuts now. "She just left. I never saw her again."

"That's not helping me . . ." he said. "That's not helping *you* . . ." He presented the bloody razor blade, well aware of the power it contained. So small, but so effective.

He counted down, "Five . . . four . . . three . . . two . . ."

"A letter!" she said too loudly.

Paolo cupped her mouth, turned his attention toward the door, and listened, thankful for the continuing commotion in the waiting room. He motioned for quiet, then released her mouth.

"She owed me some money. A hundred dollars. A pair of shoes I'd bought her. I didn't even *remember* it," she said. "She mailed it to me . . . *Cash*. Letter said, 'Thanks.' Wasn't signed. But I knew it was her."

"You're wasting my time." He moved the razor so it flashed light across her face. "Come on, Tina . . . you know better."

"I was curious," she said quickly. "On account of the way she'd left like that. Panicked and all. Leaving a paycheck behind. No explanation."

"You're stalling." He forced his free hand between her legs and filled his hand with her. Soft, and incredibly warm. He felt himself stir.

She rose to her toes and he heard her choke back a scream.

"St. Louis," she said. "A postmark . . . the envelope. *St. Louis.* It's all there was, but at least I knew . . ."

Paolo felt a wave of satisfaction and accomplishment. *St. Louis.* His erection receded. He hadn't the time for such foolishness.

"Well done, Tina."

He eased off her crotch while keeping the razor close to her face.

"I'll spare you the pain," he told her in a warm whisper into her ear.

With that, he crushed her nose with a single blow, knocking her unconscious. He used a towel to block the spray as he sliced her neck ear to ear, as he'd been taught. He let her slump to the floor, the secret of their conversation contained.

He once again felt himself engorged and aroused but knew

this was not the place. He committed Tina to memory, slumped on the floor like that, so he'd have it to draw upon when he had the time.

Then he cracked open the door and slipped out, leaving the wails and cries from the waiting room far behind.

CHAPTER EIGHT

Larson climbed the apartment stairs two at a time, his federal shield flapping against his coat pocket. He couldn't blame his pounding chest solely on the exertion. He'd been in an agitated state ever since arriving in Minneapolis. The rental car company said his credit card was no good, only to reverse themselves; he was detoured because of road construction. But his rapid heart rate and clammy hands spoke to one thing: Hope Stevens. He prayed he'd arrived in time.

At the address Sunderland had provided, Larson faced clusters of poorly parked cop cars, flashing lights, and not one, but two ambulances. He slumped, knowing without knowing. Everything about this scene implied he was too late.

The fall night air slapped him. He smelled wood smoke in the air, or rotting leaves, or a foul cigar. The trees were barren in Minnesota weeks ahead of Chicago and a month in front of St. Louis.

He reached an apartment's open door at the top of the stairs. Slowing to allow an MPD officer to mentally process his federal credentials, Larson quickly introduced himself as "Fugitive Apprehension."

The seas parted, and he was inside.

"Who's lead?" he asked the door guard, who then pointed out a man crouching by the sprawled body of an elderly woman who was simultaneously being photographed by a forensics tech in her late twenties. The photographer bounced on her haunches as she squatted, studying the dead woman with a controlled impatience before clicking off another shot.

The deceased's dress was hiked up over ashen legs revealing varicose veins that wandered like wisteria. The grape-stained bruise on her neck suggested she'd been strangled. Larson's panic gave way to relief. "Who the hell is this?" he asked.

"Who's asking?" The detective was seated by a phone, which he promptly hung up. He'd spent too much time in the sun on vacation, his well-weathered and leathery face now pink and peeling. You didn't get a tan like that in Minneapolis. He appeared to have fresh mosquito bites on his lower neck. Larson was guessing Florida or maybe the Yucatán. He'd been back a day or two, at most.

Larson introduced himself.

"Detective Dennis Manderly." He wore latex gloves and didn't offer to shake hands with Larson. Dressed in plainclothes like Larson, he stepped closer and studied Larson's credentials carefully through a pair of bifocals that didn't want to stay on his nose. "Question still stands."

"Fugitive Apprehension Task Force," Larson said, straining now to steal a look at the number on the apartment door: 3C. *He had the wrong apartment.*

Larson wasn't sure what was going on, but the clamminess crept through him again.

"I missed my mark," he said. "I'm down the hall."

"Hold on a sec." Judging by his accent, Manderly had been raised on the eastern seaboard. Boston or the Bronx came to mind. "I'm gonna need a little more than that."

"That'll have to happen boss to boss. I'd tell you if I could."

Manderly gave him a look that said, "I'm sure you would."

"Wrong apartment. My mistake." Larson turned toward the door.

Manderly called out, stopping him. "My guys are down in 3D as well. You're not going in there until and unless you, or someone above you, explains to me, or to my boss, why I've got two toe-taggers on my hands."

. . . *two toe-taggers* . . . Those words drowned out all else.

Larson charged out of the room, down the hall, and blew past a uniformed officer whose job might have been containment. He entered a fairly bare living room, where he stopped abruptly, struck by the sight of the woman spread-eagled on the floor. A blue work-out mat was indicated by four numbered flags pinned into the carpet. A television's blue screen glowed in the background.

Larson thought he knew that body. The woman's chest and abdomen were splayed open in the sign of a cross, nipples to navel. Dark, rust brown blood had run out of her and coagulated into a giant congealed scab, looking like melted wax from a candle where it puddled on the carpet. A rank and familiar odor pervaded, a stench that even an open window couldn't overcome.

"Deputy!" Manderly shouted, behind him by only a step.

Larson had to confirm her before they dragged him out of here. The razor-thin incisions needed no medical examiner to be properly analyzed. He lunged past another forensic technician in an effort to identify the victim's face.

He fell to his knees as Manderly's thick fist caught his coat collar from behind. Larson looked over his shoulder and straight up the man's arm and said, "Give me one minute. Sixty seconds. Then we'll do this."

Behind a face flushed from running and indignation, Manderly met eyes with him, released him, and stepped back.

Plastic surgery was a relocated witness's best friend, never mind Hope's pledge never to resort to it. Chin, cheek, breast, and buttocks implants, Botox, pigmented contact lenses, teeth veneers, dental work, laser hair removal, and a cutter's creative blade could so radically alter a person's look that only the lab boys could make the final confirmation. He disconnected from the victim's hair color, forced her chin flatter, her nose wider, her cheekbones lower, wondering if it possibly could be her.

He used his pen to move the woman's hair off her neck. Ears were as individual as fingerprints. This woman's right ear, smooth and perfect and clearly untouched by surgery, did not belong to Hope Stevens. Larson had once spent hours staring at Hope while she slept. This was not her ear. He exhaled.

Wondering now how he might explain himself, he hesitated briefly while concocting a ruse. "Gloves?" he asked the tech.

He did not look back at Manderly as the detective asked, "What the fuck are you doing in my crime scene, Deputy Marshal?"

"Gloves," Larson restated, motioning with his hand, awaiting delivery.

"If you're thinking of moving her head, forget it," Manderly said. But he must have okayed the gloves, because the technician deposited a pair into Larson's waiting palm.

Larson donned the gloves, slipped open the eyelids and touched the surface of the eye, looking for contact lenses that weren't there.

"Victim's name?" Larson asked.

"I'm not in a real giving mood," Manderly said. "Maybe we take this up back at the office when your boss talks to mine."

Larson snapped off the gloves and let them fall. He passed Manderly his full credentials wallet as he stood. He explained, "We thought . . . briefly . . . judging by what we'd heard of this scene . . . the address . . . that we might know the victim. But clearly we're mistaken."

"Lemme get this straight. You came here in a real cooperative mood, but changed your mind after seeing her face?"

"Why the old lady?" Larson asked. "Any theories on that?"

"Why the cross, tits to crotch?" Manderly nibbled toward the truth. "That fit the profile of whoever it is you're after?"

Larson considered how to play this. Rotem had assigned him to track down Markowitz and therefore knew none of what he was up to; if it went boss to boss—which wasn't going to happen until Monday morning—this would all come apart on him.

"Did she lease it or sublet it?" Larson asked.

"We barely just got here. Give us a minute to get her bagged first, would you?"

"I'm betting sublet."

"Are you telling me this was mistaken identity?"

"They look a lot alike."

"This one and who else?"

Larson shook his head, conveying his unwillingness to share that information.

"Yeah, that's what I thought," Manderly said. "I suppose you have a theory on the neighbor?"

"An older woman like that . . . she was probably a longtime resident of the building. When this one became a problem, he turned to the older one for what he wanted."

"And what did he want?"

"There's a contract hit out," Larson explained, stretching the truth. "I'm supposed to stop it. This razor . . ." Larson indicated the cuts. "We've seen him before."

"So have we," Manderly said.

Larson rose to his feet, heady from the fatigue and moving too quickly. But more than all his physical challenges, it was this information that made him stumble a step. "What's that?"

"We had a similar killing, a razor like this, earlier today. We figure we got ourselves a serial killer." He added, "And I'm thinking you federal boys have lost one. Am I right?"

"The other victim look anything like this one?" Larson indicated the dead woman on the floor.

"Not really. Older, maybe four or five inches shorter. Smaller overall."

Larson felt himself relax a little. Hope might look older, but she couldn't have shrunk. Sunderland had provided a possible place of Hope's employment. "This wouldn't have been an employee of St. Luke's Hospital, by any chance. Would it have?"

Manderly's face registered his astonishment. "Where the fuck did you get that?"

"I'll need to speak to the investigating detective," Larson said.

Manderly stood and brought his face close to Larson's. "You're looking at him," he said. "It's been a long fucking day, pal, and it just got longer for both of us. You're coming to the office. And if I have to cuff you to get you there," he said, a couple of his uniforms perking up and stepping toward them, "I will."

"This dumb-ass picked the wrong closet," Manderly explained. Nearly two hours had passed amid the familiar smell of burned coffee and male sweat. Cop shops weren't so different, one to the next. It had been a while since Larson had been inside an actual police department, his time typically occupied in federal facilities. But the lighting, the low hum of printers and copiers, of keyboards and muted conversation were nearly the same.

Manderly and Larson occupied chairs in a good-sized conference room with gray carpeting and an oval table that sat eight. The room's single window might have had a good view if the blinds hadn't been drawn. A computer and keyboard, a blank whiteboard, a pair of phones, and a video projector accounted for most of the room's electronics. On a separate dolly, a TV and VCR held the attention of both men.

"Thing is," Manderly said, further explaining himself, "evidently hospital scrubs make pretty good pajamas, and this closet in ER was getting hit the hardest. That, and antibacterial soap, and shit like that. So Admin gets a heads-up from IT that they can mount a wireless webcam in there for peanuts and monitor it for theft. This jerk-off drags her in there to do his thing, having no idea he's on *Candid Camera*."

On the screen, in the silent, jerky motion of low-frame-count surveillance video, to which Larson was becoming accustomed, the abduction and murder played out again.

"Either he got seriously lucky here, or he'd scouted it and took his chances, but his back is always to the camera. We never get a look at his face."

"Other security video?"

"They got cameras all over the entrance to the ER, 'cause that's where the trouble always comes from. But this turd entered ER from the main wing. We got a profile of him while he sat in a chair scoping the vic, but that's about it. And in terms of quality, it sucks. Grainy and burned out. It's true video. This webcam stuff is much better quality."

As it was, the webcam image didn't impress Larson. It blurred with any quick motion, so that when the killer moved to cut her neck it looked as if someone had wiped Vaseline on the camera lens.

"Back it up," Larson instructed, all civility gone from his voice. It felt like a ghoulish act to repeatedly watch her die.

On the fourth viewing, Larson accepted the VCR's remote from Detective Manderly, to both men a symbolic exchange of power. Larson watched a particular twenty-second section well over a dozen times. He finally said, "I can't make out any of that, can you?"

"You're kidding, right?"

"Have you got any kind of society or center for the deaf here in town?"

"Metro Deaf School," Manderly answered. "One of our captains . . ." he said, responding to Larson's look of surprise, "has a kid enrolled. They do this music thing every Christmas. Pretty fucking amazing, actually."

"Can we get someone over here?"

It had taken Manderly that long to understand the request. "Fucking A . . ." he said, his tanned face breaking into a smile. "Now *that* is fucking genius!"

Two long hours later, Larson had a ticket in hand for the city mouthed on the video by the woman who was about to be murdered in the hospital linen closet.

"St. Louis."

Back to where he'd started.

CHAPTER NINE

Wearing only a shirt, Paolo leaned back on the airport mo-
tel's crisp white sheets and muted the television's sound. On the
screen, the videotape of the yoga instructor in her pink leotard
played, just as it had been playing when he'd sneaked into apartment 3D. The woman on TV turned sideways, bent over, and practically touched her nose to the floor. But it was the way her compact
little ass flared toward the ceiling that sent Paolo's heart aflutter.

He removed the small cardboard sheath that protected the new
utility razor blade, examining its miraculous edge in the yellowish
light of the motel room's bedside lamp. In flashes, his face reflected
partially in the steel of the tiny sharpened mirror—an eye, his teeth,
another eye. He'd grown thinner in recent months, his face
stretched unnaturally over sharp cheekbones, more like the face of
a mummy, the dark eyes sunken deeply inside pronounced sockets.
The rich brown color of his eyes only revealed itself when he tilted
his head up into light. Despite the look of his gaunt frame, he'd
never been this fit, this strong, this fast on his feet, in his life.

He accepted that with crimes came punishment. Guilt gave way to confession. Release. He felt no pain, internally or otherwise, when he did these things to others, only when he did them to himself. Without pain there was no payment. It confirmed his existence.

He examined the perfection of the blade. He loved it, and hated it.

Propping his head up with two pillows, he saw past his erection to the screen where the pink leotard continued its contortions. He could picture the woman he'd killed mimicking those movements. He could smell her.

He unbuttoned his shirt. It fell open revealing dozens of raised scars. Some pink and fresh. Others dark and older. A few lucky ones had been cut repeatedly and now protruded a quarter inch or more, a geometric lump of scar tissue.

Under the glow of the lamp's dim light he placed the blade to a vacant space on his abdomen and applied pressure, gentle at first, then pressing more firmly as the skin separated and curled away from the blade. He gritted his teeth, watched the television and stroked himself.

He dragged the razor deeper, creating a red, feverish wound three inches long. As he climaxed he dropped the razor, awash in relief, a flood of departing tension, like a drain being opened beneath him. He closed his eyes, sighed deeply.

Later, when he bothered to look, he realized he'd gone a little deep with the razor. The pink leotard had been lying on her back at the time, stretching her legs up and apart. He'd overreacted. The wound would require butterfly bandages, but he carried them with him wherever he went.

For a moment he was not alone. For a moment he'd done nothing wrong. For a moment he felt at balance with the world and his own place within it. These feelings would change, would forsake him over the next several hours—he'd been here enough times to know. The kill might return in his dreams, might linger for days or even weeks. That he'd fucked her while she died beneath him only made matters worse: his moment of creation, hers of destruction. But he took opportunities when they arose and paid for them later in his own way, as he did now.

He might rest later, but now the adrenaline from this painful act would carry him. He sometimes stayed awake days without sleep, never bothered by it, never fully understanding it. He couldn't remember if or when he'd last eaten and reminded himself to eat something before continuing.

Under the glare of a fluorescent tube, he wetted a towel and cleaned himself.

His black hair wet and combed back, he left the room for a twenty-four-hour diner, envisioning pancakes and a hot cup of coffee, an aging redhead in a tight shirt who would call him "Hon."

A bead of blood seeped through and stained his shirt despite the butterfly bandages. He failed to notice it, his body numbed and distant. His mind whirring. He felt right again. And that was all that mattered.

CHAPTER TEN

Alice Dunbar's Jefferson Square loft apartment lacked a view of the St. Louis arch or the Mississippi. Instead, it looked out onto what only a few years earlier had been a needle park. Gentrification had relocated the drugs and dealers a few blocks south and east. Now the park offered Penny a place to play on the jungle gym or to swing on the swings during the steamy, sultry afternoons.

But Penny wasn't in the mood for playing. She stared at her mother, tears pooled in oversized blue eyes, poisoned by betrayal. "But we just got here . . ."

Alice packed furiously, a maternal storm leaving debris in its wake. She'd been through this before, she reminded herself, wanting to stay calm. Only months ago, in fact.

She felt bad for uprooting Penny for the third time in her five short years. This time Penny had found a set of kids at day care to call her friends, and her mother hated to lose that.

Until this most recent move Penny had pretty much kept to herself. She liked American Girl dolls and to be read the accompanying stories. McDonald's Happy Meals, her hamburgers with onions, mustard, and ketchup. She'd outgrown a macaroni-and-cheese phase. Now it was frozen Gogurts, pancakes, and flank steak when Mommy could afford it.

She liked for her mom to read to her before bed, her baths hot, and her pillowcase cold.

She'd learned to watch her mother for signals when on the bus or the street. With little in the way of discussion, instruction, or explanation, she'd intuited that they lived a secret life, a different life from others.

"It's not forever," Alice lied. In fact, Alice had no idea when they might stop running. "We're not moving, we're just leaving for a while. Like vacation."

"Not me! I'm not going anywhere! I'll run away! I will."

"That's the point: We're running away *together*, sweetheart," Alice said in as loving a voice as she could muster. "We'll be back."

Despite this outburst, Penny was significantly more mature, more worldly and sophisticated than her peers. It no doubt stemmed from their nomadic, secluded life. Whether those qualities would benefit her remained to be seen. She acted like a five-year-old, but she read at a sixth-grade level and spoke with an adult vocabulary. Though adults were impressed, Alice wasn't thrilled with what she saw developing: a precocious, challenging, willful child who acted as if she were entitled.

Garage-sale furniture had failed to adequately fill the loft space that had once housed a printing press and been home to a citywide giveaway newspaper. Alice had left the yellowed front pages of past editions stapled to the rough wood walls as artwork.

She checked the TV, tuned to CNN, wondering how often they would run the ad for the ID bracelets. She'd seen it only once, about an hour earlier, but that had been enough to make her leave St. Louis today. Possibly forever. The WITSEC deputies had drummed into her the need for her to keep up her daily watch of *USA TODAY* and CNN. And even though she'd fled WITSEC years before, she'd never stopped looking for the warning signal. If she ever saw an ad for a silver-plated ID bracelet, with the name "Johnny Anyone" on the bracelet, and the address on the mail-in form "PO Box 911, Washington, DC," she was to take immediate action. Sight of the ad today had knocked her sideways: one moment struggling through life on its typically difficult track, the next, pure panic.

Something drastic, something radical had happened within WITSEC that must have jeopardized all protected witnesses. Sadly for Alice it was just more of the same—the endless dance of reinventing herself.

She packed while containing an anxiety she hadn't experienced since fleeing St. Luke's. The unsettling existence of living with the knowledge that someone was after her, wanted to kill her, preoccupied her every thought, every movement. WITSEC tried to explain such feelings in its orientation literature, but had no idea what they were talking about.

She knew that given this unexpected move, she would not sleep for days, worried sick about Penny being a part of this, and what might become of her daughter if her enemies were ever successful. She glimpsed her immediate future. Their survival depended upon her own random, unpredictable behavior. They would live on what she'd saved until she found new work. She did not maintain a bank account; instead, she converted paychecks to cash for a fee and bought U.S. Postal Service money orders. She would keep moving, would contact no one. They would return to an isolated, unpredictable life for the next few days or weeks, however long it took for WITSEC to run a nearly identical ad to read: "Mr. Johnny Citizen, PO Box 411, Washington, DC." That combination would alert her that whatever the problem, it had been resolved. It would be safe for protected witnesses to call the memorized phone number and check on their individual status. For Alice, long since out of the program, it would likely mean choosing someplace else to resettle with Penny. St. Louis had not worked out as planned anyway.

Self-pity crept in and she pushed it away. She would not cry in front of her daughter, would not resent their situation. She was alive. She had a beautiful daughter. She would not fantasize some life other than that she'd been handed. She would not give *them* that. She would not succumb.

She and Penny were a team like no other. Best friends. Mother and daughter. Rivals. *Survivors*.

She looked up from the clutter of clothes, sorted first by necessity, given that she'd elected to try for a warmer climate this time. Fewer clothes, less baggage.

She turned.

Penny was not in the room.

She called out, the first tendrils of fear wrapping around her heart.

"Pen?"

No answer.

Her daughter had been standing there only seconds—*minutes?*—earlier.

Her feet moved independently of her. First at a walk, then a run, she hurried around the few rooms offered by the loft's layout. She checked under both beds, in all three closets, behind the couch . . . all of those places Penny sought during hide-and-seek.

Then she arrived at the front door only to find it hanging open.

Her daughter—her headstrong, precocious, adorable, frightened little girl—had run off.

Alice hurried within the building, neighbor to neighbor. Not many of them knew her particularly well—she'd made a point of not getting close. But most knew Penny just from hellos in the hall and at the mail slots.

With each successive failed attempt, her desperation increased. She was lightheaded and sick to her stomach. She steadied her balance and attempted to predict where Penny might go.

She ran three blocks to a church playground, grateful that Mrs. Kiyak, a neighbor who didn't know her well but recognized a mother's fear when she saw it, agreed to guard the apartment building's stoop in case Penny returned. Alice's deeper concern was that the elderly Mrs. Kiyak might forget why she was sitting there, for *whom* she was waiting, and might return to her own apartment unaware she was in fact deserting her post. Mrs. Kiyak had delivered Christmas cookies to her friends in the building, not a month too early, but on the twenty-fifth of September.

The playground stood empty, a blanket of fall leaves at its feet. They stirred in a light breeze. One of the swings moved pendulously on its chains. The more Alice shouted, the more anxiety flooded her.

She fought to calm herself again. If she'd covered her tracks well, and she believed she had, then no one from her past knew about Penny's existence, no one could connect either of them to St. Louis. If she'd made any mistake, it had been using her Alice Frizen social security number at St. Luke's, a mistake she had not repeated here in St. Louis. Able to manipulate computer data with ease, she'd covered her tracks within her employment records at Baines Jewish Hospital by way of a small sin she felt was forgivable, adopting the Social Security number of a woman her age and roughly her description who had passed away from cancer up in Minnesota. By the time the IRS figured that one out, Penny would have her own grandchildren.

The sounds of city traffic hummed like swarming bees. She inhaled the improbable mixture of rich fall smells: wet, loamy earth; the dry dust of brittle leaves.

She couldn't imagine Penny leaving the building without her, much less the neighborhood. But then Alice realized that if Penny had left, there was probably only one place she would go.

Remembering she'd left some cash by the phone in the apartment, and now not remembering if she'd seen the money during her search, Alice hurried back home. If the cash was gone, then she thought she knew exactly where to find her. Candy was Penny's first and only real weakness.

Discovering the cash missing from where she'd left it, Alice tried three neighborhood stores, two that sold candy and one that offered ice cream. Drawing blank looks and offers to help from each establishment, she wandered back out onto the sidewalks.

She rarely shopped the same grocery store twice in a row. The nearest lay eight blocks away—the opposite direction from the hospital. Sometimes they walked to the market, sometimes they took the bus. She spun in circles, tears now threatening as the hopelessness, anger, and frustration competed within her.

She thought of the toy store and broke into a run, slaloming through pedestrians, avoiding collisions. Then, halfway to the toy store, she skidded to a stop. Across the street she spotted Little Annie's Bookshoppe, Penny's favorite store after Crown Candy.

Torn between the two, she willed her feet to move but they wouldn't budge.

"Penny!" She screamed in such a shrill voice that she turned heads, then quickly reminded herself that she was the one the Romeros sought.

CHAPTER ELEVEN

Larson felt about hospitals the way kids do about dentists. He'd watched his mother die in one; he'd sat by his brother's side as he recovered from a freak diving accident that left him a paraplegic; he'd had his own shoulder operated on, allowing him to continue rowing. The smell, the morose quiet. The only thing good about hospitals was women in uniforms; even a woman wearing blue scrubs turned him on. Pathetic.

He entered Baines Jewish, the third hospital he'd visited since landing two hours earlier in St. Louis, bound and determined to ferret out Hope.

Trill Hampton had met him at the airport, driving one of the Service's black Navigators, an ostentatious ride if there ever were one, considering the Service's efforts to maintain a low profile.

Hampton, a graduate of Howard University, was often asked, stereotypically, if he'd played college sports—football was the first guess because of the broad shoulders and thick neck, the cantilevered brow and jutting jaw. But in fact his interest in college

had been theater arts, and to this day, he was Larson's best guy to
send into a dicey situation that required the elements of undercover
work. Like Larson, he'd come to the Service through public law enforcement—Baltimore PD—where he'd found the thinly concealed
corruption impossible to sidestep, finally turning in his shield and
keeping his mouth shut. Through this service he learned more than
he'd wanted to know about the federal witness protection plan,
eventually applying there for his next job. Like Stubblefield,
Hampton had been with Larson for nearly seven years; first on a
witness protection team, and more recently FATF.

Hampton spoke with a tight voice. "Scrotum thinks both Palo
Alto and Duke are worth a follow-up. He says you can have Wash
U since you've been on the road. All three have supercomputers capable of decrypting *Laena*, and Markowitz either contacted or visited all three right before his disappearance."

Larson couldn't put into words the way he felt. Seeing the cut
and naked body of the woman Hope's age in Minneapolis had poisoned him more than he knew.

Hampton picked up on the silence. "So . . . you really think it's
him, Razor Face, the guy who did Benny?"

Even doing eighty, Larson wished Hampton would drive faster.
He lived in a perpetual state of feeling one step behind. He'd been
here before, any fugitive pursuit felt much this same way—playing
catch-up, living with the concern a crime would go down before
you collared the guy. But this was different, and Hampton knew
that now, given Larson's silence.

"Actually, I got the go-ahead to look for Hope Stevens prior to
checking out Wash U."

Hampton seemed to buy it, or at least wasn't going to argue.
"And where's that leave me and Stubby?"

"On the road for the next few days."

"Interviewing geeks and getting hard-ons over coeds," Hampton said. "You won't mind if we wait to file our reports upon our return?"

"But if you find anything," Larson said, "that's a different story. Any possible connection to Markowitz, living or dead, I need to know about it ASAP."

"Got it." Hampton accepted that there was nothing more to be said.

At Baines Jewish, Larson negotiated his way through the disorganized parade of orderlies and nurses, doctors and housecleaners, maintenance men and visitors, following signs to Administration. He felt his chances of finding Hope alive dwindling, especially if, by now, WITSEC had sent out its national alert. Protected witnesses would have gone into hiding. Would Hope? The notion that the cutter had a head start on him, that one or both of the dead women in Minneapolis had known something about Hope, tortured him.

With a ten-acre footprint, and housed under a dozen roofs, Baines Jewish was more a small city than a large hospital. Consequently it took Larson over twenty minutes to reach the information desk capable of helping him.

Larson displayed his credentials while line-cutting.

"I'm looking for a woman who works here." He described the former Hope Stevens as, "A little taller than average. Eyes—grayish green. Thin face, a bit of a pointed chin. Nice build. Long legs. Unique laugh, like happy coughing." Reconsidering, he added, "Could be any hair color really, maybe the chin is rounder or . . ." He saw the woman's eyes glaze over. A place like Baines, there had to be thousands of employees. A little more desperately, he said, "I.T. probably. Computers, for sure. Insurance? I don't know." He realized how ridiculous this all sounded.

"I'm not sure where to start." The receptionist, polite and demure, wore a telephone headset over a French braid that vaguely resembled a topknot. "Do you have a name, sir?"

"Try Alice Dunbar," Larson suggested.

The woman attempted typing. "No one admitted under that name. Sorry." She looked past him, at the two women behind him.

"Not admitted. She *works* here," he said. "This is urgent, government business. Please. Employees. Anyone named Alice."

Her eyes dulling, she said, "We've got over twenty-two hundred people who work here on any one shift. Five, six thousand total. You're describing a white girl, right? Like the color of her eyes and her having nice legs means something to me. If you've got a *last* name, I'll put it into the system. Otherwise, you've got to step out of line."

A last name. "She might be in the ER," he said, thinking back to St. Luke's. "Try Alice Stevens or Alice Stevenson. Actually, try both Alice and Hope . . . and try Hope as the last name as well."

The woman stared across at Larson. "What's with all that?"

Larson returned his credentials to the countertop. "Please," he said.

The receptionist lost some of her earlier confidence. The gold federal shield had that effect on some people. She looked warily between Larson and the two waiting women. She started typing. Her eyes widened and narrowed with her efforts. She needed reading glasses but was too vain to wear them. She glanced up sharply, drawing Larson in, then shook her head and mumbled and typed some more.

Recognition registered in her eyes and then, more brightly, roamed from the screen to Larson and back to the screen.

"She's in there," Larson said. "Under which name?"

The woman's attitude had changed. With her success, Larson could feel her wondering if she should involve others in this process. Not wanting any such delay, Larson reached across with his long arms and spun the computer monitor to face him, knocking over a gray plastic magnetic paper clip container in the process.

The woman protested, but it was too late.

Alice Stevenson. An acronym alongside the entry: *AEDEA*. The space for a home phone number had been left blank. The mailing address, a post office box, not a street. No way to trace her to a residence. It was her. They'd taught her all of this.

A wave of guilty pleasure swept over him. She lived in St. Louis. Five years of wondering boiled down to this. Maybe the laugh at the back of the theater had been her after all. *Why?* he wondered. Had she been watching him?

Yanking back the monitor to face its original position, the receptionist asked him, "You want me to call her extension?"

Did he? He felt stunned. He answered automatically, "No . . . thank you. Is she here? On site? Working here today?"

She tried the phone next, angling her index finger to press the phone's number keys without dislodging a nail. She pressed the headset's earpiece to her ear.

Larson reached across the counter and punched a different CO button on the phone, disconnecting the call.

"Hey!" She slapped the back of his hand.

"She can't know . . ." he told her. "What department?"

"What's she done?"

"It's not like that."

The woman fixed a doubtful, disbelieving look onto him. After a short staring contest, she decoded the acronym for him. "Assistant Executive Director, Emergency Administration."

"I'll check into it myself," Larson said. Then privately: "You are not to alert her, not to tell anyone. You do, and you'll be interfering with a federal investigation." He waited for her practiced eyes to register his warning, but saw nothing.

Her face expressionless, she called out past Larson, as if he weren't there, "Next!"

CHAPTER TWELVE

Paolo didn't trust hospitals. Like the Bates Motel, people checked in but not out. Nor did he like going after a kid. But both directives had come from Philippe, and if there was one thing a soldier learned to do early it was to follow orders.

Fortunately, looking Latino remained an advantage. No one would take any notice of him. He intended to exploit this invisibility.

Paolo knew that no day care worker in her right mind was going to turn over information about a child under her care. Not to a Hispanic man. Not to a civilian. For this reason, as he had before, Paolo donned his police uniform. It was black, not blue or khaki, the word *SWAT* written over the pocket, and a SWAT insignia sewn onto the left sleeve. The trained eye might immediately note the lack of a city or jurisdiction within the badge or insignia, might identify this costume as a costume, might question the forged ID badge that hung open from the left breast pocket, slightly smeared—pink, as if blood had been cleaned from it, his own per-

sonal touch for which he felt especially proud—making it difficult to read. But who knew what a SWAT uniform was supposed
to look like? Civilians encountered cops often enough to develop
expected patterns of dress—but special forces units? Also working
in his favor was that SWAT held a certain respect, panache even,
that impressed people. It made up for any questions—voiced or
otherwise—about his ethnicity.

He entered Baines Jewish Hospital from the delivery side and
asked directions only once, then of a young woman who appeared
to be in a hurry. After ten minutes of wandering corridors and
moving between connecting structures—this place was more complicated than the pyramids—he finally reached a door marked
EMPLOYEES ONLY. Administrators had elected not to advertise the
whereabouts of their employees' children.

He found the door locked—an unexpected nuisance—and
knocked twice with authority. There would be cameras here. There
might be an armed response if his uniform were spotted by some
alert security guard.

"Officer Rodriguez," he announced himself in a hush to the
anorexic who opened the door and received him. She could have
been thirty, might have been fifty. Her teeth pushed apart thin lips.

"I need to speak to Penny . . ." he said, while digging into his
left pants pocket.

". . . Stevenson," the woman supplied. Teachers were always so
eager to know everything, so eager to please. "Regarding?"

"Police business," he replied. "We have a . . . a tricky situation.
In progress. I'm going to need to contact the mother . . . April, no.
Alice," he corrected himself. "I'll leave Penny in your care, but ask
you to keep a close eye on her once I've spoken to her."

"Penny's not with us today."

Paolo craned to get a better look past her. He hadn't been asked in. A group of fifteen kids sat cross-legged on the floor, facing an adult woman who held a book in her lap.

"Where is she?"

"I wouldn't know. Absent today. Her mother's scheduled, so we called, but there was no answer."

"I'll need her address and home phone number."

"The police don't have a home phone number and address?" Lines of incredulity damaged an already difficult face. Her eyes fell to his uniform, and he knew he'd lost her.

He jammed a straight arm, the flat of his palm against the flatness of her chest, and drove her backward and off her feet. She fell onto her coccyx and cried out sharply.

He was inside. With his foot, he drove the door shut behind him.

"Cell phones on the floor," he announced, carefully brandishing a plastic weapon in order to disguise its lack of authenticity. To his satisfaction the other two caregivers, the one reading and another neatening up a play area behind her, went slack-jawed. The one neatening up was of a sturdy, breeder build, a dark-haired wonder, well endowed in both hips and chest. He took a special interest in her immediately.

With the instruction repeated, the reader tried to speak as the breeder rose and crossed silently to her purse. The breeder set her phone down onto the carpet.

Not taking chances, Paolo holstered the fake pistol. He backed up, seized the thin one off the floor, and held her in a choke hold. She was frail enough that he could kill her by merely tightening his grip.

"Anyone moves," he warned, now flashing his razor blade in the grip of index finger and thumb, "including any of the little ones, and there's trouble for all of us." He made eye contact with each of the two caregivers now on their feet. "Are we clear?"

The women nodded. They eyed their captive colleague, and instinctively moved to corral the children.

The one Paolo held went limp, having passed out from fright—or perhaps he'd choked her too tightly. He allowed her to slump to the floor and released her. He stepped over her, approaching the two others. Both recoiled.

"Penny's mother's address. Now."

The kids stared at him, wide-eyed.

The breeder glanced toward the computer terminal on the gunmetal gray desk.

Paolo grabbed the phone off the desk and tore it from the wall, in case that had been her intention. He signaled her over, and she responded by standing and brushing herself off. Her colleague, the reader, reached out to stop her, but the gesture went unfelt. The sturdy woman walked calmly toward the computer terminal and sat down. Paolo moved around to view the screen from directly behind her. He stood close enough that had he wanted, he could have cut her open ear to ear.

"You do anything to—"

"I won't."

He watched as she called up various employee records.

He kept watch between keystrokes, first to the wall clock, then to the woman seated with the kids, then to the one still unconscious on the floor. He hoped he hadn't killed the skinny one.

She toggled through several records, a digital photo embedded in each. A minute or two had passed. Murphy's Law told him everything about this would quickly fuck up, and he'd be caught if he didn't hurry.

By purposely identifying Penny and her mother he'd shown his cards, revealed his target. In the time it now took him to reach Hope Stevens, a.k.a. Alice Stevenson, she'd be warned off, and he'd miss her again.

That was unthinkable. Not an option. He had to think of a way around that.

Then he spotted the breeder's handbag sitting atop the desk where she'd searched it for the phone, and he had his solution.

"Quickly!"

Terrified, she typed faster.

When he heard her fingers pause, Paolo viewed the record on the screen: "Penny Stevenson. PARENT/GUARDIAN: Alice Stevenson. ADDRESS:" *a PO box!*

"Her *street* address," Paolo said.

"See for yourself," the woman answered. "There isn't one listed." With a trembling finger, she pointed out the appropriate line on the screen.

"I need the *street* address . . ." he repeated. "Now!" He reached out, snatched up her purse, and then turning, the two other purses, both from cubbyholes.

The tall, skinny woman came alive, sitting up from where she lay on the floor. She tugged at the hem of her dress self-consciously. It had ridden up her pale thighs, revealing a pair of white stretch stockings that stopped at her knees. As if a part of this conversation, she told him, "I drove them home once." To her colleague at the computer she said, "That blizzard last year. The buses . . ." She caught herself. "It's a loft in Jefferson Square."

"You'll come with me," he said.

"Oh, God, no . . ."

He removed the billfolds from all three purses. The thin woman looked dazed. He'd have preferred the breeder, for entertainment value, but he'd take the one he was given.

"I now have all your home addresses," he explained, displaying their billfolds. "I have your driver's licenses, pictures of *your* children, no doubt. I'm an elephant."

All three women reacted with puzzled expressions.

"Children," Paolo called out to the kids on the floor, "what do we know about an elephant?"

A boy raised his hand energetically and called out, "He packs his own trunk?"

Some of the other kids laughed.

Paolo cued the kids, "Do elephants forget?"

"No!" a handful of kids erupted.

Addressing the women, he said, "And neither will I, if anyone tries to interfere." He tossed a box of tissues across to the thin woman, now kneeling. It landed at her feet. He asked which purse was hers and retrieved a set of car keys.

"You're driving." Moving toward the door now. "No one comes in or out. You don't make or take calls. If it comes up, your friend went home early. One of the kids pulled the telephone off the wall." He held up the two billfolds. "You continue on and finish the day as planned. You go home. For all you know, I'll be watching you. Do not call each other, do not tell anyone anything: husbands, family, no one! If the kids talk, you handle it. Tomorrow morning you can do as you please."

He glanced back at the breeder one last time, knowing the pleasure she represented.

He called out to the room: "Start singing!"

As he headed down the hall, the skinny one at his side, he heard their small voices like toy bells, off-key but lovely in their clarity.

CHAPTER THIRTEEN

"As you can see . . ." the matronly ER nurse explained to Larson, "we're a little bit busy right now, Officer."

It was deputy marshal, not officer, and Larson considered setting the record straight in order to take control. The nurse wore a set of extra-large scrubs that nonetheless stretched to contain a continental shelf of breast and a hula hoop–sized waist. She wore a St. Christopher cross around her neck. A mouth-breather, she exposed a thin slice of white teeth, like a sleeping cat. She glanced up, locked her flinty eyes onto Larson. "Do I know you?"

The question was not uncommon. People said he had a little bit of Harrison Ford in him, a little bit of movie-star quality that seemed familiar at first glance. He'd looked for it, but sadly had never seen it. But this woman didn't mean it as a come-on, but a qualifier; she was simply being stubborn.

"I need a street address for Alice Stevenson."

The woman complained, "You know how hard it is shorthanded?"

He saw her name on her badge pinned above the shelf. "Ms. Rathmore, I need your undivided attention here." He awaited those annoyed eyes of hers, then lowered his voice. "I'm conducting a federal investigation. I'm not going to throw around words like bioterrorism and national security"—he immediately won her full attention—"because you're not authorized to receive such information, but let's just say a little bit of help would go a long way, and you're not going to want to look back on this opportunity and have to tell your friends you were the broken link, you were what took more time than necessary, you were the one who cost lives."

"We don't have an address in the system," she told him. "But I can tell you this. Alice doesn't make friends easily. She's a little off, you know? I mean, who makes the kind of money she makes and still rides the bus? And with her looks . . . I mean the docs hit on her all the time, and she turns a blind eye to every one of them. So the talk is, you know . . . that she likes other women . . . and that stuff. Not that there's anything wrong with that, but there's not a lot of *them* around here. I'm not saying I feel one way or the other about that, you understand. But she does have a little daughter . . . Penny. Thick as thieves, those two."

Nurse Rathmore's mouth kept moving, the words kept coming, but Larson no longer heard. The request Hope had made for a second protected identity had been for a *daughter*, not for a husband or lover. He filled in the blanks almost automatically. He considered the timing. My god. Maybe Hope had jumped the program because of her daughter. *Our daughter?*

Larson rushed his words, a fluttering inside him like something had broken loose. "The daughter. Penny . . . Did you mention a father? . . . A nanny? . . . Who takes care of her during work hours?"

Rathmore nodded, tilted her big head. "Daycare's over in the basement of the Children's Hospital. Not so easy to find. You'll have to ask."

When she looked up, she saw only Larson's back, the automatic doors already closing.

CHAPTER FOURTEEN

Paolo explained the rules to the pale, trembling woman behind the wheel. He'd removed and pocketed all the cash, credit cards, and the three driver's licenses from the women's wallets, the rest of the contents spilled out onto the floor mat at his feet. She'd gotten the message, loud and clear.

She slowed the car suddenly. "This is where I dropped her off."

"Pull over."

The woman's glassy eyes and twitching fingers did nothing to convince him she'd heard him. Nonetheless, the car pulled to the curb and stopped.

He said, "The easy out is to kill you and put you in the trunk and steal your car." She tensed, and went yet another degree of pale. "But you're a teacher, and I like kids. I'm ready to let you go if this is the right place. Is it?"

She nodded.

"Okay, then drive home and lock your door and turn off your phone and don't talk to *anyone*. You wake up tomorrow morning and you go to work, and you deal with this shit then. You think you can hide from me?" She shook her head vigorously. "Your Alice Stevenson's been hiding for six years, and look where she's at. Keep that in mind."

She nodded, her fists tight on the wheel.

At first Paolo thought he'd done a convincing job with her, but then he took the cue and followed her line of sight to the sidewalk in the middle of the next block.

He glanced once more at the driver, then again at a pretty little blond girl facing a doorway but staring straight up at the building.

Looking lost.

The first smile in a long time curled across his lips as he thought: *God helps those who help themselves.*

CHAPTER FIFTEEN

Each time the bus shuddered to a stop, Alice was stung by impatience. Convinced her daughter had fled to the one place that felt safe to her, she was on her way to the hospital's daycare. If she'd seen any taxis on the street, any other means to reach the hospital more quickly, she would have bolted the bus in a heartbeat, but cabs weren't a common sight in St. Louis, a city dominated by its suburbs.

She chastised herself for panicking over the alert on CNN, for her lack of an explanation to Penny, who was old enough now to understand some of this. She could have handled this so much better. If she'd turned this into a surprise trip to Disney World, they'd already be on their way, riding some Greyhound toward Atlanta. So why had she reacted like that, a fit of worry?

But then again, she'd been trained to worry; trained to be paranoid. Her daughter wanted nothing of it, and who could blame her?

"The Romeros can and will find you. If you make so much as a single mistake, they'll be on your doorstep." Had Lars told her that, or one of the others? There had been so many debriefings, orientations, meetings with psychologists. She couldn't remember them all. But the warning had been convincing then, and she heeded it still. Caution was a way of life, not a switch she threw when convenient. She'd overreacted to the alert. She understood that now, but knew this was part of her programming, and her programming had kept them alive this far.

Penny was the only one who had the number to the cell phone Alice carried. It was their leash, their fallback. She never phoned out on it, never created a call history. She might have used it now to call ahead but feared that if Penny got even a hint of that call, she might run off again in protest. Anything to delay their next move. Penny was far too smart a child, far too intent on making her mother pay for their nomadic ways. Surprise remained Alice's best chance.

CHAPTER SIXTEEN

Larson entered the hospital's daycare center only minutes behind a pair of uniformed security guards. Two women, the children's caregivers, were trying to explain the events to one of the uniformed security guards, while a nurse attempted to entertain the children and a second guard, on his knees, quietly interviewed three of the kids.

Larson pulled rank and removed the two teachers from the room. The more athletic and attractive of the two maintained her composure.

"He said he'd come back and kill us and our families," she said calmly. "But we—*I*, actually," she confessed, eyeing her hysterical friend, "felt the threat to Penny and her mom was more immediate. So we called security."

Larson sought a description from her, wincing as he heard mention of the intruder's police uniform, for it stirred up his own memories of the bus attack years before. If he'd harbored any doubt, any question that they were pursuing the same cutter, this initial description sealed it for him. As she went on to describe the man as Mexican or Hispanic, lanky, late twenties, early thirties, Larson nodded. He hadn't gotten a good look at the man in the bus, but the general description combined with the razor and the use of a uniform was enough to further convince him.

He watched as his only verbal witness withdrew into herself. He recognized the aftershock of a guilty conscience, her second-guessing their cooperating with the man, her reviewing the alternatives they might have had, might have taken. Conscience is so quick to relive, so unforgiving and hypercritical of its own decision-making. Larson knew this about himself and could see it in her now, and knew better than to try to say anything comforting, for such things only solidified one's convictions that the wrong choice had been made.

Seeing this as a scene that could quickly absorb him, Larson excused himself. The moment local police heard of a federal agent's involvement, Larson would be delayed by questions he couldn't answer. He turned and made for the door.

"I know where she lives," the caregiver called out after him. "Alice."

Larson stopped and returned to her, sensing now the impending arrival of police and the need for quick information.

She spoke in a voice that sounded as if she were explaining this to herself. "I drove them both home once."

From what Larson had learned, her colleague had been dragged off because of this same knowledge.

"Debbie didn't need to tell him that," the woman said. "Shouldn't have told him. I wasn't about to tell him."

Larson took her gently by the shoulders. Human contact could have transforming results. He said softly, "I need the address." When she gazed up into his eyes, Larson added, "With your help, we can stop him."

CHAPTER SEVENTEEN

Hope Stevens, now Alice Stevenson, broke into a run at Baines Jewish Hospital, overwhelmed by the flashing spectacle of police cars and emergency vehicles. A pain gripped her chest, but she continued running. Her eyes swept side to side, her focus shifted near to deep, alert for any special attention paid to her.

Battling her maternal urges, understanding the attention she would provoke by storming into the daycare center, she forced her legs to slow, and as she did so took deep breaths to settle herself to where she could talk clearly and calmly without betraying her terrors.

She felt exposed and vulnerable. Both government agents and the Romeros could be looking for her. A day ago—just twenty-four hours earlier—she'd been rebuilding, planning, comfortable in her life here. Now, when it mattered most, she not only couldn't find Penny, but she'd driven her daughter to run away.

She reached the Children's Hospital basement by a circuitous route known only to employees. Through a series of color-coded hallways, corridors, and underground passages, she passed through the central Baines building, heading north and finally into the subterranean infrastructure of Children's, past laundry, food services, and maintenance.

She suppressed the urge to hurry, holding herself back for the sake of appearances. Reaching a clot of uniforms and scrubs that blocked the entry to daycare, she battled against her own guilt-ridden pessimism and did not ask what had happened. Instead she listened, gleaning bits and pieces. *An intruder. Wanting an address. No children hurt.* Awash with relief, she nonetheless coughed up a murmur of a mother's anguish that mixed awkwardly with despondency and a sense of reprieve.

From behind her a uniformed cop approached, trapping her between the group and her only easy exit.

Then, a voice: "Alice?"

She turned to see Phyllis's astonished face peering around a door frame. Alice quickly reached the distraught woman, passing shoulder to shoulder with the cop, who barely looked at her.

"Penny?"

"We didn't see her today . . ." Phyllis said. "A man . . . an awful man, Alice . . ."

"She wasn't here? Didn't come here?"

"Today? No. Listen . . . I'm so sorry . . ." Phyllis broke into tears, and not for the first time judging by the look of her.

Alice welcomed this news of her daughter, even though it meant Penny remained missing. "This man?"

"A policeman, or dressed like one. We wouldn't have let him in . . . wouldn't have opened the door . . ." Phyllis met eyes with Alice, hers bloodshot and tear-filled as she said, "We told him where you live."

Alice backed up and slowly walked away, not wanting to bring attention to herself. She thought her heart must have stopped completely for the pain in her chest, but the pulse-pounding whine in her ears kept her moving.

"Hey, lady!" a deep male voice shouted from behind. "You! Lady!"

She headed left, then right, then right again, and then broke into a run. She would never allow them to catch her in these corridors.

CHAPTER EIGHTEEN

"Penny?"

The girl turned around immediately, confirming her identity.

Paolo stood tall, enabling her to take in the police uniform. "I'm Officer Rodriguez."

The little girl—*she's a pretty little thing*—backed away from the apartment house's buzzer board and into a corner. "I'm not allowed to talk to strangers . . ." she said. "I'll scream if you come closer."

And well trained . . .

"And well you should, young lady," he said, "*if* I was a stranger." He took another step closer. By the look of her, she didn't have a way into the apartment building, standing by the buzzer board as she had been. It suggested Mama wasn't home. He decided to play that card. "But I'm not a stranger. I'm a policeman assigned to find you and take you to your mother. Doesn't that sound like a good idea?" Her head tilted curiously, like a dog's. "She's at the hospital. Baines Jewish." Penny seemed to accept this explanation, concern worrying her small brow. Using the information gleaned from the wallets, he exploited that concern. "Ms. Gillespie—from the daycare center—has had a small accident. Your mother is anxious to get you over there and see her."

"What happened?" The girl's curiosity won out. Paolo extended his hand toward her, again reminded of a wary street dog. "We'll take the bus," he said. "Did you know policemen ride the bus? We'll go find your mom."

Already planning ahead, he realized he would soon need to rent or steal a car—but both options presented serious risks.

Her eyes softened slightly, though she remained cautious.

"Or . . ." he said, "if you want to stay here—if you promise to stay *right here*—I could head back and tell her I'd found you, and that you were okay, but that you wouldn't come with me . . ."

He turned his back on her, knowing well what she'd do.

"Wait!" she called out when he'd taken but two steps.

Thrust, parry.

He heard the patter of her small feet, dried the sweat from his hand on the uniform's shirt, and extended it for her to hold.

CHAPTER NINETEEN

Trill Hampton affected the deadbeat, too-cool-to-get-excited deputy marshal role whenever possible. So when Hampton interrupted Larson's call in an animated voice, Larson immediately took note.

"Good timing!" Hampton said. "We just got a tac alert from Homeland that an air marshal may have IDed a guy with a bow tie scar on his forearm. Someone actually reads the alerts we put out there, if you can believe that. If it's our cutter, he was seen on a morning flight, NWA, from Minneapolis to St. Louis. Flying under the name Rodriguez."

"It's why I called," Larson said. "It *is* him: the guy who did Benny; I'd put money on it. And my best guess is I'm only a few minutes behind him. A half hour, at most," Larson explained. He weaved his Explorer through traffic. "I was calling in for backup."

"Gimme your ten-twenty," Hampton said.

"It's a Jefferson Square address." Larson recited the exact street and number.

"Me and Stubby have made some progress on Markowitz.

We'll catch you up. We're probably ten minutes behind you. We'll stay on com."

For Larson, the air marshal's spotting the tattoo connected the passenger to the Romeros. Homeland Security could now interface with the Bureau and perhaps even Interpol to track the suspect's travel, his true identity, his route, his finances; everything that could be generated and gathered.

Larson ran two red lights, narrowly avoiding a collision as he raced through the second intersection, a not-so-subtle reminder for him not to lose focus.

By the time he reached the apartment complex off Jefferson Square, he first heard and then spotted a squad car a block behind him and closing fast, siren blazing. Larson pulled over and hurried out of the Explorer. The sirens grew steadily louder and more shrill. With his third kick, he dislodged the door from the jamb and he shouldered his way through. The siren wound down—they'd reached the curb.

Larson had not seen a listing for any Stevenson or Stevens on the buzzer board. But 202 had held a blank card, and it won Larson's attention. He sprinted for the EXIT sign and the stairs he knew he'd find behind it, avoiding the slower elevator and hoping the cops might sucker into it.

He had his weapon out and at the ready by the time he nudged open the door to the second-floor hallway. The corridor was empty and quiet. He worked his way past one apartment—204—and reversed directions. 203 . . . 202 . . .

He braced himself. Hope might be dead, murdered only moments before; or the cutter might be inside the apartment with her, prepared to use her as a hostage, the sirens having alerted him; it might be empty; it might be lit on fire.

He placed his ear to the cool door. The gun's grip warmed in his hand.

Silence.

A trickle of sweat escaped down his face. A syncopated, jolting rhythm occupied the space below his rib cage.

Into the mix he now added the sound of hurried footsteps as the cops followed up the stairs.

Larson reeled back and drove his heel into the door. With the second blow, it tore open, banging against the interior wall and rebounding.

"PUT DOWN THE WEAPON!" a male voice screeched from behind him.

"Federal officer!" Larson roared as he charged into 202. He wasn't waiting around to share a moment with the two patrolmen.

Larson hurried from one interior door to the next, his weapon held in both hands at the ready. A loft apartment with an open floor plan, the wood planks creaked with his every step.

"PUT THE WEAPON DOWN! HANDS WHERE I CAN SEE THEM!" shouted one of the cops from behind him in the doorway.

If Larson failed to answer, he knew the man would enter without further warning and might shoot him out of a bad case of nerves. Nonetheless, Larson headed down a narrow hallway, now facing two closed doors to his left, and two to his right. *Bedrooms and closets*, he thought.

"U.S. marshal," Larson called back, intentionally engaging them even though it would reveal his position to anyone else inside. "You're interfering with a federal fugitive apprehension. Stay where you are and guard the door."

"Not happening, buddy. I'm coming inside, and if that gun is not on the floor . . ."

"It's not!" Larson called out as he moved down the dimly lit hallway. He reached for the doorknob of the first door.

"Drop it!"

Very close behind him now.

The tension in the cop's voice cut like a knife blade. Larson shot a glance back there, far enough to see the toe of a polished shoe.

He shouldered his way through the door and swept his weapon corner to corner, beads of sweat now trickling down from his temples and armpits.

A little girl's room. Larson felt a pang of dread. A jolt of connection. Stuffed animals. A low bookshelf crammed with thin, colorful books.

The cop was suddenly right there behind him. Larson could *feel* him.

He chose his words carefully. "Listen, Officer . . . we have one more room to clear. The apartment isn't safe until we clear that room."

"Drop the weapon."

"Guard your backside . . . Don't get yourself killed out of stupidity."

A second cop now entered the apartment, calling out now for his partner.

"Guard the door!" Larson shouted. "The suspect is considered armed and dangerous. He may have two hostages: a woman and a child."

"What the fuck is going on here?" the cop behind him asked.

Larson squatted and gently placed his weapon on the floor. These guys were too green and uptight for him to take any more chances.

Larson ordered, "Whatever you do, clear that room behind you, Officer. *Now!*" He turned slowly, to reveal his credential wallet hanging from his coat pocket.

"Fed . . . er . . . al off . . . i . . . cer . . ." Larson repeated syllabically. "Clear that fucking room, and both closets, before somebody throws shots!"

The banter increased between the two cops. The one guarding

Larson collected his weapon and required him to kneel with his hands behind his head. His partner abandoned the front door and cleared the remaining room and closets.

A minute later, weapons drawn, the two carefully followed Larson out into the hallway.

Then he heard a woman's voice. A familiar voice.

"You?" She was panting from having run the stairs.

He saw her first in a dreamlike blur—a rush of memories, love, lust, and confusion overtaking him. His only thought: *It can't be.* But it was. She was. Right there. Not twenty feet away.

Six years compressed into that singular moment as they met eyes.

And he froze.

"Where's my daughter?"

CHAPTER TWENTY

Larson and Alice climbed into his parked Explorer. This was their first moment alone together after an hour of negotiations that had included Scott Rotem in Washington, D.C., the Missouri-based U.S. Attorney, SLPD, and the regional office of WITSEC. Justice, represented here by FATF, had won custody. She was Larson's.

She displayed a reticence in closing the car door, and he wondered if he should read anything into that.

After an awkward few seconds of silence, they turned to face each other. He saw a mother's anguish on her face and realized this was neither the place nor the time to express what he was feeling—joy, exhilaration, a sense of completion—but as usual, his mouth betrayed him.

"It's incredibly good to see you again."

The shock that registered on her face told him he'd gone too far. But then her expression warmed, however briefly.

"We'll find her," he said.

"You don't know that."

"I don't mean this," he said, sweeping his hand to include

everything outside the windshield—the lights, the uniforms, the huddled discussions. "I mean you and I. We'll find her."

She fought back tears and won. "I appreciate the sentiment, Lars, I really do. But we both know that when Debbie dropped him off—" She might have managed to get the sentence out, but she couldn't complete the thought, couldn't allow herself the image of Penny at the door unable to get inside.

She'd held up unbelievably well over the past hour—perhaps her months with WITSEC had conditioned her. At some point she would need to release what she now bravely contained. But not now. She was either numb, or far stronger than he'd imagined.

She said, "I'd hoped for a happier reunion." That would be all she would offer him for now, and they both knew it. It was enough. "Yeah."

The Explorer had a view across a corner of the park to the entrance to her apartment building. A dozen uniformed police and two detectives continued to comb the neighborhood, conducting interviews in an attempt to locate Penny. The one report they had, confusing as it was to some, put a young girl matching Penny's description with a policeman boarding a city bus. The eyewitness put the policeman's uniform as blue, but Larson was betting black. He and the others knew who was wearing this uniform, since the same disguise had been used at the hospital. *Rodriguez.*

Nonetheless, the local police were conducting a full canvass of the area, both because it was dictated by procedure and because when it came to a child's abduction, all bets were hedged.

In profile, her nose turned slightly upward, her lips looked a little less full than the lips he remembered kissing. Larson adored the perfect pear shape of her ears and was reminded of the dead woman in Minneapolis. There was so much more to tell her, both personally and professionally, but first was the question of Penny's whereabouts.

Larson believed Penny's abductor might call Hope's cell phone, as Penny was believed to have the number memorized. The call wouldn't be for ransom, though. All the Romeros wanted was this woman dead.

For the moment Larson was authorized to oversee Hope's protection (he couldn't think of her as Alice) while his FATF team continued to pursue Markowitz and *Laena*. When and if WITSEC stabilized, Hope would be turned over to Justice for more permanent protection.

He said, "We can't take you to our offices because they're too public and could be being watched."

"All I care about is getting Penny," she said, looking out the windshield now. Searching.

"That's all I want, too," he said. He decided to trust her with the truth. "We think we may have a mole, either in WITSEC or FATF. We've lost something valuable to us. That's why the alert went out. While we figure out how to get Penny back, I'm taking you into a safe house to ride this out."

"Ride what out? Finding Penny, or the return of whatever was taken from you?"

"Both," he said, speaking only for himself. Rotem and others would see Penny as an unfortunate; her life would not measure well against the lives of thousands of other witnesses and dependents. While trying to ensure her safety, ultimately they would use her, lose her, if necessary. Larson could not go along with that, but neither could he tell Hope this now.

After a few painful moments of silence, during which the only sounds were her occasional sniffing back a runny nose, Larson said, "We should go."

"We can't leave. She'll come back home."

"Your apartment building will be watched twenty-four/seven. I'm in constant contact."

"I'm not leaving."

"They want *you*, Hope." He didn't bother to correct himself—he wasn't going to get used to her as Alice. "We *are* leaving. We're going to get you to safety. Every effort is being made to locate Penny. There's nothing to be gained by staying here and putting you so out in the open."

"And if I get out of this car?" she asked, her hand on the car door. "I'm allowed to do that, right? WITSEC, any kind of government protection, is voluntary, right?"

She remembered her orientation materials well. "Technically, but we can hold you as a material witness to a crime."

"Those crimes happened over six years ago!"

"There's no statute of limitations on federal capital murder cases. You're in this now."

"I'll get an attorney," she said, still resisting.

"And it'll get ugly," he shot back. "And all that energy, time, will be diverted away from where we need it most: finding Penny."

Again, she looked at Larson directly. "Do something."

Larson turned the ignition.

CHAPTER TWENTY-ONE

Larson drove his Explorer down a perfectly straight farm road. Less than forty minutes west of St. Louis, the McMansion suburban developments finally stopped sprawling and the flat expanse of generational farms took over, the small white houses and silos surrounded by brown tilled ground, rail fence, and pasture. The almost geometrical landscape looked familiar to both passengers. Six years earlier, Larson had sequestered protected witness Hope Stevens in the same Marshals Service safe house—the Orchard House—that now was his destination.

The closer they drew to the final turn, across a wooden bridge and up the hill, the more those memories weighed on him. It was at the farmhouse where they'd first found each other—and had last seen each other.

For six years he'd avoided reliving such moments, no great fan of nostalgia and unwilling to be one of those people who lived constantly with one foot in the past. But now, with her finally in the seat beside him, something allowed him to revisit another time in this same place, and he gave in to it willingly.

Larson had run the protection squad back then, and the rotation of assignments had conveniently left him inside the farmhouse with her, while Stubblefield and Hampton had perimeter patrol. He later wondered whether he'd been set up, whether Hamp and Stubby had felt the chemistry between them and arranged this one night for them. But he wasn't thinking such things at the time. He was thanking his stars.

The two-story, hundred-year-old farmhouse had not been restored since the thirties and remained in a state of neglect. It sagged, with wandering cracks, like lightning bolts, in the green-painted plaster walls and white ceilings, gaping chips drawn by gravity out of the dining room's elaborate ceiling molding, swollen black fingers of cigarette and cigar burns at the edges of much of the furniture, especially the dining room table where witnesses and their deputies had whiled away the hours with games of poker and scotch. The house had been shown little respect since its incorporation into the Marshals Service. The exterior, once a fashionable gray, was now peeling paint, curling away from the western sun and sloughing off like reptilian scales.

What had once been a proper and formal staircase led up to a narrow second-floor hallway off of which were two small bedrooms and a narrow bath wedged between them, probably originally a linen closet or nursery. Another, smaller corridor, added hastily years before and without the care given the original construction, led over a study below and into two oddly shaped bedrooms connected one to the other through an ill-fitted communicating door. A foul-smelling, twisting set of back stairs led from the added bedrooms down to the small kitchen below. Because of these additions the house had a wandering, cut-up, and unpredictable feel to it, seeming larger than it actually was.

She'd called him upstairs. "Lars?"

And he knew before arriving that despite other nights of comforting, of intimacy, that this was their moment of consummation. He knew what she had in mind not from anything said but by the pent-up energy that had been forced to simmer between them while in the company of others. He couldn't identify the moment between them that accounted for the way he felt, nor had she directly communicated to him her own emotions or desires, and yet he knew. He knew this was wrong, against all regulations, and he knew this was going to happen. Knew they wouldn't have long.

All windows in the house had been retrofitted with removable blackout cloth that Velcroed into place. The two exterior doors had blackout blankets that tied to the side by day but hung as light barriers by night. The fixtures in the house, and all lamps, burned compact fluorescents, the government's idea of how to save on energy costs; the resulting light, slightly blue or oddly yellow on the eyes, never looking quite right.

Her bedroom had one jaundiced bedside lamp aglow. The house, closed and shuttered as it was, and without air-conditioning of any kind, sweltered in the late-summer heat, with only ineffective and noisy floor fans left to stir the turgid air. One such beast was at work in the corner, grinding and clapping as its paddles scraped the wire protection meant to defend fingers from accidents. It forced a mechanical rhythm into the room, clippity-clippity-clapping and then whining asthmatically before starting the pattern again.

Hope stood just in front of the lamp, casting herself in a dark shadow. She'd shed the pale-violet blouse, one of two such shirts she alternated day to day, revealing the low-cut, sleeveless saffron tank top that held to her loosely, her egret's neck and strong arms glistening in the bedroom's heat.

"Close the door," she commanded.

The idea of locking the air in the room went against all logic. It had to be for privacy.

He pushed the door shut with a click.

"Does it lock?"

Larson's heart responded in his chest. "I don't think so."

"Will they come in the house?"

"Not until shift change."

"What if they need to use the facilities?"

She'd clearly deliberated on the obstacles that faced them.

Larson's heart continued to race. "No, I seriously doubt it." The fact was they'd piss into bushes if need be, but he didn't want to get crude at such a moment. Furthermore, both his men would keep well away from the farmhouse in an effort to not place motion near it, not bring any attention to it.

She unfastened her belt, unbuttoned and unzipped her jeans, leaving them hanging on the width of her sumptuous hips, her purple underwear showing. "I want to take a bath," she said. "Warm, not hot. To cool off, if that's possible."

Standing just inside the shut door, Larson walked toward her.

"I've slept in my clothes the past several nights. We all have, haven't we? I'm sick of sponge baths."

He took another step closer. "I'm not sure I know where you're going with this."

"Oh, I think you do," she said as she dragged the jeans lower, tugged them over her hips and down her legs. She leaned over to step out of them and her tank top fell away, offering a flash of round, pale skin and the white from her bra. She added, "Am I the only one who's been thinking about this?"

"No."

Another step closer.

"There's something about taking my clothes off, undressing. It's a moment of extreme . . . vulnerability. I'm glad you're here."

"Hope . . . I . . ."

"If you're ever asked about this, questioned . . . I know you,

Lars. You'd never lie about it. I know you could lose your job, and I know how much it means to you, how good you are at it. All those things. So you see . . . there's only one way this can happen. Between us, I mean. I'm usually not the forward type," she said, pulling off her top and standing now in bra and underwear. "Not at all." She reached behind her back and deftly unclipped the bra. "This doesn't come easy for me." As the back strap came loose it slipped half off her breasts, the shoulder straps sliding lower on her arms. "But it has to be that I seduced you. It has to be all me, all my doing. That I came up with some lame excuse about being afraid to undress in the room alone—it was all I could come up with on short notice," she said. "That I came on to you in a moment of weakness."

"It's supposed to be me protecting you," he said hoarsely, his throat gone dry, "not the other way around."

"We'll look after each other then," she said. She allowed the bra to fall. Her breasts rode high on her chest, her nipples and areolas far darker than her complexion suggested. She climbed out of the bikini briefs, and he could feel her embarrassed determination to continue. She wore only a thin silver necklace now—something he hadn't yet told her would have to go before enrollment in the program.

She stepped forward and melted into him, her arms between them, her hands already working on his shirt buttons.

He reached around to embrace her and she chided, "No . . . No . . . No . . ." Looking up at him, she suppressed a grin as she explained, "I want it to be *entirely* my doing, Lars." She mocked a response to her being interrogated about this. "He stood there stoically. He was in the room as I undressed. I asked him to be. I can't explain that, but I couldn't take off my clothes without someone there and Deputy Larson was the one guarding me that night. And, well . . ." She continued working his shirt open. She moved on to his belt and khakis. "I suppose I felt vulnerable, or in need of company, safety, security, but I found myself not heading for the bath, as I'd suggested, but instead, one thing led to another and I found myself flirting with him." In her regular voice, she said, "Flirting's far too soft a word. Not the right word at all. I'll have to come up with something better."

"Hope . . ."

"You be quiet, Deputy. We need the record clean. We need our story . . . straight." With that she had his pants open and him firmly in hand. She brought his fingers up to her chest and whispered, "This once, the first time between us, it has to be all me."

Her nipple firmed and grew puckered under his touch.

She undressed him, saying, "You're going to lie down on the bed and do your best to resist me." Again, Larson reached to embrace her, having had enough of the game, but she held him off, saying, "Please," and he understood from her tone that she was serious. Perhaps she couldn't confront true lovemaking. Perhaps it was too soon for her. Perhaps this was more born of a primal urge to dominate after days—weeks—of having her every movement controlled and coordinated by others. And all of them men, always men.

"My turn," she said, confirming his thoughts.

She lay him back on the bed and climbed atop him, dragging her warm spot against him, drawing something abstract with her soft paintbrush. She climbed over him and lowered a breast and nipple to his lips, and as he kissed her there, as his tongue raced circles, she reached back and touched him and he shuddered head to toe. She alternated breasts to his lips as her fingers explored him.

She pulled her breast free of him and raised up on extended arms and locked elbows, hovering over him on raised toes like doing a push-up, and slowly lowered herself to where it was the heat from her skin he felt first. Then her breasts lit up his skin and she slowly eased her full weight down onto him, melting down into him to where arm matched arm, belly matched belly, and thigh matched thigh. Then she rocked her hips, opened her legs and reached down there, taking hold, sliding lower along his chest, and with this motion joined them with barely any effort.

She lay there quietly, Larson fully inside her now, not a motion between them beside the drumming of their pulses, their conflicting heartbeats. She held him like a clenched fist. He tried to initiate a rhythm and she pinned down his hips and said hotly into his ear, "You're all mine."

And he was.

He grew delirious in the heat of the room. He lost track of time but never of her. They melded into this single, humming entity. A lone moth worked along the ceiling, dancing with its shadow. They must have lain absolutely still for ten minutes or more—it was like nothing he'd ever experienced. At the first sense of him losing his erection she moved one full, glorious stroke, lifting herself up to sitting, and driving him back into her, filling her, completing her, before stretching out prone and lowering herself incrementally again in that same dizzying fashion as before. Now she lay fully atop, their bodies meeting together again, both of them murmuring.

"I've wanted this for so long," she whispered into his ear. "I didn't want to waste it."

She sat up then, pulled his hands to her breasts, and began her musical rising and falling.

"Look at me," he said, and she did, and it felt like days later before her eyes rolled back into her head and the world exploded through him and into her in a perfectly timed choreography of contractions and sharp cries of satisfaction.

He awoke to the sound through the wall of her bath running, and might have believed it all a dream had not that paddle fan been grinding its way through the chorus of that same grating song.

———

Rolling swales of bleached and dying field grass gave way to slate ponds stitched together by meandering streams the color of old steel. A pair of mallards rose and crossed the road, their wings beating so fast they seemed to fly without them, veering away from the Explorer and up into a guncotton sky.

Hope sat stone-faced in the passenger seat, a knot of concern worn on her brow like a birthmark. "How do we know that will work?"

"Because we've done it before," Larson answered.

"But it hasn't rung."

"It will." He'd call-forwarded her cell phone to his secure BlackBerry, and had then shut her cell phone off, to prevent any chance of her phone being triangulated, a sophisticated method of radio telemetry. If Penny had been kidnapped, and if her captors called, if an effort was made to negotiate, Larson believed it would only be to hold her on the line long enough to electronically track her location. He dared not underestimate the reach of the Romeros. If they could corrupt the federal court system—and some said they already had—then cell phones weren't going to inhibit them.

"This drive is bringing back all sorts of stuff for me," she said.

"Yup. Good stuff."

"You sure?"

"Absolutely."

"What's her name?" Hope asked, out of the blue.

"There is no 'her.' There's a friend, Linda. It got heavy for a couple months, a long time ago, but it's friends now, and that's good." He said, "You?"

"No." She offered a mocking smile. "Not even close."

She'd overheard Larson's call to Linda, suggesting she stay with her mother for a day or two. The incident at the hospital and the kidnapping had rattled him. It seemed unlikely the Romeros would connect him to Hope, then his dog to Linda, but he'd never forgive himself should anything happen to her because of him.

Unsurprisingly, Linda had reacted calmly, her primary concern that he make sure he was taking all necessary precautions for himself.

"Did you come to St. Louis looking for me?" Larson asked. Why he couldn't bring himself to ask the real question, about Penny, he wasn't sure. The moment he'd heard the child's age, he'd known. So why the indirect questioning?

She almost smiled. "Yeah, I did. Had no clue there'd be no way to find you once I got here. You're not in information, not in any phone books. Nothing on the Internet. You're worse than I was in protection." She hesitated, as if ashamed to admit it. "I even sat outside the Federal building a couple different days looking for you. How's that for sick?"

"Not at all." He thought a moment. "*Much Ado About Nothing?* Was that your laugh I heard?"

"Don't miss the turn," she said, indicating the left.

As if he would have.

"Are you *sure* there's no way they can detect that I've call-forwarded my number? Why haven't I heard from someone?"

Good job changing the subject, he thought. But at that very moment Larson's BlackBerry chirped at his side to save them both.

Rather than answer himself, he pulled over sharply and caught a quick look at the caller ID: OUT OF AREA. Calls from anyone inside the Service came up PRIVATE on caller ID. Believing this could be intended for her, he passed her his phone, still ringing. He switched off the car as she cradled the BlackBerry awkwardly and pressed it to her ear.

"Hello?" Her eyes darted first to Larson, then out toward the landscape.

Larson leaned across to listen in and for a moment their heads touched and he felt that same sense of burning he had felt all those years ago. He withdrew quickly but now it was she who angled toward him, and again, he leaned to meet her.

"You are missing a package," the voice said. "A very pretty little package."

But the way the words were drawn out and strung together convinced Larson that the call was nothing but a ruse to buy time to trace Hope's location. Larson's BlackBerry was untraceable; and though it housed a GPS chip, that chip had to be switched on manually.

"You leave her out of this!" Hope blurted out, contrary to what she knew was required of her.

"Oh . . . but it's a little late for that now, don't you think? I wonder what Social Services would have said about you locking her out like that?"

Tracing calls worked both directions. The Romeros had to know that the full technological might and power of the Marshals Service would be summoned to locate this girl. So why play so loose with time? Caller ID was nearly instantaneous, whether the caller believed the line blocked or not. This caller had already stayed on much too long. Larson suspected that a reverse trace was under way: The caller had been advised to keep Hope engaged for as long as possible. But by remaining on the line, the caller was in fact leaving his own foot squarely in the bear trap.

Larson drew a fast circle in the air, indicating she should keep the caller talking.

"What do you want?" she asked.

"It's not about what they—what we," the male voice immediately corrected, "want. If you want to recover the missing package, I suggest you keep your phone close by your side. Instructions to follow." The line cleared.

Larson found the caller's slipup telling—from "they" to "we"—and the choice of language intriguing. It sounded as if the man had been reading from a script at the beginning and end but had improvised in between.

He took back the phone, expecting to hear from the Clayton office within minutes. The call had lasted plenty long enough for them to trace, even if some kind of switching device were involved. Sitting upright behind the wheel again, Larson turned the key.

Hope's face was streaked with tears, her arms now crossed so tightly he wondered if she could breathe.

"Don't," he cautioned. "Don't let them win. They want this kind of reaction from you."

"Shut up!" she said, ratcheting her head away from him, gazing out at the patch-quilt geometry of some farmer's labors.

"It helps them."

"Leave it," she told the tilled fields. After a moment she asked, "What now?"

"They think if you leave your phone on they'll find you, and that will end it. But, we won this round. We'll trace *them*. Maybe they know that, maybe they don't."

"So, what now?" she repeated.

"We'll get you settled in at the farm. Normally a couple of our guys would join me, but Rotem and I think that's too risky right now. Soon enough. Until then, basically, you're missing and I'm AWOL. My boss has to plug a leak. Until then, you and I remain on our own. It's best. I have some stuff to work through once you're okay."

"I *am* okay," she said.

He had the car going again. "There's a psychology to this—to abductions. I'm not expecting you to be able to detach. Of course not. But their plan is to play with you—to manipulate you into making a mistake and offering them a chance to kill you. That's all they want. They don't care about Penny the way we do," a slip he covered by talking more quickly now, "and nothing they say one way or the other about her is the truth. What we know—what we absolutely know—is how important she is to them right now. She's their passport to you. That's all that matters, all there is. She's a means to an end, and as long as we, I, the Service, keep them from getting you, Penny retains her value. Do you understand? It's important you understand this. You don't do anything without me knowing it. *Nothing*. I don't know how, but they're going to try to push you into something—we don't know what it is yet—but what I need you to keep in mind is that denying them is the key."

"Sounds like there's a lot you don't know. Not very reassuring."

"As long as they don't have you, Penny's safe." God, how he hoped he was right. "And whatever you do that they ask will only ensure that both of you are killed."

The Explorer complained as it climbed a long twisting hill, revealing pumpkin patches and apple orchards and unexpected colors brought on by early frosts that had yet to reach the city. The leaves were changing here, a swirling mix of maturing oranges, reds, and browns. Paint by number. PICK YUR OWN—3 MILES AHEAD. The Orchard House was just around the next bend. Her body stiffened once again, telling Larson that she recognized it, too.

CHAPTER TWENTY-TWO

In the motel room's dimly lit bathroom Paolo dabbed a slippery antibiotic cream into the red, raw, self-inflicted wound on his abdomen, addressing the infection. In the mirror, covered in the white flyspecks of someone else's flossing, the chaotic scar tissue, the randomly drawn bumps and lines that lay across his chest and midsection reminded him of dead worms on blacktop after a hard rain.

His eyes shifted focus in the speckled reflection. Behind him and to his left he encountered the bound ankles, knees, and shoulders of the little girl tucked into the bottom of the open booth that served as a closet. She wore a pair of his dirty socks tied around her head, the ends connected by a shoestring, the bulging knot jammed into her mouth.

Having phoned in the girl's abduction—his success—to Philippe, he now awaited instructions as to what came next. He placed down the tube of cream. The girl turned away from him as he double-checked her gag and the duct tape on her wrists and ankles. He repeated this ritual every five minutes. Kids could be tricky little things.

"I don't like this, either," he said to her, though he might have been talking to himself again. "I told you that." The girl made no indication of hearing him. "It wasn't exactly my idea, snatching you up like that." Now, for the first time, she turned her head. Her sad eyes, bloodshot and irritated to a pitiful pink, pleaded with him. Then he watched as she caught sight of the mosaic of his scars.

Whimpering, she turned away again.

Paolo slipped on a black T-shirt. He tried again. "I can remove this stuff, you know? Penny? Are you listening? The tape. The gag. You understand? You could watch cartoons. Whaddya think?"

He stood and fumbled with the remote control. "You want to watch cartoons?" He cycled through the channels, hitting mostly ads. No cartoons. He tossed the remote onto the bed, pissed off at it.

"Come on!" he said to her. "Do something. Nod, if you want me to remove the gag."

She cowered into the corner of the closet, a tight little ball of pale fear.

"Nothing I'd rather do than cut you loose. You understand that?" He studied her. "All we need is an agreement, and I can cut you loose. No screaming, no fighting—and I remove the tape and gag. Okay?" He moved closer to her, craned down to where he could smell her fear, and said, "Do you think you're helping anything?"

Her head pivoted slowly. Her nose was runny, and he went over and got her a tissue and brought it back and held it at her nose so she could blow, and she did. Not just once, but a couple of times.

"See?" he said. "I want you to be as comfortable as possible. This is going to work out."

She nodded and tried to speak. Paolo grinned ear to ear. His eyes brightened. He reached out to pet her head, but thought better of it.

"By nodding you're promising me you won't do anything stupid—won't shout or anything like that. Are we both clear on that?"

Penny nodded for a second time.

"All right then. Yes. Good." He was already loosening the gag. "Real good." The sock fell down around her neck.

Penny said softly, "I've got to go potty."

A few minutes later he'd untied her and helped her to stand. Her knees, ankles, shoulders, and wrists ached. She leaned on him for the first few steps, trying to find her balance.

"You can shut the door," he said. "But don't lock it. If I hear you lock it, I'm going to have to bust it down. And then our deal is over, and I'll have to tie you back up."

Frightened, she managed yet another nod.

"Okay. Go on and do your business." Penny entered the bathroom and closed the door behind her. She dropped her pants and pulled down her panties and sat down to pee, but her mind was on escape. She was hearing her mom telling her all this stuff she never really bothered to listen to. Over and over, the same boring stuff. Stuff about where to go if they were ever separated, how to scream and run, how to bite. Her mom had once showed her everything in the kitchen that could be used to hurt someone, telling her over and over that she was only showing her this stuff in case it was absolutely necessary, in case someone tried to rob them or *something like that*. But the way she'd said it, the *something like that* was the important part. This felt like one of those times: *something like that.*

She looked around. *Dental floss, a toothbrush, a tube of ointment.*

She reached forward and grabbed the ointment, because one of the things her mother had showed her had been all the stuff under the sink, and how most of that stuff if squirted or sprayed into a man's eyes would blind him. She squeezed a little dribble out onto her finger and held it close to her nose and smelled it. It didn't smell like the kind of stuff that would hurt your eyes. She put it back.

"You done in there?" he asked through the door.

"Almost done."

A plastic basket that was supposed to look real held tiny bottles of shampoo, conditioner, and lotion. Next to that was a brown tray with two coffee mugs and a little dish with plastic-wrapped coffee creamer and sugar. In the corner, a coffee maker.

Her eyes returned to the coffee mugs.

She finished up and pulled her clothes back up, but her eyes never left those two coffee mugs. The image was vivid in her mind because she'd been the one who had knocked the mug off the kitchen counter and broken it. Like the mug, she'd then broken into tears, made all the worse when her mother had cut her finger picking up the pieces. That bleeding finger was so present in her mind now because she'd glimpsed the awful man's stomach—all those scars and that one fresh cut—and somehow the two things connected in her thought. *Blood.*

He knocked.

It spiked through her like a jolt. "I know. I know!" She didn't need to try to sound annoyed with him.

She wrapped one of the coffee mugs in a towel, several layers thick. She could feel the man about to open the door. As she wielded the towel up over her head with her right hand, her left tripped the toilet flush, wanting the noise. Just as the toilet crashed into a gurgle, she flung the towel to the bathmat on the floor and felt the cup shatter.

Opening it, she selected a decent-sized curved, triangular

shape, handling it delicately, remembering how effortlessly it had cut her mother. She closed up the towel as the toilet finished its coughing and glugging, wrapped it into a ball. Now what? She looked for a place to hide it. She spun around in a panic. Where? she wondered.

She placed it into the garbage can. *Too obvious.*

"Okay. Open up!" Only the thickness of the door separated them.

She pulled back the garbage can's white plastic bag liner and stuffed the towel and its contents beneath the bag that she now saw held the scabby remains of an orange peel and several pieces of crumpled tissue. She returned the liner around the lip of the garbage can, wrapped her chunk of pottery in a wad of toilet paper, and slipped it into her front pocket. Then she changed her mind and put it into her sock, behind her ankle where it fit well.

CHAPTER TWENTY-THREE

"My guys are outside," Larson explained. Hope sat at the aqua-blue, linoleum-topped kitchen table, her chair a piece of porch furniture. She held her hands cupped around a mug of steaming tea that filled the room with lemon and ginger. She stared down into that tea as if it held some answers. "Two of them, but that should be enough."

"Why are you telling me this?"

"I'm leaving for a while."

His comment lifted her head as if pulled by a string. Her thumbnail rubbed at the red glaze on the mug that advertised The Home Depot. It made a thin scraping sound.

"You still like gin rummy?"

"It's been years," she said, deadpan and lifeless. "Probably in this same house, the last time I played."

"We'll play a hand tonight, and I'll let you beat me."

"You wish." She returned to picking at the glaze, a futile effort if there ever were one. "Why? Where are you going?"

"Our guys were able to trap and trace that call to you. It came from a pay phone."

"Here?" Her voice brightened. "In St. Louis?"

"Don't get your hopes up. But yes, here. The Hill. I'm going to follow it up. Guys like the Romeros, they never do something like this themselves. It'll be an intermediary, if we're able to connect it to anyone, that is." The realization that Penny might be his daughter knotted his gut, pushed him like nothing he'd experienced. Not even his love of this woman measured up against that feeling.

"A dead end."

"Not necessarily. It's a lead."

"If we know it's the Romeros," she asked, "why don't you just kick down a door?"

"There's a lot we don't know. Among which is a firm location for the Romero operations. We're talking with the Bureau—the FBI—their OC unit. See what they have."

"You don't know where they are?" Incredulity.

"We don't—the Marshals Service. Someone does, either in Justice or the Bureau. People like this are generally kept track of, but not always. Gaining access to that information isn't easy. It's compartmentalized and protected for the sake of the informers and UCs—undercover agents. I'm sure Rotem's working on it, but we're not going to sit around and wait to be cut in. Guys like this . . . when Donny was convicted . . . they know we're coming after them next. They know it's only a matter of time. And they go to ground. They make it as difficult as they can for us to find them. But they've still got to maintain control over their various businesses and interests. Half of what these families do is legitimate. The bad money finds its way to the good. The Romeros are still in business. And because of that they leave a trail. Someone will know something. That's what we're working on. That's why I'm gonna follow this phone lead."

"She's five years old, Lars."

"We'll find her."

"By dinner?"

How did he answer that?

Tears had found her again. Floated at the bottom of her eyes. She bunched her face and sniffled, and he could see her trying to keep from spilling them. He wanted to do something, but the only thing he could think of was to get going with what he had planned: follow leads, beat the bushes, stir the nest. Stubby and Hamp were off pursuing similar leads trying to connect Markowitz to the use of supercomputers, and in turn to track him down, and *Laena* and the Romeros along with him. In the back of Larson's mind was the nagging reminder that there were seven thousand others out there just like Hope. He knew a dozen witnesses personally. Their families indirectly. When the last name on that master list was finally decrypted, there would be more Pennys, more Hopes than they could possibly save. People were going to die; some of them deserved it as far as Larson was concerned: He'd personally protected dozens of guilty men, killers and loan sharks and losers he'd have rather shot in cold blood than pamper and defend. But their families, their kids, and the whistle-blowers like Hope. If the names on the list were sold off like pigs at auction, there would be untold bloodshed and carnage.

"I gotta go," he said. He handed her a Siemens cell phone. It was a new phone for her to use, brushed silver with a green screen. "Your number has been forwarded to this one now. It's also untraceable, like mine is. We programmed in my number. Speed-dial one. You and I can text message, as well. Just so you know: If they contact you—this phone—our guys will know about it, too. But call me the minute you hang up, no matter what."

"What are their names?" she asked.

Larson was stumped.

"The two guards," she explained.

"Marland and Carlyle."

"Are those their first names or last?"

"I don't know their first names."

"Do I lock the doors?"

"They're all locked. I've double-checked them. Everything's blacked out. You can turn on any lights you want. You'll dead-bolt the kitchen door behind me."

"And if they want in?"

"They won't." Larson thought she would have remembered all this.

"I don't want to be alone," she said as his hand found the cool doorknob. "Please stay."

With his back to her he said, "I can send Carlyle inside if you want."

"Send Carlyle on the errand. You stay. Please."

"Listen . . . I want Penny back, too," he said, grateful she wanted him to stay. "Right now, there's no one I trust to follow up this lead . . . no one I'm going to trust Penny's life with. But if you ask me once more to stay with you, I will." How could she still command this kind of response in him?

"I hate this," she said.

"Lock it behind me," he reminded.

Larson's head ached. He couldn't remember the last time he'd eaten. This time of evening he thought about beer. His mouth was dry and tacky.

A tourist visit to St. Louis wasn't complete without a trip to the Arch, Ted Drewes Frozen Custard, and Cunetto House of Pasta. Soon after his transfer, a few of Larson's coworkers had led him on a somewhat drunken tour of all three. He didn't like small spaces, so he stayed on the ground instead of riding to the top of the Arch but had found the underground museum and film on the construction of it enough to hold his interest.

Frank Cunetto, the restaurant's second-generation owner, was considered a friend of law enforcement. He typically offered cops and special agents and deputy marshals complimentary rounds of beverages. He loitered and rubbed shoulders and no one knew if he was a spy for the mob or just a good guy who happened to like cops. He'd done Larson plenty of favors: Cardinals tickets, Rams tickets. Even set him up with a busty Italian woman who hadn't worked out.

He turned east onto Southwest Avenue, stirring leaves under his tires, driving past the postwar-era row houses, each so similar—if not identical—to the next. Little houses, larger lives. The Hill was all about who you knew and what family you came from. Larson was an outsider here.

"Roland!"

Frank Cunetto lived inside a round face: pale Mediterranean skin, an affable smile, and a bald spot on his head that made him look older than his thirty-eight years.

He pulled Larson by the arm and dragged him past the clot of restaurant-goers who'd been waiting forty minutes for a meal.

"Lemme buy you a drink!" Excitement was a perpetual state of existence for Frank. He wore a thin white dress shirt, an undershirt showing beneath, gray flannel trousers, and an open, matching vest. He had a barrel chest and a dozen pounds he didn't need. His face glistened beneath the dim lights of the smoky bar. His uncles had started the place, after opening a pharmacy. How the two were connected, Larson wasn't sure, but black-and-whites hung on the walls in a family pictorial. The uncles looked like they went back to the fifties.

"Draft beer," Larson told the matronly waitress whom Frank

signaled. "Bud," he added, paying loyalty to the city's home brew in front of Frank.

When their drinks had been delivered, Larson asked to see the restaurant's pay phone. Frank's face screwed up into a knot of suspicion, but he maintained his cool. He talked as he led the way. Frank liked to talk. "What's this about? Anything I can help with? You guys on a case or what? I never figured out exactly what it is you guys, the marshals I'm talking about, do. Besides protecting the courts, and witnesses and all that. Not that that's not something, you understand, but tell the truth, Roland, you don't strike me as the type to stand around a courtroom all day."

The place was crowded. Linen tablecloths. The waiters were mostly old guys in black pants and white shirts. The waitresses dressed like they were from *Playboy* fantasy camp, with the white aprons, fishnet stockings, and high heels. Frank knew better than to mess with a winning formula. He couldn't hear who was singing on the piped-in music, but Larson was guessing it was the other Frank.

They passed through the main dining room and entered through a door and into a corridor where Larson had never been. Off of this room were several private dining rooms. Waiters and waitresses came and went from these, standing out of their way as Frank and Larson passed.

"You happen to see anyone using your pay phone earlier this evening? This was at 5:57, to be exact. They aren't in any kind of trouble themselves," he hastened to add, he hoped lying convincingly, "but they may have information important to a case."

"Let me think on that, Roland."

"I didn't want the restaurant getting any bad press over this," he said as the aromas from a platter of something very garlicky caught his nostrils. He was starving. "My boss has a way of playing things pretty heavy-handed."

"Who is your boss right now? I probably know him." It was this kind of prodding that left Larson and others wondering about Frank's true colors.

"He's outta D.C. You think I could get some takeout? Toasted ravioli or something I could eat in the car?"

"Not a problem."

"I'm paying."

"Sure you are." Cunetto had barely turned his head to look for a waiter before one appeared. A guy in his sixties, balding, with wet lips and an expressive face that belonged on the side of a jar of spaghetti sauce. Frank ordered Larson the toasted ravioli, to go. The waiter took off at a clip, moving well for a guy so round.

Larson finished his beer, having drunk it too fast. On the empty stomach, he already felt a ticklish light-headedness. He craved another.

At the end of the hall, Frank pointed out the pay phone. It was an old, battered thing. An exit door stood three feet away at the very end of the hall.

Larson said, "Hell, I didn't even know these private rooms existed."

Frank shook his head nervously, wanting nothing to do with this. Frank knew which side his bread was buttered on.

Larson lowered his voice. "You're a good guy, Frank. We all know that about you—law enforcement, I'm talking about. Family's important to you. The kids of this city are important to you. That soccer program you helped get started. It's good work." He paused to allow this to sink in. "This case I'm working, Frank—it involves a *child*. A little girl, actually. Time is everything in these cases—I'm sure you know that. First twelve to twenty-four hours are critical. I'm not making arrests. No rough stuff. But I need to deliver a message to give that girl any kind of fighting chance, and

I need to deliver it to whoever made that call ninety minutes ago. Your pay phone, Frank. This one, right here."

"I don't know, Roland." Uneasy.

Larson said, "You understand how this develops if my boss gets his way? A crime scene unit. Your place shut down. Your guests interviewed. Names taken down. Detectives asking to see your credit card records for the evening. You know how long it takes the federal government to let go of a bone? I need a name, Frank."

Cunetto looked dazed. "A *kid*? A little girl?"

"That's what I'm saying," Larson said, his gut turning over. "It's awful to make a kid a bargaining tool."

A waitress pushed through the far door, walked down the long hall, and delivered Larson a beer, taking his empty.

She asked, "Everything okay, Mr. Frank?" She eyed Larson like she was ready to punch him out. Might have a good chance at it, judging by her shoulders.

"Thanks, Maddie," Frank said. "Tommy put in a takeout. Make sure it's up as soon as possible."

Maddie marched off, thighs like a hurdler. A body like hers didn't work in the short skirts Cunetto's mandated.

"You don't want to get on the wrong side of this," Larson said. "That's all I'm saying, Frank. I held off my boss because I told him you'd help us out without a pile of warrants and a lot of flashing lights out front. But ultimately, that's gonna be your call."

Larson swigged the beer. Jesus, it tasted good. He stifled a belch.

"Kathleen and Bridget," Frank said. "My sister's twins. Six-year-olds." He met eyes with Larson, his sad and tight with concern. "I'm not saying I actually *saw* him use the pay phone. You understand?"

"Who?" Larson's skin prickled. "The way we do it," he explained, "is I sell whoever this is on the idea that we tracked his cell phone, that we placed him here in your place at the time the pay phone call was made. Most people—this kind of person—know we can do about anything when it comes to technology. They don't question something like that. There's no connection back to you other than his using your pay phone."

Frank cocked his head to study Larson. They met eyes again. Larson remained unflinching, knowing this was the moment.

"Dino Salvo was in about the time you're talking about. Had a drink at the bar. Left for the can. I'm not saying one way or the other, but he never came back to finish that drink. Thing about Dino?" he asked rhetorically. "He *never* leaves a scotch half-full."

Larson swilled the rest of the beer. On the way out, he handed the sweating empty to the waiter who delivered the bag of takeout. He reached for his wallet and Frank Cunetto said, "Gimme a break, Roland. It's on me."

"And I'd like to accept. You know I would. But I'm afraid I can't." He passed him two tens. "Will that cover it?"

Frank handed him back one of the bills. "We'll write you up a receipt. Nice and tidy."

"And while you're at it," Larson said, "I could use a home address for our friend, and a description of his ride."

Dino Salvo turned out to be a known man to the local cops. One phone call to a detective friend and Larson knew him as a low-grade bagman, an errand runner who was connected up in a business arrangement to a former gangbanger-turned-rap-artist, Elwood Els, or LL, as he was called on the street. LL was currently serving time for a nightclub shooting.

Salvo was believed to be supervising LL's hip-hop club in East St. Louis. He was a regular at a Friday-night low-rent poker game that the cops knew about.

Larson stopped at a gas station convenience store and bought a disposable camera and a cup of black coffee.

Salvo was registered as owning a black Town Car carrying vanity plates that read: LUV-NE1. He lived ten blocks from Cunetto's, on the second floor of a walk-up. A drive-by found the place dark, so Larson asked the detective for a BOLO on Salvo and the Town Car.

The cop called him back twenty minutes later after Larson finished the takeout and was working on a second cup of coffee. A patrol had spotted Salvo's ride outside Guneros's Pizzeria, a joint that Larson knew because it served the best tapas in town.

The salsa music seemed in direct conflict with the aroma of Bolognese sauce. Larson chatted up the hostess, slipped her a twenty along with the disposable camera, and gave her specific instructions. He then worked his way through the cluster of overly tall cocktail tables and chairs toward the back. The music changed to percussive Moroccan. He recognized Salvo from the simple description supplied him by Frank Cunetto.

Salvo wore his arrogance in the form of an overly starched, oversized yellow collar poking out of a black leather jacket unzipped to below the table. A thick gold chain showed through a forest of chest hair. His watch had to weigh a couple of pounds. He had the lazy eyes of some killers Larson had interviewed and the broken nose of someone who liked to use his fists, but something about him said more bark than bite. Dino also looked younger than he'd hoped. He wore his black hair slicked back with too much mousse. It shined in the overhead lights.

One small plate contained rolled dolmas, another, some kind of dumpling, and a third, shish kebab. The dipping bowl's pool of black ink might have been responsible for the smell of cinnamon.

Without invitation, Larson sat down across from Salvo. He placed his identification wallet down next to the man's wineglass and left it there long enough for Salvo to read it. He then slipped it back into his pocket, making sure that in the process Salvo would see he was packing.

"You like dolmas?" Salvo asked, without so much as a flinch. "Best dolmas in the city, right here."

"Pass," Larson said, "Dino."

Dino remained impassive.

"We both know you made a phone call from Cunetto's, and we both know who it was to, and that it came at the request of someone else like you: someone not worth my time."

"If you don't like tapas, they do a pretty fair toasted ravioli as well."

"There are jobs worth taking, and there are jobs that aren't worth taking, and this one falls into the latter category. You want to stay as far away from this one as possible. And all your friends do, too. You were put up to this because you're expendable, Dino. Plain and simple. What you want to do is play this smart and let the Romeros do their own business."

Dino wanted to think he was good at this, but with mention of the Romeros his eyes fluttered. Larson decided he hadn't known who was behind the job he'd carried out. Just good money for placing a phone call.

"They told you what to say," Larson said. "And chances are a man of limited intelligence, such as yourself, probably was dumb enough to write it down. And that means you threw a scrap of paper away, doesn't it, Dino? You want to think about that. Are we going to find it in a car, in a trash can at Cunetto's, tossed out on the street between here and there? It's not still in your pocket, is it? 'Cause that could be really embarrassing."

The man's blinking and the tongue working told Larson he'd struck a nerve.

"The best thing you can do right now is get the word out that there's federal heat on jobs coming from out of town. Even these small ones, like making a phone call. Big heat. Do yourself a favor, and take the money you made on that call and take a long vacation. *Anyone* found cooperating with these people will be looking at accessory charges—*child kidnapping*. Federal charges, federal courts, federal prison. It took us less than ninety minutes to find you, Dino. You need to do a lot better next time."

All this served a simple strategy. If Larson could force the Romeros to negotiate directly with Hope, he had a chance of locating the child. But it was highly unlikely his talking tough would have much effect—there were plenty of Dinos waiting in line.

He lowered his voice, leaned in across the table, and stole a dolma. He ate it as he talked, the food blurring his words. "Whoever's the first to provide information that connects to the Romeros is going to win a free Get Out of Jail pass as well as the daily number." Larson wasn't being facetious. State lotteries had been used for years to pay off informants. Ten thousand here, five thousand there—a low-level winning ticket in hand for all to see so there were no questions asked about where the money came from.

"You like the dolmas?" he repeated.

Larson's BlackBerry rang. He finished chewing, swallowed, and as he took the call, he signaled the young hostess who carried his twenty.

He was told Salvo's cell phone had received a call two hours earlier from a pay phone in Plano, Texas. Another evidentiary dead end, no doubt, but Salvo didn't need to know that. He hung up and faced Salvo.

"So now I hear that the call that was made to you—the one giving you this job—came from Plano, Texas." This much was the truth; the next part Larson invented. "We picked up your boy about a half hour ago."

As the hostess arrived, Larson scooted his chair around right next to Salvo, who was mid-bite. He threw his arm around the man's shoulders and then tossed his head back and said, "Cheese."

She clicked off two flash shots before Dino Salvo had the good sense to break the embrace. Larson stood and took the camera before Salvo was to his feet. Twenty dollars well spent.

"How long will it take LL to identify me in that shot?" Larson asked Salvo. "How about the Romeros? How long to figure you're hanging with federal heat?"

Concern creased Salvo's brow. Larson knew he'd hit a nerve.

The hostess moved off, sensing the trouble she'd caused. Several nearby patrons stopped eating and watched.

"How much of a scene you want to make, Dino? How deep do you want to wade into this?"

"LL has nothing to do with this."

"Then you'll have no problem explaining to him a wave of new charges filed against him and the five thousand dollars—a cash deposit—that moved through your bank account the day after this picture was taken."

"What five grand?" Dino Salvo wasn't the fastest on the uptake.

Loyalty was the only currency for guys like him. No matter what excuses he might make for the photograph, its very existence would plant seeds of doubt. Larson might not be able to pull off the money stunt, but Dino couldn't be sure of that.

Salvo told the waitress to leave his food as he followed Larson out of the restaurant. For a moment Larson believed the man stupid enough to start a fight. But as it turned out, he'd only sought to distance himself from the ears inside. Amid thick humidity and the distant hum of traffic, Salvo lowered his voice and warned, "You don't want to fuck with me."

"I'm *already* fucking with you, Dino. Gimme a break. You get the word out, and you get lost, and I'll *stop* fucking with you. Make another phone call for whoever paid you to make that phone call, and you'll regret it for twelve to twenty." Larson pointed at the man's yellow shirt. "You got a little spot there. Looks like sauce, maybe."

He turned his back on the man and walked away, but used a parked car's outside mirror to see Salvo already scratching frantically at the stain.

CHAPTER TWENTY-FOUR

"This is not an official review," Scott Rotem began. He faced Deputy Marshal Gilla Geldwig, an unusually attractive woman with dark, brooding features and haunting green eyes. Her body, a bit big and clunky by femme fatale standards, was nonetheless full at the top and lean in the leg, giving her an imbalanced look that would not have photographed well, but worked fine when she was sitting down, as she was now. It was her face, though, her eyes, that grabbed you, so Rotem tried his best not to look directly into her eyes, not to cave in to the compelling pull. He needed this interview—this interrogation—to be successful. For the sake of Markowitz, *Laena*, and his own career. Five protected witnesses had been executed in the past twenty-four hours. The bloodbath appeared to have started. Thousands of others were at stake. He hated her for what she represented.

It was dark outside now. Traffic on Pennsylvania Avenue slowed to a crawl, seen as two long streams of red and white lights from the one-window conference room.

They shared the oval table, Rotem sitting across from Geldwig, and to his left, Assistant United States Attorney Tina Wank, who possessed a mannequin's complexion and body type that complemented her somewhat nervous disposition.

"Do I need my representative present?" Geldwig asked.

"It's certainly your right to make such a request. You tell me: Do you need a rep present?"

"Not if there's a deal to be made beforehand."

"You've been carrying on an affair with Assistant Marshal Bob Mosley," Rotem said.

"Sue me." She contained her body language well but could not prevent the scarlet blush that moved up from her fashionable suit's shirt collar to its hiding place behind her ears.

"Mosley came clean earlier this morning, and we've had the day to review your own activities, assignments, and your overall participation within the Service. You're a hard worker. You moved around a lot within WITSEC. Now you're here. You've moved through the ranks surprisingly quickly."

"All legitimate promotions."

"I'm sure."

Tina, the attorney, took notes, her pen working furiously so that it looked as if she were a stenographer.

"What's your point?"

"Ms. Geldwig, this may have started out as some kind of game to you. I'm not sure. Maybe it was for the money, because God knows we'd all like more in this job. Maybe it was the secrecy or the joy of feeling so damn important to someone. Or maybe they—and in this case I'm specifically talking about the Romero syndicate—had collected some piece of information that they could use against you. Hold over you. Your sex life, your vices, your spending habits, your family. I mention these only because they are the most commonly seen in cases like this."

"Cases like what?" She fumbled in her clutch purse and came out with a delicate handkerchief that she used to dab at her nose, more nervous habit than necessity.

"Bob Mosley remembers everything he told you. Everything you asked."

For Rotem, the inconceivable thing in this case was that a guy like Mosley would ever believe a woman such as this could fall for him in the first place. He'd now have twenty to thirty years to think about it, and so would Ms. Geldwig, thanks to his testimony. "What you seem to be missing in this, Deputy Marshal Geldwig, is that Mosley's told us everything. The longer you play the naïf, the less time you have to get on the other side of this and help yourself."

Finally Wank joined the discussion. "You've been with Fugitive Apprehension for a little over three months, Ms. Geldwig. Perhaps you can explain what was behind your decision to transfer."

When she failed to answer, Rotem did it for her. "WITSEC might be considered the more prestigious, more interesting employment. And yet you transferred over to the FATF."

"I wanted away from Mosley. Besides, I think you're wrong, sir. This is where the action is."

"We know for a fact that Mosley told you everything there is to know about Leopold Markowitz and what came to be known as *Laena*," Rotem said. "Do you know what *Laena* means, Deputy Geldwig? Where the term came from?"

She cleared her throat. "It's Latin or Greek for 'cloak,' as I recall."

Rotem now forced himself to lock eyes with her. "And you've removed that cloak, haven't you?" He avoided mention of the recent executions—she'd lawyer up given that information. "Exposed several thousand lives to possible execution. And all for *what*, Ms. Geldwig? The seven hundred thousand dollars in commercial real estate? The time-share in Paris? We know about those, Ms. Geldwig, and we'll find out more. We've seized all your property, all your assets—or rather, Ms. Wank has. As of this moment you don't have two nickels to rub together. Are you sure you don't want to talk?"

"RICO," the attorney said.

"We own you. And you've run out of time to explain yourself."

A knock on the door was followed by an aide poking his head inside. It had to be important.

Rotem stood, walked around the table, and passed close to Geldwig. She smelled darkly sweet and earthy, a perfume designed to engorge a man. The effect lingered as Rotem reached his aide, who apologized for the interruption.

The aide, a young man in his late twenties, handed him a sheaf of papers. "Her movement through the network, sir. What files she accessed. I highlighted the few of interest."

Rotem scanned down the list of computer network addresses, all directories and files that Geldwig had accessed in the past week.

The aide said, "We can go back further as time allows."

Rotem flipped pages, waiting for the yellow highlight. On page four his thumb found the line and his eyes carried over.

"What the hell? What is this, utilities for what?"

"She'd been surfing the utility records—the billing records, sir—for our various safe houses. A change in utility consumption."

"Indicates activity at a particular safe house." Rotem jumped ahead to what this meant, but restrained himself, needing to confirm his suspicions before sounding the alarm. "And these particular billing records?" he asked.

"Are for the Orchard House, sir. But I checked with WITSEC and they don't have anyone assigned to the Orchard House at present." The young man noticed Rotem's sudden pallor. "Or do they?"

Rotem swallowed dryly. "Get Larson on the phone. Now. *Right now!* You don't send him an e-mail, you don't leave him a message, you get him *on the phone.* I need to speak to him right now."

He glanced back at the closed door to the conference room, thinking a gun to the head would serve the taxpayers far better where Geldwig was concerned.

CHAPTER TWENTY-FIVE

Paolo drove past the farmhouse and kept right on going. At first glance, his guess was that the info they'd been given was bad. From what he'd seen of the house, pushed back off the road and in a cluster of barren trees, it was decrepit and hardly the kind of place the government would use as a safe house. The feds leaned more toward motels and hotels, military facilities and public housing, not a neglected farmhouse, isolated and out in the middle of nowhere. Defending such a place would require a minimum of two, probably more like four to six, which again struck him as far too rich for federal law enforcement.

He also couldn't be sure it would be the same mark as he was after, but the assignment had been handed to him, passed along to Philippe by a supposedly reliable source, and he had to stick with it. How many witnesses in and around St. Louis could they be protecting on a given day? He followed the map, making a full circle of the area, driving close to five miles before pulling around and back up the steep hill again, and passing the same rock outcropping that looked this time like some sort of face: part human, part devil.

He'd left Penny behind in the motel, her hands taped behind her back, her ankles, knees, and thighs taped around her pants to keep her legs straight, the gag in place. He'd left her on a towel in the bottom of the dry bathtub with the sink water running, and the television in the other room left fairly loud. With the removal of four screws he'd reversed the bathroom door's knobs and lock, so that it now locked from the outside. Even if the kid got free— *impossible*, he thought, though he didn't put much past a child— she was imprisoned.

He slowed and studied the surrounding property, held in the evening dusk as if sprinkled with fireplace ash. He turned the car up a muddy, rut-covered track, stopped at a rusted metal gate, climbed out, and swung it open. The air smelled different here, the way really cold water from a bottle tasted more like melted snow than tap water. Once through the gate, he backed up and parked, tucking the car in alongside a hedgerow of overgrown, weedy trees and shrubs. From here, the track rose into the spines of gnarly, barren apple trees that cast a chill in the air, forewarning winter's approach. The hill rose up to a rocky queen's crown, the swells of the orchard below rolling, once up and then back down, before slipping left toward a crumbling fence line in disrepair, and just beyond, leveling to nearly flat ground and the fading farmhouse, now only a suggestion in the dwindling light. Paolo charted a course through the orchard to the house, committing it to memory so that he could return to the car by one of two different routes.

He spotted one tree among all the trees that would serve well as his lookout. The apple trees had been trimmed and cut back for many years, keeping them full and at a height convenient to harvest. He couldn't tell if they were alive or dead—they looked as inert as gravestones—but they'd lost that look of being tended to.

He crept carefully through the separating rows, the trees as regimented as soldiers, starting and stopping, alert for the slightest sound, change of color, shift of light or shape. Once into the tree, he climbed to the small branches, from where he could see the gray geometry of the farmhouse. Farther to his right and slightly down a hill, a large milking shed with a metal roof bisected a free-stacked stone wall, jutting into a fallow field thick with grass. The hint of an approaching moon warmed the horizon with a yellowish glow, seen through the gray haze of ground fog, just lifting out of the ground as if sucked by the retreating light.

Paolo waited, as was his way. Worked alone, as he and the Romeros preferred it. If he'd been trained in anything, it was patience. He could sit immobile for hours, never bothered by stiff joints or the urge to do something. Ten minutes passed before he detected the red pulsing light. In another season, another color, he might have mistaken it for a lightning bug, but well into October, the evening air chill, its perfectly timed flashing meant electronics, more than likely a cell phone or radio. It was clipped at a height that made sense for a belt. A waist. A guard.

He warmed with anticipation, the falling temperature meaning nothing to him. The information had been good: The dilapidated farmhouse might indeed be a safe house, given that he'd now spotted a patrol. But police and federal agents were like termites—for every one you saw there could be many more in the nest. Overcoming them one at a time presented the kind of challenge Paolo lived for. Subterfuge, stealth, baiting, razor work—all his skills would be required here.

He gave no thought of calling for backup. Of waiting hours or days. Opportunity had presented itself, and he intended to capitalize, to prove himself.

The red flashing stopped. Either the guard had turned, or the phone had been briefly exposed as he'd gone for a stick of gum, scratched an itch, or donned a sweater or jacket against the cold. A small mistake lasting no more than a few seconds, but enough to signal the warning to Paolo. *A God-given blessing.*

A few minutes later his eyes adjusted to where he was quite certain he saw the guard that belonged to the flashing red light—a large lump of black neatly attached to a tree trunk in the side yard. Then, to his delight, another such lump moved from his left to right, and then left again. It took several seconds for him to identify this pattern as circular: This guard was slowly orbiting the farmhouse clockwise. Eight minutes later, around he came again, the original guard still not moving from his post in the side yard. The repetition of this, the combination of one moving object, one stationary, told him there were far fewer deputies than he'd anticipated. As few as two. No more than three. Eight minutes later, there he came again, around the near side of the house. They were lazy, these two. Typical government agents. They'd established a pattern, well conceived, but flawed in execution. Their undoing.

Having just driven onto 270 North, Larson received the call from Rotem, still twenty minutes or more from the farmhouse.

Larson rocketed into the far left lane and brought his speed up in excess of eighty as he spoke into his BlackBerry.

Rotem said, "There's something else you need to hear. WITSEC is reporting five protected witnesses dead, all executed."

Laena, Markowitz's defection or abduction. It seemed a world away from Penny and Hope, but only for Larson. For Rotem and most of the Justice Department the recovery of *Laena* was now a matter of national security.

Larson heard small sparkles of static on the line. "Why only five?"

"You catch on fast," Rotem said. "Now add this into the mix:

The Bureau's OC unit is reporting increased chatter among the top West Coast crime families. A meeting has been called for this Friday. All the big guys. Undisclosed location."

Larson put it together. "So the Romeros sold off or gave up those five witnesses to prove they had the real thing—that they could deliver the master list."

"And now they intend to auction it off."

"*This* Friday?"

"Two days," Rotem confirmed.

Two days to find Markowitz. Two days to locate the Romeros. How long would they keep Penny alive?

"Listen," Rotem said, "there's one other thing, we don't know how much weight to give it, if any. It's a compromised source . . ."

"What's going on, Scott?" Larson didn't appreciate all the qualifiers.

"This source appears to have accessed utility records for our safe houses—including Orchard House. But . . . and I want to emphasize this: There's no indication that information went any farther."

"Jesus, Scott!" He disconnected the call.

Larson had to warn Carlyle and Marland that Orchard House may have been compromised.

He tried Marland first but when Marland failed to pick up he called Hope.

"Hello?"

"It's me. Everything all right?" He worked to keep his voice level and calm.

"Fine."

"Listen, the house may be compromised. I couldn't raise Marland so I'm going to try Carlyle next, but I wanted to get to you first."

"You want me to go find them?"

"No!" he said a little too loudly. "*Do not go outside!* Not under any conditions. Not for any reason. You keep the doors locked until I arrive. Hide somewhere inside."

"Hide? You're scaring me, Lars."

"Just until I get there. It's *serious*, Hope. Okay? Don't hide anyplace obvious. Not under the bed or in the closet. Find a place you can be comfortable without moving around." He told her to put the phone into vibrate mode and then double-checked that she'd done it correctly. "I'll be there in minutes."

"What aren't you telling me?"

"I can't tell you what I don't know myself," he said.

Paolo went well out of his way to approach the far side of the house and lie in wait for the deputy on the circular patrol, costing him valuable minutes. He was warming to the kill now, and so took little notice of the sustained hush delivered into the wilds by the further setting of the sun. Only the very distant barking of a dog, almost a howl, interrupted the night's still, quiet air—a yap-yap-yap that paused for a half minute before barking out into the void, a male no doubt, longing for company. The ground fog lifted like bedsheets, rolling and twisting and yet languishing at chest height. Paolo's movement broke these plumes like a finger through cigarette smoke, creating feathers of vapor that slowly dissipated and dissolved.

The farmhouse, now within a stone's throw, continued to appear empty and uninhabited. He couldn't help but wonder if this was all an elaborate trap to snare him—leak the location, set up a patrol, lure him in. So he again practiced his patience, in no hurry to find himself in federal custody.

He allowed the circling deputy to pass, to complete yet another full loop, but decided against such foolishness. He wasn't going to blow his chance by being overly cautious. He belly-crawled GI-style into the overgrown perimeter shrubbery that surrounded the farmhouse and lay low, razor at the ready.

When it came time, he felt no great adrenaline rush; to the contrary, he found a quiet stillness within himself, an immediacy that led him into a graceful movement, a silent, one-man ballet, choreographed to deliver death.

A moment later it was over, the deputy gaping soundlessly like a beached fish, his body twitching and sparking through the throes of death as he bled out from the neck. Paolo considered taking the man's gun but, recalling the barking dog, decided against its use for fear of alarming a neighbor. He did take the dead man's cell phone, but disconnected the battery. He would study it later for programmed phone numbers, call lists, and might even use it for a call or two.

Now, for the time being, he assumed the role of the circling deputy, picking up where the man had left off. He came around the front of the old farmhouse, ears alert for any sounds whatsoever inside. He heard only the yap-yap-yap, *pause*, of the baying dog.

Charged with exhilaration, Paolo headed straight for the tree behind which he hoped to find and kill the second agent. Only at the last moment did he realize he'd chosen wrong as the agent stepped out from behind the tree to Paolo's right . . . not where he expected him.

"What's up?" this deputy asked in a whisper. In the thick black of night, both figures were silhouettes.

Paolo said nothing, having no idea what voice to mimic.

"Hey! What's up?" the deputy tried again, his voice clear and tight, more strained than before, perhaps sensing, as some animals can, his own demise, even before taking precautions against it.

Paolo took two last strides, suddenly much longer strides than he'd used in his approach, so as to throw off the deputy's timing. One moment he was a smudge in the ground fog, the next a blur of arms and limbs, a slicing blade behind extraordinary leverage and strength. The deputy managed two defensive blocks, both of which cost him long gashes down the palms and wrists of both hands. As he opened his mouth to scream, Paolo's hand flashed before his face, slicing his tongue and lower lip. Containing him in a choke hold, Paolo spun the man, drove his right knee into the man's lower back, bending him backward, and in that moment of pas de deux, drew a hot, angry opening across the man's jowls and larynx, issuing a sound like a steam pipe bursting behind a crimson spray that joined the fog and painted the tree bark scarlet.

He dropped the man like a bushel of apples, not looking down to see if the job was complete. He knew his work. Instead, his back to the bark, he opened his senses like a flower to the sun. Every sound, every swaying branch and rattling leaf was a part of him. He waited for the backup, for the threatening glow of an infrared rifle sight tracking the tree and trying to find a kill spot on his body. He anticipated surprise, braced himself for the unexpected.

He kneeled, glanced once at the dead man, and pulled open his windbreaker. He found the man's weapon, chambered a round, and shoved the gun into the small of his own back. This for inside, if needed.

The dog stopped barking, as if somehow silenced by the scent of fresh blood on the wind—Paolo pissing on his territory; the dog wisely unwilling to challenge. Well off in the distance, he could make out the low, insect hum of interstate traffic. A jet rumbled. Fallen leaves tumbled and rolled and swirled at his feet, offering faint applause.

Paolo sensed there was no backup coming. He would face one more inside the house, and beyond him the prize. At any second, any minute, the deputy inside would attempt his scheduled contact with those on perimeter duty. Never longer than ten- or fifteen-minute intervals.

Paolo moved through angular shadows, dodging across the lawn toward the farmhouse.

The dog started up again, his nose revealing the truth. Only the dog, far off in the distance, stood witness to what had been done.

Larson drove all but the last mile with the retrofitted light system in play, his parking lights, taillights, and headlights alternating right to left and left to right in a dazzling display that identified him as an emergency vehicle. From inside the car's front grill, bright blue and white bursts of warning marked him as law enforcement—not fire or medical.

He'd called for backup—federal, not local—not knowing how traffic would affect his ride. As it happened, he reached Orchard House first.

He pulled off the road a quarter mile short of the farm and set out on foot.

Paolo ducked and crossed below the window, intent on reaching the front porch as quickly as possible. The ground floor would not only be highly secured, but would be where the remaining agent would keep himself. *Herself* was more likely, he thought, since they were protecting a female witness. This gave him more confidence.

The second story looked best. Even if it came down to breaking glass to gain entry, the time it would take a deputy to respond would be in his favor—he'd be inside and at the ready before anyone could make it upstairs.

Once onto the porch, he climbed atop the railing and pulled himself up a column, leprous white paint flakes peeling away and floating to the autumnal vegetation like moths that had ventured too close to the light. He climbed with all the sound of a snake, slipping up onto the porch roof, and from there the steeper main roof, to the first of several dormered windows, all pitch-black. He moved carefully and slowly, one window to the next, feeling vulnerable. The construction was old. Rope-and-weight double-hung windows. A barrier had been hung just on the other side of the glass—some kind of blackout material. He hoped this fabric might mute the sound of breaking glass. When the windows proved impossible to jimmy open, he drove his elbow just above the lock. Pieces of glass tumbled down, caught by the blackout curtain.

The window opened. His razor led the way through the rubbery vinyl covering, and he squeezed through the slit, into the interior.

The room was dark. A simple bed, made. A corner sink from a hundred years ago. A mirrored dresser. No suitcase. No clothes. He crossed to the door, soundlessly, ears alert for the sound of a guard rushing up the stairs.

Nothing.

For a moment—only a moment—he allowed himself to believe the woman was not here, that this accounted for the informal patrolling of the perimeter, that these two had not been protecting someone but defending a structure. Another possible explanation for this complete silence was so tantalizing that he barely allowed himself to consider it. Were there only the two guards, not three? Had they adopted the format of one moving, one stationary because of these minimal numbers? Was the witness here, armed perhaps, but all alone?

It seemed plausible. The Service could be in chaos. How many deputies could they spare for a single witness when thousands of witnesses were at stake? But this optimism got interrupted by a second thought: The remaining deputy could be more clever than he'd given him credit for. Perhaps he was not the type to charge upstairs and force an encounter. What if he/she was lurking somewhere inside, ready to spring a trap and gain the element of surprise? Added to his sudden uncertainty was the idea of timing. Payment for his killing the two deputies outside would come due. With communication lost, the Service would respond, either by helicopter, car, or both. He might have five to ten minutes. After that, he couldn't be sure. It was a big house.

He went to work.

Through the whine in her ears that whistled like a teakettle, Hope thought she heard something. Larson's warning had tightened the screws at her temples, fixing her jaw to where she ground her teeth, her prickling skin feverish with fear. She'd worked so hard all these years to control such reactions, but this time, isolated in a strangely familiar place, without Penny for company, she panicked.

Outside. Close by. On the roof?

A location. She'd thought of little else since his call. In her various residences over the years she'd always created clever hiding spots for herself and Penny. Not panic rooms, but a nook or cranny, a false wall at the back of a closet, cleared out shelf space in the kitchen cabinets. But here, in this place? She considered the back bedrooms, for they gave her a shot at the back stairs if she heard someone coming up the front. She thought she might even engage in hide-and-seek by using both stairways and constantly keeping on the move. But Larson had told her to seek out a spot and stay put, and as much as she resisted being told what to do, she knew instinctively this made sense.

When she heard the muted but distinctive sound of glass breaking, she moved without further thought. The point was to find someplace out in the open yet hidden—how many times had that been drummed into her? Not a closet or an attic.

She spotted it that same second, her imagination fast at work given the breaking glass. She grabbed the bolster in this first of the two back bedrooms, the room having been converted into a television den. She unzipped the zipper the full length of the long round pillow that sat atop the twin bed converting it into a makeshift couch. Inside was a tube-shaped filler that she quickly hauled out and wrestled into the room's only closet, pausing as she found herself faced with two buckets of cleaning supplies, and on the shelves, in typical government fashion, another six cans of each cleaning product, all neatly lined up like little soldiers. Deodorant. Toothbrushes. Aspirin. Tylenol. Tampax. Toothpaste. Hand cream. A mini-pharmacy. How many times had she schooled Penny on using readily available household items as weapons?

The words on a green-and-white can jumped out at her: *Oven Cleaner*.

Paolo opened the bedroom door a crack, his back against the wall and away from the door in case someone threw shots blindly. He sneaked it open to where he could get an eye out.

An empty hallway. No guards.

Razor in his left hand, the borrowed gun now in his right, he moved down the hall, his back to the wall. He paused. He tried the next door. A bathroom, longer than it was wide. Empty of people, but not of their presence—a tube of toothpaste and a toothbrush, both new, on the sink.

Another bedroom, next door, near the top of the stairs, its bed made, but ruffled. Someone had lain there. The air smelled cleaner, less dusty, less trapped, and Paolo could picture Hope Stevens airing out the stale air ahead of the blackout curtains being hung.

He took a glimpse down the staircase. With the hallway being empty, if there were other guards they were downstairs. Was she down there with them, or had he missed her somehow? But the woman was most likely upstairs. He retraced his steps, hurrying down the hall past where he'd come from, only to discover an unexpected hallway that emptied quickly into a television room.

He stopped cold. He smelled her: the sharp tang of fresh sweat. The pungency of woman. Close now.

He raised and lowered the gun as he stepped toward the room's closet.

He yanked it open, gun now aimed into the darkness. Found a string dangling and yanked it. A bare bulb flashed on, revealing two plastic buckets and some rags on the floor. All kinds of personal items and cleaning supplies on the shelves. A regular storehouse. A long white pillow, like a bolster.

Paolo jerked his head to his right: the bolster on the bed. *Misshapen.*

He followed along the zipper with his eye. A small gap at the very end, the zipper not quite closed.

There.

Weapon in hand, Larson accidentally smeared the doorknob with Marland's blood as he cracked open the farmhouse's back door and slipped inside. Panic had invaded him and he couldn't shake it. He left the blood-smudged key in the lock to avoid making any more noise than necessary. *Settle down*, he told himself, but he found it impossible. He'd come across the body of only one of his fallen deputies. It had been too dark to identify him, though he believed it to be Marland.

He'd abandoned Hope here. Left her. Again.

He moved, cautiously and alertly, through the kitchen. *Clear.*

He surveyed the living room. *Clear.*

As he passed through it and crossed the hall and continued into the small study, the structure's old floorboards creaked beneath him with every step. No matter how fancy he got with his attempts at delicate footfalls, the boards still complained, some loudly. He decided distraction wouldn't be such a bad thing. He cleared the study, now focusing on the staircase to the second floor. Climbing those stairs would leave him exposed and vulnerable.

His lower back pressed against the handrail, his shoulder blades dragging on the peeling wallpaper, Larson started up the stairs.

They announced his every step.

With the first of the sounds, the reluctant bending of unwilling wood, Paolo turned toward the improvised hallway and the second-floor banister beyond. Someone was coming.

Hope saw the intruder fix on her. He'd not so much as given the bolster a second look until he'd seen the pillow that belonged in it at the bottom of the closet floor. Then he turned and looked right at her—right at the tiny gap in the zipper through which she looked. Right into her eye.

He took a cautious step toward her. Then another, to the edge of the bed.

As a sound in the hall distracted him, she made her move. With her left hand, she stripped the zipper open. With her right, she pushed the can of oven cleaner out of the bolster, sitting up simultaneously.

He sensed her and turned.

She threw herself forward, aimed for his face, and pressed the button, the can issuing a hiss of white spray that grew into foam as it contacted his skin. The cleaner covered the right side of his face, bringing a scream of pain, and she kept spraying.

The burning began at once.

With the pain, Paolo's finger involuntarily flexed on the trigger and the weapon fired wildly. Its recoil sudden and more than he'd have expected, his wrist was jerked violently back and, as he reached to stem the agony in his right eye, he dropped the weapon completely.

He lashed out blindly with the razor in his left hand, transferring it effortlessly to his right, and continuing to slash the air. The back of his calf caught the low coffee table and he went down backward, first to sitting, then rolling off the table.

Footsteps charging up the stairs.

The burning in his eye and on his nose and lips was more severe than anything he'd imagined and only grew worse. More spray hit him and again he lashed out at his attacker. Coming to standing, he caught blurry sight of the open door to the next bedroom and, feeding down from it, a second stairway—a back stairs. Everything inside him resisted turning his back on someone approaching. The person would shoot him dead.

He leaped for the door.

Larson, now at the top of the stairs, ran toward the gun's report. He slipped on the hallway rug, banged into the doorjamb of the small television room, and an arm came down onto him as a gray blur. Heat penetrated the back of his right hand and his gun fell out of his hand as he realized he'd been cut.

Hope lay on the floor in some kind of sleeping bag, struggling to get her legs out.

A swipe came at his neck.

Larson jerked away from the attempt. He kicked out and connected with the intruder, who slammed against the open closet door but came back at Larson like a boxer off the ropes.

The razor whooshed past Larson's right ear. He ducked and kicked out again, this time spinning the man.

Larson regained his balance and delivered the tight knot of a fist squarely into the space above the man's hip bone, pounding deeply for the kidney and bending him backward in pain as he connected.

Incredibly, the intruder spun as if never struck. Their arms tangled. Larson defended against the razor by first blocking an intended blow and then grabbing the man's wrist. They banged together like a pair of wrestlers, still on their feet. Larson won purchase on fabric and pulled. Buttons flew. Fabric tore. The intruder's shirt tore open. Two dozen red raised scars screamed from his bare chest. Random lengths and shapes. Some old and thick and hardened, as if recut many times. Some pink and raw and new.

Larson froze. He'd never seen anything like this.

The intruder caught him with a toe in the groin, snapping Larson over in pain. Inexplicably, he did not feel the razor run its course down his back. Instead, he heard the familiar sound of feet fading away from him. A crashing downstairs.

Then, *gone,* as he glanced at a wide-eyed Hope.

"Are you hit?"

"No."

"Get the gun," he said, sliding it across the floor as he retrieved his own. "Into the bathtub for cover—lock the door—*now!*" His last words faded behind him as he entered the mouth of the stairs and scrambled down into the waiting darkness.

A locked house proved as difficult to get out of as to get into. The intruder—Rodriguez?—made for the kitchen's back door, but struggled with the antique twist-knob dead bolt, found it an impasse, and turned. This in the same time it took Larson to descend the steep back stairs.

Larson got off a round—given the angle more of a statement of his presence than a kill shot. The bullet took out an old hand-painted plate in the hutch on the far wall. Splintered pottery rained down, tinkling and clinking as it landed. Larson raced down and into the kitchen but slowed as he reached the door that connected through to the front entry in case the killer planned any surprises.

He heard the front door—a rattle of chains and locks. A loud *bang* as it thumped the wall, reeling on its hinges. The *humph, humph, humph* of the intruder running off the porch. And then, as the man hurried away, the crackling of sticks . . . autumn winds.

Larson, like someone late off the blocks in a track meet, now followed behind as fast as his powerful legs would carry him, as fit and as solid as he'd ever been, the morning training on the river engorging his muscles, arms pumping like pistons as his right hand still clung to the weapon, slightly warmer, it seemed, from his firing that shot. A hundred yards and closing the distance, judged only by the sound of the other, the smudge of gray charcoal that might have been a man obscured in the foggy haziness of night.

Larson made it another fifty yards before his own voice, whispering dryly from the back of his brain, asked about Hope and who was guarding her now, asking how certain he was that there'd been only one intruder. With the killer went a chance to find Penny. And Markowitz. Guilt-torn and fearful, his groin aching, his nerves raw from having discharged the weapon, the smell of cordite still bitter in his sinuses, Larson slowed and reversed directions. He pulled out his cell phone but then thought better of it.

Compromised. Rotem had said so himself. How many other such moles? How many secrets leaking from FATF's splintered hull? He put his phone away.

His priorities certain now, Larson returned to the farmhouse, intent on getting her out of here. Rotem would have to handle the cleanup. He and Hope would sleep, if they slept at all, in a downtown condominium a friend had been trying to sell to Larson since the middle of summer. He'd say he'd picked up a woman downtown, and if there was ever a time for him to demo the place it was on this night of all nights. He would arrange for the key to be left. See no one. Make contact with no one. There would be no more connection made between Hope and him and the Service. They would go it alone.

Some old dog began barking as a car fired up far in the distance.

Thoughts competing in his head, Larson hurried inside and called out for her.

CHAPTER TWENTY-SIX

Blinded by the corrosive chemicals in his right eye, Paolo drove one-handed, covering his bad eye to block the blurring double vision that turned the interstate into a rainbow of stretched lights.

He headed for the motel but missed a turn somewhere and finally exited off 270 south onto Manchester Road, which teemed with traffic even at this late hour. He drove east, past the onslaught of strip malls and chain stores. Spotting a Shell station on his left, he pulled up to the back of it, hoping for a restroom accessible from the outside, only to realize he would have to go inside if he wanted water on his face, and inside meant witnesses and security cameras.

Then he spotted the automatic car wash—three minutes of peace, a chance to collect himself, maybe even water for his face. But getting his car caught in an automatic car wash made no sense. He crossed back into traffic and found a McDonald's. He pulled the car around to the drive-up microphone, his eye stinging and throbbing, leaking tears like a faucet. He ordered fries—feeling he had to pay for something—and a large cup of water, no ice.

He awaited change at the first window, keeping his head aimed down, and his hand up to screen any sight of him. Dodging the change from the two dollars might make him memorable. Once in possession of his order, he tossed the fries onto the passenger seat and raced the car ahead to a parking space. Hanging out the car door, he doused his eye. As the water hit, he clenched his teeth, the pain hot.

He sat up, switched on the interior light, and aimed the rear-view mirror. He saw a red, swelling mass, oozing yellowish fluid. He pried his unwilling eye open between trembling fingers, gathered his courage, and touched the eyeball itself, in an effort to clear it. But the plastic of his contact lens had melted and adhered to his eyeball. Real terror ripped through him. *Blind?* The end of his career. He'd be relegated to sweeping sand traps on the Romeros' eighteen-hole golf course.

The fear encouraged more pain, the pain more fear.

He knew he had to extricate the lens. To leave it invited infection, possible blindness, and unbearable pain. Leaning out of the car, he once again splashed his face and eye, once again cringed. He stabbed at it with his fingers, squeezing and pinching, but it was no use. The excruciating pain left him feeling faint. It was glued onto his eyeball. He was stuck with it.

He had to get to the motel. Had to handle the little girl. Had to handle his eye. Still had to take care of Hope Stevens, Alice Stevenson—the mark.

His fear graduated to panic; pain to agony. His world caved in around him. Philippe would recall him. He'd be sweeping tennis courts. He'd be the guy *with that face*. The mirror showed blisters already forming on the rim of his eyelids, his nose, and the corner of his mouth—anywhere the chemical came in contact with him. The red swelling now included most of the right side of his face. Any such memorable features were impossible for a man of his trade. Anonymity was crucial. He had to fix this before it changed his life forever, and by the look of him, he had to do it fast.

He needed soap and water. He needed the contact lens removed. *Painkillers.*

Through shifting, blurring colors of passing traffic, streetlights, and walls of neon, swirls of light, he spotted a building across the street that represented some help: Mason Ridge Veterinary Clinic and Animal Hospital.

He carefully backed the car out of the spot.

For now, the girl would have to wait.

CHAPTER TWENTY-SEVEN

Penny lay in the bottom of the bathtub on top of the towel, her knees taped together. She couldn't bend her legs and reach the piece of broken crockery hidden in her sock. Couldn't cut herself free. She'd been here for so long she was beginning to wonder if the man with the scars was ever coming back, or if he'd just left her for good. The tub was slippery. She could rock back and forth but could not get her legs up and out and over the edge, could not get out of the tub.

She'd tried a dozen different things, at one point accidentally rolling over so that she lay facedown on the towel. It had taken her several tries to get back over onto her back. Her flailing efforts reminded her of a turtle she'd had—*Cheyenne*—and how her mother had made her leave it behind on one of their many moves.

If she could get out of the tub, even taped as she was, she thought she might hop to the door, maybe bang her head against it as someone passed. *Do something.* But trapped in the tub she felt helpless.

Frustrated, Penny rocked and bucked, which only served to bang her head against the tub, and that hurt. She quieted again, remembering her mother's lessons on patience, that everything took time, sometimes more time than we wanted, and there were "more ways than one to skin a cat."

At that moment, at the height of her telling herself to be patient, her mother so fully in her mind that it felt to her as if she, her mom, were sitting on the toilet while Penny took a bath, her mom finger-combing her hair the way she did when she was tired and talking to herself, Penny heard her mother say, "Look for the obvious." "Don't fight the easy answer." It was then, at that moment, that Penny finally did see the obvious, saw what had been facing her throughout her entire ordeal, facing her like a giant's eye, and she thought that without Mommy she never would have seen it, and that made her sad and all the more desperate to be out of here.

The tub's faucet, its single lever right before her eyes.

She wiggled, moving herself incrementally toward the drain, stiffened her elbows, and rocked her bottom like playing bucking bronco. Her feet jumped up, though she could not hold them there. She tried again. And again. The third time, the tape around her ankles snagged on the pull-up lever on the top of the spigot, a lever that started the shower. Her feet were held aloft.

One more heave, and her toes smacked the faucet.

Cold water trickled out.

Another try and the valve opened and the water gushed out.

Shivering, she wrestled her feet free of the spigot.

She felt the water collecting. When the maid had finished cleaning, she'd left the tub's stopper down, plugging the drain.

The tub slowly filled with cold water.

A moment later she felt the first tingle of her body rising with the water. Floating toward the top of the tub.

She cried at the thought of seeing Mommy again; her freedom might now be within reach.

CHAPTER TWENTY-EIGHT

Paolo roughly broke through a glass window using the corner of a shipping pallet at the back side of the Mason Ridge Veterinary Clinic and Animal Hospital. The sounds of barking dogs erupted from within. Hearing a burglar alarm, he moved quickly. These kinds of suburban neighborhoods were well patrolled, especially along the commercial district. The cops were typically bored and appreciated a good break-in to pick up a slow night.

Stepping through, he found himself in a small bathroom. He grabbed a pair of latex gloves from an open box and donned them. The dogs continued to battle the alarm. Door by door, he worked his way past two examination rooms, an office, and the waiting room. The place smelled of dry dog food, medicines, disinfectant, cedarwood shavings, urine, and feces.

Having marked his watch at the moment of break-in, he estimated he had less than five minutes before the police arrived. In New York City or Los Angeles he might have had twenty to thirty minutes. Not here in Middle America.

He found the stockroom, located a pair of locked cabinets, and used a stainless-steel surgical device to pry it open. He trained his one good eye toward it in the dim light: The shelves were stacked with cloth-wrapped surgical gear. As he turned his talents to the second cabinet, he noticed he'd ripped open the surgical glove on his right hand. *Fingerprints!* He glanced behind him, attempting to quickly catalog all the surfaces he'd touched. *When had it torn?*

As it happened, the idiots used their sirens. He heard the mechanical cries growing louder, but they still sounded far off.

The second cabinet succumbed.

He searched the five shelves of prescription drugs, reading for the base compound instead of the brand name, as vets called their drugs by different names.

He pocketed some high-dose antibiotics and finally, mercifully, located a synthetic opiate—*a painkiller*.

He would have liked to search for a salve for the blistering on his face, but no. The wash of headlights on the windows signaled the arrival of a patrol car far sooner than he'd anticipated.

He hurried back through the building to the window through which he'd come, not trying for his car, eager to disappear up into the woods on the hill behind the small clinic.

Minutes later, he dry-swallowed two of the large pain pills and squirted saline solution onto his swollen face.

Never resting, he pushed up through the woods, reaching a clearing shared behind three large homes, all with garages.

Garages meant cars or bicycles.

From a distance, he could see down to the roof lights of the patrol car flashing red, white, and blue across the vet clinic.

The painkiller wouldn't kick in for a half hour or so, and by that time he hoped to have ridden a bus back to the motel, hoped to be numb to the sensation of the razor's edge, and the punishment he so craved.

He would still have to deal with the little girl.

He wondered how tough she was, how badly she wanted her freedom, and whether she possessed the courage to remove the melted contact lens from his swelling eye.

CHAPTER TWENTY-NINE

"What now?" Hope asked. She carried a small bundle of in-timates and clothing cradled in her arms. "You want me to wash yours as well, you're going to have to get out of them."

"No thanks."

"You could use it."

"This is all I've got," Larson informed her.

"That's my point," she said.

He'd risked a quick stop at Target to buy them both some clothes. She was laundering what she'd changed out of.

The condominium they occupied overlooked construction on a new baseball park for the Cardinals, and, beyond it, the tiny moving lights from Highway 40. From the corner of the living room, they had a view of a gambling casino on the Mississippi, an eyesore in Larson's opinion.

Larson took a minute to don the sweatpants and sweatshirt. Their clothes joined in the washer. He thought this oddly signifi-cant. Wondered if this was but the first of such nights together.

He heard her setting the timer. She seemed more settled.

She returned to the kitchen, searched the refrigerator and the cabinets, but of course no food. "We're going to have to order in."

He wondered if this ease of hers had come with the shower or the attack on her. Or had she simply resigned herself to the fact that he now represented her daughter's only real chance? Or, like him, did it run deeper than that?

She slid down into an IKEA chair and placed her elbows on the table. "Let's say they never call me back," she proposed from a distance. "How do we go about finding her?"

Larson took a chair facing her. "It's a two-step process. Our best shot, our most likely prospect, remains Markowitz."

On the way to the condo, he'd told her all he knew about Markowitz. Hope already had a better grasp of the computer and technology aspects of the case than he did.

"So you're saying the Romeros got to Markowitz."

"Or they didn't have to because it could have been his idea in the first place. No one is saying Leopold Markowitz walks on water. He could be bent. He could be broke. He could have approached the Romeros for protection while he went about stealing the list. We won't know until we get there."

"Are you saying if we find Markowitz, we find Penny?"

"It's a possibility, yes. If the Romeros are behind this—and I'm convinced they are—then finding Markowitz gives us the Romeros, and we're that much closer to Penny."

"And how do we find him?"

"WITSEC is convinced he'll need a supercomputer to accomplish the decryption."

"If it's one-twenty-eight-bit or higher, then, yes," she said, interrupting. "It would be painfully slow, even on the fastest PC."

"And with such computers in short supply," he continued, "that makes them a good lead. We have guys spread out from accelerators at Stanford to cyclotrons at U of M, Indiana, and Duke." He saw a sparkle in her eyes. "What is it?" he asked.

"By now, knowing you guys, you've confirmed where he last was seen?"

"Stanford—Palo Alto, yes. Just before that, Wash U. And he was in any number of places before Palo Alto. We're still chasing his travel, his finances, and the like. It's a job even tougher because Justice is not eager to let anyone know he's missing."

"But that's stupid!"

"Government work," he said, as frustrated by it as she was.

"What department at Wash U.?"

"Planetary Sciences, I think it was," he answered.

"Makes sense. Weather prediction. That would be a Silicon Graphics or even a Cray. Those machines create processor reports, ways to determine a machine's activity, even if they're not showing Markowitz himself as having been logged on."

He welcomed her excitement, her computer expertise surfacing. "I'm assuming we've checked all that," he told her.

"I can't just sit here," she said. "Can you?"

"No." For one thing, he'd fall asleep.

A look of defiance overcoming her, she said, "Good. Then let's check for ourselves. I'll need access to the processor reports. We can start at Wash U."

"I can't take you out in public."

"I thought the best place to hide a person like me was out in the open."

He felt himself losing ground. She had the will of seven. He felt a heat hanging between them, wondering if she felt it, too.

"Trust me," she said, "I've become something of an expert in the art of disguise."

He told her if she slept for a few hours, he'd consider it.

She nodded her assent.

Larson double-checked his BlackBerry. No messages. Rotem would understand his going AWOL, would contact him when he was certain FATF was safe again, the internal threat contained. Fatigue was getting the best of him, he realized.

Hope brought him out of it. "The point being that if they aren't going to bring Penny to me, then we're going to find her without them. I haven't spent a single night without Penny since she was born. Not *one, single night.*" Her lower lip trembled despite her efforts to keep it steady. "This is my first." She looked up at him then, her eyes carrying anger, frustration, and a mother's pain.

Her hands were right there on the table, and seeing them Larson felt compelled to reach out and surround them with his, which he did. Of all he'd done that day, he considered this his biggest act of bravery. Hope did not pull her hands away. Instead, just as the awkwardness of the moment required him to let go of her, she looked up and they met eyes, and his hands stayed where they were.

"Thank you," she said.

CHAPTER THIRTY

The bathwater continued to rise, and Penny along with it. Lifted, it seemed to her, by the fingers of angels come to rescue her. Extremely cold at first, she'd managed one more bump into the faucet to make the handle point up at twelve o'clock, resulting in a lukewarm stream. Even so, Penny was cold, shivering cold, and she wanted out of the tub.

At a little over the halfway mark, the rising water hit the overflow drain, forcing Penny to wedge her head in front of the soap dish mounted into the wall tile in order to then hold the toes of her right foot over the vent in the drain and allow the water to continue to fill.

Water still seeped out, but there was more water coming in than going out. The tub continued to fill.

She peed in her pants, into the tub, unable to hold it. Sight of the yellow stream motivated her. Soaked through, the duct tape had lost some of its stickiness. The tape at her knees came loose, her knees able to bend, her ankles wiggling.

She hooked a knee, rolled over the edge of the tub and crashed onto the floor of the bathroom, face-first, a splash of bathwater following with her. As she sat up, she saw the water on the floor was pink. Blood pink. Her nose screamed with pain, and she screamed right along with it—a muted, worthless cry forced through a knotted sock. The thin puddle of water grew as she kneeled. A dead fly floated past. This all but yanked her to standing.

Then, her knees giving out, she sank back and collapsed onto the toilet with a loud bang. Try as she did, she could not get hold of the chip of pottery she'd hidden in her sock. It took her several minutes to get feeling back into her legs. Her strength returned, she kicked and fluttered, and tried everything to break the tape at her ankles, but it held.

Soaked through to the bone, more determined than ever, she rose, held her stance, and hopped toward the bathroom door, angling like a penguin to use her right hand, still taped to her waist, to try to open the door. Locked.

She remembered the man with the scars reversing the doorknob. On her side of the door the knob now had a hole in it. But Penny knew such doorknobs. More than once she'd locked herself out of her room and then watched as her mother did the clothes-hanger-in-the-hole trick to pop the lock. Another time she'd used a paperclip.

Penny spun, hopping like a rabbit. She looked for anything that might work as a pin or nail to shove into the doorknob and free the lock. And there it was, right on the bathroom counter: a thin piece of silver metal. She moved, and it moved. A mirrored reflection of her own belt.

Her arms and hands held to her sides with tape, she nonetheless fingered the belt and drew it around her waist toward her fingers. The buckle caught on the first belt loop. But this proved close enough for her to deftly unfasten her belt with outstretched fingers. It did not go smoothly. She fell back onto the toilet twice, losing her balance, only to stand again and continue with her efforts. Finally, the belt buckle came open and Penny sprang forward, hopping a little to position herself before inserting the buckle's metal tongue into the doorknob. She pushed and nothing happened. She pushed again. *Click.*

She had to push her arm against the knob and slide down to make it turn. It took four tries before the door finally came open, the bedroom lit only by the shifting colors of the TV.

Her face exploded into a smile: She'd done it. Better, she'd done it *herself*. Along with the fear, the dread of Him returning, came a gleeful sense of accomplishment. Usually Mommy did everything; told her what to do; made all her decisions. Somehow, this one act of floating herself out of the tub and winning her freedom was the best feeling she'd ever had.

Wanting nothing more than to find her mother and tell her everything she'd been through, all that she'd accomplished, Penny hopped toward the motel room's door, determined to open that one as well. She was on a roll; why stop now?

She was just past the bed, past the TV bleating out its news, when the door seemed to jiggle.

She stopped, frozen.

The door didn't just *seem* to jiggle, it *was* jiggling. And it wasn't the loud TV making it move.

She wanted to turn and head back to the bathroom, would have given anything to mop up the dark stain of bathwater that now loomed at the junction of the door, her wet footprints where she'd hopped across the carpet. But her legs would not move, would not cooperate.

The door came open.

Again, she screamed one of her muted screams.

It wasn't Him.

In the blue flickering light of the television, she saw the blistered face and red dripping eye of a two-legged monster.

CHAPTER THIRTY-ONE

By the time the morning sun set the Mississippi ablaze, bro-ken only by the rolling brown *V*s cut into it by slowly moving river barges, Larson and Hope were eating bagels wrapped in butcher paper and drinking OJ from plastic bottles in the second-floor of-fices of Grossman Iron and Steel, five acres of dirt dedicated to mountains of scrap metal. Beyond the yard, a massive twenty-foot wall had been erected forty years earlier by the Army Corps of En-gineers to hold back the river's spring floodwaters.

Skip Grossman was a rowing buddy of Larson's from Creve Coeur Lake. Mike, who worked the graveyard shift and sat guard on the yard's gate, knew Larson well enough to admit him. It wasn't the first time Larson had stashed a witness for a few hours in this brickyard neighborhood that had risen from the Mississippi's banks at the birth of the Industrial Revolution.

The two ate their bagels in silence, both lost. It was a matter of waiting now, until Washington University's Earth and Planetary Sciences department opened. Their hunt for Markowitz was about to begin in earnest.

———

In its heyday, in 1904, St. Louis hosted a World's Fair, the Olympics, and the Democratic National Convention all in the same year. Hundreds of stone mansions that had been erected during this golden era still stood in the area, including a long line of such homes along Lindell Avenue on the northern boundary of Forest Park. Immaculately kept lawns spilled down to what had once been a busy cobblestone thoroughfare.

"You can almost picture the carriages, the gentlemen in top hats, and the Victorian women with their parasols," she said.

"Gateway to the West," Larson said from behind the wheel of the Explorer as they made their way toward Washington University. "Anyone heading west resupplied here. It made it a very rich city."

At the far western edge of the park, just across Skinker Boulevard, the pale stone buildings of Washington University rose in dramatic fashion, showing off a neo-Gothic architecture that rivaled the Ivy League colleges. The buildings stood amid towering oaks, maples, and a few elms that had survived Dutch elm disease. Larson had attended its night-school MBA program, though he had dropped out in the middle of a difficult protection six years earlier—a protection he couldn't help but be reminded of, given the woman next to him.

"Where are you?" she asked.

"I was thinking back six years ago. And then I was thinking that Penny's five years old."

She applied makeup to her face using the small mirror in the back of the sun visor. She slowly created the look of a hollow-eyed woman ten to fifteen years older.

"Do you want to know?" she asked.

"Of course I do."

"Then find her. Take a good long look at her. You'll know."

His chest tightened as his heart ran away from him at a full gallop. "I've known all along," he said softly. He wasn't sure she'd heard him.

"And I've waited for you to ask."

"And I've waited for you to tell me."

"I thought it would be cheap of me. Manipulative. Unfair. 'It's your daughter, so do something.' How could I say that?" She didn't take her eyes off him. "Are you okay with this?"

His throat caught. He found himself overwhelmed with wonder. Curiosity. Anticipation. "I'm great," he managed to whisper.

"Light's green," she said.

He took an enormous risk by bringing her along. But it seemed a bigger risk to leave her behind and without protection. He could easily justify her being here because of her computer expertise, but what good would justification be if something went wrong?

He drove.

"Why haven't they called?" she asked yet again.

"What's she like?" he asked.

She pursed her lips, looked away from him, and attempted to conceal her eyes, now glassy with tears. "Not now. You wanted to know. That's as far as I can go right now. Please don't push me on this. The more I think about her . . ."

He said, "Look . . . they probably don't know what to do next. They never meant to have Penny instead of you. They tried to trace your phone and we cut that off, and now all that's left is to hunt you down while we hunt them. They're not going to try to negotiate Penny's release until they've figured a way to beat us, and there is no way to beat us. They know that. We know that."

He pulled to a stop at the next light, the university now directly in front of them.

She fidgeted in her seat. Larson pulled through the intersection and found a place to park. He shut off the motor, and she popped open her door.

"Which one is Earth and Planetary Sciences?"

"Macelwane Hall."

"Which one?"

"We'll find it."

She was out of the car. Larson climbed out, locked up, and caught up to her on the sidewalk. The neo-Gothic architecture towered over them.

Her shoulders slumped, she trudged, head bent, up the incline.

He caught up to her for the second time. "You came to St. Louis because of you and me. For Penny." He waited. "Tell me why you came to St. Louis, Hope," he persisted. "Did you want me in Penny's life, or both of your lives?"

"I didn't choose it for the weather," she said. "But do me a favor and don't go all warm and fuzzy on me because I don't think I can handle that right now. Okay?"

He moved closer to her as they walked. He held his hand out to her.

And she took it, their fingers interlaced. Entwined.

Larson squeezed, and she squeezed back. Just for a moment it felt as if he were floating.

"We can't do this," she said. "We can't get everything all confused."

"Sure we can," he said. "It can't get any more confused than it already is; it can only get better."

"Later," she said, increasing her pace to keep up with him.

The Earth and Planetary Sciences office was staffed with a combination of salaried assistants and graduate students. The walls were lined with photographs of tornados and satellite images of hurricanes. Dr. Herman Miller, a man in his late sixties, had sad brown eyes, wet lips, and a runny nose he tended to with a white handkerchief. He wore a navy blue cardigan sweater populated with pills of yarn, some the size of bunny tails.

"Why more questions about Leo?" he asked. "I spoke to someone just yesterday."

Larson introduced Hope as Alice. "She's our contract I.T. specialist."

"We're interested in reviewing your mainframe's access logs," Hope said. "Specifically, the past six weeks."

"And we've been looking them over, just as your guy asked. 'No stone unturned,'" Miller said to Larson. "That's how your other guy wanted it."

That was Stubby by the sound of it. Trill Hampton was too street-cool to bog down in clichés.

Nonetheless, Hope and Miller got started, talking their own language. ID log-ons, pattern recognition software, spyware, keytrackers. Hope pushed for specifics each time Miller fired off too quick an answer.

Miller asked rhetorically, "Could Leo Markowitz get in and out of the Cray and the Silicon Graphics without our knowing it? Of course he could."

"But if Markowitz is on the system, decrypting these records one by one, which we know for a fact he has to do because that's the way he set it up in the first place—and there are *thousands* of records, don't forget—then your processor logs are going to reflect that, even if they don't tell you exactly who's doing it."

Larson asked for a definition of a processor log, and at the same time both Hope and Miller met him squarely with expressions of exasperation. He took a step back and let them go at it.

A few heated exchanges later, Miller said something like: "If you want an exercise in futility, be my guest."

"Thank you," she said. "Lead on."

Miller, annoyed with her, walked down a hall covered with

weather-radar printouts and time-lapse photographs of lightning. They passed through a steel door and down two flights of stairs that took them into a subterranean lab. They arrived at a door where Miller used his ID card to gain access.

The expansive room was chilly and the equipment it contained— mostly rack-mounted black and blue and yellow boxes with thousands of multicolored wires—hummed loudly. Row after row of them. Wires and lights, routers and hubs, all interconnected.

"Your networking," Hope said.

"Our routing center," Miller answered. "One of three such hubs on campus. On any one day, we have around fifteen thousand PCs hanging on this system. Every student, every department that wants access."

Hope glanced down the long rows of machinery and narrow aisles. She studied the racked routers as Larson and Miller continued on without her. Eventually, Miller turned back toward her to hurry her along.

Familiar with that searching look in her eyes, Larson placed a hand on Miller's arm to silence him as he was about to call out to her.

"The Cray is down this way," Miller finally said.

"Dr. Markowitz is a *systems expert*," she said, repeating what Larson had originally told her.

"A description that hardly does him credit," Miller added from a distance.

"He served as a consultant here?"

"Yes. Our weather simulators, our forecasting modules." He walked a few steps back toward her. Larson followed. "Leo is far more than a systems analyst. He's a designer, a code writer. Custom apps, source code. He ramped us up to full integration. He identified nearly thirty percent more processor headroom than we thought we had. Stabilized the platform. All without touching the Cray."

"The additional processing power," she said. "Did he, by any chance, set up grid computing for you?" Before Miller could answer, she asked, "Has anyone checked the network logs?"

"Good God," Miller mumbled. To a confused Larson he said, "I assure you the oversight was unintentional."

"What the hell are you two talking about?"

Miller held up a finger. "She just might be onto something," was all Miller would give him.

Miller's office, a sanctum of order, overlooked a campus lawn and intersecting pathways. An extra chair had to be brought in, crowding the space.

Miller worked behind his desk, consulting two computer screens and an accordioned stack of printouts.

Hope explained to Larson in a hushed voice: "Grid computing is the poor man's supercomputer. Any personal computer or server, at any one time, is only using about fifteen percent of its processing power. You link machines together, you take advantage of the headroom—the unused processing power. You link together a thousand, or ten thousand, you have what amounts to a homemade supercomputer."

"What we've just established," Miller explained, "is that our grid, the one Leo set up for us, has shown massive additional usage from midnight to seven A.M. for the past three weeks."

"Markowitz has been using the system undetected," Hope interjected. "With everyone asleep, he has six or seven hours of power processing available. He's been working the swing shift."

"We were focused on our Cray and our Silicon Graphics. But someone tapping directly into the grid? It's so obvious in hindsight, but at the time—it's so new to us—it just wasn't on our radar."

"Can we shut him down?" Larson asked.

Miller looked up sharply, meeting eyes with Hope, who then said, "No, no! You don't want to do that."

"Yes, we do."

"Each night he stays on the system for hours," Hope said. "Dr. Miller can peek behind that curtain and trace what port he's coming in on, which Internet provider he's using."

"We've collected enough data points—six nights' worth. We'll identify the ISP and, with their help, should be able to nail down his exact location. If he's moving around, that may not help you. But if he's stationary . . ."

"Of course he'll keep moving," Larson said. "He's not going to give us a way to find him."

"Unless he's innocent." Miller made sure he met eyes with Larson. "You're in such a hurry to prosecute him."

"He could be being watched, or like me, maybe they hold something over him," Hope said. "He doesn't dare send out a distress signal, for fear of being caught, but he's smart enough to leave us an electronic trail to follow."

"We've interviewed his extended family," Larson said. "There's nothing they gave us to suggest extortion."

"Nothing the family's willing to share, at any rate," Hope said.

Still working the printouts, Miller observed, "Only Leo would understand the risks involved by using the same entry port, the same ISP, night after night. If he is remaining stationary, if we are able to trace it, then it has to be intentional. He's leaving you a string to follow." Looking up from the paperwork, his finger still marking a spot, Miller said, "And if you're smart, you'll follow it."

CHAPTER THIRTY-TWO

A woman with bright green hair passed Rotem's office. She wore a black cape and had pointy ears. He thought she must be part of the secretary pool, but the lime green hair threw him. *Do they have Goths working here now?* He hoped like hell she wasn't one of his deputies.

Reminded then of yet another Beltway Halloween he felt burdened by his responsibilities as a father, restricted by the twenty-minute drive to a safe neighborhood where they'd trick-or-treat with friends, the fathers drinking a little too much as the mothers went door to door with the kids. He felt the day slipping away from him, the quitting hour quickly approaching, even though it was barely after lunch. He slid the well-marked legal pad in front of him and reconsidered his list of priorities. He drew a few arrows and then pushed the pad away, feeling helpless. The discovery of a mole in their midst, and the ongoing investigation into damage done, had crushed morale within Fugitive Apprehension. Rotem's mood wasn't much better.

He'd had a latte and some biscotti for lunch and was already beginning to feel hungry again. With four meetings scheduled this afternoon, he had his work cut out for him.

Wegner entered his office without knocking. A redheaded man so thin he couldn't find shirts to fit, Wegner's boyish face belied nearly a decade of experience in the department. His deodorant failed to mask his body odor. A desk jock devoted to intelligence gathering, he approached his job with the eagerness of a field operative.

"May have something." When overly excited, one of Wegner's most annoying habits was his tendency to either truncate his sentences, leaving the recipient to decode them, or talk so quickly you couldn't understand a word. Or both.

Rotem had not heard from Larson. Nor had he tried to make contact. He had two dead officers—murdered—and a safe house that was no longer safe. Larson would find cover and check in. He'd recalled Hampton and Stubblefield, who'd both been pursuing Markowitz leads. With Rotem's department in disarray, Wegner's enthusiasm seemed surreal.

The man placed a printout in front of Rotem, gave him about an eighth of a second to examine it, and then began talking at a furious rate. Rotem slipped on a pair of reading glasses.

"ATC. General aviation aircraft. Flight plans, into the greater St. Louis metropolitan area. Last thirty hours. Current as of one-zero hundred . . . a little over an hour ago."

Rotem had reported the missing child to the FBI's St. Louis field office, requesting they make it a priority. He'd not told them who Penny was, nor how she connected to WITSEC or FATF, nor that *Laena* was missing. Train stations, rental-car agencies, bus stations, truckers, truck stops, and state troopers were all on the alert, as were the general aviation airports and St. Louis International.

Rotem didn't recall requesting that one of his guys work with Air Traffic Control's computerized flight plans. He hadn't asked anyone to filter general aviation for first-time visits to the area, but he wasn't complaining.

"Give me the short form," he told Wegner. "And slow down."

"Homeland Security requires ATC to track every bird in the sky for variations from their regularly filed flight plans. Since the abduction of the Stevenson girl, ATC has recorded a half dozen first-time single-engine aircraft into the St. Louis area, and we've accounted for the pilot and the reason for the visit in each case. Eleven twins, most of which simply landed and refueled. Employees at FBOs are encouraged to keep track of passenger pickups and drop-offs, something initiated by Homeland. All FBOs have been advised of the little girl. Intel gathered an hour ago from ATC concerns"—he leaned over Rotem and turned the page, directing him to a line about halfway down—"a fractionally owned private jet. In and of itself, it's not too remarkable; in the past day we've logged seven privately owned jets landing there for the first time. But in *each* case, the paper trail made sense—that is, the fractional owner was a corporation, or at least a known entity, and the passengers listed on the manifest checked out. This one," he said, tapping his finger strongly on the open page, "is the exception. We've been on the horn with Sure-Flyte, the corporation that sells and maintains the fractional ownership fleet, and we've also run a background on the fractional owner—a corporation out of Delaware—and it's murky, to say the least. Past flights, and there haven't been many, have been Seattle to Providence, round trip. Seattle to here, Washington, D.C. Seattle to Reno a half dozen times. Always originating with a passenger in Seattle. The passenger names listed on the manifests are for people who certainly exist—of course they do—but I'm betting ten to one they're recent victims of identity theft. You look at their incomes, these people did not ride a private jet around the country."

"Is Homeland involved?"

"They'll be all over this once they hear about the aliases."

"Let's delay that for now," Rotem said. "Where's it scheduled to land?"

"That's what caught our attention. The pickup is Washington, Missouri. It's a small strip west of St. Louis, just big enough to handle a jet like this. And get this: no tower, no FBO. No witnesses. Sure-Flyte has never, let me repeat that, *never*, landed one of their jets at the Washington strip."

"A private jet of dubious ownership," Rotem repeated, "landing for the first time at a strip just out of town where no one is likely to see who gets on or gets off."

"And the first time a passenger flight for this company did not originate in Seattle. Which is why I brought it up here in person rather than put it into the paper mill."

Wegner lived in an office cubicle where the only light came from fluorescent tubes and the only smells from his armpits or the coffee machine. For a reward, Rotem felt tempted to bring him as a field-side spectator for the day—to see his efforts in action—but decided he needed him on the front line of paperwork.

"You may have saved a life, Wegner." Rotem watched as the man grew a few inches taller. "Maybe more than that. Maybe many more."

Wegner lingered a little too long.

"Now get back to it," Rotem said, already growing impatient with him.

CHAPTER THIRTY-THREE

A thunderstorm cracked wildly with twenty minutes to go before the scheduled landing.

With the small girl bound and gagged in the trunk of the stolen car, Paolo sat off a farm road across a small poured-concrete bridge to the east of, and with a good view of, Washington Memorial Airport's landing strip. He'd rigged the car's jack to make it look as if he were dealing with a flat. In fact, he could drive away, leaving the jack behind if needed. By car, he was less than five minutes from the tarmac and the sole hangar. On foot, they would have to cross a farmer's field, ten to twelve minutes if the girl stayed on her feet; but this option would allow him to abandon the stolen car in the woods along the creek and thereby limit the evidence connecting the kidnapping to this airfield. He waited. Which would it be? He'd been told the pilot had his cell number.

He couldn't get the image of the girl out of his mind: dripping wet head to toe, caught between the motel bed and the TV, a stunned look of surprise as he came through the door.

He'd waited for her to say something. And she, him.

Finally, he broke the silence. "Get out of those clothes and dry yourself. You'll catch cold."

She turned around and headed for the bathroom.

"I need you to do something for me," he called after her.

She stopped just outside of the bathroom and turned to face him as if expecting more from him.

"It's the duty of every prisoner to attempt escape," he said. *"Once,"* he added, "and only once. I'd have done the same thing."

"I want my mommy."

This stung him but he said, "I'll hurt you if you do that again. Hurt you bad. Count on it. But no one's going to kill you, Penny. Least of all me. That's a promise."

The kid never flinched. "I want my mommy."

"Get out of those clothes. The motel has a washer/dryer. You can wear one of my T-shirts."

"I don't want to."

His eyeball had swollen and blistered to deformity. Yellowish fluid leaked in bursts down his cheek. For a moment his eye would actually feel slightly better; then the stinging would return, escalating to unbearable pain, and then it would squirt out its foul juice, and the cycle would repeat itself.

"I need you to do something icky," he told her. "Something's in my eye, and it has to come out."

"I don't like icky things."

"Neither do I. But you're going to have to do this."

A few minutes later she had changed and opened the door for him. Her clothes lay in a heap by the front door—all but her socks, which she refused to take off. She wore his Oakland Raiders T-shirt like a dress.

He mopped up the bathroom floor with a towel and had her sit on the counter while he held his damaged eye open to the bright light.

He described the melted contact lens and pointed to it. "You're going to have to pinch it, and pull it off," he instructed. "I tried, but I couldn't see what I was doing."

"I can't do that."

"Yeah, you can."

"No, I can't."

"You act like this, and you're going back in the closet. You help me out, and there's ice cream and cartoons."

"What if I hurt you?"

"You're going to hurt me, but it's not your fault. Just pinch and pull, okay?"

"It's disgusting."

He tried to think of other kids he knew—kids who lived on the Romero compound. He said, "What if it was a kitty cat with something in her eye? Would you help the kitty?"

A reluctant "Yeah?"

"So forget it's me. Pretend it's a kitty cat, and you're the only one that can help it, the only one who can save it. Can you do that?"

"Maybe . . ."

"We're going to do this now. You and me. Ready?"

"I guess."

"Okay." He pried open his bad eye, gritted his teeth, and watched as the two little fingers converged, blocking what little sight he had.

A moment later he screamed. It stuck to her finger like stubborn mucus, and when she shook it off it landed on the bathroom floor, a little glob of yellowish goo.

"I got it!" she said. "I got it." Without thinking what she was doing, she almost hugged him, then shrank back.

"You got it," he said, swallowing a scream. His one good eye met hers, and for a moment, neither knew what to say.

———

The assigned hour of 2:37 P.M. growing near, Paolo checked his watch repeatedly, his good eye rotating from the distant airfield to the airspace above the field, to the rearview mirror, and back again. He'd covered the injured eye with an athletic headband worn askew on his head, a makeshift eye patch.

Arrangements had been made immediately after reporting he'd lost all sight out of the eye. He'd hoped Philippe might simply decide to send him a partner, possibly with some medical supplies, so that he could complete the original assignment. The jet coming either meant anxiety over the hostage situation or a loss of faith in him, so he looked ahead to the landing sick with nerves. His future was in the hands of others, the outcome a plane ride away, and Paolo felt desperately out of control.

The first car he saw could have been nothing. It pulled off the two-lane road on the north side of the airstrip and into a dirt turnout in front of a farmer's maintenance shed or hay barn. When no one climbed out, Paolo kept his eye on it.

But it was a second vehicle, a dark four-door much like the first, that got his heart pounding. If he had it right, and he wasn't sure he did, he'd seen this same car already. It had driven past the airstrip's entrance. Now it had backtracked and entered. It drove up to the strip's only hangar, where a man wearing a sport coat climbed out. A moment later the hangar's electronic door opened slowly, and then this car pulled inside, meaning there was a second man behind the wheel.

Before the hangar door came fully shut, Paolo had his motor going. He rocked it off the jack and backed up across the small bridge. He took a rural road south, into farm country, having plotted this course as an escape route in advance. It was hilly and wooded out here, an easy place to lose a tail if necessary. He drove fast, but not too fast, his one good eye jumping from the road ahead of him to the road behind.

Cops or feds, it hardly mattered: Philippe had been clear about what he should do should anything go wrong.

Radio silence—no phones, no attempts to contact the compound. No e-mail. No faxes. He was on his own, his only assignment to get the little girl to the compound as soon as possible.

Crossing the stream for the second time, Paolo slowed and tossed his cell phone out the window into the water, ending any possibility of triangulating his location. It landed with a small splash.

He and the girl were on their own now. Bad eye or no bad eye, he had an assignment he intended to carry out. He felt strangely relieved. By the grace of God he'd been given a chance to redeem himself, to prove his worth.

He crested a hill, already planning how to replace the stolen car in case it had been reported. He tried not to think of the implications of what he'd just witnessed at the airstrip, how close he had come to being caught.

Tried not to think of what he'd do if Philippe ordered him to kill the little girl.

CHAPTER THIRTY-FOUR

In a surprisingly short time, Dr. Miller traced Markowitz's Internet access backward from the university grid to a physical address in Florida. Armed with that address, and hoping the Markowitz-Romero-Penny connection would hold, Larson drove Hope to Springfield and chartered a King Air twin engine to Tampa, topping out his credit card and forcing him to call in for a "preapproved" home equity loan.

Late that same afternoon, Larson drove a rental car past a cattle farm's unmoving windmill that stood in a field of lush green grass intermittently shorn by gray longhorn cattle looking worse for the wear in the Florida heat.

Stretching high above the flat green horizon, eighty-foot-tall telescoping steel poles held clusters of powerful gas-vapor highway lights that trained down onto the cloverleaves and rest areas. A blessing in hurricane season perhaps, but an eyesore on any other day. The occasional building crane loomed in the distance, reaching for the rare cloud like a bony finger. Randomly placed cell towers also rose from the green jungle, looking for all the world like derelict oil rigs. The only other break in the perfectly blue sky came from a musical staff of high-voltage wires strung across the highway. These were images one absorbed on the flatness of Interstate 75, heading south from Tampa: orange construction cones; bumps of black road tar in a sea of powder gray concrete; a set of smokestacks belching in the far distance.

They passed a sign indicating they'd entered Manatee County. Larson upped the rental's speed, desperate now to reach their destination.

"You're not coming to Useppa with me," Larson said, having delayed it as long as he could.

"Of *course* I am."

"I've arranged something. A buddy of mine will look after you."

"That's ridiculous."

"At the end of this it would be nice if Penny had a mother."

She bit her tongue and said no more.

Larson had left Dr. Miller both his own and Hope's original cell phone number—the number now call-forwarded to the Siemens he'd given her, and therefore it was impossible to triangulate. Miller and Hope spoke the same language; she would be the one called with anything technical.

"Tell me she's okay, Lars," she said at last.

"She's okay," he said.

"Tell me again."

"They have not hurt her. Guys like this, it's all about profit and loss. There's no profit in that."

She unstrapped her seat belt and moved over the gap between the seats so that she could lean against him.

Larson drove on in silence, holding his breath. With each mile, he pressed the rental a little faster, and she leaned more heavily against him. He could have just kept driving.

Ninety minutes later, now on the island of Gasparilla, a hotel bellhop, clad in khakis and a green golf shirt, awaited them with a brass luggage dolly and a look of impertinence. Larson's rental blocked the hotel's semicircular drive, other arrivals now idling behind him.

The night air rang behind a chorus of cicadas and tree frogs. The Gasparilla Inn's white antebellum facade loomed large before them. Hotel guests came and went, climbing into golf carts used on the island in lieu of cars, a parade of salmon and lime green Bermuda shorts, Tevas and leather deck shoes, spray-on tans eager for the real thing, diamonds and silicone.

"Tommy'll take care of you," Larson said.

"I don't want Tommy to take care of me." She turned intentionally childish.

Larson had bunked with Tommy Tomelson during a two-week in-service training at the FBI Academy a couple years earlier. He'd stayed in touch enough to know that the man had lost his wife to cancer and had subsequently taken a year's leave from the ATF, then a short nosedive into a rum bottle, and finally sobered up enough to live the grief-stricken existence of a charter-boat captain. He was currently operating a tarpon charter out of Miller's Marina, which served Larson's needs well.

Tommy was up there on the veranda, smoking a Marlboro and drinking something dark, watching the tight buns and the halter tops pass by while waiting for Larson to sort things out. He was a big guy, with a fisherman's tan and a quarterback's shoulders, his sun-leathered face covered now by a pervasive veil of discontent and loneliness.

"When and if I find her, you'll be the first to know. All right?"

She held on to his arm.

"Listen to Tommy and do as he asks."

"At least take *him* with you, if not me. Please don't go alone."
She squeezed his arm.

"This is not heroics. It's simple numbers. Tommy stays with
you." He'd gone over this a dozen times in his head. The smarter
call was to wait for Hampton or Stubblefield to fly down here.
Maybe both—to take on the house on Useppa Island with as strong
a force as he could currently muster. But Markowitz logged onto
the grid at night—and with the meeting of known crime families
called for the following night, the list had to be close to being fully
decrypted. Larson didn't have twenty-four hours to wait.

"You call me the minute you know anything."

"Same there," he returned. "If Miller should call—"

"You'll hear about it," she said. She leaned away from him,
then changed her mind and craned across to kiss him. Larson
turned to meet her lips. There was nothing particularly romantic
about it, but he felt it long after.

"Don't do anything stupid."

"As if I have a choice," he fired back. "This is me we're talking
about."

The first hint of a smile began, but then she hid it well.

She paused, the car door now open a crack. "If you find her—
when you find her—she won't trust you. We talked about getting a
dog, she and I. We were going to name it Cairo. Like Egypt. Use it.
It may help."

"Cairo."

"Yeah. Ever since she saw a picture of the pyramids she's
wanted to go there." Her eyes grew distant as if watching a film run
inside her head.

Larson walked her up the hotel's front steps and introduced her
to Tommy Tomelson.

As he left, he felt horribly alone.

Tommy Tomelson had used some of the life insurance from his wife's passing to buy the twin-engine inboard-outboard four-hundred-and-forty-horsepower *Christine*, judging by both the name and all the bells and whistles he'd added. GPS satellite navigation. Sonar. Weather radar. SailMail e-mail. Larson read his own e-mail off the BlackBerry as he navigated the channel cut into the shallow bay between Gasparilla and Useppa. Fishing craft, cigarette boats, and pleasure cruisers stayed to the dredged channel, crowding it. Larson opened it up once he'd cleared the speed-controlled areas. Dusk was an hour off, the sun burning harshly to the west, the air holding that twinge of change that came with approaching twilight.

Larson hoped to make the return crossing before darkness fully descended. He wasn't keen to test his maritime skills on a friend's six-figure investment.

Tying up at Useppa, a private spit of old island luxury less than a mile long, required permission. Tommy, who often chartered for the island's guests, had called ahead for Larson. With no bridges connecting it to the mainland, and only the marina for access, Useppa was as remote a place as could be found. It made great sense as a retreat for Markowitz.

Walking off the immaculate dock and onto the island proper, Larson stepped back a century, entering an enclave like nothing he'd ever seen. No cars here—only golf carts used for everything from maintenance to transportation. Larson climbed a sidewalk set amid a lush botanical garden of wild orchid, mangrove, tropical fruit trees, and flowers in garish colors. Tiny lizards scurried through the underbrush, sounding to Larson like rats. Single-story shell-white houses carried names instead of street numbers, black shutters, and screened-in porches. BEGONIA HOUSE. THE BOUGAIN-VILLEA. THE ROSE COTTAGE. Larson ducked beneath a heavy overhanging branch that ran tentacles back to the ground like a shredded curtain. Lights already glowed yellow behind a few windows. The air smelled of perfume. Small waves lapped on a crescent-shaped man-made beach below and to his left. A few sailboats were tied up to moorings there. The encroaching dusk foreshortened distance and softened edges, giving everything a look that for Larson usually followed two or three cocktails.

He stepped off the path, making room for a middle-aged tennis couple with a perky teenage daughter in tow who offered Larson a smile full of braces. The sidewalk terminated in front of a hundred-year-old inn, from which emanated the sounds of a busy bar and dining room. The lush life. Tony Bennett crooned about lost love.

Bit by bit, byte by byte, it was to here, Useppa Island, that Dr. Miller's information quest had led them. The technology had been explained to Larson—using Internet service providers to trace Markowitz's digital identity to a Direct PC high-speed Internet account.

The address was The Sand Dollar, Useppa Island. Larson had been expecting a hotel, not a private residence.

Larson found the look of the place intriguing, its isolation and privacy perfect for hiding, an ideal location from which to decrypt *Laena*.

Near the end of the path he reached and entered the Useppa Inn. Paddle fans and linen tablecloths. A wood bar with a dozen varieties of bottled rum hanging inverted in a metal rack. Larson slid up onto a stool and ordered an Appleton Estate rum and tonic with a lime wedge. Two women sat at a window table nursing what looked like iced teas while a pair of elderly fellows shared beers by an overhead television with the sound off showing a prerecorded golf match. One of the women wore a witch's hat and green nose. The other wore Harry Potter glasses and had a wand sitting on the table. Halloween with the elderly.

Ten minutes passed and Larson ordered another rum. Knowing he shouldn't drink on an empty stomach, he added a basket of french fries to the mix and called it dinner, capping it off with a double espresso. An octogenarian entered, sat alone, and ordered a vodka up.

Larson daydreamed of the St. Louis Rowing Club on Creve Coeur Lake, missing the spiritual exercise as much as the physical. He felt bone-tired, though the french fries had helped to wake him.

The house detective, an older, florid-cheeked man named Harold Montgomery, whom Tomelson had phoned ahead of time, doubled as the dinnertime maitre d'. Smelling of lime cologne with an afterglow of gin and tonic, he offered Larson a damp, soft-fleshed right hand and the two men greeted one another by sharing a few stories about Tomelson. Montgomery wore dark trousers, a white shirt, a navy blue tie with anchor insignias, and a sheen of perspiration across his brow. His sport coat was a mean-spirited, shocking green better reserved for highway work crews. He had a piece of food stuck in his top teeth. He'd missed a few spots shaving. His white hair was front-combed in a failed attempt to hide his baldness. Montgomery raised his right index finger to signal the bartender and was quickly delivered a gin and tonic.

"To absent friends," Montgomery said in a tight voice, clinking glasses with Larson.

"Let's talk about the layout of The Sand Dollar," Larson began.

CHAPTER THIRTY-FIVE

True to his training, Tommy Tomelson guarded Hope's second-story room from the hallway, occupying one half of an old-fashioned love seat located beneath a set of windows that conveniently overlooked the hotel's semicircular driveway. He'd checked her in under the aliases Stephan and Elizabeth Storey, so as not to identify her as a single woman and to keep the wolves off the scent. The room's windows, long since sealed shut for the air-conditioning, were behind closed blackout shades. If a killer wanted in there he'd have to go through the glass, and Tomelson would be on top of the intruder before the guy hit the floor.

Soon after she entered her hotel room, Hope's cell phone rang. She scrambled to answer, praying it was Penny, only to hear the voice of Dr. Miller.

"I can't talk long," Hope said. "I need this line free for a call I'm expecting."

"He's online," Miller said. "And I've IDed his port."

"Right now?" She checked her watch.

Miller confirmed.

"He's early."

"Maybe not," Miller said. "More likely I was a little sloppy, a little hasty in my analysis. I was working fairly quickly this morning. By coming online early evening he picks up another five or six hours of processing."

"But if he's online right now," she repeated, "and you've identified the port he's using, are you saying I can communicate with him?"

"He has no firewall in place. No protection. You realize what that means? I know Leo. That's no accident. If he didn't want to be found, I wouldn't have found him."

"But . . . then why not contact us directly?"

"Technically speaking? For one, they could have a key-tracker in place that would tell them anything he typed—they'd know what he was working on. Or they might have certain applications blocked. Or they might be watching his screen. It's hard to say. Why don't you ask him?"

"Me?" she gasped, thinking immediately of Larson.

"Certainly not me," Miller said. "You apparently know what this is about. I do not. If you people . . . if the federal government is interested . . . the way the world is right now . . . then that's enough for me. Do you have an Internet connection? I can give you a URL and a password, and that's about all there is to it. It's all handled on this end—on the grid."

Her heart quickening, Hope glanced around the room, found the hotel directory, and tore it open, the receiver cradled between her shoulder and ear. Flipping through some notebook dividers, she saw that the inn had a business center, but it closed at 5 P.M.

"I'm fifteen minutes late," she mumbled into the phone. "I could call the manager, plead my case."

"Any laptop would do."

She thought of Tomelson, just outside her door. A guy like that would have some way to connect to the Internet. "I'm going to need a minute."

Then, as she turned toward the door, she noticed the folded advertiser that stood up on its own alongside the withered rose that was trying its best to look fresh. NINTENDO! ON-DEMAND MOVIES! WEB ACCESS FROM YOUR TV!

She practically tore the doors off the armoire. A wireless keyboard sat atop the television, two elaborate joysticks on the shelf to the right, their wires tangled. A duplicate advertiser sat atop the TV.

She switched on the TV. It took too long to warm up. Finally a menu appeared, and, sure enough, INTERNET ACCESS was there on the menu.

"I'm on . . ." she said less than a minute later. "What's the URL and password?"

"You understand," Miller said with great reserve, "that once we do this, a window is going to appear on his screen. We can't predict how he'll react."

"No firewall," she said, handing him his own earlier argument. "That has to be significant."

"Of course it is," he agreed, each building the other's confidence.

She asked Miller to give her another minute and called Larson using the hotel phone, but the call went straight to voice mail. He either had the phone shut off—doubtful—or he'd moved out of cellular service range. Her maternal fears decided it for her.

"Okay, let's do it," she said.

Sounding excited himself, Miller dictated the specifics and she wrote them down. She worked the keyboard and, a moment later, a small window appeared in the center of her browser.

"I've got it."

"Again, there's no gentle way to do this," Miller warned. "Once I patch you in, you're just going to show up on his screen, uninvited. What he does with you at that point is anybody's guess. Likely he'll kill that window and log off the grid, and that's the last we'll see of him."

"He'll talk to me." She sensed her child's fate at the end of her fingertips. She felt torn about doing this before contacting Larson. If she succeeded, they both would celebrate. If she failed, he would never forgive her, and she would never forgive herself.

"Are you ready?"

"Ready."

"If he's using sniffers—spyware—he already knows I've accessed his port. But he hasn't broken the connection. He may already have both of our IP addresses. Let's start now and get this done quickly."

She took one more furtive glance toward the door. "Go ahead," she said. "Put me on his screen."

CHAPTER THIRTY-SIX

Larson slipped a photograph of Markowitz onto the hotel bar and left it there briefly. Larson returned the photo to his pocket and said, "The Sand Dollar then?"

"The only two I've seen from The Sand Dollar," Montgomery said without missing a beat, "are city types that don't belong here. They come and go this time of night or later. You don't see them outside during the day. They order lunch and dinner delivered."

"From here?"

"We're the only game in town."

"Two of them?"

"Yeah, but the meals are for three, so maybe it's that guy," he said, pointing to Larson's jacket.

"Kid food or adult food?"

"Adult, far as I know."

"Do you happen to cover the residences as well?"

"I'm all there is for island security, if that's what you're asking. So, yeah, when residents vacate a premise, they slip me a little something, and I keep an eye on it. That's all. Vacationing teens are the biggest concern. The closest thing we get to a crime here is what we call a DWI—drunk while intoxicated." He lifted his glass and sucked down a fair amount. "We go about ninety percent occupancy Christmas to Easter. We're what you might call inbred. I see the occasional pissed-off spouse armed with a golf club or tennis racquet out for revenge. High crime. In my five years we've had a couple broken noses, unlimited in flagrante delicto, and maybe a dozen shattered egos, and that's about it."

"Sounds nice . . . for you."

"It pays. It's steady. They got good health care and a pension, though I won't stay long enough to qualify. Over half the year we go down to a maintenance level of about twenty percent occupancy. It's a ghost island with an open bar, and that's fine with me." He hoisted the gin again and worked to below the quickly melting ice cubes. "To absent friends," he repeated.

"Is there a dinner order placed for tonight?"

Montgomery blinked his rheumy eyes a couple of times. Larson pushed what remained of the rum away for the bartender to clear. Despite the beauty of the place, this was exactly where he did not want to end up twenty years down the road.

"Standing order. Every lunch, every dinner. They call in to check the specials."

"Can you check for me?"

Montgomery didn't look pleased. But he climbed off the bar stool and disappeared through a door to the kitchen. Emerging a few minutes later, he saddled back up. "If you're fucking around with me," Montgomery said, "I'd prefer you didn't."

"I'm not."

"The order for three dinners was cut back to two, not ten minutes ago. But I suppose you already knew that. What's going on here, Deputy?"

Larson had not known anything of the sort but did nothing to correct the man's opinion. "How exactly do I get to The Sand Dollar?"

"South end of the island." He pointed. "Eye-talian family owns it, name of Valenti. But mostly it's their guests that use it. There are a couple homes down there, all of 'em pretty much off by themselves. You didn't answer my question," Montgomery said, "about what he's done. Why a U.S. marshal's interested?"

"Deputy marshal," Larson corrected. "And no, I didn't tell you."

"Hey, I can keep it to myself."

"I'm sure you can," Larson said. "If one of them left the island, would we have any way to know it?"

Montgomery didn't answer, at least not outright. Instead, he signaled the bartender, who delivered a phone to him. He dialed a three-digit number and waited for an answer on the other end. "Charlie," he said, not bothering to introduce himself, "is the Valentis' boat in or out?" He paused and listened into the receiver, nodded his head, and said, "What? Just a couple minutes ago, am I right?" Paused again. "Thought so." He hung up, pushed the phone away, and worked on his drink. "One of your guys took the boat out not five minutes ago."

"Hence the changed dinner order." Larson checked his cell phone. No reception. He made change with the bartender and used the hotel's only pay phone to call Tommy Tomelson, but got voice mail. He tried Hope's phone next and got a busy circuit. The recorded voice told him to try later.

When Larson returned to the bar, Montgomery was leaning back and drawing a pattern on the sweating glass with a stubby finger. Larson complained about the cell phone service on the island.

"It's hit-and-miss over there," Montgomery admitted. "There's one carrier that's better than the others, but for the life of me I don't remember which one it is."

"How soon are those meals being delivered?"

A tanned older woman with the stretched skin of too many face lifts eyed Larson over a clear cocktail. He wondered what it said about him when seventy-year-olds were making eyes at him. He smiled awkwardly back at her.

"Every night, seven o'clock." He checked his watch. "You got ten minutes to kill."

Larson didn't appreciate the terminology. "Who's delivering?"

"Probably Orlando tonight."

"Don't tell him anything about this. We want the delivery to go just as it does any other night."

"Got it," Montgomery said. "South end of the beach, there's a road to your right. Follow it to the end. The Sand Dollar is second on the left. It's marked. You want my cart?"

"I'll walk."

"Orlando'll drive a cart down there a couple minutes before seven," the old guy said. "Make sure he's gone before you do anything, 'kay? He's a good kid. He doesn't need any trouble."

They shook hands, and Larson was gone.

CHAPTER THIRTY-SEVEN

—Dr. Markowitz?

    —Who is asking?

Worried her actions could cost Penny's life, Hope wondered what she'd gotten herself into as she debated how to answer that query. Her fingers hovered over the keys. Finally, she typed:

    —A mother. The Romeros have taken my daughter. I need your help.

    —No. I cannot help you.

    —You left the port open on purpose.

    —Yes.

    —So you want help. So do I. Is my daughter there with you?

    —No.

    —You must help me.

The line remained blank, the cursor blinking like a winking eye.

—They took my grandson, Adam. If my daughter—her family—says anything, they threatened to kill him. Rescue my grandson and I will do anything.

Hope stared at the flashing cursor on her screen, her fingers suddenly frozen. His answer was so unexpected, she wasn't sure what to do. Finally she wrote the only thing she could think to write.

—Where is my daughter?

The question sat on the screen, the cursor blinking. She waited for his line of text to come beneath hers.

—Follow the e-mail.

As she lifted her hands to the keyboard, the dialogue box suddenly disappeared. At first she thought it was a malfunction. With Miller still on the line, she said, "What just happened?"

"Terminated." She heard the furious clicking of a keyboard. "From *his end*," Miller reported. Then, just as quickly: "Oh, shit." He blurted it out like a man unaccustomed to swearing. "They just pinged you!"

"What?"

"Shut off your machine! Lose the connection *right now!*"

Hope stood from the edge of the bed, the keyboard spilling from her lap and crashing to the carpet. She lunged for the television remote, left on the small circular table by the windows. She pushed buttons, but nothing happened, only to realize she had the remote aimed backwards. She turned it around, hit MENU and worked through the choices. When she hit RETURN TO LIVE TV, an episode of *Seinfeld* appeared.

"Dr. Miller?" she inquired, back on the phone now.

"They pinged you. Do you understand?"

"Follow the e-mail," she said, repeating what she'd read.

"The port had to be open, you see? Unsecured, to do this." He seemed to be talking to himself, apologizing. "By pinging you, they went straight back to whatever machine you're using. Understand? There was nothing I could do about it."

"What e-mail is he talking about?" she repeated.

"That ping will return a unique ID for you."

She thought of Larson. "They'll be under arrest before they can do anything about it."

"We don't know that."

"Yes, we do, actually. Now, calm down and think," she told him. She was close to Penny now—she could feel it. "We need to concentrate on what he told us. *Follow the e-mail.* Can you trace any e-mail he may have sent through your network?"

"I've put you in danger."

She pulled the phone away from her face and took a deep breath, then resumed. "Doctor, I need you to concentrate."

CHAPTER THIRTY-EIGHT

Lizards scampered noisily through the brittle dead leaves amid the overgrown tangle on both sides of the lane. Dusk had ridden away while Larson had shared drinks with Montgomery. The sky retained a smoky blue haze as a few determined stars struggled through. Rum pulsed inside him, competing with adrenaline and the lingering effects of the espresso. He longed for backup, but he'd already made that choice.

Despite what he'd let Hope think, he doubted he'd find Penny with Markowitz. The Romeros were too smart to lump together their assets. But Markowitz remained a possible link—a lead worth following—and Larson was intent on making that connection.

He moved off the narrow road of sand and crushed shell and ducked into the tangle of jungle plants. The ground was soft here and spongy beneath his feet.

OSPREY, the house sign announced above the front door. No lights on. No electric cart out front.

The sand in front of the home was cratered with water marks

from heavy rain, undisturbed by either wheels or footprints and suggesting the OSPREY stood empty.

Larson carefully picked his way through the undergrowth, coming up on the north side of what, from Montgomery's directions, was The Sand Dollar. Constructed on stilts to survive a storm surge, the first floor of these homes stood twelve feet above sea level. Larson would have to climb either the front or back stairs to get any kind of look inside. Caged in by white-painted lattice fencing that surrounded the ground-level carport, a crusty golf-cart charger sat on the sand, its dial glowing, wires like sleeping snakes. The cart itself was missing, driven down to the marina—Larson thought—supporting what Montgomery had told him: One of the three had taken off unexpectedly. Alongside a rust-brown propane tank, two air-conditioning units rumbled and a pair of vinyl garbage cans overflowed with trash.

Above the loud drone of the air conditioner, Larson heard hurried footsteps overhead. Someone going up and down stairs. Shouting, although too muted to make out the words.

What if the other man had not left the island but instead was bringing the Valentis' boat around in order to load up and evacuate the professor? What if Miller's electronic probing had somehow been detected? Or what if Markowitz's work was complete: *Laena* now fully decrypted? What if Markowitz himself was expected at the upcoming mob meeting?

A room light glowed from the first floor. Larson reached down and touched the butt of his Glock but did not arm himself.

For the next ten minutes he patiently awaited delivery of dinner from the inn. His ears whined. The air smelled sour; everything on this island was rotting at a different pace. A motor grumbled at a distance, and Larson thought he'd been right about the evacuation plan. But as it grew louder, it sounded more like a plane, and then all at once a seaplane flew past, low to the water, lights flashing, not thirty yards away. Larson took advantage of the noise and distraction to climb the back steps to The Sand Dollar.

There, his fears and his theory were confirmed as he nearly tripped over two rollerboard suitcases and a cardboard box stacked outside at the top of the stairs. Through a kitchen door that was primarily glass, he saw the kitchen countertops in disarray, glass and plastic bottles of every variety, from peanut butter to cranberry juice, some empty, some not, all lined up on a center island like soldiers. *Fingerprints*, he realized. Any surface capable of carrying a fingerprint had been brought out of the cupboards and sequestered. Wiped down, no doubt.

Close by now, the seaplane's engines groaned in bursts. The aircraft had landed and was taxiing. Its engines finally wound down and fell silent. Larson had seen a long dock off the crescent beach and believed the seaplane likely had tied up there.

At that instant, a golf cart's dim headlights broke the darkness of the lane. The vehicle motored silently up to the front of The Sand Dollar and a college kid climbed out and carried a tray up the front stairs. Larson heard the bell chime through the walls and waited first for the sound of feet approaching. A man's back appeared, heading away from Larson down a peach and turquoise hallway toward the front door.

With the man's back to him, Larson stepped around the luggage to the kitchen door and tried the knob. It turned. He pushed through and stepped inside, working to shut the door soundlessly behind himself.

Two careful steps took him deeper into the kitchen and away from any line of sight from the front door.

He connected the seaplane to the packed bags out on the porch. Markowitz's handlers were moving him.

He slipped quietly into a small dining room. A large mirror was centered on the longest wall and held in a seashell frame. In the mirror's reflection, Larson saw the man at the door in profile as he tipped the college kid, accepted the tray of food, and then, closing the door, set the tray on the floor. He turned away from it, showing no intention of eating it.

Larson heard the man's quick ascent of the stairs and his arrival on the second floor. "Get it done!" the man hollered. "What the fuck is taking you so long?"

"It's on its way now," came another man's strong voice. Older perhaps. Defiant. "It's a large file. Several minutes at least. Just pack or whatever. Don't rush me."

Markowitz.

"They're here now!" the younger voice said. "Just landed. They'll be down here any minute to pick up our stuff. Hurry it up!"

"I said it's on its way!" the old man replied. "There's nothing I can do about transmission speed."

Larson heard the distinctive clicking of furious typing at a keyboard. *It's on its way.* Was that *Laena* he referred to? *Transmission speed.* Where, and to whom?

Seeing no other choice but to make his move, Larson withdrew his weapon and rounded the corner into the hallway. He slipped past the smells of a fish dinner and edged toward the staircase that rose to the second floor.

He took his first tentative step, his weapon aimed straight up the tunnel toward the two—*possibly three*—arguing men, heard but not yet seen.

CHAPTER THIRTY-NINE

Tommy Tomelson let himself into the hotel room with his own electronic key card. He was sweating, a sour, bitter odor coming from him, as he turned and both locked and barred the door. He clutched a maid's black-and-white uniform under his left arm. Extending the dress to her, he instructed, "Put this on. And hurry!"

She stepped toward the bathroom, but Tomelson blocked her advance with an outstretched arm.

"No need to undress," he said. "Besides, I don't want you trapped in there." He pointed first to the drawn blinds, then to the door behind him. "Windows and the door. Quick egress." He turned his back to give her privacy, facing the door. "Keep your clothes on. Just get the dress on over them."

"What's the hurry?"

Tomelson's eyes said it all.

"Someone's here?"

"A guy at the front desk asked some questions," he told her. "No idea how he found us so fast."

Hope glanced back at the television. For the past forty-five minutes she'd been agonizing over what to do. Before running she wanted Larson back. She wanted Miller to call with more information about the e-mail Markowitz had mentioned.

Tomelson said, "I'm not taking any chances."

She considered explaining what she'd done but ate her words. She tried to pull her pants up on her calves, but it was no use; the pant legs would stick out from beneath the dress. She inspected the garment, unzipped it, and pulled it on over her head. The top of the dress hid her shirt, but its skirt, with a mock apron sewn in place, stopped at her knees. She reached up under the dress and, kicking off her shoes, unfastened her pants and slipped them off, stepping out of them.

Tomelson located a hotel laundry bag in the closet and handed it to her. She put the pants into this bag.

There was music playing somewhere nearby. Children's voices shouting, "Trick or treat!" Only a few days ago she and Penny had had such plans for this evening. That recollection overpowered her.

"The shoes are wrong," she said, looking down.

Brown slip-ons with a black uniform.

Tomelson didn't dignify that with a comment. Instead, he said, "You'll go calmly down the hall. Use the stairs. You'll leave out the back of the hotel, by the putting green. Head down the bike path. It's crazy out there because of Halloween. Find someplace nice and public. When you do, call me."

He scratched out a phone number, tore off the corner of the magazine he'd written it on, and passed it to her. His hand was shaking, either from alcohol or nerves.

Hope pocketed the number in the front of her maid's apron.

Behind Tomelson, the door kicked in and she felt the thunder of shots fired.

Hope dived to the floor, so dizzy with fear she couldn't see.

CHAPTER FORTY

Larson was halfway up the stairs when all the shouting stopped. The sudden change froze him. He became acutely aware of the big-breasted white-porcelain mermaid figurine on a small table at the top of the stairs. She seemed to be looking right at him. Laughing.

Then, ever so slightly, the mermaid rocked side to side, a nearly imperceptible movement. The flooring had moved; and with it, the table; and with it, the figurine. Someone up there was moving toward the stairs.

All these realizations collided in Larson at the same instant, combining to loosen his knees and move the barrel of his Glock slightly to his left. He crouched and raised the weapon. A man appeared at the top of the stairs, already firing.

Larson squeezed off two shots and then intentionally slipped his toes off the stair tread, sliding backward and down the stairs toward cover. White plaster from exploding Sheetrock filled the air like smoke and fell like snow. Larson's third shot, aimed at the belly, took away most of the man's knee, and spun him around like a dancer. Hit, the man fired off three more rounds, lost to the walls.

Larson reached the bottom of the stairs and stopped moving. His arm steady, he fired again, but the man was turned, his profile reduced. The porcelain figurine erupted off the table into a thousand floating shards.

A splash of flesh erupted out of the shooter's back. He buckled forward and collapsed. Then the top stair splintered, as did the fifth stair down.

Larson had not fired either of those shots. Montgomery had given him the wrong head count.

A younger man appeared at the top of the stairs, a black semi-automatic gripped in both hands, arms extended. Eyes squinted nearly shut. Early, early twenties, still with bad acne. Freckles. Reddish hair. He looked like an altar boy, not a killer. Fired a gun like one as well. He'd shot the other one—accidentally, no doubt—while wildly running through a full magazine. His shots continued down the stairs, wood and carpet jumping, debris flying.

Larson dropped him with single round, a gut-shot that staggered him back and pushed him to sitting against the wall by the table where the figurine had been. He stared straight ahead as he slumped to the side and fell still.

Larson moved into the downstairs hall for cover.

"Dr. Markowitz?" he shouted, when he'd regained his breath. "U.S. marshal. Hello? Dr. Markowitz? I'm coming upstairs. Hands on your head, knees on the floor, or I will shoot! Dr. Markowitz?"

He worked his way slowly up the stairs, his attention committed to the two on the top landing, wondering if either of them had enough left in their tanks to extend the firefight. Two steps later he felt fairly certain the younger guy was dead, and a sense of outright anger flooded him, for he'd felt compelled to defend himself, and the kid had no sense of guns whatsoever.

The first one, the one now folded forward in a pose of contrite prayer, had been gut-shot and was losing blood badly. He was unconscious, though somehow balanced and stuck in this position. Larson reached the landing, kicked the weapons away. One tumbled downstairs, clattering as it landed. He glanced around for a phone. Perhaps they could medevac this one to the mainland.

In searching for the phone, Larson spotted Markowitz, recognizing him even from the back. He shouted to him, "Dr. Markowitz! Hands where I can see them, please."

It was only then that Larson noticed the small trickle of red below the man's curly white hair. He recalled the first shooter's wild shots as Larson had taken out his knee, the sound of bullets penetrating walls. One of those bullets had found Markowitz.

"Dr. Markowitz!"

The old man still had his fingers on the keyboard, but they weren't moving. He was dead as well. Whatever progress he'd made in decrypting *Laena* remained to be determined.

Larson quickly but thoroughly searched the house, closet by closet, room by room, in search of Penny. He looked for clues of the girl's presence in the food stocked, the laundry washed, bath toys, beach toys: anything he could think of—but found no indication of a child. He returned upstairs to Markowitz, hoping for a disk or storage device, but was faced with only the laptop computer beneath the man's hands. Larson disconnected the laptop and its power supply and took them with him. There would be hell to pay for leaving a shooting—but to remain behind and suffer through a day of statements and inquiry was unthinkable.

As he stole through the night toward the marina, Larson called Montgomery at the Useppa Inn and told him to call every law enforcement agency he could. And an air ambulance. Larson left behind the carnage, but not its aftershock. For along with Markowitz, Larson realized he'd lost his connection to the Romeros, and with it his best and perhaps only chance of finding Penny alive.

CHAPTER FORTY-ONE

Having slept only two hours in the past twenty-four, Jimmy
Oyer rose from his bunk at the back of the Peterbilt with the sour
aftertaste of modafinil in his dry mouth and a raging temper bulging
at his temples.

"What the fuck?" he screamed at whoever was banging on the
driver's side window. He cleared his eyes, squinted, and searched
for his glasses. When he spotted the silver badge, he mumbled,
"Oh, fuck it," and climbed down and over the front seats to unlock
and open the door. Cops!

A fist pounded on the window for a second time.

"Hold your horses . . ." he mumbled, collecting himself. He
tried to think what he'd done wrong, if anything. There was that
whore in the trailer park outside of Omaha, but he'd left her with an
extra fifty after playing a little rough, and she'd told him that put
things right enough. He fought against his clouded head. What kind
of badge had that been? He hadn't gotten a good look at the thing.

An interstate violation?

But hell, he'd stopped at every weigh station as required, and they'd signed off on this load—washers, dryers, dishwashers, and stovetops—so what the hell could the problem be?

He snorted and swallowed to clear his throat, found the lock, and opened the door.

"What is it?"

The guy reached up at him incredibly quickly—his hands like a point guard's. Jimmy felt a line of heat on his exposed neck and clutched at it, as he found it hard to breathe. He sucked for air but it was his *neck* doing the breathing, not his nose or mouth. When he exhaled, he sprayed a mist of blood onto the window and door. He'd been cut! Coughing, he tried to call out, but it just sprayed more red rain.

The cop was a little guy with dark skin, a burned face, pinched eyes, and a three-day-old beard. He shoved Jimmy back and into the cab with incredible strength.

Jimmy carried a few extra pounds. His being lifted like this, up and over the seats and back onto the bunk, shocked him. He swung out with his right hand, but the intruder grabbed him by the wrist—with incredible strength—twisted and turned in one sharp motion, and Jimmy heard something snap as he felt more pain than he knew his arm could suffer. Then he was being bent and rolled over, and the little guy hog-tied him with the wire from the CB radio's microphone.

Lying on his stomach like a rocking horse, in his own cab's sleeper bed, Jimmy gasped wetly for air as he watched a pool of blood spread onto the bed pillow. *His* blood, from *his* neck.

As the guy left the cab, Jimmy's lights were dimming. He rocked and groaned, but the pool beneath his head only widened with each passing second. Deep green and purple orbs formed at the edges of his eyesight, like holding a camera wrong and putting a finger in front of the lens. Jimmy regretted the whoring, regretted all the mistakes, wanted nothing more than to be home with his wife.

The greenish purple crept in from the edges, now nearly all he saw. He felt the cab door open. He heard the little guy straining with something. For just a flicker of a second Jimmy thought he saw a pretty little girl in the shotgun seat, silver tape around her eyes, a knotted rag in her mouth. But maybe that was just dreaming about his own kids.

Engulfed in sadness, drowning in his own blood, Jimmy Oyer succumbed to the sounds of Vince Gill on the four-hundred-watt stereo he'd paid for himself.

CHAPTER FORTY-TWO

Larson swerved out of the way of some teenage trick-or-treaters as he drove the rental car around the bend in the road by the hotel's golf course, running the wipers to clear the windshield of sea spray that had collected in only a matter of hours. The strobing blue and red emergency beacons caught his eye and filled the faces of dozens of onlookers, many in costume.

He'd picked up decent cell reception halfway across the bay. Neither Hope nor Tommy had answered their phones, leaving him pushing Tomelson's charter boat to warp speed. Stomach acid bubbled in his throat. He saw himself as a murderous failure. He'd arrived with only noble intentions of saving his daughter, protecting Hope, carving out a future for them. Seeing himself as part of that future.

But this?

He pulled the car over and went the rest of the way on foot. Clearing the front corner, arriving at the hotel's covered porch, he was met with bedlam.

He'd been gone a little shy of three hours. He returned to a different world, he realized.

Already a busy Halloween night, the emergency lights had brought the locals out like moths. Fifty or more had gathered, held back by the staff of college kids in their green golf shirts.

He found the dense Florida night air as suffocating as St. Louis in August. He tugged at his collar, only to realize it wasn't the fabric constricting him. He strung his federal shield around his neck by the wallet's string. It bounced against his chest. His throat tight, he cautioned himself not to give anything away. Practiced in the art of lying, the identity of a witness to protect, he crossed the porch, for the first time bringing attention to himself.

"You!" an older guy wearing a wrinkled khaki uniform called out. His khaki shirt was buttoned incorrectly, the collar opened beneath the loosened knot of black necktie.

He wore CHIEF on the pinned-on nameplate. He had the bone structure of a drill sergeant. The look came complete with a buzz cut of gray hair and the requisite crooked nose. But age had softened him considerably. Beers on the back patio hung from his jaw like saddlebags. He held contempt in his flinty eyes, barely containing a pissed-off attitude brought on by his night being ruined.

There were too many younger kids in the crowd. Spider-Man. Catwoman. Power Rangers. Larson swallowed dryly, knowing you didn't drag the chief of police out of his house, along with what had to be every emergency vehicle for a few miles, for anything less than a crimes-against-persons felony.

Beyond the crowd, filling Gasparilla's only access road, Larson saw bumper-to-bumper vehicles backed up more than fifty yards behind the stop sign at the crossroads. Among the trapped vehicles, a NEWS 7 step van stuck out, its ungainly antenna lying on its roof like a giant corkscrew.

Sight of the news van told Larson he was at least an hour behind whatever had happened here.

Squinting at Larson's shield, the chief said, "Come with me." It was not an invitation.

"Vacationing?" the chief asked sarcastically, noting Larson's Marshals Service shield.

From behind the registration desk, a pale, nervous woman in a hotel uniform caught Larson's eye. She looked sick, and Larson quickly felt this way as well.

"What's going on here?" Larson asked.

"I thought I was the one asking questions." The chief made a half-assed effort to stop and shake hands while walking. He squeezed too hard.

"Floyd Waters," the chief introduced himself. "You are . . . ?"

"Visiting friends," Larson said. "I saw the cruisers."

The chief led the way.

Black-and-white photos hung on the hotel walls and spoke of another era. White dresses and wooden golf clubs. Children in knee socks and bow ties.

The chief turned left at the top of the stairs. "Where you out of?"

"Washington." Larson found the lie easy, he'd made it often enough. He had no desire to identify himself as FATF just now.

"Where do your friends live?"

"On the bay side. I'd rather leave them out of it."

"I bet you would."

The chief rudely pushed past one of his officers. Larson braced for the sight of her sprawled out on the floor. He lowered his eyes, unable to look.

"Medics stabilized the white guy and took him off island by ambulance. One in the leg. One in the lung."

The white guy. The description echoed in Larson's head: Tomelson.

The dead guy on the floor had pale Mediterranean skin. Clearly not purebred enough for Floyd Waters. He'd taken a bullet under the chin that would have killed him instantly. Tommy had either fired from the hip or from the floor.

"He say anything?" Larson asked. "The one that lived?"

"Unconscious when I seen him," the chief answered.

The chief pointed a dull toe of a black shoe at Tomelson's nine-millimeter Beretta, partially beneath the bed. He said, "That's a 92FS. Military officers and federal law enforcement." He looked up at Larson and said dramatically, "I'm going to ask this once and only once. Did you know this white guy?"

"Are you going to give me a name, or should I recognize his piece?"

The big man leaned in close, apparently thinking he might intimidate Larson.

The armoire doors hung open. Larson noticed the TV's remote on the bed and then, to his surprise, a computer keyboard upside down on the carpet.

Larson scanned the room. On the floor, not two feet from the chief's pant leg, a hotel laundry bag hung partially open. He recognized Hope's pants as the ones he'd bought for her at Target.

Had she been abducted? Fled? He felt his breathing quicken.

Larson needed to find a quick and believable way out of here. He thought the dead man on the floor to be the missing Markowitz guard. The man had hurried to the marina, barely an hour after Hope had checked in. Did the Romeros have someone on the staff of the hotel? Was there some other way they might have learned Hope had checked in?

His eyes returned to the keyboard, wondering what that had to do with anything.

"Room's registered to a couple," the chief said, studying a piece of paper he'd been handed by a patrolman. "Is this something a U.S. marshal might arrange?" He tried to engage Larson in a staring contest, but Larson wouldn't give him that. "A marshal carrying a 92FS."

"I carry a Glock myself," Larson said. He patted his side, indicating the hidden weapon. "So does everyone on my squad."

"And that squad is . . . ?"

"Based in Washington."

"The laundry bag contains a pair of women's pants, size four."

For playing into the stereotype, Waters didn't miss much.

Larson said, "So where is she? If we're looking at abduction—kidnapping—then I'm required to notify the Bureau . . . as are your guys." It was the only card he could think to play, the threat of federal involvement. He hoped it might buy him an invitation to leave without further questioning.

The chief studied Larson a moment with an unwavering eye. Judging by his breath, the man had been party to a few nightcaps earlier in the evening. "Who'd you say your friends were?"

Larson hadn't said. "The Kempers. They've got a pair of beautiful daughters," Larson added. "Both married, but things change. I try to keep my toe in the door."

"As long as it's just your toe," the chief replied, thinking himself clever.

"Why don't you head back on over to your friends and wait for the morning paper? Might be better for everyone."

"Better for me," Larson said.

"You got a card or something?"

Larson did have a card, but it listed St. Louis as his office address. "I'll write it down for you."

He stepped around a patrol officer who was serving as crime technician and found a magazine. A corner of the back page had been torn off. Larson studied this a moment, finding it of interest. The inn was too classy a place for torn magazines to be lying around.

He scribbled out the main Washington number—Rotem's number—on a subscription solicitation and handed it to Waters.

"You've got business cards right behind your shield," the chief said, pointing to Larson's chest.

Larson had forgotten he'd hung his shield out, and of course there were also cards in his ID wallet. He quickly said, "And I'd be happy to give you one if you're willing to spend the next three days in Tallahassee going through debriefing."

"I know who you are," the chief said.

Larson doubted he had a clue, though many cops associated the Marshals Service with witness protection, so it wasn't impossible. "That makes us even. You're going to get a phone call some time later tonight, tomorrow morning, and you're going to want to talk with me. Call this number first, *before* you make a mistake."

"I don't take orders from you guys," Waters said.

"Then take some advice." Larson said no more. He walked past the man and left the room, wishing he could have taken Hope's pants with him. Wondering if they offered him any clues to what had become of her.

Larson hurried out the back of the hotel, stopped in the middle of the practice putting green, and turned to inspect the roof outside Hope's windows, wondering if he might see her cowering up there, hidden in a shadow. He did not. Plagued by concern, he walked around the street side, leaving the relative quiet of the back to return to the more noisy congregation at the front. Dismayed by the circus atmosphere and not seeing her anywhere, he returned to the rental car.

Only then did it occur to him to check his BlackBerry—silent for the past hour except for his failed outgoing calls—only to realize he'd never turned the ringer back on.

The icons showed he had seven e-mails and two voice messages waiting.

Behind the wheel now, he called his voice mail. Hearing Tomelson's voice was like stopping time.

> *Larson, it's Tommy. Listen, there's someone*
> *nosing around here at the hotel, and I don't like it.*
> *I'm going to relocate the package in a little*
> *Halloween costume of her own. Call me.*

He deleted the message. An automated woman's voice said, "Second message . . ."

> *Lars . . . It's me.*

She sounded out of breath, frightened.

> *Something's happened. To your friend, I mean. It*
> *was horrible. Whatever you do, don't go to the*
> *hotel. I'm in a bar. It's a restaurant called*
> *Temptation. Green and white, across from a bike*
> *rental place. I'll stay here . . .*

Her voice paused. He could feel her checking her watch or a clock.

> *. . . an hour at most. After that, I'm not sure. Call*
> *me, or come by.*

She paused.

> *Hurry.*

"To delete this message, press seven. To save it, press nine. To reply . . ."

Larson disconnected the call, checked the BlackBerry's message area and saw the two missed calls, the second of which had been made fifty minutes earlier when he'd still been on Tomelson's charter boat. He kicked himself for having left the ringer off.

He called her back as he drove around the tiny village looking for the bike rental place or a green and white awning. This time she answered. They were barely into their conversation by the time he caught up to her outside the restaurant.

She climbed inside. Able to let down the front for the first time in hours, she nearly collapsed. "It's all my fault. I blew it. Miller warned me they could trace me. But I wanted to—"

"Miller?"

"Find somewhere to pull over. We've got to talk."

Larson drove straight to the public beach. Hope told him about her brief connection with Markowitz through Miller, and Miller's detection of the electronic ping that quickly identified her. She detailed Tomelson's actions in the hotel room. Larson explained the shooting on Useppa, and the setback it dealt them. He indicated the laptop computer at her feet, and Hope got to work as they talked.

"His family should have told us about the grandson," Larson said. "That explains so much."

"Markowitz, dead?" She mulled this over, Penny's life in the wind. "He would have kept a disk, a backup of some sort."

"I looked around. Didn't see anything. Patted him down, thinking it might be a USB disk I'm looking for. Nothing. So I took the laptop."

"The list will be on the hard drive." She had the computer running now. "Though in and of itself, that doesn't help us much."

"It may help others." Larson wondered about a system that placed the innocent in hiding from killers who remained in open society, the twisted logic in that, and his own willing participation in its perpetuation. Now his flesh and blood was a part of it, and this seemed to him penance for his failure to question the moral authority of such a practice. He'd so readily focused on Hope, and then Penny, that only now did the full importance of stopping the sale of *Laena* hit him. There were not simply tens or even hundreds of Pennys out there, but thousands. Many had hopefully heeded the alarm as Hope had and were now well away from their homes, harder to find. Hundreds? Thousands? But even these still carried an assumed name, and those names were on that list, on credit cards, checks, bank accounts, vehicle registrations, school enrollments. How many would have the wherewithal to drop all that like a stone? How many of the thousands had never seen or heard the alarm? How many were still at risk?

"If you're the Romeros," Larson speculated, "and you've hidden this old guy away on a remote island with virtually no access, but therefore no escape route either, what protections do you take to make sure someone like me doesn't walk away with the list?"

She thought about it. "If I'm the one in charge, I'd want to see daily progress. And I don't want the only copy of that list in his possession."

"Exactly."

Hope suddenly understood. "Follow the e-mail! Markowitz e-mailed the newest part of the decrypted list each morning."

Her fingers were typing furiously now. The light from the screen washed her face.

"And you're not going to trust something as important as *Laena* with a surrogate," Larson said. "Not when it's worth tens of millions of dollars. It's got to be e-mailed directly to you. To the Romeros."

"Follow the e-mail," she repeated. Her hands paused above the keyboard. "Shit!"

Larson glanced over at her, then back into the darkness of the beach.

"You said there was a techie there with him."

"That's how it looked," Larson told her. "A young guy. Nerdy. I can't say for sure."

"Well, this thing's clean," she said, slapping the laptop. "That guy's job apparently was not only to monitor Markowitz's progress, but to wipe the files . . . to reduce the chance of *Laena* or those e-mails being lifted if someone like you *did* come along."

With her finger she drew a line in the condensation on the inside of the car's glass. An old lighthouse at the end of the parking lot threw a dim beacon out to sea, swiping their faces with each pass. She disappeared from him between the pulses.

"So we're screwed?"

"No way to tell yet," she said. "His e-mails aren't on this machine. He must have erased them as he went. His mail is hosted on a server—another way to reduce the security risk if the laptop was taken. The deleted information may still be on here somewhere, but it will take days, weeks, to drill down in and find it."

"Then we *are* screwed."

"Now wait," she said, as if talking to Penny. "The e-mails would have gone through the same connection. Through the university's grid. Miller's network. That's what Markowitz was telling me about following the e-mails. They leave a digital ID at each phase of transmission. There's no way to completely erase an e-mail once it's sent. It sticks to every server and relay it touches."

"So Miller can help us." Larson started the car, a sense of purpose finding him again.

"He read the exchange between me and Markowitz." She turned her face into the sweep of white light. "My guess is: a guy like him? He's already on it."

CHAPTER FORTY-THREE

His right eye had not improved. If anything, it seemed to Penny to have gotten worse. He kept it covered most of the time, and because of this, whenever he turned his head to check the truck's driver's-side mirror he had no sight of the back berth, no sight of her whatsoever. They passed a sign welcoming them to Colorado.

Penny had discerned a pattern. The monster (which is what she called him, ever since he'd killed the poor man who owned this truck) was tired and playing games with his left eye, his one good eye, in order to stay awake. First he looked out the passenger window into the truck's right-hand mirror; then, out the windshield; then out the driver's-side mirror. He returned his attention to the highway for another couple of minutes and then started the pattern all over again. Always the same.

He'd put her onto the comfortable bed in the back, ankles and wrists taped together, but no gag for most of the day. She appreciated having the gag off and didn't say a word, knowing if she did, he'd put it back on. He'd dragged the dead man into some bushes alongside a deserted road well off the highway, late, late at night. She tried her best to forget about that.

She now lay with her knees bent facing the front so she could see what he was doing, where he was looking. Her nose was still thick with clotted blood, badly bruised but not broken. Inch by inch, she moved her knees up closer into her chest, her sock and the broken shard of pottery nearly within reach now.

She slipped out the broken piece and gripped it tightly and sawed at the silver tape, working only for those few seconds he eyed his outside mirror. As the edge of the tape was cut, it tore. He had country music playing. Its sound covered the small sounds of the tape tearing as her ankles came free.

Working her wrists free felt impossible. Twice she dropped the shard of pottery into the bloody sheets, a jolt of panic flooding her until she came to realize he'd all but forgotten about her. He seemed occupied with staying awake and overcoming the pain in that eye.

She waited three more hours for him to pull over, the digital clock in the truck's dashboard seeming slower than ever, the expanse of elapsed time excruciating.

He never stopped at rest areas. He peed or did his business in the woods along empty roads that he'd sometimes take forever to find, driving around on farm roads well off the highway, until for one reason or another he settled on a place. He left the truck and did his stuff first, then returned to collect the Tupperware pot he made her use while he watched—the only time he removed the tape allowing her hands and legs to separate. She never left the truck.

Until now.

This time, he glanced back at her on the bed, said, "Same program, little one," for that was what he called her. "I'll do mine, you'll do yours, and we're out of here."

She nodded and groaned, since she was now facing away from him, for this, too, had become part of their routine.

He left.

She sat up and pushed aside the black curtain and watched him hurry into the rocks bearing a roll of toilet paper. With two quick jerks, she had the silver tape off her. She couldn't believe the pain in her limbs from not moving. She rolled and fell into the front seat, slid beneath the enormous steering wheel, and clicked open his driver's door.

She lowered herself and climbed down onto the pavement, the fresh air the first thing she tasted.

But what now?

Her plan all along had been to get free. Now that she was, she had no idea what to do.

Nothing but vast farm ground as far as the eye could see, with nowhere to hide. The only place to hide was the tangle of boulders and rock into which he'd disappeared. She saw snow-covered mountains in the distance, but they had to be a million miles away!

There! She spotted it. A huge metal tube that ran under the road. Without a second thought she ran over to it and off the road, and tucked herself into a crawl and scurried inside. It was dry and sandy in the bottom, and spiderwebs stuck to her face and hands as she pushed in farther, now centered between the two large openings at either end.

She waited, not knowing what else to do.

It seemed like forever before she heard the clap of the cab door open and close. Then open again. Then close. Heard his feet move this way and back that way again, and she could sense he was searching the underside of the truck's trailer.

The monster did not call out for her, and this surprised her most of all. She waited to hear him drive off, to look for her. But instead she heard his feet approaching. She heard him . . . *laughing*. Chuckling to himself.

Then he called out loudly, "You really think so?" A moment later, closer yet. "You really think this will *work*? You think I will let this happen, little one? Is there even a remote *chance* I will let this happen? THERE IS NOT! And the longer you hide from me, the longer you go before your next meal. You HEAR ME? This is your choice and you're making it! So think about it." Another long pause. He was closer still. Now his face appeared at the end of the long pipe in which she hid. She shuddered and pulled into a ball.

He dared to smile at her. "We're not so different, you and me. I like you."

Penny began to cry.

CHAPTER FORTY-FOUR

Larson lost most of the day to making arrangements. Dr. Miller had once again come through, this time working through the night to follow Markowitz's e-mails. Those e-mails, all with encrypted attachments, had been sent from Useppa Island to Mountlake Terrace, Washington, north of Seattle. While the private jet was being refueled early in the afternoon on the outskirts of Denver, Larson sat in a black leather chair in the passenger lounge, speaking on the BlackBerry's cell phone.

He should have felt a pit in his stomach over the seven thousand dollars it cost for him and Hope to fly charter from Tampa to Seattle. If he was not reimbursed for his expenses over the past twenty-four hours, it would take him a couple years to repay the home equity loan. But with Penny's life in the balance, none of that mattered.

"I tried Rotem: Got his voice mail. You're stuck with me," he informed Trill Hampton.

"Where the fuck have you been?" Hampton complained. "That mess out at the Orchard House flattened us here."

Larson knew the pall that hung over operations following the loss of a fellow deputy. The double homicide must have been devastating and would have long-lasting repercussions.

"I dropped two of Romero's men last night, and one of them shot and killed Markowitz in the process."

"That *was* you," he said, as if this possibility had already been raised.

"It was ugly. I walked—had to—and I didn't report it. I'll pay for that."

"The FiBIes are apeshit."

"We're a step ahead of everyone."

"We? As in you and the witness?"

"As in," Larson confirmed. "We haven't determined how much of *Laena* he decrypted, but with this meeting called, they must have most if not all of it. How losing Markowitz affects the Romeros, we don't know. But in all probability, it has sped things up for them. We've traced Markowitz's e-mails to an address north of Seattle." Larson read the exact address. "Another four hours or so, we'll be on the ground there. I need you to get the place under surveillance until I arrive. Use our guys if possible. Use local law only if you have to." Larson didn't love the idea of Seattle's finest being part of the operation. "I want you and Stubby with me. Rotem as CO. We converge on this place ASAP. There's at least some chance the Romeros have one or two children held hostage—Markowitz's grandson was nabbed about the time of his disappearance."

"Son of a bitch."

"The kids are our top priority, so this is *not* a crash raid. You got that, Hamp? No matter what, we do not crash this place."

"Got it."

"And no one goes in ahead of me."

" 'Kay."

Larson read him the address provided by Miller for a second

time. He said, "The three of us—you, me, Stubby—go in after
dark. Tonight. We'll need full gear. No SWAT guys ahead of us.
No crash team. But we'll want them all—we'll want the fucking
Russian army—as backup if it comes to that. The best guys we can
assemble."

"I've got it all down."

"But you, Stubby, and I are lead."

"And if Scrotum balks at that?"

"Then you need to give me a heads-up, so I can work the alternatives. Don't leave me hanging."

"You got it."

"You're going to have to move if we're going to do this tonight. You're on a plane in the next two hours. If Rotem's right
about this meeting—this auction—taking place tonight, then this is
our only window. Markowitz's grandson has lost his value. We've
got to act now!"

"So what are you doing keeping me on the phone?" Hampton
complained.

CHAPTER FORTY-FIVE

Towering cedar, lodgepole pine, and Douglas fir climbed the low hill behind Katrina Romero, looking like ivy on a ruin. The low pewter clouds, broken into patchwork, streamed overhead while the sunlight that pierced through felt summer-warm and sublime. The breeze carried the smell of burning leaves and the cackle and chirp of chipmunk and squirrel competing to shore up their supplies before winter fixed its grip.

Katrina rode the buckskin with the dusty white tail. She wore a black riding jacket over a tailored white shirt with a dozen small mother-of-pearl buttons running down its front. "Mother-of-toilet-seat" an instrument-builder friend of Philippe's called the plastic substitution. Katrina held herself erect, the cream riding pants stretched tight.

Philippe Romero, by blood her husband Ricardo's uncle, but in life a younger half brother, stood below her, looking up. He was a smallish man in his late twenties, with dark features and thoughtful eyes. He glanced at the leather patch on the inside of her thigh, rubbed smooth and polished by hours of her locked embrace with the saddle. She leaned down and handed him the CD-ROM, a small disk in a plastic jewel case.

"This is the last one," he said. "Seriously, Katie, I can't thank you enough."

"What's wrong? Why's this the last? And don't tell me 'nothing.'" She'd been burning these disks for him every day or two for the past three weeks. "You don't look well, Philippe."

"We suffered a great loss," he said. "Not a lot of sleep last night for me. But what we have—this last disk—is more than enough for our needs." He sensed a change in her.

"Then after tonight, you won't need me."

"To burn e-mails to disk? No. But I don't like the sound of that. What's going on, Katrina?"

"Why don't we ride together?" she asked, looking to the woods beyond him. "Do you still ride? How long since we took a ride together?"

"I'm not sure Ricardo would love that."

"Do you actually think he is capable of love?"

Stunned by the question, especially directed at *him*, Philippe felt he had no choice but to watch as she tapped her heels and rode off. Rising and falling in that saddle, timed perfectly as the horse trotted, in such a suggestive way that Philippe believed it had to be intentional.

Stretching back over her shoulder, she called to him, "Red Rock in half an hour?"

The choice of that place as the rendezvous set the record straight. He wasn't imagining any of this.

The thirty minutes passed quickly as he readied a gelding to ride, left a few messages, and made a few calls to buy him time. He selected a circuitous route through the cedar forest—past the eighth green, a half mile out the Winifred trail, and then off-trail several hundred yards south to a small outcropping of rock covered in red lichen.

They'd shared this as their secret place while growing up as teenagers, the site of a coming-of-age sexual encounter that remained the most explicit and vivid sexual memory of his life. A violent summer rain. The two of them tucked into a small cave, her shirt soaked through, her nipples puckered and firm and inviting his fantasies. As he now rode closer to that spot, he recalled her crossing her arms, and his own embarrassment at having been caught staring. Her sudden change of heart, as she uncrossed them, stood with that proud posture of hers, and then disrobed right there in front of him. No words, no explanation. Never breaking eye contact with him, her nakedness revealed only in his peripheral vision.

She'd ordered him over to her: "Come here," or something like that, leaving little doubt who was in control. Her sharp tan line from the point of her darkly tangled hair—and so much of it!—to the sloping curve on her chest.

As teenagers, they had kissed until his mouth burned and she'd whispered for him to touch her, and then, miraculously, had moved his hand to her breast so he might know what to do.

Their one and only encounter—not that he hadn't want to relive it. She represented the sum of all good in this world, and he'd slowly driven her away with his need of her.

And then came Ricardo and her, in this same cave—Katrina saying it was forced, Ricardo saying otherwise. A child. Marriage.

As Philippe arrived this time he found her with her back pressed up against a fir tree, sheltered from a light drizzle, their situation not so very different than all those years before, a fact not lost on either of them.

She made no move to her mare, apparently had no intention of taking that ride she'd proposed. He dismounted and tied off the gelding and ducked under the heavy branches to join her in the muted light, the clouded light playing on her face. He never felt entirely comfortable around her, always on the edge of an apology.

"So," he said softly.

Her eyes hardened and she said, "I saw the boy."

"That wasn't supposed to happen."

"It happened. They thought he was sick. They asked me to have a look."

"They shouldn't have done that." He'd heard nothing about this.

"How could you do such a thing? Kidnap a little boy, little Donny's age?"

"It's not something to discuss." He had no doubt how she would feel about the young girl now in Paolo's care.

"Of course it is. You, of all people. I'm leaving," she announced. "Tonight. During your meeting."

He had trouble catching his breath.

"It's the one time I'm guaranteed of Ricardo, of all of you, being that distracted. I'm taking Callie and Remy."

"Not tonight," he begged.

"Yes, tonight. It's perfect. His full attention is on this meeting you've called."

"But why?" he asked. "I can't let you do this. Not now."

"This place is like a prison. His men drive my children to school. Pick them up. My only chance is tonight."

"That's ridiculous. You can come and go as you please." He turned to go, not needing this.

"Not with the children. They never leave the children."

"And tonight?" He had no time for this. He'd come here hoping to be seduced, only to find himself betrayed. Ricardo—already unpredictable and dangerous—would be impossible if she left.

"I overheard them. They're assigned to this meeting of yours. This is my opportunity, Philippe, my one decent chance, and I intend to take it."

"You're overreacting."

"As if you know what he's like."

"I have a fair idea, believe me."

And there it was again: that same unbuttoning of her blouse. For a moment they were sixteen and seventeen again. For a moment he couldn't think. But then the shock of her believing she could buy his participation in willfully letting her go so revolted him that he took a step back to signal his refusal. Yet by the fifth button, the first of the bluish patches appeared. By the time she allowed her blouse to hang open the discoloring began beneath the stark, bleached whiteness of her bra and spread down, covering both sides of her, unmistakable handprints across her ribs.

"Against my will," she said. "It's his way of punishing me, I suppose. Some shrink will work it all out into neat little boxes, but it's not so neat and little when you're on the receiving end. And I'm done. I'm out of here."

He failed to speak.

"The trouble with him—with *both* of you—is that it's all about the money. How much is enough? I ask Ricky that and he can't answer me. What good is the money if all it buys you is higher walls and more bodyguards?"

"It's not the money."

"That's a lie, and you know it."

She buttoned the blouse and tucked in the tail, her hand stuffed low into the crotch of her riding pants, and despite himself he wanted to take her right there and then—no better than Ricardo. She'd driven Ricardo half-mad with her open contempt of him. He wondered how he would have fared under such reproach.

"So go," he said, the words tasting foul in his mouth.

Her face brightened beneath the gloom of the tree. "I was thinking the back gate."

"Were you?" He realized she wouldn't have left him like this if she hadn't seen their hostage. "Life is not without its irony." He climbed back onto the horse, already feeling a soreness in his ass. His efforts to wrestle—some would say steal—control of "the company" from Ricardo had largely been based on his fantasy of one day winning this woman back for himself. Now, all for naught. She was leaving, with barely a good-bye. If she hadn't needed something from him would she have lured him out here like this?

As he rode away, he imagined her calling out to him, imagined her laying herself down beneath that tree and opening herself to him, that same wet, warm pleasure he'd tasted. Once. He imagined her begging him to come away with her.

But in fact that sound was nothing but a bird or some other wild thing out there alone in the forest, hungry for company, contemplative, mistrustful of all things foreign and new.

CHAPTER FORTY-SIX

The late-afternoon sky darkened with the threat of storm, leaving ghosts and false images on the small black-and-white television screen.

The tall wrought-iron fence, supported every thirty feet by a column of rock and mortar, contained the rolling swales of fairways, the out-of-bounds populated with towering cedar, white pine, and hemlock. The bleached sand traps surrounded the greens like neck pillows. The black pavement of a road rolled out like a tongue through the columns that supported a heavy gate over which hung a swirl of metal fashioned in twisted curls forming an *M* over a solid line with a *W* reflected beneath it.

Larson took his eyes off the television monitor. He had parked a rental a half mile down the road from the Puget Sound Energy truck they now occupied. Hampton had done his best to call ahead and find a federal strike force capable of immediate surveillance, but in the end had settled for the Seattle Police. Larson checked his watch. Hampton and Rotem would be landing at Sea-Tac any minute.

"Wireless cameras?" Hope asked.

The Seattle sergeant was dressed in pressed jeans and outrageous cowboy boots. "Exactly. Used to be you wanted to watch a place, you parked across the street. Now we're three-quarters of a mile away, watching the tube."

The cop wore his long curly brown hair almost to his shoulders, looking more like an icon from the '70s than one of Seattle's finest. A brown mustache overpowered his mouth, and he had Mediterranean eyes that looked deceptively sleepy.

He said, "Of course, they've probably got cameras, too. Watching that fence, the fairways, the various roads. So what you've got yourself right here is a real Kodak moment: cameras watching cameras."

Headlights from a passing car illuminated the far left of the four screens, and then moved one to the next. The compound's gate was seen in the third monitor, where the vehicle passed.

The sign out front read: MERIDEN MANOR.

"It looks like a country club," she said. "But that sign makes it sound like something from the Cotswolds."

Larson didn't appreciate how these two hit it off so quickly. To him it looked more like a fortress and sounded like something made up.

"If the Romeros are in there, it's news to us," the sergeant told Larson.

"Sorry, I've already forgotten your name," Larson said, maybe a little too intentionally.

"LaMoia," the sergeant said. "This is Billy and Duke," he

added, reintroducing the technician and the van's driver, who sat behind Larson facing out toward the road. "This Meriden Manor is a corporation. If the Romeros are in there, maybe they've changed their names or had a couple of Mexican face-lifts, maybe they've paid some people off to look the other way, because we should have been all over that, otherwise."

"Penny's in there," Hope stated. LaMoia looked over at her. "My daughter," she explained.

Larson cringed, seeing clearly in LaMoia's surprised reaction that this was more information than he'd been supplied.

"Is that so?" He gave Larson a look.

"It's entirely speculative," Larson was quick to point out. Technically, Seattle Police were here at the request of the Justice Department. But those lines could get real fuzzy with a young girl captive and the smell of headlines in the air.

Hope hit Larson with a stinger of a look, intended to hurt him, but he knew what he was doing and looked right back at her, condemning her for her honesty while begging her to let him handle the sergeant.

He didn't have any sense of the future beyond that he wanted to spend it with Hope and Penny, if they would have him. He hadn't given any thought to what shape that would take, only its importance, the connection with his daughter intense in spite of the fact they'd never met. He'd not even seen a photograph, as Hope never carried one in case she were ever caught or killed by the Romeros.

"It's down as an assisted-care facility," LaMoia told them. "Health care corporation. We've got no record of ever having set foot in there—SPD I'm talking about. We got a request in to King County, but I'll bet it comes back the same. Whoever they are, whatever goes on in there, it's all theirs. And they've kept it nice and private."

"That fits for the Romeros."

"Yes, it does."

"And if we need your guys in there?"

"You give us probable cause, and we can put ERT inside."

"Does my daughter count as probable cause?" Hope asked.

"No," Larson answered, pained to do so. "Not until I get inside and confirm she's there."

LaMoia explained to her, "He's federal. Right now there's some AUSA working up papers to justify his snooping around. For us it's a different story."

"There are bound to be people coming and going," Larson said, thinking of the meeting. "I'd like to get her"—he indicated Hope—"closer to the gate. She was an eyewitness several years ago. It may help us with probable cause if she can make a face."

Hope's look of total confusion nearly wrecked things. Larson tried to quell her expression with one of his own: a scornful drop of the brow and a hardening of the eyes. Yes, it was a gross exaggeration—a lie—but he needed them out of this truck and closer to the estate. Thankfully she caught this, and stopped herself from saying whatever it was she'd had on the tip of her tongue.

LaMoia instructed Billy to reposition the camera that covered the gate. The image moved as the camera—mounted temporarily atop a telephone pole, it appeared—panned to the left. LaMoia pointed out an area on the screen. "You should be able to make your way up into this ground cover by crossing the road right where we are and going it on foot. Through the woods maybe a quarter mile this direction. Just make sure you stop well short of where you might be seen." He pointed again. "About here. You know the drill."

"Yes, I do." Larson knew LaMoia might offer advice but would not try to stop him. If a federal agent wanted to take a damn fool position, LaMoia was ready to allow him that mistake.

But not without a word of caution, as it turned out. "If you decide to go in there without a call from the U.S. Attorney's Office—well, it's clearly posted as private property. Without some kind of warrant, that makes you the criminal, not those assholes. We get a call, and we gotta come bust you, not them. So think about that."

For Larson, it was a matter of getting free ahead of Rotem's arrival, of establishing that Penny was captive and getting a firsthand look at the setup.

He, Stubblefield, and Hampton were going in there, and he wanted a firsthand look, not Spectravision.

The woods were dense. Slow going. Deadfall and thornbushes caused them several detours as Larson fought to maintain his sense of direction. After ten minutes they arrived at a spot with a distant view of the gate. Larson hunkered down.

"How are we going to get in there?" she whispered, echoing his present thoughts. The two of them were on their haunches with a view of the gate now.

He wished he'd come alone, that he'd left her safely behind in the step van.

From within his coat pocket, he removed her original cell phone and its battery.

"Hey," she said, recognizing it. "What are you doing?"

"I'm putting the battery back into it."

"I can see that."

"We have to consider another possibility."

"The first possibility being?"

"Maybe we weren't as smart as we thought," he told her, clearly frustrating her with his obliqueness. "I'm thinking now we may have been suckered into that mess in Florida. That it all went horribly wrong for them but that Markowitz not using a firewall was no mistake."

"They wanted us to find him?"

"They wanted *you* to find them. To lure you there. What have they ever wanted? You dead, right? Listen," he said, answering her doubting expression, "it's just conjecture. But they were so quick to get over to the hotel, and they only sent the one man. I'm just saying there are a lot of things that don't add up perfectly."

"So they've lured us here." She made it a statement.

"I'm just saying they wouldn't mind if you walked through that gate."

"Penny's not in there," she moaned. "Is that what you're saying? It's all a trick to get to me?"

"I hope not, but I can't rule it out."

Indicating the Siemens phone, he said, "The point is, in terms of psychology with guys like this, you work their blind spots as much as possible. You exploit their weaknesses. You feed them what they want, but not when or how they expect it."

"You're losing me."

"We've kept your phone off, meaning they had no way to locate you," he said, clicking the battery in place. "And we'll keep it off until we want them knowing you're here. At that point, I'm convinced they'll try to track you down and kill you."

She laughed at that. "Whose side are you on?"

He placed the phone into the pocket of his black windbreaker, waiting to activate it.

"Once it's on, it shouldn't take them long to know where you are. At that point, if Penny's in there, they'll want to reinforce her position, or even attempt to move her."

She speculated, "And by doing so, they reveal her to us." She nodded, understanding his thinking now. "And if they don't react as you want them to, aren't we seriously outnumbered? I count five of us, one of whom's a video technician and another a driver."

"There're more than that," Larson assured her. "The radio tech had a list in front of him with seven call signs—handles—written out. He keeps LaMoia in radio contact with his teams."

"I didn't catch that."

"That could mean seven to fifteen or twenty of their guys around here someplace," he speculated. "There are only two ways to do something like this. You go in small and quiet or big and noisy. If you go big, you have to go very big."

"And you obviously don't like that."

"My squad is small, but we work very fast."

"Hampton and Stubblefield."

"That's right."

"So we wait for them?" Her voice returned to anguish.

Headlights.

Larson reached out and placed a hand on her forearm. She was unusually warm, the shirt damp from the thick air.

The headlights were from a car on the inside of the compound. It slowed as it approached. The gate opened—perhaps automatically, perhaps not—and a sedan pulled through, turning out onto the road. A high-end Mercedes four-door. It stopped at a stop sign twenty yards to the right and then continued on.

When it was well out of earshot, he tugged on her and whispered, "Okay, let's go."

She shook off his grip. "Go where?"

"Back to the van."

"I want to stay here!" she protested. "This is the closest I've been to her. I'm not leaving."

"You're cold."

"We stay here until your friends arrive. I'm not going back to that van."

He stripped off his windbreaker and made her accept it. It was heavy on the side with the phone.

"When do we turn on the phone?"

"Soon."

In a sudden burst of light, the gatehouse and entrance were illuminated as a pair of overhead lights came on.

For the second time he noticed the ornate ironwork above the gate. But this time it wasn't on a small TV monitor in the back of a stuffy van that smelled like a locker room.

His breath caught in a gasp as he picked up the significance of the *M* and the *W* encircled in an oval of twisted wrought iron.

He mumbled, thinking aloud. "That's not a *W*. It's an inverted *M*. Meriden Manor."

Hope followed his line of sight and turned her attention to the logo as well. "Yeah?"

"*M*," he said, "and *M*." Sounding foolish. "Meriden Manor." He made the fingers of both hands into *W*s and connected them.

"Yeah? So?" She didn't see it.

He spread his fingers, making what vaguely looked like a diamond. Like a bowtie.

"The scar on the cutter's forearm."

Then she saw it.

A gleaming razor's edge sparked across Larson's memory. He felt it like a clean cut down his spine.

"I think we've got the right place."

CHAPTER FORTY-SEVEN

Philippe Romero steered the sleek Mercedes sedan onto the I-5 southbound ramp and located the abandoned truck stop along a dark, winding road that aimed west toward a seaside town that had once been a lumber port. The truck stop's back lot consisted of a pale, claylike mud and deep potholes that looked to him like open wounds in the moonlit surface. Derelict gas pumps, now nothing but sawed-off pipes protruding from the ground into hulks of rusting sheet metal, rose like headstones from the ooze.

Philippe pulled around back of the boarded-up restaurant and mini-mart, per instructions, facing a rusted-out Dodge pickup truck and an eighteen-wheeler with Iowa plates. He carried a Beretta semiauto in the door's leather pouch, a round chambered and ready to fire. He had another weapon, a .22 meant for target practice, tucked into the small of his back inside the black leather jacket. A hunting knife warmed in his right sock.

He pulled alongside the tractor-trailer and a moment later a male figure stepped out of the broken-down Dodge. Paolo came toward him in the headlights. He opened the door and climbed inside. His face glowed blue in the light of the dashboard. He smelled foul. His face looked like he'd bobbed for apples in a deep fat fryer.

"You were smart to call," Philippe said. "We don't need a stolen eighteen-wheeler on the property."

"You want her in the trunk?"

"No. Put her in the backseat with the kiddy lock on. We're decent people."

Paolo didn't move.

"She's okay, right?"

"Yeah, she's fine."

"You haven't done anything to her, right?"

Paolo leveled his blister-encrusted eye at the driver. "I'm not going to hurt this kid. You understand me? You want that done, you're going to have to ask someone else."

"Okay, okay. You can relax now. We'll get you fed and cleaned up, all right? You smell like low tide and your face looks like you're still doing Halloween."

"I stay with the girl."

"You do what I tell you to do." Philippe felt his hand slip toward the leather pouch. It brushed the stock of the gun. "We've got a hell of a night ahead of us. Don't make trouble for me, Paolo. You've done good. Keep it that way. We'll get that face looked at. That's got to hurt."

"I've got pills."

"Get the girl." Philippe reached down to the dash and switched off the car's interior light so it would not come on when a door was opened. "And no names when she's in the car. You got that?"

Paolo didn't answer. He climbed out of the car, shutting his door, but then opening the back door a moment later.

Philippe leaned over. He felt the .22 at his back. "Put her behind me, so you can keep an eye on her."

Paolo shut that door and came around and opened the opposite door. He moved heavily, under the weight of great fatigue.

Philippe put all the windows down to air it out.

It stank in there.

CHAPTER FORTY-EIGHT

Hope and Larson crouched in the bushes less than twenty yards from Meriden Manor's front gate as the headlights approached.

"Sit absolutely still." Larson hoped they were far enough back in the thicket not to be seen. White skin showed up easily at night, especially in a collage of green and black.

With their eyes now adjusted to the darkness, it took several seconds for Larson to establish it was the same black Mercedes they'd seen leaving the estate less than twenty minutes earlier. The car rolled toward the gate, the driver's side toward them. For a fleeting second, just a momentary flash, they saw a young girl's profile through the rear side window. Hope heaved forward and off-balance, and Larson caught her and clapped his hand to her mouth to hold back the sobs that began involuntarily. That profile had been Penny's.

The car window went down as driver consulted the gate guard and Larson committed the face behind the wheel to memory. Male.

Late twenties. Short, perhaps. Dark coloring. Roman nose. The large black gates yawned open. Taillights quickly receding.

Larson had to think fast. He slapped his BlackBerry into her hand, while peeling his windbreaker from her shoulder and slipping it on. He zipped it, containing his upper body in its black fabric. In nearly the same motion, he retrieved her original cell phone from the windbreaker's pocket and switched it on. Hope's number had previously been call-forwarded to the untraceable Siemens he'd supplied her. He changed that now, call-forwarding that number to his own BlackBerry, now in Hope's possession.

He explained in a forced whisper, one eye tracking those receding taillights. "Can't wait for those guys. If Romero tries to call you—and he may, because I've just turned on your phone—you'll now get the call on my BlackBerry. I'm taking both yours and the Siemens." He took the phone off her hip without asking. "With the BlackBerry, you can send me text messages." He showed her quickly how to do this, though she cut off the demonstration. "I need to know what's going on out here. Make your way back to the van, and keep me up-to-the-minute. When I establish her location, I'll send for Hamp and Stubby." He seized her by the shoulders, unclear if she'd heard anything he'd said. "We're going to do this," he said strongly. "We both saw her in the car: She's okay. Right?"

He waited for her faint nod, said, "Okay," and then he took off low and fast through the dense undergrowth.

Whether a nine- or eighteen-hole golf course, Meriden Manor covered far too much ground to be patrolled effectively. For this reason, Larson worked his way quietly through the woods for well over a hundred yards past where he'd seen the fence turn a sharp corner. Now he crossed the road and stayed low. He entered the woods and cut an angle to intercept the fence. He reached a chained gate—spiked wrought iron—used for dumping lawn and garden debris into the woods. The gate offered a good chance to get into the compound, but he was haunted by LaMoia's description of a "Kodak moment," and feared a video camera watching the gate.

The fence was likely intended as much for keeping deer out as for blocking intruders. He continued down the wall until spotting an overhanging limb. He climbed the tree, worked his way out the limb precariously and dropped over the other side.

LaMoia had infected him with paranoia. He imagined night-vision video and infrared "trip wires" set at waist height to avoid raccoons and dogs but to catch intruders. He envisioned silent alarms and legions of security guards patrolling the grounds, though in fact he didn't see any such boxes or wires running up trees or any evidence indicating any such equipment or personnel. It was probably just fantasy. With the Romeros having called a meeting for some heavy hitters, they would concentrate their manpower around wherever that meeting was scheduled to take place.

He began crawling. Hands and knees into the center of a fairway, believing the wide-open, grassy expanses the most difficult to electronically survey. Fairways were sprinkled, even in rainy Seattle, and sprinklers would trip alarms as quickly as any person would. The smart money put security sensors—if there were any—across the cart paths and at intersections between holes. He crawled on.

A hundred yards farther he arrived at what was marked as the eleventh tee. The course had been cut out of forest. Stands of tall, mature trees separated one fairway from the next.

Minutes later, he crested a small embankment, peering over at the clubhouse.

An enormous Tudor structure loomed close by. Built a hundred years earlier and standing amid a ring of towering pines, this was clearly the original Meriden Manor—perhaps imported from England beam by beam, brick by brick. He imagined it as a family home belonging to a lumber tycoon or shipping baron. Running away from it were more structures, some private homes, some looking more like companions to the manor house, though built more recently. It looked more like the campus of a private boarding school, now that he had a closer look. Places like this went through a dozen such uses, one owner to the next. The Romeros had bought themselves an enclave.

To his left, one road stayed on the level and appeared to service the private homes. Another fell down and away from the manor house, into the clutch of the dark woods. He could imagine barns and maintenance sheds, workshops and garages and buildings dedicated to equipment storage.

Not five minutes later, headlights appeared from the woods to his left. What appeared to be the same Mercedes he'd seen at the gate climbed into view and parked in the manor house's porte cochere. Larson couldn't make out details well enough at this distance, but two men climbed out.

No Penny.

Larson glanced quickly left down the hill. Penny had been dropped off—or *disposed of*.

He broke into a run. He would have to improvise.

CHAPTER FORTY-NINE

One of Philippe's guys hurried over to him. At first Philippe thought he intended to valet the Mercedes around back, but his face indicated otherwise.

"What is it?"

"Her phone's up. The mark—the Stevens woman. Her cell phone logged on to the PacWireless network a few minutes ago."

Philippe's face tightened. It was too good to be true. The timing couldn't be coincidental. "Now? After what, three days?" He thought a second. "They know about the meeting. They're using this to try to distract us. They don't want this meeting taking place." He looked for what else it might mean. "Do we have a fix?"

The guard lowered his voice and spoke quickly. "The phone is transmitting from here on the compound."

Philippe felt it as a blow to his chest. Eyes darting, looking for an answer in all that darkness, he muttered, "Not possible. *Impossible.* Here?"

"Here," the man answered, feeling obliged to say something.

Philippe's eyes landed on the tortured face of Paolo. The man's objections to the treatment of the girl rang loudly in his head. "Oh, shit," he said, under his breath.

He carefully instructed the guard to show Paolo into the study and for him and one other to stand by once he had Paolo inside.

Philippe suppressed a rush of panic. The one-eyed dog had betrayed him, had carried her cell phone with him in order to lead the marshals to his doorstep. He composed himself, struck a solid, confident expression and pose, not wanting to reveal any of his suspicions. He glanced around one last time, peering into the darkness, and strode inside.

CHAPTER FIFTY

Crawling toward the fringe of woods that bordered the road
descending from the manor house, Larson witnessed part of the im-
promptu meeting between the driver of the Mercedes and a body-
builder type. He wondered if it had anything to do with him. The
brief flash of terror in the driver's eyes had felt good.

A moment later the driver spoke into his cell phone, and within
a few seconds, two other men sped down this same hill at a run.

At great risk of being seen, Larson rose and cut through the
woods and paralleled these two, now confident that they'd been ordered to beef up Penny's security. A trap for Hope and whomever
she brought with her.

His shoes soaked through, wet from the ground cover. He
caught a glint off the two black leather jackets as the road snaked
gracefully down the long throat of the hill.

At the bottom of the decline, the paved road crossed a noisy
creek before rising again. Larson stopped short as he came across a
formidable obstacle course—wooden walls with hanging ropes; car
tires lashed together and suspended over a sand pit; a series of low

stone walls; a shooting range with standing targets. It looked like something from an army boot camp.

He slipped through the course, using it as cover, keeping the two guards in sight. As they approached a double-wide trailer home, a floodlight came on, triggered by a motion sensor.

The guards arrived at the top of a set of raw-lumber steps and knocked.

Larson drew closer, careful now of each footfall.

The door was answered by a guy in a T-shirt and black jeans. Larson saw the blue flicker of television light. That, in turn, told him the windows were blacked out from the inside, just like the farmhouse. That alone told him he probably had found Penny.

A sense of triumph and fear mixed in him as a cocktail. He felt the first trickle of sweat catch up to him. His mouth was dry.

He glanced at the face of the Siemens, wondering if Hamp and Stubby were on their way.

Larson needed a look inside the double-wide. But he didn't want to walk into their trap. Instead, he needed to set one.

CHAPTER FIFTY-ONE

"Talk to me," Philippe said, stepping through the study's door, his back now covered by two men, unseen, behind him. The room smelled richly of oiled leather and bookbinder's gum. Three thousand volumes of rare books ran floor to ceiling, encased in imported library shelving complete with air-bubble glass-panel doors and brass fittings. A single Heriz covered the parquet flooring. An antique globe and an Englishman's partners desk faced a pair of worn leather chairs that dated back to American independence. Paolo occupied one of these chairs, looking completely out of place, a mutt among the pedigreed. The light fixture, four fogged-glass orbs, had been converted from gas to electricity at the turn of the twentieth century. A land baron, looking vaguely unhappy, loomed large in an oil portrait that hung over a wrought-iron grated fireplace.

"You said you'd get me a doctor," Paolo said. He delicately touched the skin near his eye, then withdrew his hand.

Philippe reached up under his coat and pulled the .22 out from the small of his back. It wasn't much of a weapon, but it was loaded with live rounds and was accurate. He remained out of reach of Paolo, knowing his fast reaction time. He did not provoke him, did not aim the gun directly at Paolo, but its presence said it all.

"Empty your pockets."

"Sure." Paolo, confused but not about to object, did as he was told. He placed several credit cards and some bills and change on the edge of the desk. The stub of a pencil. A small pocket watch with a badly scratched face. His cell phone.

"Behind your belt."

"You said my pockets."

"Everything."

"Whatever." Paolo slipped the razor blade out from behind his belt and placed it on the desk. He kept it within reach, his eye on the gun in Philippe's lap.

"Show me the phone."

Paolo took the phone off the desk. It was a clamshell design, not powered up, its small screen dark. This didn't fit with what Philippe had just been told.

"Turn it on."

"But . . ." Paolo said. "I mean, think about it. If they have a lock on me, they'll pull a location. Why risk that?"

Philippe reached forward and swiped the phone out of the man's hands, knocking it across the room. The battery came loose as the phone hit the floor. "When and where did they get to you?"

"What the fuck?"

Now Philippe aimed the gun directly at him. "When . . . and where?"

"How about who?"

"You needed a doctor," Philippe said. "I can understand that."

Paolo turned the injured side of his face toward Philippe. "Does this look like I've seen a doctor? What's going on here?"

"The more you stall, the more you piss me off." He made a point of the weapon. "Never piss off—"

"—the guy holding the gun." Paolo knew Philippe's inside jokes better than his teacher knew them. "I've had no contact with them. You hear me? None! They did *not* turn me." He said earnestly, "Don't you get it? All I want . . . all I want *more than anything* is to do this job for you. This woman . . . she did this to me." He touched his face again. "It's my turn."

"What did you do with her cell phone?"

"I never had her cell phone. If I did, she'd be dead, and I'd be offering it as proof."

Philippe had trained the man well: He showed no signs of breaking even under the threat of the gun.

"Let me help fill in some of the blanks," Paolo offered.

"That's the idea."

He extended his arms. "Are you going to do this or not?"

Philippe lowered the gun. Paolo might have hidden her cell phone in the Mercedes, so that it wouldn't be found on his person. But a second explanation presented itself, however improbable. "If it's not a plant, then it's her. She's here. Could you have been followed?"

"No way."

"Could the girl have signaled someone, gotten word to someone?"

"Impossible."

"Because if she's here, you have to tell me how she found us, you see?" Philippe talked to himself, working this out. "One of our guys could have given us up, I suppose." He answered Paolo's puzzled expression: "We suffered a setback last night in Florida. It was messy. Two of our guys and the professor. The phone could be her and this marshal, I suppose." He considered this further. "Might even be intentional on their part. Or just plain reckless. We'd be stupid not to find out—to pass up the opportunity, if that's what this is."

"If she's on this property, I owe her," Paolo said. "Cut me in on this."

"Your face? Your eye?"

"Can wait."

"Collect your things," Philippe said. "Hurry."

Paolo scooped his belongings off the desk and jammed them into his pockets. All but the razor, which he delicately returned to its hiding place behind his belt buckle.

Philippe's hand shook slightly as he returned the .22 to the small of his back. On this, of all nights . . .

"If she's stupid enough to show up at the house, I'll call you. We've got it locked down tight for the meeting. One marshal and a witness are not going to present much of a problem. You back up the bunkhouse, just in case this marshal's luck holds out a little longer."

"Consider it done."

Philippe debated calling off the auction, but to do so would be a sign of weakness. He had ten men; Ricardo, another six to ten. If possible, they would sweep the property one more time before the meeting. He could put off canceling until then. If they caught and killed Hope Stevens in the process—the only remaining living witness who could give them all jail time—he'd have a major announcement with which to open the auction. This might help him to cover that he had only a partial list: eight hundred witnesses and their three thousand dependents. And it'd be a major public victory for him personally.

"Did you say something?" Paolo stood at the door to the study.

Had he? He wasn't sure.

"The bunkhouse," he said, then watched as Paolo walked briskly away. A man on a mission.

CHAPTER FIFTY-TWO

Larson moved before the double-wide's motion-sensitive lights switched off because after that, if he approached the building, the sensors would bring the lights back on. Although the windows were blacked out, he couldn't rule out a visual or audible alert connected to the lights on the inside.

He worked around the near side of the building past four plastic trash cans, some discarded truck tires, and pieces of plywood used for target practice. Wedged between the trash cans were the cardboard and Styrofoam from packaging that had contained a microwave oven.

The double-wide was a glorified shoebox with a flat roof that extended in short eaves on every side. Larson followed with his eyes a black wire that attached to a video splitter under the nearest eave. Next to the cable wire ran a power line extending from the same pole.

To crash through the door and attempt a rescue was not going to help anyone. Even if he reached Penny—doubtful—they'd never make it off the property. He had to get inside quietly, and sneak off the property with a five-year-old in tow. Possibly Markowitz's grandson as well. Might as well throw in a tap-dancing elephant.

Where were Stubby and Hamp?

Larson found a stout branch to use as a club, preparing to carry out his developing plan. He then crept to the back of the structure and placed his ear to the glass, hearing only the low rumble of television and nothing more. No small voices. No kids crying.

The front floodlights clicked off. But because of his continuing movement, the back lights remained on. He wondered if this gave him away.

He leaned the wooden club against the trunk of the tree nearest the structure and climbed quickly. Several of the evergreen's stout branches hung over the building's sloped roof. Larson reached five branches up and then worked his way out along the thickest of these to where he could make the transfer from tree to roof. The back lights now went dark, leaving Larson literally out on a limb over the roof in the pitch black.

He could sense that the limb he stood on was taxed by his weight. It sagged too low, bent too far. Somewhere just below and to his left was the edge of the roof. One last step was all he needed. But if he jumped in the dark, it would make for a loud landing.

Slowly his eyes adjusted. First, geometric shapes. Then, the branch. The roof, directly below. The roof's edge.

Larson slid his left foot out and stepped off. On the roof now, he moved like a ballerina toward the eave and lay on his stomach. He reached under the eave and fished around until he found where the cable was attached. He unscrewed the cable from the splitter but only partially removed it.

Inside, the television had either lost its picture or gone extremely fuzzy. That would be significant. Larson knew protection work. Live by the tube, die by the boob tube.

The darkness left nothing but shifting shapes and made the going difficult as he worked his way over the edge of the roof. He squatted, prepared to jump.

He could hear grumbling and bumps from inside. He waited.

When the front floodlights popped on, Larson let himself drop to the carpet of spongy pine needles.

A male voice complained loudly to the others inside. "Where's the fucking cable again?"

Larson grabbed the club like a bat and stepped up to the plate.

CHAPTER FIFTY-THREE

DELMONICO'S *DELIVERS*

Hope read the name on the back of the panel truck, her patience draining. She stabbed the small keys on the BlackBerry, spelling out:

caterer? @ gate

and sent the message to Larson.

She'd not returned to the van as Lars had asked. The next time she saw Penny, she'd throw herself onto the road if necessary. She was too close now to go sit with *the boys* while they played with her life. She'd been through too many months of such treatment. That part of her life was over.

The panel truck was kept waiting while the gate guard, dressed head to toe in black, circled it. Finally arriving at the back, he rolled open the back door and shined a flashlight inside. Hope was prepared for a team of military operatives to storm out, take down the guard, and open the gate. Instead, the powerful flashlight beam found stacked plastic boxes, collapsible tables, flats with serving trays, and bags of ice. His inspection concluded, the guard pulled the rolling door back down. In his haste, he did not secure it, and as he rounded toward the gate, the back door bounced open, first a crack, then a foot or more.

Hope looked left and right. *Nothing*.

With Penny inside the compound and this truck her best chance at getting inside, she slipped out of the bushes, used the truck to screen her from the gatehouse, and sprinted across the road. She reached the truck's partially open back door before the gate had fully opened.

CHAPTER FIFTY-FOUR

The guard rounded the corner, looking up toward the eave, straining to follow the thin black TV cable.

Larson, both hands gripping the broken stick like a Louisville Slugger, stepped into the swing and put the man's unsuspecting forehead into the nosebleeds. The guard fell on his back with a *whomph* of released air, clearly unconscious before he landed.

Larson considered tying him up, gagging him, but feared he had no time. If he could bag all three guards, then he'd return to this one. He rolled the man onto his side, so he wouldn't drown in his own vomit, and left him.

With no choice but to risk it, he entered the glare and hurried up the wobbly front steps. He thumped an elbow onto the door and said in a gruff, intentionally muffled voice, "Hey, help me out here . . ."

As the door came open, he thrust the broken limb like a battering ram into the gut of the guard, connecting just below the *V* of the rib cage. He stepped inside, past the one staggering back, and clipped the skull of the next, who, at that moment, had been kneeling in front of the TV, his back to the door. The one behind him went for a gun.

Larson broke the man's wrist with the stick and, as he cried out, dimmed his lights by breaking his jaw. The guard's eyes rolled back into his head, and he slumped. Out cold.

Sweating profusely now, Larson surveyed the fallen. He kicked the door shut, and breathed for what felt like the first time. He rounded up weapons and pocketed their magazines.

He'd bought himself a few minutes at most.

The guard with the broken wrist moaned himself awake, grabbing at his flapping hand. Larson raised the club above his head and lowered it like a camper going after a snake.

The shabby interior reeked of years of cigarettes and beer. It reminded Larson of a crappy college dorm lounge. A Formica galley kitchen offered a two-burner stovetop, a microwave, and a fridge under tube lighting. The building's modular design left the kitchen and living room at one end, a bath, and two other doors off a narrow hallway lit by an overhead fixture missing at least one bulb. Larson's heart remained in his throat as he carried the bloodied club with him down the hall. The doors seemed to stretch farther away the more he walked.

He threw the first open, club hoisted and ready.

Two sets of bunk beds, complete with sheets and wool Pendletons. Signs of bachelor life: Ashtrays that needed emptying. Copies of men's magazines with cover shots of bare-breasted starlets. Soiled laundry in a far corner, looking like an animal's nest.

Clear.

He hurried to the second room, threw this door open, expecting either the fourth guard or the expectant eyes of the two kids. Another bunk room, not dissimilar to the first.

No kids.

He tried to wrap his mind around all this. The speed with which the two guards had fled the main lodge had convinced him they'd taken the bait of Hope's phone coming online.

The most pressing thing now was to buy himself time to find the children. He could bind and gag all three guards, leave the one out back, perhaps behind the trash bins, the other two here in the bunkhouse.

He felt a rumble in his legs and knew it to be a vehicle. He switched off all the interior lights and cracked open the front door in time to see only the back of a panel truck up at the top of the hill, rounding the north corner of the lodge. He couldn't make out its writing on the back from here.

He shut the door, set down the club, and grabbed for Hope's mobile.

    caterer? @ gate

Party time or a Trojan horse, courtesy of Rotem? Something was wrong: Hope should have been supplying him with more information than this.

Where to go from here?

He spotted two rolls of silver duct tape—further evidence of the kids, or wishful thinking?

No matter, he would put them to good use.

CHAPTER FIFTY-FIVE

"What the fuck is this?"

Philippe watched the panel van disappear around the far corner of the lodge. But his attention was elsewhere, out into the night, down the hill to the bunkhouse, which he couldn't see from here.

Paolo would reach the bunkhouse any minute. Philippe had the rest of his guards patrolling the manor. Representatives from the other families were due any time now. All this should have made him feel more confident than he did. But the mark's cell phone coming alive while *on this property* did not sit well. That had yet to be explained, and was the most troubling of his concerns.

Ricardo, older than him by a year, but technically his nephew, answered from behind him. "Jimmy Nans decided to make a little contribution to your meeting."

"I don't want his contribution."

Philippe had never learned to feel comfortable around Ricardo. Never had. Never would.

"Not the way to play host," Ricardo chided.

"They'll set up upstairs. Then I don't want them anywhere near the meeting."

Philippe decided to follow the van around the building and make sure his guys were on it. "Where you going?" Ricardo called out. "You got something going with Katie?" Philippe stopped in his tracks, then decided that the worst response was any at all.

"She's a nervous twitch. Can't stop moving around the house. You know what's up with that?"

"Katrina is miserable, Ricky," Philippe answered, using a nickname Ricardo loathed. "Everyone around here knows that. We've known it for a long, long time. But at least you don't have to worry about losing her."

"How's that?" Ricardo asked, suddenly all the more curious.

"Because you never had her."

CHAPTER FIFTY-SIX

Prostrate, Hope peered out of the back of the catering truck. By the time it rounded the second corner of the lodge and descended down a small ramp, she anticipated its coming to a full stop and slid out, feet first. As her shoes made contact, she fell onto the pavement, tucked into a ball, and rolled an ugly back somersault. She quickly came to her feet and stuffed herself into a cave of steel formed between two massive Dumpsters. The catering truck continued another thirty or forty feet, its brakes squealing as it stopped.

Odds were that Penny was somewhere inside this building.

She heard a male voice first: "Stupid shit . . ." Then the rolling open of the truck's back door, the driver angry at the gate guard for leaving it unlatched.

A smallish man not with the catering crew walked within inches of her and started shouting at people. Hope leaned back, put her hand into something disgusting and had to bite her tongue to keep from groaning out loud.

The one barking orders explained that the caterers would be let

inside. The back door would be opened for them. If caught anywhere in the building other than the basement or the first-floor dining room, they were told they'd spend the rest of the night in the
truck, under guard, and could say good-bye to any tip.

"And I'm a big tipper," he said, his voice fading into the building.

She wondered if she could pull off being part of the catering
crew. She picked out the voices of two women and a man, all three
having arrived in the truck, she assumed. The back door now open,
they went about unloading the truck. Hope sat up into a crouch,
brushed herself off, and poised herself.

Prepared to head to the back of the truck, pick up a crate and
act like she knew what she was doing, she willed her feet to move,
but they remained frozen to the pavement. Terrified, she collapsed
and hunkered back down.

She couldn't do it.

It was then, sitting there between the two Dumpsters, with only
a wedge of visible landscape and sky in front of her, looking out
across an empty golf green where sprinklers made rain with random precision, that she spotted a flicker of movement high in a tree
at a great distance. She saw a low stone pillar that supported the
wrought-iron fence. This tree was on the far side of that fence.

There! Another similar movement, about twenty yards to the
left of the other, also high in a tree.

She stared and stared. No more movement.

And then she understood.

Hands trembling, she removed the BlackBerry, shielded it carefully before lighting up its screen, and began typing.

CHAPTER FIFTY-SEVEN

Having taped and gagged the three guards, Larson finished with the unconscious one outside and moved across the road and higher up the hill in order to see three cars arriving in succession. As Larson finished binding the guard outside, the headlights of arriving cars lit the treetops, the light dancing and shifting as it advanced one crown to the next. Criminal royalty, if Rotem's information were correct.

Frustrated at having used up time and energy, Larson wondered where Penny could be hidden. A search of the trailer had yielded nothing.

He scrambled out from under some bushes and broke out onto an open fairway, dividing his attention between several things at once. The house. The edges of the fairway. The fairway itself. The possibility of more guards, people, cameras, dogs.

He caught movement well down the fairway and slightly to his left, moving right to left. He lay on the damp grass.

A lone, dark figure—female, he thought, judging by her walk—moved quickly between two large white pools—sand traps, he realized. He rose up slightly onto his hands and, as he did so, caught sight of a massive roof, well out of bounds from the golf course. A barn.

He added this up. A woman, not using any flashlight, heading toward the barn. Nearing midnight . . . Eccentric at best. Secretive came to mind.

To check on sleeping children? he wondered.

Yet another car pulled up to the lodge, another passenger dropped off. That made five or six just in the past ten minutes.

Then, on the cart path, not thirty feet away, a man's silhouette. Larson angled his face away from the man, to hide the white of his skin, while he simultaneously hid his hands beneath him. Larson froze.

Judging only by sound, Larson determined the man continued walking a few more yards. Larson braced for his own discovery, plotting a course toward the woods.

"Katie!" the man called out.

Larson saw that the woman in the distance stopped. She seemed to turn but then moved on, continuing down and out of sight, toward the barn.

"Shit." The man seemed to give up. The soles of his shoes ground sand onto the cart path as he headed back toward the manor house at a brisk pace.

The substitute cell phone vibrated in his pocket. Larson rolled onto his hip to put it completely beneath him, compressed and silent.

The footsteps stopped. "Who's there?" the man called out toward Larson. But his mobile chirped and he answered it. Over the device's speakerphone a man announced, "The visitors have all arrived. Assignments, everyone."

The man's footfalls faded as he headed away from Larson and back toward the lodge.

Larson scrambled a good forty yards and into some woods. Well concealed, he withdrew the mobile, reading the text message sent from his own phone.

2 men in trees. Police?

He found the message in some ways welcome, but disturbing as well. If she was in the police van, shouldn't she *know* if these were police or not?

Torn between the confusion of the message and his instincts that this woman he'd just seen would lead him to Penny, he crept to the edge of the woods and then hurried after her toward the barn.

Such a perfect place to hide a child, he thought. All little girls love horses, and a few errant noises from a barn would not attract attention. Wouldn't surprise anybody.

CHAPTER FIFTY-EIGHT

"What have we got?" Rotem asked the long-haired detective who sat at the console in the back of the now-crowded Puget Sound Energy truck.

The civilian, Billy, operated the equipment. The long-haired plainclothes homicide dick, who had a wiseass disposition, mustache, and exotic-skinned, cream-colored cowboy boots, clearly considered himself in charge.

Rotem had his work cut out for him.

The man on the green nylon camp stool to Hampton's left was the deputy Special Agent in Charge, a man by the name of Forsyth. He wore a business suit with a blue handkerchief in the breast pocket. The heels of his polished Oxfords showed a great deal of wear. Pronated. He had a fairly good attitude—unlike the detective—able to let Rotem tug the reins. The wheelman was an SPD officer whose name Rotem had missed. He occupied the driver's seat on the other side of a blackout curtain that lay on Hampton's back like a cloak. There were two opposing consoles of electronics.

The men gathered around the four television monitors as if watching a Sunday game.

"Birds aloft," Billy reported. "We've got two men in place with visual. They're looking over the wall, down into the compound."

"Can we put them on speaker?" asked Rotem.

With the flip of a few switches, everyone in the van could not only hear the spoken words of the two Emergency Response Team officers, both Seattle police, both twenty feet up trees overlooking the compound, but the fourth television monitor now carried fuzzy green-and-white still images returned from the electronic-assisted night-vision binoculars each man wore.

The officer described a quiet golf course with a main clubhouse beyond. Those in the van saw still images of two, possibly three, individuals off-loading a panel truck.

"It might be food," an electronic voice reported.

"Copy that," the other field officer said, agreeing.

Rotem double-checked his watch. A catering truck and five cars had entered the premises in the past fifteen minutes. The information they'd gotten on the meeting—the *auction*—appeared good. A small but necessary step forward.

The long-haired detective took a call on his mobile, stripping the headset away to allow himself to hear. He ended the call, turned to Rotem, and reported, "Plates on the third car come back a livery service with known OC ownership."

Organized Crime. Looking better. What they were seeing fit what they'd been told: an exclusive compound; luxury cars and limos arriving. The fact that there might be one or more child hostages on-site was the one wild card on Rotem's mind.

"We still need probable cause," the long-haired detective said, "in order for my guys to go in. A license plate is not going to cut it."

"Agreed," said Forsyth. "Let's work on that." He looked over at Rotem as if he might pull a rabbit out of his hat.

"You've got a deputy inside," the long-haired detective said. "Has anyone tried calling him?" This slight to Rotem and his operation did not go unnoticed.

"We have," Hampton answered. Stubblefield groaned a complaint from the passenger seat on the other side of the blackout curtain. He was far too big to fit into the back with the others. "He's not picking up."

"His presence remains unconfirmed at this point," Rotem said. He racked his brain for probable cause, even a *suspicion* that might entitle him to appeal to the AUSA for a phone warrant.

One of the two ERT operatives checked in.

The detective, a hand to his headphone, informed Rotem of the communication. "We got a set of high tension lines crossing the property," he said.

"I've forgotten your name, Sergeant," Rotem finally admitted.

He lifted an ear of the headset. "LaMoia," he said. "No sweat."

"What about these power lines?" Rotem asked.

"High-voltage overheads crossing the property. Might be for irrigating the course. Thing about tension lines . . . they're well-hung." A knowing smile curved under the mustache. "As in they're strong enough to support an adult male—two adult males to be more precise." He added, "My guys go in suspended from Skyjacks—motorized rubber-wheeled pulleys—so there's a bit of a noise factor, hum of the motors and all, but it's not much."

"Skyjacks? You've done this before."

"ERT learned the technique from Search and Rescue. The idea is to be able to move people between existing buildings at high altitude. Urban warfare. It's Homeland Security shit. We've used it for some surveillance as well."

The man's tone implied not all was told. Rotem resented the tease. "I'm sure you'll enlighten us, Sergeant. We're somewhat pressed for time here."

"You'll have to go through the AUSA to get the paperwork, right? So maybe that will make it different for you guys. But we've had a ruling in Washington state that the airspace above private property is not the property's. The catch here is that all power lines, and all equipment relating to the transmission of power, is the sole property of the power company, in this case, Puget Sound Energy. Get it? We don't violate any rights by using those tension lines."

Rotem connected the threads of the sergeant's logic. "You're saying if we get the power company's permission to use their lines, we're good to go?"

Forsyth caught on. "No one ever actually touches foot on the soil below those lines . . ."

Rotem met eyes with LaMoia in the dim light of the glowing communications console.

LaMoia grinned. "No trespass. No probable cause requirement as long as you keep to surveillance."

"How very creative of you."

"It wasn't my idea, but I'll pass along your appreciation. Once you're in, if you're lucky, you use the surveillance to find probable cause, and then you're really in."

"Providing you get lucky and happen to see something." Rotem wasn't complaining, but it wasn't a gimme.

"There's always that," LaMoia admitted. "But if they happen to see *you,* it's amazing what kind of felonies take place. The bad guys never love to see SWAT guys dangling from their power lines."

"That borders on entrapment," Rotem said, but seeing how easily one thing might lead to another and win them their probable cause.

"That's showbiz." LaMoia winked. "You want my guys to pull out the Skyjacks, just give the word."

"Word," Rotem said, already dialing his cell phone to roust the Assistant United States Attorney in order to push for the power company's cooperation.

CHAPTER FIFTY-NINE

Hunched low to the ground, Larson headed past the out-of-bounds markers and down the grassy slope toward the barn, now fifty yards away. The urgency of finding Penny only increased as the prospect of an armed federal raid of the Romeros' meeting loomed. Things would likely get ugly, and he didn't want Penny caught in the crossfire.

This end of the golf course hosted the occasional fairway home. It seemed possible the woman might have come from one of them. Perhaps nothing more than a pregnant mare or a sick horse explained her late-night visit in the dark, but Larson had convinced himself the barn was worth pursuing, and there was no turning back.

Below, a set of windows lit up. A tack room, office, or storage room—any one of which would work for sequestering a kidnapped child.

Reaching the barn, Larson moved away from the glowing windows, avoiding what Service field instructors called the "moth syndrome." He held close to the barn wall, moving quietly. More interior lights switched on directly overhead, the yellow glare spilling out and revealing to his right a thick stand of sixty-foot evergreens. Larson passed an open-ended enclosure where bales of hay were stacked. There was a pitchfork stabbed into one, and for a moment he debated bringing it along. He rounded the far corner and encountered two enormous twin barn doors, a slice of bright light escaping. He placed his eye to this crack and saw the woman—quite the beauty—walk quickly down the stable aisle toward him.

Mid-twenties. Well postured. Mediterranean or Hispanic. A brazen confidence in her dark eyes and pursed lips. She stopped at a stall and slid its door open. She stepped inside.

Larson hurried now, coming fully around the far side of the barn. Alert for guards—for if Penny was here, there should be guards—but saw none. He also failed to spot video or security devices. Reaching the barn's other end, before rounding the corner he saw a trapezoid of light spread out onto a pad of pavers, suggesting opened doors.

It was here that the horses were groomed and washed and saddled, sheltered from the area's persistent rain by an enormous roof overhang. He saw now that the first windows he'd seen lit indeed belonged to a tack room. Still no guards. No trap. It doused his earlier optimism.

But then another thought: Horses meant riding trails. Even on a large estate like this the trails probably led off the property and into the surrounding woods. This meant a safe means of escape for Penny should he find her.

Feeling he'd blown it by following her here, he peered down the stable's well-lit aisle, determined to make something out of it. What he lacked was information. The strong-bodied Italian guy who'd been driving the Mercedes, who was almost certainly the man who'd come so close to him back on the fairway, had shouted at this woman. If indeed she proved to be Katie—his wife? sister?

associate?—it implied an intimacy between the two. She could know something of value. He'd wasted too much time not to seize even this small opportunity.

Most of the stall doors remained shut, some with lead ropes hanging outside them. A few stood open.

He ducked inside the first open one he found, hid in the shadows with the potent, but not unpleasant, odor of manure and hay and horses enveloping him. Open stall by open stall, Larson moved closer to her. Was it possible that this woman *was* the guard? That she'd been caught off her post and been shouted at by the boss?

At once, her whispering voice carried in the air. "I'll miss you so much. They'll treat you well. I promise."

Larson buoyed with hope, riding a seesaw of emotions. First failure, then possibility. Penny's guard might be in the stall with her. Perhaps she was sick or needed an adult woman's attention. Perhaps Larson was closer to finding her than he thought.

He moved to a stall directly across from the one he believed she'd entered. He listened for the sound of a child's voice, twice nearly convincing himself he heard it.

Then silence. Two excruciating minutes of it. He stole a look across the aisle through the wrought-iron bars. Saw nothing. Quietly he drew his weapon, wondering if he was the reason for the sudden change. The gun hung heavily in his hand. He realized how tired he was. He summoned a deep breath, gripped the weapon in both hands, and prepared to cross the aisle.

At that instant, the stall door in front of him slid quickly and loudly shut, a roar of steel wheels on tracks. Larson jumped back, surprised by it. By the time he recovered, the door was now closed. He heard the fading, hurried patter of footfalls on the dirt aisle.

Larson tugged on the door, but it didn't move. Locked, from the outside.

He stuffed the gun away. He'd been jailed.

She would signal the others. He would have an army after him. Any chance of saving Penny was lost.

He jumped up and pulled himself over the stall's eight-foot walls topped with ornamental ironwork. Up and over and gracelessly down.

Larson crossed the aisle, tore open the opposing stall door, and faced a chestnut mare.

The woman had been saying good-bye to a horse.

He sprinted and first caught sight of her again outside the barn. She had a good twenty yards on him and was a fast runner. If he allowed her to reach the top of the hill, it was over. She glanced over her shoulder, and he gained a step or two on her. Agile, and quick on her feet, she coughed as she cut left into the woods. She slowed a step, a sprinter, not a marathoner.

Larson closed on her.

CHAPTER SIXTY

Faint cracks of light were all Penny saw. Dust in the air, like when her mom shook a bedsheet by a window, little sparks of light like fireflies. Something cold and damp upon which she sat in this new prison. The sweet smell of lumber mixed with other scents foreign to her and unpleasant. Sour. Tangy. The taste of metal in the cool air.

Where was she?

Her ears rang and her toes felt numb, which was to say they didn't feel at all. She had to go potty and she was fiercely thirsty and stomach-growling hungry. Afraid of the dark, she shut her eyes against it, finding her private darkness more tolerable than the blind darkness that faced her. Silence like a sponge, soaking up any hint of life, even the sound of her own breathing.

And then, as she dared to open her eyes again, dared to face that demon of darkness that had for so long made her shut her closet door before bed, there in the swirling grays and formless blacks, a shape slowly took form. And she gasped.

She was not alone.

CHAPTER SIXTY-ONE

Larson followed Katie into the woods. Still running, she gave away her location with the crunching of broken sticks and the thrashing of undergrowth.

Larson cut an angle to intersect her route. Having been raised in a house that bordered nine acres of Connecticut woods, he effortlessly negotiated his way through the stands of pine and fir and cedar, moving like a deer. He sprang as he ran, landing and rebounding, moving far more quietly than his prey, who crashed and banged her way more deeply into the thick.

She did not scream or call out, suggesting to him that for whatever reason, her visit to the barn was off-limits, or there was someone here she feared more than a stranger running after her. And that gave him the chills.

He bore down on her now, able not only to hear her, but finally glimpse her as a darkly moving shadow that strobed between trees. Paired now like rabbit and hound, they darted through the trees, the rare foam of gray light penetrating from the houses beyond. Larson caught a flash of skin as she looked back, her face a reflector. He could hear her panting as she ran.

Larson pushed harder, finding a sudden burst of energy. He vaulted a pile of dead limbs. Again, the woman glanced back, never breaking her stride. She looked behind a fraction of a second too long.

"Look out!" Larson called out, instinctively.

Too late.

She collided with the trunk of a fir tree, a great *whoosh* of escaped air as her chest impacted. Larson skidded to a stop, mesmerized by the surreal effect of seeing a human body in motion so suddenly still and quiet. Her shoulders slumped as if unconscious, yet she remained standing.

A grotesque gurgle arose from her, a wet, sucking sound mixed with escaping air.

Struggling to catch his breath, weapon in hand, Larson reached her and found her eyes open and blinking. Her right foot was angled down, touching the bed of pine needles with the toe of her shoe. She was weightless. Unsupported. Not standing and yet erect. A stain crept out of her, like something living, and spread down her left side. He holstered his weapon. Her mouth opened and shut but no sound came out.

In the limited light that reached into the forest, she seemed cut into several long pieces.

Another step forward and he saw it. She had impaled herself on a stub of a broken branch that held to the tree like a dagger, a jagged, splintered, six-inch blade of weathered wood. The wet gurgling coincided with the slight rise and fall of her shoulders. It had pierced her blouse, cleaved her ribs, and punctured her lung.

"Federal agent," Larson whispered, simply to identify himself.

Fear was their biggest enemy now. She could live through this, but she needed medical attention immediately. "I'm going to get you help. Do you understand?"

Her dark eyes moved slightly.

He realized that by helping her he would likely get himself caught, perhaps killed. Penny would be lost. For a moment, he considered leaving her, resentful that a stupid accident—her own damned fault—would cause him to lose everything. But he could not pull himself away.

He slipped off his belt and withdrew his handkerchief from a back pocket in advance of grabbing her around the waist from behind, lifting her slightly and pulling her off the stub. She shuddered and fell into his arms, and he laid her down on her back.

He tore open her blouse, and mopped around, finally finding the wound at her ribs. He held his handkerchief there, and used the belt to secure the handkerchief, applying pressure.

"Okay?" he asked, their faces only inches apart.

Again, her eyes moved vaguely. In shock, she was barely with him.

"He would have left me," she said hoarsely. When the words came out of her mouth some blood did as well, and Larson felt himself flinch.

Whomever she meant, Larson thought not. No man would leave this woman.

"There's a girl. A little girl," he said, knowing that his chances were slim to none, but clinging to hope. Perhaps he could pass something along to Rotem or Hampton before he was caught. "She's my daughter," he said, his throat constricting.

Her mouth moved, but he heard no words.

He scooped her up and carried her in his arms, amazed by how small and light she was. He navigated out of the woods, carefully up the incline, the dense forest giving way to the clipped grass of a fairway.

She grew heavier in the silence. Larson felt his legs and back straining.

"A boy," she said so breathlessly he thought he might have imagined it himself.

Larson paused.

"They have a boy," she said.

He continued climbing, reaching the crest and moving across the fairway. No one approached him. No one arrived to detain him.

"A young boy," he said, thinking of what Markowitz had written to Hope.

Her eyelids closed and opened—her way of nodding.

"Where?"

"They'll kill you."

"Probably," he said.

She shook her head and went silent.

"Where?"

She managed to point out a medium-sized home that bordered the golf course, one of the ones he'd seen earlier. Her home clearly. There would be a road on the far side of the house. A car in the garage. A way out for her.

She shut her eyes and grew much heavier. She'd passed out.

He walked through low bands of ground fog that had appeared in just the past few minutes. The fog shifted like chimney smoke and swirled at his waist. The air felt noticeably cooler.

His shoes and socks soaked through, he reached the cart path and crossed it, into her backyard. He saw a swing set and a toy lawn-rake and a wheelbarrow heaped with leaves.

She came awake in his arms, risen from the dead.

"Leave me . . ." she muttered. "The porch. A . . . housekeeper."

He carried her to the back porch where a porch light shone. "Okay. You're here. Now tell me: Where's the boy?"

He stepped toward the porch doorbell. He looked at her for a response before ringing it.

"The bunkhouse," she said. "It's down the hill from the manor."

Larson rang the bell, then pivoted, hearing footfalls approaching the door. He had to leave and yet couldn't tear himself away until he was sure. "The double-wide."

Katie's eyelids fluttered and closed.

He heard the lock come off the door.

He ran.

CHAPTER SIXTY-TWO

Hope's maternal instincts soon drove her out of her hiding
place and toward the back of the catering truck. If she didn't get inside, she told herself, she had no chance of finding Penny.

Larson's BlackBerry buzzed yet again—area code 314, St.
Louis—and again she ended the call to keep the device from vi-
brating and giving her away. Wedged between the Dumpsters, she
was in no position to strike up a conversation. Had it been area
code 206, Seattle, any possibility of being the kidnappers, she
might have dared answer.

The two caterers came and went from the truck in roughly two-
minute intervals. Hope reached the back of the truck, snagged the
corner of a plastic cooler, and carried it by its two handles. Bravely
now, and with great resolve, she approached the building's back
door and thumped her foot against it, knocking. She knew the faces
of both caterers from having observed them. She was glad to see it
was one of these women who opened the door for her.

Hope explained herself. "They asked me to help you out." She
offered a perfunctory smile. "I'm on the wait staff here. Where to?"

"I'm Donna."

"Alice," Hope supplied automatically.

"We were told there'd be six of you."

"Well . . . I'm the first," she said brightly. "The others will be along." A stopwatch started in her head. By the time someone determined they had seven waiters and waitresses, not six, she would have to be gone.

"We're setting up in the kitchen," she was told.

Hope pressed past the woman holding the door.

"We were told it was black bottoms, white tops."

Hope noticed that Donna had stuck to the uniform. "Yeah. I'll change into my stuff after load-in."

"Midnight to two," Donna said. "You always work these hours?"

"We see it all here, believe me," Hope answered, the cooler growing heavy in her arms.

"At least the pay's right."

"For *you* maybe."

"These guys are real pricks about us keeping to the basement—"

"And the upstairs dining room," Hope completed, having overheard this condition. "Same old, same old."

Donna shut the door behind herself as she stepped outside.

Hope hurried down the hall and followed a line of water drops like a mouse after crumbs. She paused at the kitchen door. An exit sign, straight ahead. A small elevator—no, a dumbwaiter—to the right of the kitchen door. A set of stairs that beckoned her.

She stepped into the busy kitchen, set down the cooler, and wondered what came next.

CHAPTER SIXTY-THREE

The Odessa Room had once been a library and still retained the floor-to-ceiling shelves of leather-bound books, broken only by mahogany slabs bearing oil paintings under the warm glow of brass tube lights mounted above their frames. For years it had doubled as a more intimate dining room, for parties of less than thirty. Some time in the early 1930s, its recessed ceiling had been installed, an elaborately engineered panel with curving sections that met in the very center, surrounding an oval-shaped, hand-painted depiction of a fox hunt. On its north wall was a marble mantel and its matching hearth, a working fireplace. The mantel was shored up by twin stone columns, carved into which were two nude angels bearing baskets of wheat above their heads of flowing locks. Atop the mantel, two silver candelabra, their new candles unlit, protected a dried arrangement of deep-red roses, wheat straw, and burgundy fruit blossoms.

Around the polished rectangular cherry-topped table sat ten men ranging from thirty to eighty and in every shade of skin: African, Native American, Far Eastern, Caucasian, Hispanic.

They represented Reno, Sacramento, Los Angeles, Oakland, Portland, and points in between. They were not unfamiliar to one another.

Philippe, at the head of the table, brought the meeting to order. He thanked them for coming, reached into his black Armani sport coat, and withdrew a plastic jewel case containing a gold CD-ROM, a computer disk capable of storing ten thousand documents. "The highest bidder takes home the entire list. Subsequent sales of the names of individual witnesses, or groups of witnesses, are at the discretion of the buyer."

A Mexican, who wore a collarless shirt open to a gold chain bearing a St. Christopher, said, "My people tell me a general alarm was put out, that most of the people on that list have fled by now."

"And that may or may not be true," Philippe said. "But even so, do you run every time you hear an alarm? Do you uproot your entire family? This list includes *everything* there is to know about these people. Not just new identities, but employment, banking, known associates. It would take months, years, to regenerate all new data for these people. Whether they run or not, they're out there, and they're leaving trails to follow." He paused, swallowed once, and said, "The bidding will start at ten million dollars."

A knock on the door—no cell phones, no weapons, were allowed in this room—and Ricardo, who sat to Philippe's left, was summoned by one of the guards.

Philippe considered Ricardo's departure carefully, wondering what trick he might be playing. He didn't want him outside this room where he couldn't see him.

As the door shut behind Ricardo, Philippe heard whispers that included the words ". . . *your wife* . . ." Fast-moving footsteps followed. It was everything Philippe could do to remain focused as he turned to face the group of raised hands.

"Do I hear fifteen?" he asked.

CHAPTER SIXTY-FOUR

The Skyjacks operated as motorized trolleys, a battery pack powering a high-torque motor with an oversize pulley-wheel that ran atop the steel aviation cable supporting the four black high-voltage lines. Each of the two ERT operatives hung suspended from one of the devices in a harness that featured quick-release carabiners that allowed them to bail out one-handed and rappel via a weight-balanced recoil, falling toward the ground, if need be, like frightened spiders.

As they entered the estate's airspace, each carrying a semiautomatic rifle slung around their shoulders, they surveyed the property with high-power night-vision headsets with wireless technology that transmitted the digital images back to the command van. The hands-free radios and earbuds allowed continuous communication between all parties.

"You getting this, Flyswatter?"

"A picture's worth a thousand words," LaMoia's voice came back to the dangling operative.

In the night-vision's eerie green-and-black, viewed alternately between the Vs of trees, they saw a small parking lot crowded with luxury SUVs, Town Cars, and two stretch limousines. A cluster of darkly clad drivers and chauffeurs, some of whom were smoking, loitered by a door to the building.

"We need more than a couple cars and chauffeurs," LaMoia told his two men. "Keep looking."

At each pole, the operatives were required to suspend themselves from the cross-ties and move the Skyjack past the pole to the next length of cable. Such transfers consumed three to five minutes, conducted with the utmost care, to avoid being electrocuted.

"Off-line," announced the lead operative in a hushed whisper.

In the command van, Rotem had had his fill.

"We're not going to get anything out of this," he announced to no one in particular.

"Give it time," LaMoia said. "Our guys know what to look for."

"When that meeting breaks up," Rotem said, speculating, "we lose what we're after." He had yet to explain, and never would, the loss of *Laena*. "By then we need legitimate reasons for stopping each and every one of those vehicles. And that's not happening in this lifetime. If this goes down as a win, we're going to have to take them as a group, while they're still in that meeting."

"It's a catered event," LaMoia reminded. "It's not going to be over in a half hour. They're probably not even set up yet," he said, completing his argument. "Give 'em a minute."

"There's baggage," Hampton advised from his uncomfortable seat.

"What about your guy inside?" LaMoia asked.

"That's unconfirmed," Rotem said. But then hearing himself say this, he ordered Hampton to try Larson's cell phone again, muttering, "I've waited long enough." ERT officer Peter Milton, sus-

pended by a woven nylon climbing-strap from one of two wooden
booms that supported four high-voltage electric lines, was in the
midst of transferring his Skyjack to the next length of cable when
he spotted a small stainless-steel box screwed into the wooden
pole, and recognized it immediately. He'd moonlighted weekends
for Cablevision.

Milton radioed his discovery to the command van and waited to
see if LaMoia understood its implications.

LaMoia swiveled on the small stool and faced Rotem. "You
may need our help on this one, Marshal Rotem—state law versus
the feds, and all—but my officer just stumbled upon the unexpected. It seems someone in that compound is pirating their cable
television."

"Television?"

"A black box," LaMoia explained. "Unauthorized intercept of a
coaxial cable. It could be to steal high-speed Internet or a television
signal, but state law's the same either way."

"Are we *sure*?"

"Milton knows his stuff, believe me. If he says it's a black box,
it's a black box. And I don't know about Washington, D.C., but in
Washington state that's a no-brainer for a search-and-seizure: 'to
confirm and record the use of the unauthorized interception of radio or television transmission,'" he quoted. "More to your favor is
that our guys typically make such raids evening or nighttime—like
right now—when people are in their homes. It's not going to ruffle
any judge's feathers to cut us the paper this time of night."

"Let's make the call," Rotem said with reservation.

LaMoia could see through to his concern. "As CO, I'm free to
solicit the assistance of any law-enforcement personnel that, in my
judgment, will better protect my field personnel. A couple federal
marshals joining up won't raise many eyebrows. We've got that li-

cense plate, that link to OC, to give us good enough reason to go in hot."

Rotem had his phone out. He told Hampton to get word to Larson to keep his head down because they were coming in.

"I've tried him, like, ten times," Hampton said.

"Well, try him again."

CHAPTER SIXTY-FIVE

Hope spotted a tray holding ten empty water glasses and two pitchers with ice. Scooping it up, she headed into the hall and turned left toward the stairs. She climbed quickly, arriving into the dizzying smell of oiled wood, leather, and the lingering sweetness of cigar and pipe tobacco. Golf championship plaques lined the walls, some dating back to 1910. Yellowed black-and-white head shots of officious-looking men in blazers and club ties filled in the gaps between the plaques.

She forced herself to walk slowly. With all the activity in the basement and the dining room being on the first floor, she assumed Penny was being kept somewhere here. The first two doors she encountered were closed. She dared not open them. The third was open a crack. She peered into an empty secretary's station, the anteroom of an office. The sound of male voices down the hall won her attention and drew her past two more doors. The hall opened up then into a large trophy room with pennants hanging from the crown molding. Clubby, with brown leather couches and overstuffed chairs, chess sets, and backgammon tables. An armoire concealed a television.

Hope cut across this room and into an opposing hallway where she came across a small window in a swinging door. She peeked through and saw a narrow stairway.

She pushed through and climbed to the second floor, knowingly out-of-bounds. She hoped a simple excuse of being lost might get her by. Stopping at the landing, she heard the elevator's electronic groan. Peering out into this second-floor hallway, she saw the room doors were farther separated than on the ground floor. Bedrooms or billiards or card rooms, perhaps. The stairs continued up to her left. She knew she was in dangerous territory.

The tray grew increasingly heavy for her.

Out in the hallway, she heard the spit of a radio intercom. "Khakis, brown sweater."

She didn't have to look down to realize she fit that description.

She set down the tray, pushing it into the corner, and quickly climbed to the third floor.

From below she heard a male voice. "Hey, I got a tray here. Glasses. Pitchers. Fresh ice."

If something was said back to this man, Hope didn't hear it. She pushed through the door and stepped out into the third-floor hallway, struck by the immediate smell of a hospital ward. She wondered if Meriden Manor was serving as a retirement home for mobsters.

She darted past medical equipment, convinced her pursuer was coming through that door behind her at any second.

The smell of old people intensified, like a grandmother's house on a winter day with the windows shut tight.

Through a partially open door she caught sight of a luxury

suite of rooms and the back of a bald head—a man wearing hospital pajamas.

Not assisted living, but *assisted dying*, she thought.

Penny might be locked up in any one of these suites, held hostage in front of a color television with room service of ice cream sundaes and grilled cheese sandwiches. How simple here to keep a young child placated and free of complaint.

Burning with resentment, hungry for her daughter's freedom, she retraced her steps, trying each and every door. All locked. Slots for key cards like hotels. The Meriden Marriott. She opened the first door without a lock, albeit cautiously.

A storage room containing linens, a pair of upright vacuum cleaners, and two rolling buckets with a variety of string mops.

Out of the corner of her eye she caught the door to the stairs swinging open. Reacting, she ducked inside and pulled the door shut. She collected herself into the corner, crouching behind the pair of vacuum cleaners. Hunkered down.

A muffled male voice. A guard on a radio checking room to room.

The complaint of the hallway's parquet flooring presaged the doorknob's twisting. Hope ducked farther down, her eyes trained to the floor, head as low as she could manage.

The door opened, the room flooding with light. She could hear his breathing. The light lessened as the door started to close.

The BlackBerry lit up and buzzed in her pocket. She slapped a hand over it, tried to squeeze the buttons through the fabric of her pants. The vibration of the plastic continued.

The room lit up as the door was flung back open.

"Come out from there," a tentative male voice ordered.

She heard a bucket kicked out of the way. Another crash, extremely close to her.

"Do . . . not . . . move," the voice demanded.

She looked up slowly, just as the BlackBerry stopped buzzing.

Head down, she managed to get three numbers typed into the device quickly and hit SEND.

He was just a kid: twenty, twenty-two. Dark skin. He held a gun aimed at her head, the barrel's small black circular hole staring at her like an unflinching eye.

CHAPTER SIXTY-SIX

After twenty minutes of watching the bunkhouse, Paolo saw something in the dirt by the far end of the structure. Only as he came up to him did he see it was one of his team—Todi, they called him. Out cold.

Paolo patted himself down, looking for his phone, only to remember Philippe had stripped him of it in the study, and he'd gotten out of there without it. He patted down Todi—he had a gun but that was all. He untaped the injured man, for all the good it would do.

Paolo entered the bunkhouse with his razor gripped tightly in his right hand, ready for a fight. With his one good eye, he saw two more men, also hurt and unconscious, tied up and stretched out on the floor. He decided to clear the building. He didn't need anyone coming up from behind him as he untied his buddies.

He moved like a wraith through the small corridor, room to room, his shadow bending as it followed. Finding each of the rooms empty, he proceeded to where he'd left the little girl.

He stood above the crawl space access door in the back closet of the back room. A fabric loop protruded from the carpet. The carpet had been cut perfectly to match the pattern.

Paolo pulled on this, lifting the trapdoor. He stepped back, anticipating a gunshot. A cool wind wafted up through the crack. Nerves tingling, he stepped forward, prepared to jump.

He'd practiced such tunnel raids in his training, though he'd never used the skills. He counted down from three, jumped into the dark space, and rolled upon impact. He crashed into a pony wall of lumber that braced the trailer's central support beam. With a vertical clearance of less than four feet, he squatted on his haunches, his razor held out in front of him. He struggled to see clearly.

Two low cots with sleeping bags. The girl was awake, sitting up, eyes wide, looking right at him.

The crawl space was as large as the bunkhouse itself, framed in with plywood and blue foam insulation. The floor consisted of dirt and rock. Several electrical boxes, strung together with Romex wiring, ran from one porcelain light fixture to the next, dividing the structure in half. Light from the hole seeped down, just enough to see dimly corner to corner.

They were alone here, the three of them.

How that was possible, he wasn't sure. Had whoever had tied up the guards missed the trapdoor?

Clunk. A sound from above. The trailer's front door came softly shut, though not softly enough.

Paolo replaced the carpeted trapdoor from below, sitting it into its frame. He duckwalked over some plastic pipe and took up a position to afford him the greatest surprise. He trained his one good eye toward a spot in the blackness.

The razor pressed tight between his fingers.

Come and get it.

CHAPTER SIXTY-SEVEN

Bloodstained from his rescue of the woman, Larson had reached the far end of a darkened fairway with a partial view of the double-wide below. The more he thought about it, the numerous guards, the isolation, the more it made sense. Somehow he'd missed where they held Markowitz's grandson, and if he'd missed him, then maybe he'd missed Penny, too.

He reentered the bunkhouse, his gun at the ready. He had no time. A woman being badly wounded on the property would sound the alarm, no matter what she might tell others. Within minutes this bunkhouse would be swarming with guards.

As he passed the bound guards, one looked conscious, but he made no appeal. Why so complacent? Larson raised his weapon. Someone was here with him.

He moved stealthily and cleared two small bedrooms and a bath in a matter of a half minute or less. Arriving at the closed door to a room he recalled as a bunk room, he tensed. He counted down in his head and kicked the door open. It rebounded off the thin, hollow wall and he blocked it with his wet shoe. He sighted down the gun, finding every pattern in the room that worked against his expectation, nearly squeezing off a round into what turned out to be a pillow angled awkwardly.

Clear.

He moved toward the closet. Looked down, and there it was: a loop of fabric. A crawl space.

A single guard sleeping in the bunk room could easily defend such a crawl space. Simple. Efficient. Practical.

Larson bent and reached down for the fabric loop. He could not only *feel* guards hurrying toward this bunkhouse, but he also sensed at least one down this hole, a man charged with defending the space until help arrived.

Larson would be a target from the moment he entered.

Ten, fifteen seconds of precious time ticked off, Larson longing for a stun grenade. He retreated and switched off the hallway light behind him, evening the playing field by ushering the bunk room to pitch black. He let his eyes adjust, then he slipped his key-chain penlight from his pocket, hoping to use it as a diversion or decoy. He held the penlight in his right hand, along with his gun, the Glock.

He knew he'd be fired upon the moment he jumped down in there. He had no doubt of this, and the stupidity of such an act briefly froze him. But with no time, and no options, Penny's survival on the line—Larson dropped into darkness.

He landed awkwardly, his gun smacking a metal pipe. He tossed the penlight to his left as a distraction while rolling right.

No shots fired.

As he rolled, his gun released its magazine into the gravel floor. His thumb touched the gun's metal: the contact with the pipe had sprung and bent the magazine's release switch. He fumbled to locate the magazine—wondering if the gun would accept it with the broken lever. He had one round in the chamber—one round he could count on.

The weak light showed a pair of collapsible cots, and on them, the blond head of . . . *a little girl*.

"Penny!"

A head of red hair popped up. A boy.

Sight of the two kids stole his attention as a figure sprang toward him from behind. Larson took the blow to his right wrist and the Glock tumbled free. Fire sprang from that wrist, and he realized he'd been cut. He recoiled, cowered, a flinching reflex to ward off the inevitable. He kicked out with his bent right leg, moving awkwardly because of the limited space. Blind luck connected that blow to the man coming after him. Both men fell away from each other. Larson smacked his head against the short stud wall.

The four-foot limitation of the crawl space restricted movement to a squatting, crouched shuffle for both men, like crabs attacking each other.

As his opponent sat up, recovering from the kick, the penlight's dim beam moved across his face, revealing chemical welts that occluded his right eye.

Larson knew the razor came next.

With his gun and its ejected magazine somewhere to his right, Larson started in that direction, but his opponent skillfully anticipated the move and blocked it, placing himself between Larson and the cots. He then lunged at Larson with incomprehensible speed and sprang back out of reach just as quickly.

Larson's left forearm went warm and stung. In that split second, he'd been cut again.

Another darting move, like the flick of a frog's tongue. Larson's left leg was bleeding.

If he stood here any longer, the cutter would pick him apart, one quick cut after another. Larson would go down, not from a single wound but the combination. He'd have his throat slit, and he'd bleed out in a crawl space, where they'd bury him a few hours later. Perhaps Penny and Hope at his side.

A thought flickered through him: *the bad eye.*

Larson feinted to the man's right—his blind side—freezing him, and then dived toward the cots, somersaulted, and came up with the penlight. He twisted it off.

Darkness.

He felt around, hoping for his gun, and came up with a scrap of a two-by-four, nearly puncturing the palm of his left hand with a bent nail. Held from the other end like a baseball bat, the nail then served as a weapon. He lunged and rolled, guessing at a location, hoping to turn the man toward his blind side. Larson swung the board blindly. He missed on the first swing but connected with the second, landing the nail into flesh. His opponent cried out.

Larson delivered it again, and again felt the nail connect with flesh.

The razor drew a line down Larson's left shoulder. All at once, Larson picked up a vague orb of black movement. Light from a front room seeped through the poorly laid plywood flooring.

Larson kept moving, working toward his opponent's right. He bumped against the cots. He heard the ruffle of sleeping bags.

"Stay back!" he hollered, having no idea where back was. "U.S. Marshal!" he called into the dark as he once again swiped the two-by-four in the general direction of the dark shape.

No contact.

He rotated to his own left again, his thighs cramping and burning from the awkward stance. He worked toward where he believed the gun had fallen, simultaneously trying to keep Rodriguez from it. But suddenly a sound came from *behind* him—feet moving impossibly fast. The weight of a man crashed into him. Larson fell forward onto his face. The razor tried to flay his back but hung up in the black windbreaker's ripstop fabric.

Larson rolled and swung again. Roll and swing. Roll and swing. The board and nail bounced off either bone or lumber as Larson felt another burn, this time along the side of his right calf, the cut deep and painful. Larson miraculously blocked the next attempt with his left forearm.

Five or six hot spots on him, all glowing, all bleeding. Crabwalking, he scooted away. He couldn't afford more cuts—he was light-headed already.

The cutter sensed an opportunity and attacked. Larson raised the board with both hands and swung. It lodged in the man's head—his cheek? Neck? He wasn't sure. The cutter jerked backward and cried out. Slippery with blood, the board came loose in his hands, and Larson lost it.

Frantic now, without a weapon, Larson furiously patted the ground around him—the Glock had to be here somewhere! He touched rocks and small chunks of lumber.

The magazine! He pocketed it. Still, no gun.

Movement. This time to his left. The kids?

Larson scrambled back, cramping and dizzy. He smacked into the pony wall and tried to collect his bearings. He'd lost all track of his gun.

Every ounce of him resisted returning toward that razor.

He paused, the silence suddenly alarming. Larson held his breath and listened in the dark. A girl's whimpering. The kids had been cowering over by the cots.

The cutter now had Penny.

A night-light came on unexpectedly. Blinding him. Markowitz's grandson, dressed in cowboy pajamas, cowered. But it was he who'd turned it on.

The cutter was crouched behind an upended cot. He had his left forearm hooked around Penny's throat. The two-by-four and its bloody nail lay on the dirt floor to his left. The man's right hand clutched his neck just below his left ear, attempting to plug the wound where he'd taken the nail. It looked arterial. A bleeder.

The boy continued to cower. Penny trembled in the man's grasp.

No one said a word. No one moved. The gun lay a full body-length away, to Larson's *left*, over by the boy, not at all where Larson had expected to find it.

The razor glinted, held to Penny's neck. One pull across that soft flesh and she was gone.

But in that dim light, in that instant as they connected, he saw her mother's eyes in the child, and he ached at their similarity. She was scared out of her mind.

"*Cairo*," Larson said to the child. "You hang tough and I'm going to get you that dog."

Those frightened eyes briefly filled with surprise. Relief replaced terror as she looked down to take in the wrist of the man holding her, and Larson knew what that child's mind had planned as her lips parted and her teeth bared.

The boy courageously, but stupidly, moved toward the gun.

"Don't!" Larson called out sharply to the boy.

But the kid's move was to the cutter's blind side, forcing him to pivot to track the boy. His one good eye flicked back and forth between Larson and the boy. Whether he understood what he was doing or not, the boy had stretched the cutter's resources thin.

Occupying no more than a couple of seconds, the boy moved and Penny lowered her chin and bit through to the bone.

Larson threw a handful of dirt at the one remaining eye as he dived straight forward, never losing sight of Penny, while his right hand clutched onto the nail board. The cutter, reeling from the bite, misjudged Larson, expecting him to go for the gun.

Larson swung the two-by-four for the cheap seats, driving the nail squarely into the side of his opponent's head.

Penny broke free.

A gunshot rang out. *The boy*.

"STOP!" Larson cried out.

Click, click, went the empty weapon.

He was atop the cutter now, who lay on his back, the nail board stuck to his head. He pounded his fist down into the man's disfigured face.

The razor glinted, but Larson had the man's wrist pinned. He dared not let go, but the hand moved like a claw, his fingers extended like pincers and, both of their arms shaking from waning strength, the razor twitched and cut into Larson's wrist. It dug deeper and more painfully.

Shifting his weight, Larson swung his elbow and connected with the nail board, hammering it more deeply into the man's temple. The white of the one good eye rolled into the back of the man's head with each blow of Larson's elbow against the board.

He went still, but Larson didn't trust it. An animal like this could feign unconsciousness. Larson pinned the two wrists, both limp and lifeless. He came higher and dropped a knee into the man's chest, but saw nothing on his face.

The razor came loose and fell.

Larson wanted the gun—the useless gun—wanted to kill the guy once and for all. But then he saw two terrified kids staring at him, one his own daughter, and he knew he couldn't do this in front of them. His vision darkened momentarily, no doubt owing to blood loss. He saw the boy's terry-cloth robe and belt on the dirt floor.

"Your belt," Larson said.

He heard footsteps above them.

One, or two?

Larson tied up the unconscious man's hands behind his back. The knot wasn't much, due to the thickness of the cloth tie. He doubled it, then crawled over to the boy and retrieved the gun from where he had dropped it. He quickly tried inserting the magazine, but it wouldn't stay. The gun's slide was jammed open as well.

"Cairo?" Penny whispered. "Mommy?"

"She's waiting," he said. Then he held his finger to his lips and shushed them.

He moved to screen them from the rectangular hole in the crawl space's ceiling—the closet floor. Each of his multiple wounds rang out in sharp, hot pain.

The overhead footsteps hurried toward them.

Larson raised his open palm, indicating the kids should stay put. He moved to just below the opening, reversing the gun in his hand, its butt held like a blunt, metal club.

The footsteps stopped, immediately above.

Larson motioned for the kids to crouch down, and they did.

He waited.

And waited . . .

Movement from the other side of the hole. Larson imagined a man going down onto his knees, preparing to either jump or peer down inside. He drew the gun back over his shoulder.

As the man's head lowered through, and he took a look, Larson waited for him to turn to face him. The head slowly pivoted, and as it did, Larson delivered the butt of the handgun squarely into the bridge of the man's nose, centered between his eyes. The body slipped through the hole like a sea lion into water. Larson reached for the limp arm and took hold of the man's fallen weapon as the first of two shots came through the floor from above.

Both shots sprayed into the dirt.

More footfalls above, as the man up there took off for reinforcements.

Larson beaded down the barrel. He picked up the parallel rows of nails sticking down through the overhead chipboard. The hallway. His aim tracked the footfalls fluidly, first catching those sounds, then leading them slightly.

He popped off two quick rounds. They sounded like loud handclaps. The third round caused a sharp yelp of pain, a collision, and then silence. Neither the kids nor Larson made a sound. No one was breathing.

From above, a groan.

Larson led with the weapon and poked his head out the trapdoor. His first chance at standing, his legs throbbed with cramps.

"Come on," he ordered the kids.

"You stay in the closet," he told the boy as he pushed him up through.

And then he bent to pick up Penny. His hands touched her little waist. He felt it like an electrical charge. She placed hers on his shoulders.

"You're bleeding," she said as Larson clutched her and lifted her through.

"Never better," he said, following her up through a moment later.

He checked the hallway. The man he shot writhed in pain. He'd taken one in the leg and one in the lower back. Larson tied him up with a lamp cord and left him.

The boy had peed his pajama bottoms.

"Shoes?"

Neither child answered, looking up at him with blank faces. It was mostly fairway. They'd go it barefoot.

He led them past the two downed guards in the front room, peered outside, and they made a run for it. With shots fired, although far from the manor house, he expected others.

The three of them running now across the dark fairway, the kids keeping pace, Larson felt sweat reach his wounds. He steered them for the unseen barn.

He pulled out his phone as they ran. He slowed, allowing the kids to run a ways in front of him. But at that instant the phone's face lit up—neon blue—and announced the arrival of a text message.

Hope!

The sound of a stream grew close. They were nearing the barn.

Desperate for word from her, he read only a number on the small screen:

911

CHAPTER SIXTY-EIGHT

"Shots fired," LaMoia reported into his headset. He told those in the van, "The spiders report hearing six to eight shots fired."

There was no longer any need to await the AUSA's warrant.

"Hampton and Stubblefield. Over the wall!" Rotem ordered. "NOW!"

All those in the back of the police van had spent the last ten minutes preparing for the raid. Hampton and Stubblefield, already having donned Kevlar vests and radio headsets, were handed white-phosphorus grenades and stun grenades by members of SPD's elite ERT squad.

LaMoia said to Rotem, "Say the word and you've got twelve of our best special ops on the field with them and two sharpshooters with positions on the lodge."

"How long?"

"Give me seven to ten minutes."

"Okay, go, but I want no mistake. Your two spiders and three of my guys are going to be on the ground. No friendly fire. Positive makes or no shots."

"Understood."

Rotem also directed LaMoia to call up cruisers or patrol personnel and to seal every gate. Anyone attempting to flee was to be detained as a material witness.

Hampton and Stubblefield took off toward ladders set against the wall. Rotem's phone rang, and he stuck it to his ear, too excited to hear at first, then stunned by the voice he heard on the other end. "SHUT THE FUCK UP!" he shouted, too loud for the small confines of the back of the truck. The men went immediately silent.

"It's Larson," he told the group. They'd heard the name bandied about, but probably did not understand the significance of the call.

"Go ahead," Rotem barked into the phone, a trickle of sweat rolling down his cheek.

CHAPTER SIXTY-NINE

Philippe suspended the auction at seventeen million five hundred thousand, two families having formed a quick alliance across the table and pooling their money to win the witness protection list away from a Reno hotelier unwilling to bid higher. The hotelier's father, brother, and two first cousins had all died of mob hits, and he believed the names of their killers were on that list.

Philippe called a ten-minute break, encouraging everyone to try the catered food. He'd done so not out of greed, but because this time one of his own men had interrupted, calling him from the meeting. First Ricardo, now him: embarrassing as all hell. But a few words whispered into his ear convinced him he'd had no choice.

"We've got the Stevens woman upstairs."

For a moment he was dumbstruck, the news nearly unfathomable. He had men out sweeping the grounds while the Stevens woman had infiltrated the manor house?

He rounded the landing on the first floor in time to see outside: Ricardo climbing into the back of a black Navigator. Philippe hurried to get a better look. Katrina was propped up in back wrapped in blankets, her face smeared with blood, her eyes blinking but unseeing. The door shut and the car motored off, Ricardo calling out, "Back gate!"

"What the fuck?" Philippe asked his nearest soldier.

"Thrown from a horse," the man reported.

More likely Ricardo had been pulled from the meeting because Katrina had been caught leaving him, and this was how he'd punished her.

"How bad is she?" Philippe knew it then: He'd kill Ricardo.

"Stab wound right below the tit," the man said. "Like a fuckin' machete got her, is what I heard."

Philippe climbed the next flight of stairs heavy with concern over Katie's condition, asking his guy to keep her situation monitored *by the minute.* He arrived into the empty suite of rooms on the third floor to see Hope Stevens sitting in a comfortable chair. She jammed her hand down into a crack in the chair and Philippe signaled his man over to inspect. He came up with the blue BlackBerry.

"You let her keep that?"

"Keep what?" the young kid said. "I never saw it."

"You patted her down?"

"Of course I patted her down."

"But not her crotch, did you?"

"What?" The man mistook the question, believing himself accused. "Listen, Mr. Romero, I did not in no way touch her in that kind of way."

"Get the fuck out of here," Philippe ordered him, disgusted.

Just before the man left the room, Philippe stopped him and asked for his gun. Alone with her now, he stepped closer.

"You have been one major pain in the ass, Ms. Stevens."

She held her head down, her hands gripped firmly, pressed between her legs. "Let my daughter go."

"Shut up."

"Do what you want with me, but let her go."

"Shut up."

"She's a *child*." She looked up at him then, her eyes glassy but not tearful. "What's the point in killing a child? What can it possibly gain you?"

"There's nothing to discuss with you. You've wasted far too much of my time and resources as it is." He came around the back of the chair.

Hope no longer could control herself. Her entire body shook. Her teeth chattered, and she heard herself whimpering. She so wished she could have been stronger at this moment, could have found the words to defend herself and put him in his place, this human monster who was behind her daughter's abduction, her years of running, her loss of life despite her living. She managed to say, "You took away my life once already." Then she added the words that were the most difficult of all to say; words she had practiced reciting from the moment she'd been discovered down the hall.

"God forgive you," she said.

At first she thought he'd fired the shot and blown a hole in her head, that somehow she'd transformed herself at that moment, feeling no pain, rising above her own body to hear the gun's discharge more distant and disconnected, more like a round of fireworks than the last sound she would ever hear.

But then a flash of light entered the room and she realized she could *see* that light. More fireworks went off. Only to realize he'd not pulled the trigger. He'd spun around to face the window frozen at the spectacle outside.

The younger man who'd found her burst through the door, a look of panic in his eyes. "Boss?"

Now she heard gunfire as well—short handclaps and staccato pops through the window that sounded nothing like she thought they should.

Philippe was frozen, picturing his guests on the first floor panicking at the sound of small weapons fire and fleeing for their cars.

CHAPTER SEVENTY

"Hang on, guys," Larson told the two children, the first bursts of light bouncing off the low clouds up by the manor house. It reminded him of the Fourth of July, of festive holidays and drinking too much. Weak and faint from the loss of blood, his every wound stinging unmercifully from the salt of his sweat, Larson looked and felt far worse off than he was. Most of the cuts were shallow, none life-threatening, and yet he felt himself fading fast.

Penny rode bareback in front, gripping the mane. The boy—Adam, he'd finally told Larson his name—held fast around Penny's waist, a stranger to horses. Larson led the quarter horse by the halter, first at a walk, then a trot, following a westbound trail. He'd discovered a laminated map of the compound's trail system posted outside the tack room and followed it now in his head. There were three major forks he would face—two rights and a left—in order to reach the estate's western boundary. It was there he was to rendezvous with SPD, although he wasn't ruling out seeing Rotem himself. Hamp and Stubby would be sights for sore eyes. But being with Hope and Penny together was all that mattered now.

With the detonation of the ordnance, he believed Hope's chances greatly diminished. With the compound now under attack, any extra baggage would be dealt with quickly. He might have believed her already dead had it not been for the second message from the BlackBerry:

MM, 3rd Fl.

Meriden Manor, Third Floor. It had arrived just before the first explosions. It at least gave him faint hope that she'd escaped or had bought herself time.

"Firefly!" he heard from behind him.

Two black-clad SWAT operatives converged on Larson from behind. One took the horse's reins from him. The other, wielding a semiautomatic rifle, continued sweeping the surroundings, forward and back in constant motion.

"As far away as possible," Larson instructed, "as quickly as you can."

"Copy that."

He reached up and touched Penny's small hand. "You're doing great," he said.

"But where's Mommy?" she said. The two kids had held up amazingly well, Penny a leader throughout.

"I'm gonna go get her," Larson said.

The SWAT guy took off at a jog, leading the horse. The kids hung on.

Larson turned back down the trail, and started to run.

CHAPTER SEVENTY-ONE

LaMoia waited at the estate's back gate, waited for the driver of the Navigator to climb out and unlock it. He waited for the exact moment the man inserted the key into the padlock and twisted. Waited for the lock to pop open and the man to remove it and the chain from the gate.

Then he stepped out of shadow and calmly announced, "Police."

The driver jerked from the surprise and reached for a weapon. From just over three feet away, LaMoia squeezed the trigger and blew the man's kneecap away. As the driver spun around, screamed, and fell to the ground, LaMoia saw someone inside lunge from the backseat up into the driver's seat. He could have fired on the man, but until a gun came out either window, he had a better option.

Instead, he counted silently in his head—singing, actually—to exercise the proper patience. Right when the man slipped in behind the wheel, LaMoia fired repeated rounds directly at the car's front bumper. One, two, three, four . . . With the fifth round, he hit the G spot and the front airbags deployed, inflating and snapping the driver's head and body back into the seat like a sixteen-ounce glove on the fist of Muhammad Ali.

He strode forward then, the gun trained right into the face of the would-be driver, ready to send the first person who twitched to his Maker.

He tore the driver's door open, not seeing the woman in the far back until the interior lights came on. That one needed medical attention. He might drive her himself—the Navigator was a nice ride.

He recognized the man behind the wheel as Ricardo Romero. He'd been doing his homework.

"Sorry," LaMoia said. "Road closed."

CHAPTER SEVENTY-TWO

Larson had no craving to run headlong into a firefight, but he accepted it as a necessary evil as he chugged uphill with a pronounced limp.

He reached a gridlock of confusion as a stable of black vehicles battled for position. One car backed up onto the grass and shot off in twin rooster tails of mud. Another followed. Both came within a matter of feet of Larson, nearly running him over, yet no one bothered with him. Perhaps no one saw him. Perhaps he wasn't there. Maybe he'd died beneath the double-wide and was now living out a final fantasy that was nowhere but in his head.

Rotem had orchestrated quite the show. To look at it, to hear it, one would think a hundred agents had stormed the compound, when Larson knew it had to be many, many fewer. Lacking any organized defense, shots were returned sporadically, with many of the estate's guards already apparently AWOL.

Amid this hellfire, Larson made directly for the mansion's front door. Once inside, he left behind what looked, smelled, and sounded like a small war and entered a world of opulence and grandeur. In their seclusion within this estate, the Romeros and others had spared little expense.

He glimpsed himself in the entranceway's oversize, gilded mirror, wondering at the walking horror there, and turning away from it. He didn't recognize himself. His sleeves and pant legs shredded, blood darkening even the black windbreaker he wore, Larson entered the grand staircase and climbed, his legs dragging, barely willing to cooperate, unmoved by the desperation that drove him.

He marched toward the third floor, another man's gun in hand.

The lack of electricity was no doubt Rotem's doing. Close to the manor house now, several percussive stun grenades exploded, rattling windows and shaking the foundation. Designed to throw shock waves meant to rupture sinuses and puncture eardrums inside enclosed spaces, the use of the grenades outside, where they were less effective but impressive as pyrotechnics, smacked of Hampton and Stubblefield and his squad's methods of overwhelming a fugitive prior to a final strike.

The harsh white light from those flares burned through windows and lit the upstairs hallways. He climbed beneath the ostentation of a dozen portraits of jowly old men looking proudly officious with their golf clubs.

In the distance now, the first whine of approaching sirens. *Backup.* A stupid tactic, given Hope's captivity. The sirens would panic Hope's captors and shorten her life considerably. If she wasn't dead already.

CHAPTER SEVENTY-THREE

The man held her in a one-armed necklock, swinging first toward the room's windows and then the door, back and forth like a drunken dancer.

It sounded like Normandy Beach out there.

His words muddled, he spoke aloud for the sake of hearing himself reason. "All this time of wanting you dead for what it is you claim to know . . ." A half minute or so passed before he completed the thought. ". . . and here you are, more valuable to me alive."

She knew better than to try to speak, for each time she opened her mouth he cinched down harder on her windpipe and drove her toward unconsciousness. In these brief few minutes under siege, Hope had come to understand that she would not die the overpowered victim. Though overpowered, she playacted now, offering no physical resistance while she searched for opportunity, the tendrils of her training as a protected witness creeping back into her consciousness. Elbows. The heels of her feet. The opponent's groin. His windpipe. She'd been told it took less than twenty pounds of upward pressure to tear a human ear away from the head, to grip it by the lobe and work it like a stuck zipper. Flooded with such thoughts, her mind had reached an uneasy calm, where time and sound and action seemed to slow, and during which time confidence grew in her. She had come this far on her own.

You shouldn't have let me live, she thought.

Her moment came sooner than she'd expected, and when it arrived she knew it, she saw it as a gift, and she had no intention of allowing it to pass. It came as a one-two punch. First, a blinding flash, much more vivid, more present than what had come before. A ball of light so bright it flooded the room in a bluish tint that went beyond pure white. This was followed, nearly instantaneously, by a concussive sound wave that found its way deep inside her bones while shattering two of the windows and cracking the third. Glass rained down, sounding like a waiter's misfortune. Hope rocked forward, using her bottom as a fulcrum, and then snapped to attention, catching the man's jaw with the crown of her skull. She spun to her right, away from the elbow that clamped down on her throat and broke the viselike grip, never hesitating for a moment as she sped to the first of the shattered windows and paused only long enough to clear the jagged mouth of broken glass that rimmed the now-lopsided frame. She went out through that window like a hurdler, one leg stretched before the other, bent over toward her extended thigh like a diver, three stories up and falling, arms flailing now as she saw the two Dumpsters slightly to her left and realized she'd misjudged and chosen the wrong window. But no matter, she was free of him, in freefall, hands out swirling like a teenager leaping from a high rock into the pristine lake below. Her lake was asphalt, and her landing, horrific.

In total disbelief, Philippe watched his one remaining negotiating tool fly out the window like Peter Pan. The sheer nerve of her jumping out the window—an act he could never have done himself—so pissed him off that he ran to the open wall, leaned out, and trained the gun down on the collapsed and broken form below. He fired off a round, not seeing well enough amid the smoke and confusion to have much of an aim, and then fired again. Missed with both. He sighted more carefully this time, determined to end this, finding the bead and locking it onto her sprawled frame.

Then, out of the corner of his eye, he saw a red firefly light onto his chest, his first reaction, like anyone's who spots a bee or wasp on their person, to swat it off. But it did not fly, for it was no insect. His last thought was recognition of what it was: a sharpshooter's laser sight creating a red circle at the center of his chest.

And then, a hole. A ripping and shredding as a large-caliber-rifle slug exited a cavity five times larger than it entered.

Philippe was thrown back off his feet as if struck by a truck, arms out to his sides, on the bed of broken glass that jumped around him like sparkling fairies on the floor.

CHAPTER SEVENTY-FOUR

As Larson arrived at the far end of the upstairs hallway, he heard two shots exceptionally close. *Bam . . . bam . . .* the sound of an execution. He arrived at a door and kicked it in, gun extended, only to see a well-dressed man lying dead in a sea of broken glass. Not bleeding, eyes open, and dead.

He might have moved on had he not seen the blue plastic of his smashed BlackBerry on the carpet in front of an empty overstuffed chair.

He checked closets. He spun around in the center of the room, convinced she was here. And then his mind reassembled the shattered windows, the dead guy in the tailored clothes killed where he was, and Larson rushed to get a look outside.

If his mind had been free of emotion, if he'd been able to clinically abstract how it was that this man could lie dead on the floor, he never would have approached the open window. But he was desperate for her now, and he knew without knowing, understood without any evidence whatsoever, that Hope had jumped.

He saw her there down on the asphalt, writhing in the pain of broken bones. And she saw him as well, just before it happened. He made that connection with her, somehow eye to eye, or perhaps heart to heart, from that great distance, the Glock in his right hand.

A red bead lit his jacket. Like a firefly.

His head snapped up to face the edgy sharpshooter somewhere out in all that darkness, and then . . . the heat of a bee sting, and the world went silent.

CHAPTER SEVENTY-FIVE

The sound of applause. Ethereal. Or the beating of wings.
The swirling white lights of angels, and a heavenly chorus rising like a whine. Then, blackness broken by a flickering gray wind and the faces of red pulsing demons all looking down at him. He, the center of attention, the focal point. It was how he'd imagined it might be, all but the strained faces of Hampton, Stubblefield, and Rotem glaring down at him like he'd done something wrong.

"Leave me alone," he wanted to say. "Let me die in peace."

If this was death, it felt anything but peaceful.

"He caught the insignia." It was Rotem, shouting above the roar of the Bell jet helicopter—for that turned out to be the source of the wind and the drumming applause and the flashing red lights. The white spotlights came from the news choppers high overhead.

"Their sharpie caught the insignia on your jacket." Rotem pointed out the white Fraternal Order of Police insignia on the chest of Larson's borrowed windbreaker.

"Just as he fired, he jerked," Hampton shouted. "Took your collarbone and a piece of your shoulder, but left you your heart."

They had oxygen on him and intravenous in his arms. He tried to speak but could find neither the breath nor the ability to form any words. It was as if he were in someone else's body and didn't know the right controls.

The paramedics hoisted him up and passed him off to their colleagues in the helicopter.

"We're right behind you," he heard Hampton shout.

Larson felt his stretcher turned and placed down. A flurry of hands in thin plastic gloves rose above him as straps were pulled across him and tightened. If only he'd been able to ask, someone might have been able to answer, and so he tried again, his lips unwilling to cooperate, his brain a tangle of life-after-death and prayer and penance. An incomprehensible moment.

The red and white lights still flashed rhythmically, the only real things convincing him he might indeed be alive. How much a dream? How much wishful thinking?

And then he knew it had to be a dream, for as it turned out, the helicopter was made to carry two, not one. Two stretchers side by side with overhead stainless-steel hooks for the bags of intravenous fluid. There beside him she lay, her eyes open and moving to find his, which absolutely meant she must, too, be alive, or they were both dead and somehow sharing this moment, which wouldn't have surprised him at all.

He saw on her legs inflated splints, and in her eyes a loving-kindness that confirmed in him this must be heaven, and he didn't mind a bit.

Finally words did come, or at least he heard himself speak, and he would wonder in the days and weeks and months to come if he'd actually said anything to her. "She has your eyes," he said.

Her hand twitched, its fingers stretched at the end of an arm bound by nylon straps. It reached for him, for his, and he too pushed with all his strength to move his index finger toward her.

Her eyes brimmed with tears, which rolled down her cheeks, clearing tracks through the smudged dirt on her face.

Their fingers did not touch, only wiggled out in space toward each other as the helicopter shook and rattled and thundered as it lifted off. Larson tried to force the snarl of pain into something resembling a smile but didn't know if it took.

CHAPTER SEVENTY-SIX

Larson pulled on the oars, working the stubborn tissue and tightness in his left shoulder to the point of pain, and then backing off to where it was manageable.

There was something about Michigan's Upper Peninsula. The smell, maybe, or the darkness of the water. The way the forest crept right to the edge of both the mainland and the island, the trees reflected like tall soldiers.

There were bugs in the air and the smells of early summer—the perfume of fruit blossoms carried on winter's freshened air spilling out of Canada. He heard a red-winged blackbird's sprightly, lilting song, heard the rhythm of the oars carving into and scooping the lake's mirrored surface, heard her joyous squeal and the thrashing of her feet on the island trail as she endeavored to keep pace with him. Penny was a fast little runner.

He looked to see her blond hair bouncing, her smart little body sprinting the trail in a pair of pink shorts and a white T-top. White sneakers and socks her mother had mail-ordered.

"Break . . . fast!" she called across to him when she knew he was looking.

He met her at the dock and she helped him stow the scull in the old boathouse and wipe down the oars and rigging. She told him of a dream she'd had in the night, spoken in one continuous monologue—of princesses and magic potions, and trees that could talk—that lasted from the boathouse clear up the trail to the sprawling log cabin known only as Baby's Breath. As they approached the back deck, buttoned down with tubs of recently planted annuals, Hope was there to greet them, a pair of binoculars in hand. Larson slowed as he saw her. Penny rushed past, drawn by the scent of cooking bacon. Hope was clearly distressed.

"What is it?" he asked.

"The launch," she said, pointing at the white dot of a distant boat approaching. Beyond it, the steady green of the mainland. Through the binoculars the launch carried a distinctive bright-blue flag. Hope knew of what she was speaking: The rules were strict concerning the waters around this island. "You ordered it, or it wouldn't be coming here."

"Yes," he answered, "I called for it. But I'm not going anywhere. It's not like that. Come with me?"

Rotem had convinced Larson and Hope to remain in protection through not only the trial of Ricardo Romero, but his sentencing as well. With the trial now less than ninety days away, pressure from Justice remained high for them to maintain the "zero profile" they'd kept over the past few months. The man driving the launch was on the federal payroll.

"It's not time for a rotation," she reminded.

The nearest town was across three miles of lake, around a bend to the southwest, about a twenty-minute boat trip. Provisions were delivered twice a week. Two marshals remained on the island 24-7, rotating in three shifts a day.

"Just bear with me, would you?" Larson asked.

She slung the binoculars around her neck, crossed her arms defiantly, and joined him in the walk down to the dock. "I thought you were leaving us," she said.

"Yeah, right."

Hope said nothing on the way down the path. Larson drank in the sounds, the sights, the smells. "This is a special place," he said.

"Only because we're sharing it," she said.

"Damn right."

"Are we going to talk about it?" she asked.

A pair of squirrels cackled and chased each other overhead, their running up the trunk scratching against the heavy bark.

She said, "*Laena*? Your all-important list."

Sworn to secrecy, Larson nonetheless owed her an explanation, even if lacking in detail. He'd put it off until she'd asked; and now she had.

"The disk that was being auctioned took a bullet. It was in Philippe Romero's breast pocket."

"Seriously?"

"Swear to God."

"The sheriff with the Bible in his coat?" she questioned skeptically.

"Only it didn't save him," Larson pointed out.

"But the list itself?"

"Katrina Romero's computer was seized. She had compiled the list for Philippe. It was her e-mail that Markowitz had been sending it to. She was convicted on a number of counts, but to my knowledge hasn't been sentenced."

"And the witnesses?"

"We've lost some. Fewer than we'd feared. Justice has relocated something like five hundred prime targets. A huge undertaking. There have been some early retirements, transfers within WITSEC itself."

The water came in and out of view. He never got tired of looking at it.

He said, "The computerization of the list is under review. There's no way they'll go back to paperwork, so it's only a matter of encryption and how they prevent something like this from happening again. It's the government, don't forget. It'll take them a couple years to come up with a plan, and by then it will be outdated. The list will always be vulnerable to some extent."

"What about the children? Katrina's children?"

He stopped on the trail, turned and faced her.

"I don't have an answer for that," he said.

"They shouldn't end up the victims."

"No. No one should end up a victim."

"But children!"

"I understand."

There was no mention of Paolo. No mention of Larson's having attended the cremation because he had to see the man reduced to ashes. Seventeen members of Ricardo Romero's former "family" had been captured and imprisoned. Like Paolo, Ricardo's empire was ashes.

Larson led her down the trail to water's edge.

They reached the dock and Hope used the binoculars to confirm the launch driver, passing the opticals to Larson so he could do the same.

"It's Neville," he said.

"I have to tell you I did not like it one bit. Seeing that launch." She didn't look at him as she said, "I don't want to lose you, Lars."

"We're going to rejoin the world. You realize that, don't you? Six months, a year? We've talked about this, I know, but don't lose sight that it'll be different when we're shopping for our own groceries, and taking the dry cleaning, and driving Penny to soccer games. As awkward as it is to be this isolated, we've been pampered. It's going to be a whole hell of a lot different."

"And I, for one, can't wait."

The launch slowed, the wake lessening, and putted in toward the dock, taking longer than either of them would have wanted.

"So this is some kind of surprise, I take it?" she asked Larson.

He said, "A promise made is a promise kept."

She viewed him curiously.

Neville, the boat's driver, coaxed the vessel into reverse, foaming the water, as Larson snagged the bowline and tied it off to the dock.

"Special delivery," Neville announced, as he then secured the sternline as well. He moved forward and opened the cabin and descended a steep set of steps, disappearing. He reappeared a moment later with a sand-colored puppy under his right arm.

"Oh, Lars!" Hope said enthusiastically.

"She's a mutt. Part shepherd, part hound dog."

"Looks part Afghan."

"That's the hound dog: Saluki is the breed."

Neville passed the pup to Hope, who then cuddled it and brought the dog's nose to her face, and was generously licked. She laughed and the dog licked some more.

"Meet Cairo," Larson said.

Hope looked up with tears in her eyes.

Neville handed Larson several copies each of the *New York Times*, the *Wall Street Journal*, and the *Detroit Free Press*, and Larson thanked him.

"Covers the past four days," Neville informed him. He brought up a large bag of Puppy Chow and several shopping bags of accessories including two books on dog training.

There was no mail to be delivered, even for Larson. For all the world, he'd disappeared after that night north of Seattle. Even Hampton and Stubblefield did not know his whereabouts.

"See you Thursday," Neville said as Larson untied first the bow- and then the sternline.

Larson pushed the stern away from the dock, and the boat's motor gurgled. Larson offered a small wave of thanks. Neville mocked a salute, and the launch motored off.

Larson left the food, but got the bags.

"She's going to flip out," Hope said.

"I hope so."

Larson switched hands with the bags and threw an arm around Hope. He was going to hate leaving this place, though not what it represented. He planned to ask Rotem if there might be a way to buy it from the government someday, if his finances allowed. No law against dreaming.

"Isn't she cute?" Hope bubbled.

Larson held her just a little bit closer. "Yes, she is," he said.

And the two walked back up the trail toward the cabin.

FOLLOW THAT MAN